MW01255847

PuppyLove

A novel by

Cheryl Cherne

* * *

Cover art thanks to L. Muller

ISBN: 9781697631227

Some have a tribe; I have a pack.
This is for them.

The Beginning

Humming. The woman was actually humming. To a song that only she could hear, to a melody tonally unrecognizable to my ears, the woman was h - u - m - m - i - n - g , humming!

And me? There I sat there her captive audience, held within a silver wire mesh cage, unable physically and incapable mentally to escape her unmelodic vocal wanderings.

My eyes rolled back in my head— Ahhhh! Such torture!

There had to be some way to liberate myself.

I closed my eyes. The cage disappeared— Ah-hah!

Tilting my head back slightly, the draft from the A/C vent carried fragments of outside air into my prison. My nose detecting the scents of long-awaited, much anticipated freedom— Freshly cut grass, newly turned soil from just planted, mulched, and watered flowerbeds, furry little rodents, the neighbor's fat cat— HEY! Wait one second! That cat had more "out" privileges than ME!

My eyes sprung open. My reality came rushing back. Myself confined within a 3x4xZERO space with hummed elevator music as ambiance. With my latest attempt at freedom sabotaged, there was no other choice— EXACTLY! Can't escape 'em? Then, join 'em! Sooooooo, I harmonized with The Hummer, adding vocals that she did not appreciate.

I did appreciate that my mother thought of me, but I was reluctant to take another responsibility into my life. I was already so busy with my job managing the estate in New Jersey, commuting between there and my apartment in Manhattan, while juggling an active social life with a two-year-old.✧ It was enough.

However, the sound in my mother's voice, when she called… I could not refuse. So, one late summer afternoon, I found myself speeding along the thruway, weaving in-and-out of slower traffic, the top down on my little red car, tunes on high, singing along.

I was singing along, harmonizing the best I could with her pitchy tunes. But she, Mrs. I-Hummm-Alone, refused to acknowledge my melodic efforts— Ughhhh.

In fact, not even the slightest glance made my way! Usually by this time she'd have said something, done something, or simply left the room. BUT, she just kept right on *h-u-m-m-i-n-g*!

✧ Dog. Black miniature Schnauzer to be exact.

Ahrmphhh.

Why couldn't she see that I was tired of being locked up?

Hello— He-LL-oo— Hellloooo!!! I am talking to you! The only person here! You did not really think that I would be talking to myself?! I am not you, Ms. Hummm-To-Myself-With-NO-Regard-To-Others!

If she would only let me out, I would be silent. Promise.

Why was she forcing me to be like this?

Humphhh.

Enough. Time to be myself. I was totally over this sing-a-long thing. Time to change MY tune.

Volume spiked to high, check. A shrill spine-tingling pitch variating between a wailing plea to short crying yips, check. A discordant melody, check check check.[♫]

Oh yeah! This should do it!

Finally, she turned to me— Success!

And smiled— Ughuhhh.

I had never seen her smile and certainly never needed to see it again. The toothy grin, enough to choke the joyful sound right out of me.

Walking over to my cage she bent down and cooed through pearly-white caps, "Not my problem anymore. Enjoy yourself while you can, little puppy."

[♫] Homage to Phillip Glass. So young at the time, I must have been a prodigy to compose such brilliance.

A little puppy was the source of my mother's "troubles." After only a few short weeks, it was driving her insane. Supposedly the "little beast" was too energetic, strong-willed, untrained, and shed like crazy. Half the time my mother was crying from frustration and the other half from allergies. She said that it was a well-bred dog and she wanted to keep it "in the family" rather than sacrifice it to an uncertain future at the local animal shelter.

My heart went out to them both. So, pedal to the metal, I was on my way.

When I arrived at my mother's house, she was already outside waiting for me. Parking the car in the driveway, I came up the front walk and greeted her with the usual hug and kiss.

As she asked me about the drive, my attention was pulled to an intensely expressive howling sound coming from the house. Looking at my mother with eyebrows raised, she explained that the dog must just be excited to have company.

Together, we continued up the walk to the front door.

As the doorknob turned, all the noise stopped as if some void, like a black hole, had been created sucking every sound from my mother's kitchen.

I opened the door and could not believe my eyes.

Before me, sitting inside a training crate, was the most beautiful creature I had ever seen.

I had never seen this one before. Smelled her, yes.× But, never a body to go with the scent.

Interesting— She had direct eye contact, unwavering focus and was coming my way.

I sat in complete stillness. Without a single blink, my eyes locked on hers willing her closer.

Hypnotizing her with the mantra in my stare, "free me free me free me free me."

She came closer and closer and closer still.

Sitting down "Japanese-style"☯ at the door to my cage, she lifted her hand. With one movement, the door swung open. All the time her eyes fixed on mine. An unchanging gaze.

Oh, oh! Perhaps, I hypnotized her too well!

× I had been on a "looking for things to chew on" expedition, earlier that week, which led me to an upstairs closet. She had excellent taste in chewables.

☯ I prefer to say that she knelt down, prostrate, in my presence but "they" said that was "inappropriate."

Even with the door wide open, I dared not move and break the spell.

My freedom was before me, but then so was she! What to do?! Why wasn't she moving? Or talking? Is she even breathing?!

AACKKK!

In my panic, I blinked.

An eternity passed— BUT NOT my anxiety!

I blinked again and the spell was broken. She started to laugh.

She kept her eyes on me and I realized that she was looking at all of me at one time!

Creepy, but cool.*

She spoke to me. Her voice so smooth and sweet, bouncing with laughter— a cadence driven by the rhythm of happy emotion. I was almost lost in her words when I saw that held within her open palm was a piece of cheese. I went for it, but her fingers closed tight.

My fingers closed tight, but that didn't stop her from trying. Needle-sharp puppy teeth sank into my knuckles instead of the treat. Ouch!

---

* Note to self: I must learn that trick.

From restraint to impulsiveness... rrrf! Such character, I liked it!

She started to whine. No manners. That, I did not like.

I snapped my fingers and grunted sharply. She fell silent and attentive again. Smiling, I opened my hand and said, "Okay!"

Gently, she took the treat only to devour it in one gulp. Oh well, baby steps with puppy paws.

We played, rough housing, for a while. Very interactive, responsive, and engaged, this puppy showed lots of promise.

Once her pent-up energy was brought down to a more manageable state, it was time for a real assessment. She was already 5 months old and no one had ever really worked with her. I wanted some idea of what I was agreeing to. As we flew through the training basics with alarming speed, it seemed too good to be true✧.

"Sit" and "stay" firmly under her grasp, we played a little game of hide-and-seek. My mom watched the

✧ And, it was. But, you have to appreciate the art of the con and the artist herself.

puppy to make sure that she "stayed," and I went to go hide. Once I found a spot, an "Okay!" with a little whistle meant the game was on.

The puppy was exceptionally good at this too. She seemed to enjoy the "hunt," Sniffing her way through the house, following my trail, and prancing with delight at the discovery of me and a treat!

After a few rounds, it was time for walk. I secured a prong collar around her neck and we went outside.

Outside! FINALLY!!! I was having fun with the New One, but rain or shine[*] there's nothing better than the good ol' outdoors and fresh air. I started out on my usual path— BAP!

She jerked me back alongside her and went the opposite way!

HEY! There are places that I want, need to check out. I've been so nice, listening and following along. Now, it's MY turn!

I pulled back. She pulled forward.

I pulled back. She pulled forward.

I sat down.

---

[*] At that time, I was too young and meteorologically unversed to include other types of inclement weather such as snow, ice storms, Nor-Easters, "les tempests", etcetera, etcetera.

She said, "Come on, let's go!"

I pretended not to understand.

She tugged a little. I stayed put.

Heck NO! Time to set precedence. There's MY Way or there's NO Way!

She laughed, said, "Okay," picked me up in her arms and continued walking!

O-M-G!

I was completely horrified. No more grass in my paws. No more exploring the ground for new and old scents. What would the neighborhood think?

I wiggled around in her arms, but her hold was solid. She walked past a few of the neighbor's houses including Fat Cat's. This was now painfully embarrassing.

Taking a few steps more, she then paused, squeezed me tighter,° and put me back on the ground

Woo-Hoo! Back to earth!

I shook myself‴ and let her lead the way.

Although on a shorter leash than with The Hummer, we kept a brisker pace and went farther AND longer! There were soooo many other things out there than what The Hummer had ever shown me. I think that I rather liked The New One after all.

° Ok fine. You're right. She "hugged" me. To this day, I cannot tell you which was worse being carried or that 1st public display of affection.

‴ Obviously, to get rid of the cooties.

After all that playing and training and walking, I sensed a bond growing between us and knew this puppy was exactly what I never knew I wanted until it was there. Besides, I had fallen under her spell at first sight.

On her papers, her name was "Azura." Ugh. I could hardly pronounce the name and doubted I could ever wrangle it out fast enough to grab her attention if necessary. The thought of having to say it every day, of telling people the name repeatedly, of explaining and spelling it out for them… No. Just not happening.

I mused on names, fictional characters, people I knew, people I wanted to know. Absolutely no frou-frou names and nothing too obvious. Just when I was tempted to settle for the ordinary, I was mentally scrolling through movie titles and serendipity! "La Femme Nikita." ✧

Nikita! How perfect!

Here was this little savage, untrained beast who no one could handle or manage. Her future:

✧ The 1990 French version directed by Luc Besson.

uncertain. However, there was potential. A strong spirit that with nurturing, firm and loving guidance, could be refined into a well-trained and poised canine. The situation mirrored the film perfectly. La chienne, Nikita.

Nikita, Nikita, Nikita.

Nikita, Nikita, Nikita. Ever since this afternoon, it was the one-word refrain to every spoken verse. Over and over and over again — a very, very broken record, indeed!

The New One would look at me, smile, and say "Nikita." She said it before she gave me food. She said it before she said "come" or "sit" or "stay" or whatever else she was yakking about. She said it repeatedly!

Was it my name? My given name?

Hmmmmm.

I had been called many things since I came to this house*, but never this AND I liked it! There was a certain ring to it.

Ni-*ki*-ta.

I was flattered. She cared enough to find a name that suited ME— to perceive me as more than just a flawless beauty with a free spirit, the heart of a gypsy.

Perhaps, I ought to consider her as more than the "New One." Maybe, she had a name too—

---

* For privacy, safety, prudence, and legal issues, I am not at liberty to divulge and will leave these adjectives, nouns, mixed with the occasional expletive to your imagination.

Huh! Yeah, WHATEVER! De*lir*ious! I must be tired, if I'm getting mushy. Best I stop right there before my train goes farther off track!

I went over to the quiet corner set up for me A.K.A. My Personal Space.

Curled up tight into a ball, closed my eyes, and followed my dreams to my new life— with my real name, with The New One.

*

Nap over. I opened one eye. Then, the other.

The room was dark except for the flickering of the TV. They were all watching something. No one noticed that I was awake.

Oh, yeah!

Noiselessly, I sat upright on my bed. Still, no one noticed.

I stayed quiet while my thoughts raced. I hadn't chewed on anything all day and there were those chewables in the upstairs closet and maybe *she* brought new ones and there was the rug that needed more rearranging and there was the tempting scent of leftovers on the counter top— BUT, this was also my 1st opportunity to surreptitiously observe The New One.

There was something different about her. She did not get frazzled or easily riled like The Hummer. She had zero tolerance for my shenanigans, but hadn't yelled OR cried OR broken down in hysterics. Her voice maintained a soft, yet firm and commanding energy. ALL day, laughing and playing games!

True everything had to be her way— But equally true, her way was fun!

Hmmmmm.

My eyes fixed on her.

Where were her buttons? Where could they be hiding?? There had to be at least ONE. Some weakness, somewhere. No one could be that nice AND related to The Hummer.

I re-concentrated my focus. Scanning her for any discrepancy, my x-ray vision blazed through the darkened room.

Through the darkened room, two red eyes blazed in my direction. This might not be Sunnydale and I definitely was not Buffy, but there was a demon inside my mother's den. Its penetrating eyes fixed on me! Yikes!

Shivers ran up my spine. My breath caught in my throat.

Ohhhh... No. It was just Nikita.

In the darkness, her blue eyes reflected the light from the TV.

However, she was staring at me... not blinking... completely motionless. It was quite unnerving. I was beginning to understand why my mother wanted the little demon dog out of her house.

I reached over to turn on a lamp. As light filled the room, the possession was exorcised. My Ni-ki-ta was back, bouncing around like the puppy she really was!

Reenergized from her nap, Niki now needed to unwind and sort her puppy beans before bedtime. Grabbing my coat, we went for an evening walk.

Much to my surprise, by the time we returned to the house, my mother had managed to move Nikita's crate downstairs next to my bed. And much to Niki's surprise, a few moments later, she was locked in her crate for the night.

A long day, I was completely exhausted and snuggled into bed. As my eyes closed, Nikita sang us both to sleep with a traditional lupine lullaby. Oh, lucky me.

* * *

It was time for me to take Nikita home. While I was busy packing up the car, my mother offered to take Nikita for one last walk. They were gone no more than 5 minutes when my mother returned to the house with a funny smile on her face.[✧] The leash was still wrapped around her hand, but the prong collar was empty.

According to my mother, she and Nikita had been enjoying their walk. Niki was a very "good girl," quickly finishing all her "business." They were headed back towards the house when Niki suddenly stopped to investigate a patch of grass. As my mother continued walking forward, Niki-Houdini moved backwards while bowing her head, releasing her from the prong collar. The last my mother saw of Nikita, she was sprinting through the neighborhood headed towards the canal.[✧✧]

I did not know whether to laugh, cry, or scream.

I did, however, throw on a pair of sneakers, tied the laces up tight, and bolted towards the front door. I flew through the doorway onto porch.

BOOM!

Sitting on the front walk was Nikita. Her head tilted slightly to one side, not a wisp of emotion in her sky-blue eyes.

[✧] Not the scary smile she is so well known for, but the sick, "oopsy!" something's not so right smile

[✧✧] Erie Canal, if you'd like the reference.

As soon as I began to approach her, she bounced up, pivoting mid-air, and sprinted around the townhouse towards the road. Not wanting to lose her again, I gave chase.

Reaching my car, she turned, winked at me, and in one clean, effortless movement sprung into the convertible. She had chosen me. A smile spread over my face and into my heart.

The car now fully charged, I kissed my mother good-bye and promised to call once we arrived safely. As we pulled out of the driveway, I could've sworn that I heard my mother humming "Oh Happy Day."

Oh Happy Day! This was the very best day EVER! The convertible riding thing was Grrreat!

I spent the entire trip with my nose in the air▲and trying to ignore The New One who talked all the way. Yakkety — yakkety — yak!

▲ Maybe it appeared a little snobby and aloof, but whatever! I was recording all the new scents and places just in case she got lost.

She told me about the place we were going. She told me about my new family. She told me what she expected from me. She told me about things too private and too embarrassing to repeat. In fact, EVERYTHING told in excruciating detail AND she told me her name. Finally!

But, I was to call her "Mistress."

Huh?! If she thought for one moment, if she even had the slightest inclination that I would be her "canine slave," she was gravely mistaken— On the other hand, it was much, much better than "Mother." Let's be honest, I was sooooo much better looking than her, NO ONE would ever believe that we were in any way related! Hah!

For the time being, I kept my silence and enjoyed the fresh air allowing it to clear my mind. Unfortunately, she did NOT do the same!

After countless hours, her soliloquy AND the car finally came to an abrupt halt when we arrived at The Farm.

The Farm

The Farm wasn't exactly a farm, but an estate located in rural NJ. Hidden from a roadside view, the house sat on top of a hill overlooking the idyllic countryside. The closest neighbors were a dairy farm to the south, a horse ranch to the east, and a couple of smaller properties, an historic home and a "in-law" house, at the base of the driveway.

I managed The Farm for a family who used it as a weekend and vacation property. It was a perfect place for Nikita and my employers welcomed the idea.✧

Niki had been so excited during the trip that almost the entire ride down, she had kept her nose up catching the air as it came off the windshield. Personally, I was just happy that her puppy bladder could hold all the excitement.

✧ Mostly, they hoped a "wolf dog" would ward off the deer that munched on all the new and pricey landscaping.

Now that we had finally arrived, she was looking around wild-eyed. Untying her leash from the armrest, I kept a firm grip. Before I could open the door, Niki bounced out of the convertible.

I wanted to walk her a bit to get her settled down and adjusted to the new home before she met everyone else.

No such luck.

All the other dogs come running over to say "hello" and meet their new sister.

Thankfully, Nikita was eager to meet them, too. Siberians can be very strong willed and dominant, not always the most "social" of breeds. I had been very anxious to introduce her to the existing pack: King and Queen, 2 Collies that had "ruled" The Farm their entire life, and Gizmo, my miniature schnauzer.

Much to my relief, there was a lot of bottom sniffing and tail wagging. All very amicable. The only hiccup was Gizmo who bared a little fang.✧✧ But, Niki had completely ignored the inappropriate gesture.

All in all, things seemed to be going well.

✧✧ No gold stars for her today. Such the enfant terrible, Gizmo was always instigating trouble.

Things seemed to be going my way. My new home was much more than I had imagined. There was lots of space to run and explore. The first chance to be off leash— TAK! I would be ALL paws ALL over it! And, there was the house itself— Which was H-U-G-E !

The only exception to my content was the contempt of that little dog, Gizmo. She actually had the nerve to "welcome me" by lifting her lip and showing her puny little incisors— Huh?!

They might have been impressively white set against her black beard, but any favorable impression ended right there.

I was about to show her mine☺, but My Mistress had been watching AND before I could properly react— SHE corrected Gizmo for her audacious behavior.

Gizmo shot her a huffy look.

My Mistress fired right back. Quicker! Harder! Longer!

Zing! Bang! BOOM!

Cool!

Firmly put back in her place, Gizmo slunk off muttering obscenities under her breath.

What a miserable drop-kick sized piece-of-work! Oh, well— Whatever! There would be time later for me to deal

---

☺ Which were truly impressive! Even if they were only baby teeth, they were whiter, larger, and I could pull my lips back more to show more.

with her, personally. Right now, time to stretch my legs and mark my territory.

*

My first few weeks were not exactly what I had expected. Here I was in paradise. There were cows and horses and wild turkeys and deer and groundhogs and voles and a lawn and a field and a barn and a pond and a stream and a woods and I spent most of the time literally tethered to My Mistress. Ugh.

Of course, I did not mind too much when she was cooking. She was quite the disaster area chef with food regularly falling off the counter. My duty, my pleasure, to help maintain a tidy kitchen.◈ But, other than that, I had ZERO desire to spend soooooo much time with her!

When I was not attached by a nylon umbilical cord, she had me "in training."

TRUE, I excelled at the monotonous routine.

TRUE, I enjoyed all the attention and praise.

AND TRUE, Gizmo was burning with jealousy because My Mistress was spending so much time exclusively with ME!

But, intensive daily training? What for?! Where was I going? Hellloo!

I have simple desires. *PL*-ease just leave me alone to roam and explore— maybe even visit with the cows!

AND, there were so many things that she wanted me to learn— command after command, verbal directives with and without hand signals!

◈ Mmmm. Messy, but a good cook. She served up a fresh breakfast for me every morning! My favorite way to start the day? An egg cooked over-easy placed on kibble, then sliced open allowing the yolk to run all over it. Mmmm.

HUH?! Did she really think that I was going to do whatever SHE wanted when SHE wanted it? Especially, when there was NO treat involved— *Delusional!*

For the moment, I was "playing along" and humoring her. But, the very instant she felt comfortable and let her guard down OR I just couldn't stand it any longer— I'd assert myself. Until then, I would be on my very best behavior— HEY! Did someone just say "Scooby snack?"

"Scooby snack!" I called out while simultaneously flipping a liver treat into the air. Niki's eyes followed the arc of the treat. Just as it began the descent, she opened her jaws and extended her head forward slightly to catch it. Brilliant. By far, the most graceful puppy I had ever seen, a thing of beauty to watch her in motion.

Since arriving at The Farm, we did training every day for about an hour. Niki quickly grasped and retained each command. After a just few lessons, she was routinely responding to hand signals without verbal prompts and had learned a few tricks, too. The rest of the day I had her attached to me, at the ankle, by a leash.

I had read in a training manual✧ that it was a good method to bond with your new puppy. Especially since I had taken Nikita after that ideal bonding age, it seemed like a perfect and simple solution. And in theory, it was. Reality was a much different story.

Niki was not the "most agreeable" puppy. Already with a mind of her own and a will to match, she could be extremely difficult. The times she resisted and could not be cajoled into moving, I felt like a tugboat on high seas having to use all my strength to tow her along. Throughout the day, I alternated between my left and right ankle to balance "the load."

And honestly, it was little joy having a dog attached to me everywhere I went. The mornings were the worst. Either she was not ready to wake up and move or she was sniffing and trying to lick me. The bathroom became a combat zone as I batted off her inquisitive nose.✧✧

✧ *Mother Knows Best*, by Carol Lea Benjamin. It's my "go to" dog training manual. An easy to read, easy to follow common sense guide.
✧✧ Realistically, there are just some places I never want any dog's nose… Or wet tongue, for that matter.

After a few weeks, it was enough. I wanted to forge an emotional connection with Nikita. However, the intensity of our "together time" was beginning to fray my nerves.

One late afternoon, we sat side-by-side on the porch watching the sunset cast a deepening crimson light over the fields. My favorite time of day at The Farm, when no one around, I'd indulge myself with the quiet time and the majestic view watching the day come to a close.

Nikita was leaning her body against me. I wrapped my arm around her, my fingers running through her thick, plush coat. Her sky-blue emotionless eyes stared forward at the darkened field, now sparkling with fireflies. She acknowledged my attention only by leaning a little more heavily into me.

Taken in by her display of affection, the beauty of that moment, I made my decision. She would be allowed free time every day. With over 80 acres to roam, I prayed that she would stay on the property and within my sight.

Freedom was within my sight— WooHoo!

After weeks of together-time torture, I was OFF-leash! FREE to roam. FREE to chase wild turkey. FREE to hunt deer and field mice alike.✓ FREE to visit with the cows. Now, this is "The Life!"

After a moment's rumination, I headed off to find King and Queen. Since they had already lived here at least a hundred years, they should know ALL the best places and things to do.

I found them in the juniper bushes.↓

Hmmmmm.

They were really quite odd. Maybe, this was not the best place to start.

As I approached Queen, she bowed her head, lowered her body to the ground, and slinked off in the opposite direction.

What?! Are ALL the females in this house anti-social? Or, wait! Perhaps, she's simply recognizing my supreme dominance! Uh-huh, that's right! She might be The Queen, but I am The Dauphine—Exactly! Younger and prettier!!

King, however, remained motionless. Staring at me. Mouth open. Drooling.

Eewwww!

Trying to ignore the puddling at his feet— Hoping that he was not incontinent, too— Giving him extra space just in case

✓ That's right, without discrimination! I am an equal opportunity hunter.

↓ Over the century, King and Queen had forged an intricate labyrinth, including rooms and passageways, through the branches and leaves of the Juniper bushes that surrounded the house.

he was— I asked King for his opinion on the best places to explore.

He opened his mouth and this choking-croaking sound came out.

Freaky weirdo!

He shook his head, opened his mouth again and nothing came out!!

O-M-G! Am I the ONLY normal dog here?!

Finally, he recovered enough of his senses and motioned for me to follow him. Leading me around to the back of the house, he went up to a screen door and made an odd grunting sound while shaking his body every which way.

Again, Frrrreeeeak!

The door opened and I "officially" met the Chinese housekeepers.

The man looked at me with squinted eyes and kept his distance.[9] He turned his head and screamed some nonsense inside. A woman appeared moments later. She started cooing and bent down towards me. The man tried to pull her back, but she turned on him like a viper. When she finished hissing viciously at him, she turned back and sweetly cooed some more.

Nice.

The woman motioned for me to stay put and disappeared into the house. There were some clanking noises, some drawer sliding, some more nonsense yelled back and forth, and then she reappeared proudly holding a bucket.

Was she daff?! WHAT would I do with a bucket? Did she think that I would collect King's drool so she could make a glutinous soup??? Blahhh!

---

[9] Not too articulate, mostly the only thing he ever said was "oohhhh, ohhhh, oh , oh, oaahh."

She turned the bucket upside down. Kitchen scraps and leftovers came tumbling out all over the deck.

Ahhhh. Heaven.

Without hesitation or a single thought towards me, King lunged at the goodies.

Oh no! No! NO!!

He was going to learn manners. We were going to establish protocol, immediately!

I firmly placed one paw forward and looked at King with eyebrows raised.

He understood my objection and my objective.

Without contest, King lowed his head and backed away allowing me first choice.

Mmmm-mmmmmm— What a fabulous feast! Beef bones, chicken claws, gizzards, raw liver, duck fat, a little cabbage tossed in, fish skin, seaweed— So much more exotic than my usual breakfast of kibble and ground beef! Now, if only King would stop whimpering, I could enjoy it!

I rolled one baby blue in his direction. Immediately, he fell silent.

Ahhhhh. True bliss. Silence and hierarchy firmly established with one simple glance.②

Finished with my snack, I thanked the woman by allowing her to pet me.

1-2-3 — OK, enough of that!

Without further adieu, I set off to check my territory.

As I marked my way across the backyard, my nose caught wind of that delightful, unmistakable fragrance. Oh yeah! The cows were out! WoooHooo!!

Leaving my work for a later time, I sprinted into the field to play with my bovine buddies!

---

② Now, all I had to do was to settle things with that miserable little black furball and life would be Grrrand!

Leaving my work for a moment, I went outside to play with my little canine buddy. My eyes scanned the property as I stood on the back deck with a dog toy in-hand looking, calling, and squeaking for Nikita to come.

There was no sign of her.

There were birds flying. A groundhog doing, well... whatever it is that a groundhog does. I even watched a squirrel fly from tree-to-tree. At the far edge of the property, on the other side of a wooden fence, the cows were grazing in the pasture. But, Niki was nowhere to be found.

Then, I noticed that there was one cow moving very oddly and very fast for a cow.

I squinted my eyes. Through the tall stalks of grass, I could make a white tail circling the bovine.

OMG! Nikita!

I watched as the cow danced around in the field, its head swinging side-to-side trying to catch a glimpse of its Husky shadow. The rest of the herd was slowly moving farther away, leaving the poor beast to fend for itself.

A comedic improvisational bit, yes. However, no matter how funny it was to watch, I had to pull myself together. Those dairy cows lacked my sense of humor and did not react kindly to distractions. One sidekick and Niki would be broken in two. Equally humorless was the shotgun wielding farmer who would shoot the "wolf-dog" first and, maybe, ask questions later.

I whistled sharply. Nikita froze in her tracks.

Then, her tail went down and she disappeared in the tall grasses.

Walking out into the backyard, I kept my surveillance on the pasture and the cows, continually searching the field for movement.

Nothing. No sign of Nikita.

Standing in the middle of the backyard, I called out a few more times while scanning for any peculiar movement.

Still nothing. My puppy had just vanished into thin air.

Shrugging my shoulders in defeat, I turned to go back to the house.

BOOM!

Nikita was right there sitting behind me.

I blinked in disbelief. Her innocent eyes fixed on me.

Relieved to see my Niki-Houdini, I threw my arms around her and squeezed tightly. Hug over, I flipped her on her back and roughed her up a little bit.

Thinking it best to keep her close for the rest of the day, I took Nikita by the collar and led her into the house. After a short "time-out" in her crate, we spent the afternoon playing a new game.

After a little snooze, My Mistress challenged me to a new game.

Acting completely terrified, Mistress Method-Acting-101 would scream "Ahh! Oh, no! It's a Vicious Dog! Ahhhh!" Then,

she would back away slowly to the count of 1-2-3, turn and sprint in the opposite direction.

My job? To chase and corner her.

Hellloo! Is that supposed to be challenging?! You are aware that I am a Siberian Husky! Only a generation, OK maybe two generations removed from wolves!

Exercise? A little. Fun? Sure. Good sport? Maybe. But, definitely not an Olympic qualifier. It was so ridiculously easy.

Once cornered, she would beg me not to hurt her. Naturally, ignoring her pleas for mercy, I advanced slower and slower. My eyes fixed on her. The prey about to be slaughtered.

Standing up on hind legs to my full height, I placed one paw on one shoulder— one paw on the other. Nose to nose. Moments of tension. Her eyes full of fear. Mine void of any emotion.

We stared at one another waiting to see who dared to make the next move. Until— I gave her a great BIG kiss!

HAH! Gotcha!

Obviously relieved, she'd start laughing, "That's enough, that's enough, Niki. What a good girl!"

Pushing me away, to straighten her clothes and hair, once she thought that she approached something more presentable— she'd make eye contact, scream some more, and we'd start all over again. We played and played the entire afternoon!

Cool!

Cooler still, she never won! Never once![◡]

Gizmo, who was always just lying around the house, spent most of the afternoon spread out on the couch eyeing us watching me play with My Mistress, wishing she could be a

---

[◡] That's right, I am the champion. [Cue in the victory song.]

winner, too— As beautiful, as fun, as loved as ME! Oh well, maybe in her doggie daydreams! Hah! Snooze away little fattie![1]

Of course, she did try to join us a couple of times. What a joke! Her? A vicious dog? *PL*-ease! She was nothing more than a speed bump— EXACTLY! A little, fat, black, out-of-shape, short-legged, even shorter tempered obstacle that s l o w s y o u d o wnnnn. ONE minute playing and she was o u t o f b r e a thhhh.

The only thing on Gizmo that was in shape was her mouth. It was always moving. When she wasn't eating, Gizmo was constantly muttering to herself— Blah, babblah, babblahhhh.

I did feel a little bit sorry for her. After all, there was No One else who would listen! So, so sorry for you— So, so happy not to be you, Mumbly-Lumpy-Bumpy! Ha-ha!

HEY! Is that Chinese chicken soup I do smell?

Oh yeah, snack time! Mmmmm-mmmmmm— Black chicken claws, my favorite! Xiè xie.[*]

*

Life at The Farm was becoming more and more difficult for me.

At the beginning, I had reconciled myself. Checked my ambitions, allowed her the lead— Exactly! Humoring her by "playing along." BUT, as often the case with lesser beings, the illusion of power was too great for her to handle. My Mistress? She was OUT OF CONTROL!

Rules! Rules! RULES!

---

[1] *Tales of the Great Gizzard Wizard*, a collection of true and outlandish adventures happening to one seemingly normal dog, will be available in hardcover Fall 20-never! Hah!

[*] The woman housekeeper was kindly teaching me some useful words and phrases in Mandarin.

Ughhhh.

The more "freedom" she gave, the more rules she imposed. I was trying my best to keep current, BUT there were always more RULES!

ALL I want to do is play and run and hunt and run and play— And let's be honest, OK? I am the boss of me and I am the ruler of my world! I have ZERO need of HER rules!

Worse still, Mistress Helicopter began monitoring my "free time." If she saw that my friends were out, she would immediately bring me inside OR tie me up!

Hellloo?! It's supposed to be FREE TIME! FREE from you. FREE your tyranny! FREE to play play PLAY!!!

I miss the cows. They're my only buddies! Sure, they may not be size appropriate— And sure, they're pretty *moo*-dy! It's true, they're quite odorific— And it's true, they live on the other side of the fence— But, there's NO ONE else!!!

I tried to make friends with the others. However, ALL of my efforts were pointless! My friendship not welcomed, not returned with the smallest gesture!

Queen refused to make any eye contact, always slinking away the minute I approached. King couldn't stop staring or drooling long enough to play. And Gizmo — well, honestly? She was just too fat to play AND too miserable to be around.

Rumor has it, Gizmo used to be the belle of the ball— friendly to all, flirtatious, and even beautiful WITH an hourglass figure! Cars stopped for her. Males marked for her. Of course, NOT that you would guess any of that by seeing her now— But, that was the rrrrrrumor!

Ready for "the real scoop?"

Gizmo had been madly in love, carrying on with some equally little, drop-kick sized dog. Together, they dusted the sidewalks of Manhattan, hosted play dates, and reveled in each other's company for hours at a time.

Ughhhh. What-everrr!

And then one day, the love of her life disappeared. POOF! He just left. No word. No note. Nothing. Gizmo looked for him and asked about, but there was nothing. Of course, it wasn't long before Gizmo came to the obvious conclusion that he had taken an "extended vacation" from her!

With no one there to share her pathetic little life, Gizmo stopped. Stopped playing. Stopped caring. Stopped living. Instead, she began stuffing the void in her heart with food and began talking to herself to fill the silence. With every morsel, with every syllable, spiraling deeper and deeper into a self-propelled madness.

So sad— Nah! So pitiful! But, what a Grrreat story!

Ahhhh— Look! There she is now! Waddling around the backyard. Out of breathhh AND out of her mind! Ha-ha-ha!

I skipped over to see if she wanted to go with me to visit with the geese. They had just flown in from Canada. They talked kinda funny— Eh? But, were most excellent swimmers and thought I was "just wicked!"

Gizmo shook her head and reminded me that My Mistress did not want us going to the pond. It was a part of the "forbidden zone."

Ooooh! What-ever! Mistress Micromanagement is not watching. And, what she does not know, will not hurt ME!

Now, come on, Gizzz! Let's go!! You don't even have to swim— just wade out a little bit until your paws don't touch the muddy bottom. With all your extra padding, you'll obviously float!

That did it! Though, not exactly what I had intended.

Gizmo got so ticked off that she waddled faster in the direction of the house, literally barking mad sounding the alarm for My Mistress to come.

Grrrrrr.

Go! Run all the way home little piggy! I'm off to learn more Canadian, eh?!

I sprinted off towards the pond before My Mistress could step outside.

I stepped outside and caught sight of Nikita just before she disappeared behind the trees. Ugh… Not the pond again. Niki was already too far for me to yell. Pointless anyway. There was no stopping her from her little adventures.

Nikita knew that the pond was "off limits." It was too close to the road and impossible to see from the main house. She also knew that the cows were "off limits." They were dairy cows and not to be agitated or they'd stop producing milk. But, nothing I did quelled her wanderlust.

Some days, Niki would stay by the house playing, chasing critters, snooping around, and digging holes.[✧] Other days, she'd simply disappear leaving me no clue where she went.

Although most days she was home by dinnertime, the hours that she was MIA were completely nerve racking. Butterflies filled my stomach, flying up into my throat every time the phone rang. Smart as she was, Nikita had a puppy brain and did not fully understand the dangers that were out there.[✧✧]

As a Siberian Husky, it was Nikita's nature to wander. I just wanted to find a way to nurture some of that out. Not to break her spirit, not keep her permanently chained to the house, there had to be a solution between the two extremes. None of the training books adequately addressed the fugitive dog issue. And, Niki was becoming a repeat offender.

I was beginning to feel overwhelmed and frustrated. Aside from her wanderlust, Nikita was also cultivating a dominant streak. I understood that she wanted to establish her rank in "the pack" and I had

---

✧ Much to my employer's discontent, the backyard was beginning to look like a meteor shower hit it.

✧✧ Aside from speeding cars and trigger-happy farmers, we also had black bears, hunters with their rifles and traps, and real wolves.

no intentions of interfering, but my sweet puppy was morphing into a little bully.

Most of the time, her dominant behavior was focused towards King and Queen. Niki would start playfully enough, but if they did not "reciprocate" she'd turn on a dime pushing them around and trying to block their escape.

So far, so good. Cool, with a Zen-like disposition, Queen would lower her head and slowly back away. King, he had such a crush on Niki that he'd let her do anything. My concern was for Gizmo.

She had assumed the alpha dog role, on grounds of seniority, and was not about to rollover. Schnauzers are infamously stubborn and Gizmo was certainly no exception. So far, Nikita had not pushed any issue with Gizmo, but she hadn't backed down either. I kept guard, watching warily as Niki eyed Gizmo as if sizing her up, waiting for an opportunity.

The few times Nikita had tried to assert herself with me, I would put her in her crate for a "time-out." No excitement. No anger. No words. My rule: Zero Tolerance. I was the "ultimate alpha."

I went back outside to the porch to watch the sunset and relax. Much to my surprise, Niki had already returned and was surveying the backyard from her bed. I sat beside her.

As I wrapped one arm around her, the other reached for the lead. Tied up for the night, Niki was not going anywhere this evening. I stayed by her side until the sun dipped below the trees, enjoying our quiet time together.

I was enjoying my quiet time alone— Until, she came out and sat beside me.

Ughhhh!

NO free time! NO quiet time! NO privacy! Was there anything sacred?! Obviously not! Because then, it got even worse— EXACTLY! She did it!

Pet - pet - pet!

She just could not keep her mitts to herself! I tried to ignore her, but she just continued!

Touch - touch - touch!

Sure, maybe it did feel good— and sure, maybe my muscles were a little sore from running around all day— But, please stop touching me! I want to be ALONE! Don't you get it?!

I was already so upset. The geese had left. Such a short visit AND no goodbye! Well, hopefully they would come back with some manners— Eh?!

As if the entire situation was not disturbing enough, Gizmo came outside. A wistful look passed over her bearded face as she saw My Mistress cuddled up with me.

Humph! You seriously like this stuff?

She sat down in front of us and keeping her back towards us, started to sighhhh.

Oh please. Such drama!

My Mistress began to motion for Gizmo to come over, but I pressed my body harder into her. Tilting my head slightly, I gave her a great, big kiss— Muah!

As expected, she wrapped her arms around me forgetting about the sighing heap before us. The disgusting display of affection was totally worth the look of jealousy burning Gizmo's face.

HA HA HA! Rejected again? Surprised?? Really?!

With one loud snark, Gizmo stomped off.

See ya! Would NEVER want to be ya!

Once Gizmo was out of sight, I pulled away from My Mistress creating some breathing space between us— hoping she would get the idea, but no such luck.

An eternity later, she finally got up and left me alone. When she re-appeared, she had a plate with her. Placing the dish at my feet, she wished me, "Bon appetite, ma belle."

Ahhhhh! Room service— And, eggs-over-easy, my favorite! Well, at least she got something right.

*

This morning I woke up in a bad, BAD mood. Even worse? I was twisted like a pretzel inside my crate AND no one else was awake— That's right! I was stuck ALL crunched up until My Mistress leisurely rolled out of bed and into the kitchen.

Grrrrr.

Last night, I had wanted to sleep in my bed outside. But, "Nooooo, not possible," My Mistress said.

Humph! What does a wind chill of -10 really mean? *PL*-ease! I am a Siberian Husky. My people thrive in Artic conditions! My people live off the frozen tundra! My people come from a land so cold that vodka freezes! Hellllooo!! Get it? Got it?! Good grief!

So what if I woke up with frost tipped ears? They were my ears! At least I'd be able to stretch my legs, be able to "relieve" my-self!

Enough.

Who was she to decide what was good for me?

Sure, she gave me food, a nice cedar bed outside— And sure, she finally gave me some privacy. NO ONE, not even Her Majesty was allowed inside my crate— But all the constant attention and interference in my life needed to end. Now!

I had had it! I could stand it NO longer! This time, she had pushed me TOO FAR!

ALL this goody four paws nonsense— let's learn something new today nonsense— let's play a game nonsense— was NONSENSE! Making me dull dull dull!!! Might as well fatten-me-up, paint-me-black, make-me-ugly, and call-me-Gizmo II!

DOUBLE GRRRrrrr!

No more "good girl" for me! The time had come for My Mistress to understand who is the "Real Boss." The time had come for My Mistress to assume her position as beta dog— Of course, if she wanted to be gamma, delta, or even omega, that would be her decision! Ha! See, even I made allowances for personal choice!

All her "attention" and "concern?" I did not need any of that— Exactly! I do not need her! I do not need the others! NONE OF THEM!

Queen always walking away, never wanting to play— never even attempting to look me in the eye— King always standing there. Watching. Drooling. Farting— Gizmo always clinging to My Mistress for protection, waiting for her to leave, and then teasing me before running back to the "safety zone"— Little-fatty-tattletale-troublemaker!

And her, My Mistress?! The absolute worst! It's always about her! Her rules! Her lessons! Her way! "No!" to the cows. "No!" to the geese. "No!" to any fun— Grrrrrrr. Who was she to choose my friends? To censor my entertainment?

Some days, I had most seriously considered leaving forever. Didn't even have to go that far! After all, I could live in the barn— Exactly! Visiting freely with my friends, catching field mice and voles, and drinking fresh milk every single day!

Of course, there were the few-and-far-between better moments with her. The silly games that I excelled at, the occasional quiet time together, the constant adoration which made Gizmo jealous, the home-cooked meals, yummy Chinese treats, my private room, my cedar bed— AND it was My Mistress who saved me from The Hummer and the murky depths of absolute boredom— But who would save me from her and Her Tyrannical Rule?!

AAACKKKK!

If only My Mistress could learn to respect my individuality, to respect my autonomy— We'd be just peachy! Well, I'd certainly be happier!

Finally, she was up— Yea!

At long last released from pretzeldome, she took me for a very, very short walk.

Really?! Ahh, come on! Only ONE hour! I need to s t r e t c h my legs! This is ridiculous!

Back at the house, she prepared breakfast. Bowls ready, she went to feed Gizmo FIRST!

Grrrrrr— Are you serious? It's supposed to be me! Me! ME! I am the Alpha!

I pushed Giz out of the way.

Gizmo snarled.

I snarled back

My Mistress told us BOTH to back down.

Gizmo stood her ground.

No surprise there. Not a single scrap of food ever escaped those wonder jaws.

I stood my ground.

My Mistress told us BOTH more firmly to back down.

I turned and told her to back down.

BOOM!

ACKKKKKK! NOOOO!

O - M - G! I was flat on my back! My Mistress had so quickly employed this fancy maneuver that I never saw it coming. The sheer audacity of it! Now, pinned to the ground by my scruff, she brought her face down to mine. Her never blinking eyes burning with a fury which I had never seen before.

Gulp.

I could not hold it.

I blinked once— Twice.

Fine. Her trickery allowed her this win, but not again. I was no longer going to play along. Nope, no more "sweet little puppy." Game Over.

The honeymoon was over. My sweet little puppy no more, Nikita and I began a new ritual. Every single morning, she would try some new angle to "establish herself" as leader of the pack. And every single time, 1 2 3... Niki would be on her back, scruff pinned to the floor. My face in hers, we began ritual #2: a staring contest.

Once she relaxed and looked away, I would place her in her crate for a little "time-out". Afterwards she would behave herself more or less, until the next morning when it started all over again.

I had promised to take care of Nikita, to give her a good home and solid training. But, this daily drama was not what I signed up for and with each passing day the "stare-fest" became longer and longer. Although she was still a puppy, Nikita could hold an unblinking stare for upwards of two minutes! Even if I growled, she was unfazed. Her resolve remained as fierce as ever. Some mornings, my eyes filled with tears from the intensity. Still, I refused to yield. This was a pivotal moment in her training. If I gave up now, I would forever have an un-mannered, un-manageable 4-legged monster on my hands.

*

My nephew came to visit and Nikita was once again a "happy puppy." Originally, she had been "his" dog. In the very short time that they were together, he must have imprinted on her. Because, for the first time since I had taken her, Nikita was completely involved with someone other than herself. She shadowed my nephew throughout the day until night, when they both collapsed into a deep sleep. Just shy of two years old, he was still too little to walk around and play with Niki; but, that did not discourage their playtime in the least.

Standing tall in his baby walker, my nephew would push a ball off in Niki's general direction. She'd make this big fuss over the ball, which had dropped and rolled at best whopping 2 feet. Jumping on it from one side, then the other, throwing it in the air, catching it, throwing, catching, throwing it farther, pretending not to see where it landed. My nephew the entire time laughing, clapping, laughing, clapping, laughing.

Eventually, she would bring the ball back to my nephew. Then, she'd back up, sit down and wait for him to "toss" it again.

The entire time my nephew stayed with us, I watched Nikita as she showed herself to be the dog I always wanted and knew she could be. No more dominance struggles, no more running away, listening attentively and obeying every command. Niki had once again become "perfect."

Perfect! My Little Person was back! MLP* was in da house— WooHoo!

Happy happy happy to see him again! He had grown a lot, but still smelled like formula and pureed plums. I wanted to bring him to the barn to meet my friends and try some fresh,

---

* To be honest, I have always referred to him as "mini-me". However, the lawyers say there seems to be some trademark infringement worries when placing it repeatedly in written text. Whatever. I know he's the original and he's much cuter, with a much kinder, gentler disposition. So there!

warm milk. Mmmmmm— However, My Mistress had confined him to this rolling contraption.

Poor Little Person, I knew exactly what it was like to be trapped in someone else's idea of safe and secure. Fact was, stuck in that thing he was in constant danger— Exactly! Easy pickings for Wonder-Jaws A.K.A. I-Like-The-Taste-Of-A-Baby-Yum.

Once, I left his side for a moment— Really, just ONE moment! I had "private matters" to attend to. When I came back, Gizmo was already there! Licking him and nibbling on his toes! Her eyes rolling back in her head with sheer delight, completely engrossed in her gluttony!

My Little Person was struggling— pushing her away— trying to save himself! Tears streaming down his usually happy, smiling face. Tasting the sweet liquid saltiness, Gizmo intensified her feeding frenzy. Now, lapping up the tears directly from his chubby, little cheeks!

O-M-G! Have you no shame? Zero scruples?? Zero sense of propriety?!

BOOM!

In a flash of movement, My Mistress grabbed Gizmo by her scruff and removed her— Finally!

As she walked away with Gizmo dangling mid-air, My Mistress gave me "the eye." And, for once, she was right— It had been my responsibility to guard My Little Person. My neglect of my chaperone duties proved disastrous and almost fatal!

Head hanging low, I sheepishly approached My Little Person⊗ apologizing for my carelessness, my negligence, begging his forgiveness.

⊗ Stop right there. Absolutely no jokes. I am not a wolf and this is not a fairy tale. OK? Let's keep it real, folks.

Closing my eyes in deep and most earnest prayer for forgiveness, I nuzzled my head into his belly.

Time stood still.

I waited. And waited. And waited.

Finally, his little hands grabbed my ears.

Pulling my head to his, he wiped his tears off on me— Ahhhh, my pardon.

From that point, I was on my very best behavior. Nothing would ever separate me again from My Little Person. Side-by-side, the two of us spent our days playing together. I tried to teach him "hide-and-seek" and the "catch" game— But, that wheeled gadget continuously hindered his full potential.

When he needed changing, I would call for My Mistress. She insisted on that particular honor. At mealtimes, I was especially vigilant— making sure that Gizmo stayed far, far outside the established perimeter. And, while he slept, I would rest at the foot of MLP's crib keeping one eye open to make sure there were no unwelcomed Gizmos during the night.[*]

Just when we were really having fun, they strapped My Little Person into the backseat of a minivan! I already had two paws in, when My Mistress grabbed me and pulled me out.

Like static cling, she stuck herself to me begging me to stay— Ughhhhh!

Such a disgusting, undignified display of emotion. You would think at her age, she would have some self-restraint! But then, to be left all alone with the little garbage pail-on-four-paws never knowing when you'd be the plat-du-jour— My sympathies were with her. And, I could discern that telltale aroma from the downstairs kitchen, The Givers of Good Food cooking a Feast— Oh Yeah!

Soooo, I indulged her insecurities and stayed.

---

[*] You do remember what happens to a "gremlin" when they eat after midnight! LOLOLOL

In recognition of my sacrifice, My Mistress began to extend more courtesies. I now wandered freely, exploring the terrain as I chose. She would serve me dinner 1st instead of I-could-afford-to-miss-a-week-of-meals Gizmo. And, some evenings she even let me sleep outside!

Those mornings, I would wake up before the dawn and watch and wait as all the little animals began scurrying out of their homes completely unaware that I too was awake.

Watching.

Making notes.

Waiting.

Those afternoons, I'd go a-hunting. It was almost too easy. After all, I had meticulously studied my prey, learning all their habits, all their alliances, all the routes, all the homes, all the entries and exits. Still, it was so much fun!

I loved the thrill of the chase, the rush of adrenaline. Moments after I caught a critter, it would spasm in my mouth like a squeaky toy gone wild— Until, there was nothing.

Hey! Not my fault! Blame it on fear!* Yeah, that's right! Fear of inevitable doom. Fear of pain yet unknown. Fear exacerbated by my razor-sharp teeth piercing its hide, the life force slowly trickling down my chin, onto my bib— Hah!

Sometimes, I had the good fortune to capture a critter with stamina and a strong constitution. I would be able to play with it for a while. Tossing it into the air and catching it, tossing and catching— Or, just let it thunk onto the ground, watching it swivel around dazed and confused, whapping my paws down to the left to the right stunning it further, blocking any feeble, frantic attempts to escape, before it seized!

Game over. Prey lifeless. I would rip the carcass open and remove the defunct, faulty squeaker, kindly donating the pelt

---

* Fear. Yet another example of a useless, counterproductive emotion and THE great motivator of nonsensical actions.

and body to King or Queen or Gizmo or any other unfortunate who did not possess my extraordinary skill set.

These past few days, the leftovers were disappearing as quickly as I could kill them. Gizmo did not look any more bloated than usual, Queen had not been in the vicinity, and it was much too fast to be King Dim-Wit. There had been a funny looking cat wandering around. Its body was normally sized, but the legs were rather short. I had observed it a few times walking around the property. And every time this cat was around, everyone else would leave. Fearless and friendless— Just like me!

I placed this morning's trophy critter at the edge of the bushes and resumed my position on the deck waiting to meet the profiteer. Hopefully, I would not have to wait too long. Thankfully, I did not.

Yep. It was Stumpy Legs. I went down to introduce myself.

Smaller than the cows, all black just like Giz, and obviously lived "on-site," maybe My Mistress would approve of this friend— WooHoo! Finally, someone purrrfect to play with!

The cat was rather surprised that I approached it so readily. He must have been much more isolated than I originally thought. Poor Stumpy! In fact, as soon as I was close enough to say hello, he scampered away.

WAIT! Don't run away! I come in friendship!

Stumpy the Scaredy Cat hurried off so quickly that he forgot to take today's trophy with him.

Whoa! Whoaaa!

The lingering odor from my new friend was quite noxious. No wonder he had no friends! This was no ordinary smelling cat. Well, if he wanted to continue our friendship, Stumpy the Stinky Kitty would require an education on the importance of hygiene. Oh yeah, most definitely!

All too easily, I tracked the stench trail back to my new friend's home. Setting up post, I kept some distance not wanting to frighten Stumpy any further by my presence and self-assuredness. The forgotten carcass placed near the entrance, but far enough away that this time I would have the opportunity to properly greet my new neighbor and friend.

Eventually Stumpy Kitty came out, cautiously keeping one eye on me as he nibbled at his present.

Ahhhh, what a good kitty. We're going to be simply Fabulous Friends!

When he finished, I stood up and came closer. Close enough now to admire his thick, plush midnight black coat. Of course, my coat was much softer and better groomed, but his had a pearly white running stripe cleverly placed down the center of his back— Cool!

Stumpy Kitty took center stage, presenting me with an elaborate song and dance routine in gratitude for all the presents— hissing and stamping away, to a beat identifiable only to himself! The spectacle finished with his tail in high salute!

Wow! What a show! Bravo! BRAVO! I really like this kitty cat!

As always, Gizmo came over to ruin the moment. Raving incoherently about something, kibble crumbs falling out both sides of her muzzle.

What? Run? Leave my new friend? Are you kidding?

Typical typical. She just wanted everyone to be just as miserable as her.

I turned to apologize for Gizmo's behavior and saw that Stumpy Kitty still had his tail held in high salute— Wow! What a super cool c-a-t!

Leaning in for a customary sniff, he spritzed me with stinky water!

Huh? This stuff smelled worse the artificial crap My Mistress hosed herself with every morning!

PSSSSSSST!

Again? Totally un-acceptable. This is no show of friendship! I shall teach you decorum!

Grabbing Stinky Kitty by the scruff, I shook him until he stopped his spraying. And then, I shook him some more. When I was certain, 100% positive that he had learned his lesson, I whipped him around a few times for good measure and flung Bad-BAD-Stumpy-Stinky-Kitty into the bushes.

Lesson over, there was one hiccup— I stank, really stank. Worse than when I played with the cows. Yep, even worse than my new friend, himself!

No worries, though. Knowing a few things about cleanliness,[/|\] I went down to the stream, waded in and rubbed myself against the rocks, drying off in the sun.

The stench remained.

Buggers. There was only one who could help me now.

I sat at the front door and waited for My Mistress to open the door.

She was not too pleased. The door slammed shut.

Door open again, she emerged covered in garbage bags secured by rubber bands. Obviously dressed for some occasion, she looked absolutely ridiculous! No fashion sense. No common sense.

Grabbing me by the scruff, she marched me around the back of the house and into the shower room, next to the pool. Then, she poured out hundreds of cans of tomatoes, dousing me from head to toe.

[/|\] I had already been told many a time, "No mud boots allowed inside!" My choice, either I wash myself or she would. Honestly, as much as I enjoy it, I do not always have the patience for a full shampoo and blow-out.

Hello! Are you cuckoo?! I am not a plate of pasta! I do not want to taste good— I want to smell like a dog again!

I did look pretty cool though— As if fresh from battle, the juice running down my sides like my victims' blood, chunks of tomatoes sticking to me like pieces of raw carnage!▪ Ahhh! Excellent!

Ahhh… Excellent! After 3 hours of soaking and shampooing, emptying every jar of tomatoes in the pantry and an entire 64oz. pump-included bottle of herbal shampoo, Niki smelled more like a wet dog and less like a skunk. Still, I knew it'd take several weeks for the underlying "musky" odor to fully disappear. I really hoped that she had learnt her lesson.

I loved Nikita and most days I was happy that I took her in. However, on days like today, I rued the decision. She was maddening. A walking juxtaposition, I never knew which dog was going to appear: the sweet, lovable, attentive, obedient Nikita or the cruel,

---

▪ Cut! Photo op. Facebook shot! Instagram that!

vicious, obstinate wild beast Nikita. Never a dull moment.

The problem was I needed a few dull moments so that I could do my work rather than cleaning up after another fiasco. Prior to the arrival of the family or any company, I would have to sweep the grounds for rotting carcasses, hiding the evidence of Nikita's bloodlust. Honestly, I was impressed by her natural instincts, but I was concerned as to what extent they would lead.

One late afternoon, I found Nikita lounging on her outside bed, gnawing on a "dinosaur bone." Funny thing was, I didn't remember buying or giving her an over-sized bone recently. As I got closer, I saw she was chewing on a hoof still attached to the deer's leg! Ughhh…

Thankfully, she wasn't moody like Gizmo. But, she was capricious. Nikita did whatever pleased Nikita at that particular moment. When she wanted to explore or to be alone, she disappeared. When she wanted to play or to have some attention, she was there. If she was hungry at dinnertime, I'd find her in the kitchen. If she was hungry between mealtimes, she'd be downstairs pestering the Chinese housekeepers for a treat.

Now, it always pleased Niki to be friendly and playful with strangers. Particularly fond of "making an appearance," she'd sneak up from behind. Like a charm it worked each and every time, frightening the newcomer or surprising the return guest.

Later, I'd spy Nikita playing catch, graciously waiting to be fed a treat, cuddling up, soaking up the attention, acting like the "perfect dog." With me, however, she still remained aloof. In fact, nothing ruffled her feathers more than a little TLC from me. Unless, it came on a plate. The look of gratitude in her eyes when I cooked an egg-over-easy was the closest thing I got to returned affection.

Our morning dominance ritual remained firmly intact and, as of late, with a reprisal in the afternoon or evening. Her relationship with the other "pack members" was not blossoming either. With Queen it was non-existent, with Gizmo strained. As for King? It was just pitiful to watch him oogle her.

I had not seen Nikita since lunchtime. She had scrounged a bit of food and went running off. I wondered where her pleasure had led her this afternoon. Most likely, into the woods. No worries. Those days would soon be over.

I had arranged for an "invisible fencing" system to be installed. From then on, all the dogs would be confined to an 11-acre area surrounding the house. No more woods. No more pond. No more cows. No more drama.

The phone rang. My heart skipped a beat. My stomach dropped and butterflies rose. On the other end, a woman was screaming at the top of her lungs. "This is yaw neighbah! Yawr dawg is botherin' my heifers, again! Do you 'ear me? Again! Get ovah now! Do you Hhhear me? Get yaw dawg, NOW!"

Concerned for Niki's wellbeing in the hands of that mad, mad woman, I immediately jumped in the car and drove over to neighboring farmhouse. Waiting for me in the middle of her driveway, was the woman, holding at arms-length what I hoped was a mud-covered dog.

Oh Niki, what have you done now…

What did I do now?! Honestly, this is positively just another misunderstanding! Please, allow me to explain.

I was thirsty after lunch. My water bowl emptied by Gizmo— Was there anything which she did not consume in totality? And, as usual, the afternoon bowl service was rather negligent. You see? I had no choice, but to run over to the barn and wash my food down with some fresh milk. And allow me to confide, not the first time, either! Luckily, my bovine friends are very generous, always sharing. However, the new cow got a little nervous— As if she'd never met a milk drinking Siberian Husky before! *PL*-ease.

She was all fussy. I tried to calm her down, but she cried, "Wolf! Wolf!"

Well, that did it. Now, everyone was all agitated. Pushing each other around and panicking because no one could see the wolf!

Duh! It was only sweet little ME!

Then, this shirt un-buttoned, exposing her not full-coverage enough bra in all its glory, granny burst through the doors screaming something about move out of the way so that I can get a clear shot.

Wow! This half-dressed, hopping mad nut-job has no sense of priorities! This is certainly not the time for a photo! [*]

As I turned to escape the crazy jumping lady, I slipped in a misplaced mudpie. Scrambling to get up, I plunked down into the manure again!

---

[*] Good thing she did not catch me drinking from the milk bucket or she might have spontaneously combust! BOOM! POW!

Holy Buggers! When would these cows learn not to poop where they live?!

Too late now.

The crazy lady grabbed me, sliding me through the muck and straight out of the barn.

While we were waiting for My Mistress, she lectured me on the disturbance I had caused— that dairy cows need to stay calm, relaxed or the milk's no good— that I had no place being there— that the next time, she'd have her shotgun loaded— BLAH BLAH BLAH!

What-ever, lady! I am not the problem here! You were the one in the barn all excited hopping about with buttons popping off every which way AND why not educate "your cows" on the difference between a "dog" and a "wolf!" And, while we're having this friendly little chit-chat, double-check those twins are securely strapped into their car seat AND *pl*-ease, cover up!

Ughhhhh!

My Mistress arrived just in the nick of time. My ears were starting to bleed from that crazy, half-naked, old lady's pitchy rant. Thankfully, wordlessly, she put me in the cargo hold of the SUV.

Our distaste for dirtiness the ONLY thing we shared, My Mistress drove directly to the back of our house and without delay escorted me into the shower room.

A nice shampoo-body massage-power jet rinse-towel rub later, I emerged pristine looking and smelling good again— And, I had just enough time to catch the last rays of sun! WooHoo!

Nestling on a sunny patch of grass, I closed my eyes trying to relax from this afternoon's ordeal.

No matter how hard I tried, friendship kept eluding me. There were countless impediments to my friendship with the cows. I had not seen or smelled Stumpy for weeks now. The geese never came back from Florida. Gizmo might be "family," but certainly was no friend. Queen was always keeping to herself, walking away from my attempts at friendship. And honestly, I preferred to keep a safe distance from King. Such a freaky pervert, he was always close by lurking, watching, drooling— Nasty! As if he had a chance! Not even if he was the only snowball in Hell! Hah!

Plop. Plink.

I stretched my head back and opened an eye.

Oh please, not again!

King was there. Only a few yards away, a puddle of drool quickly becoming a lake.

Ughhhh. Is it even possible to have a single moment of peace and quiet?!

I closed my eyes again, but the sound of the Lake Collie forming dribble-drop by dribble-drop was ratting my nerves— Enough.

Standing up slowly, I stretched my front legs forward while arching my back, tail high in the air. Holding the pose, I sighed and rolled a baby blue in the direction of misguided affection. Taking a long, deep breath, I batted my lashes and walked towards King.

Time to play a little game. Time to teach the old freak a lesson. Just watch this!

I could not believe what I was watching. Neither could King who began to whimper.

With her tail high in the air playfully swishing back-and-forth, Nikita's eyes locked on King as she began to slowly walk towards him. The closer she came, the more he trembled. His dream girl headed straight for him.

Closer and closer yet, they were now almost nose to nose. In anticipation of that next step forward, King inhaled deeply.

Without pause, without changing her gaze, Nikita gracefully floated right past King.

OMG! She had been focused on some point just beyond her lovestruck admirer. Where and when did she ever learn to be a femme fatale? Her namesake more than ever…

Never an object on her affections radar, a completely devastated King finally exhaled. Groaning with the pain of such blatant rejection, he slunk into the juniper bushes where he stayed hidden for weeks.

*

Clearly, Nikita needed some "socialization." So, I called a friend who had a puppy almost a year younger than Niki and invited them to The Farm.

Clea was a Sibercollie, a Siberian Husky and Border Collie hybrid. Standing slightly smaller than Nikita, Clea's fine coat was softly mottled black and white. Her eyes were literally half brown, half blue. Top half brown, bottom half blue. They were amazing, but gave her a somewhat dopey or half-baked look.

With an easygoing nature, Clea happily followed Niki's lead. The indefatigable duo were as thick as thieves usually staying close by the house, running around, and getting into minimal trouble.

The best part: for two entire days after Clea's departure, Niki would sleep. No drama. No fiascos. Forty-eight hours full of dull moments.

Naturally, I arranged for Clea to visit as often as possible, even organizing some "sleepovers". It was such a blessing.

What a blessing! Someone to play with and stamped "MISTRESS APPROVED!" Friendship was mine at last! WooHoo! And not just any friendship, but a real BFF! Her name was Clea— which is a little quirky if you ask me. But then, not everyone can be crowned Ni-ki-ta!

A girl just like me— not as pretty and definitely not as smart, but full of boundless enthusiasm. Faithfully, unquestioningly following my lead, Clea posed zero challenge to Me and My Reign! We got along marvelously!

From time-to-time, Gizmo would try to join in on all the fun, but we moved way too fast for the waddling wonder. Sometimes when we were tired of chasing things and running circles around The Giz, we would tease King. Slowly walking past, side-by-side, our tails weaving in & out, waving back & forth, or going over to his food bowl and with our heads nuzzled together eating his kibble piece-by-piece.

Always so much fun, I could not understand why Clea did not come over more often or on her own. Her "story" was that she was attached to her house by an invisible bungee cord and could only get so far before she'd have to go back.

Huh? Are you making some obtuse reference to your collie heritage and shepherding instincts?

"No," she insisted. "There's an invisible bungee cord."

What-ever! Just zip it and let's play!

The best part: every time Clea came to visit, My Mistress was uncharacteristically nice. She'd leave us alone to play, make a special meal, even come around with treats— Oh yeah! Garden-side, hostess-tray service with a smile!

One evening, My Mistress had "other plans" and before leaving closed Clea, Gizmo, and me in the game room.[*] By far,

---

[*] Why she insisted on leaving Gizmo with us, I will never understand. Let's be honest, okay? Giz was always the third wheel, only barrel shaped! LMTO

the largest room in the house, there was lots space to run around, furniture to jump on, a gigantic TV, a pool table, and even a shuffleboard table! But, after the movie was over, there was nothing to do! How often can you leapfrog over the furniture? How many times can you play toss the cue ball before something breaks?

Gizmo took out another video, but all she could do was rip open the cover. And come on, "Point Break" again?!

Clea suggested that we check out the rest of the house.

Hello, cute but stupid! The door is closed!

"But, not locked," she added.

Gizmo and I watched as Clea clamped her jaw on the door handle, twisted her head, and leaned forward— PRESTO! The door opened.

With surprising speed, Gizmo ran out, sputtering "mineminemine," and butted the door closed again! WHAT?! GRRrrrrr!

Clea, ever cheerful, wondered why I was so perturbed and offered to teach me how to open the door.

Ughhhh. Sometimes, she was so simple.

Rolling my eyes several times for emphasis, I dolefully explained to her protocol and decorum— A princess is always first. A princess never opens a door. The metallic taste of the doorknob is far too offensive for our refined taste buds. Most importantly, that every whim becomes a reality once the princess wishes it. So, a true princess finds the door is always open!

Clea smirked and mouthing the handle again turned her head this time in the opposite direction.

Gizmo's all-time favorite movie. She claimed that it reminded her of the good old days wave running on Venice beach. I think that she had a soft spot for Keanu. Every time he appeared on screen, she'd start singing. Ouch!

Door open, I bolted through and headed straight towards the kitchen where I found Gizmo standing on the table, the plates already licked clean!

Her mouth dropped open in astonishment and a burp escaped!

Ewww! Disgusting. Obviously, not of royal lineage.

My eyes locked on Gizmo. Her behavior was unacceptable. She knew better AND we had a guest!

Giz started to threaten me, but I quickly reminded her that I did not require any assistance to be on the table and that no one was around to save her this time.

Gizmo froze. Even her wonder jaws were unable to move.

Clea bounced into the kitchen, "Hey! Looky looky here!"

Forget about the Sibercollie thing, my BFF was half monkey-half dog! Not only had she been able to open the pantry door, she had successfully emptied ALL the shelves.

Most excellent. Very nice work, my friend!

Gizmo's stomach growled, her eyes gleamed, in expectation of the renewed feeding frenzy.

Oh *pl*-ease! You've eaten enough for 3 lifetimes and you may not even make it through this one!

Easily enough, I convinced Clea to push the chairs in tight, confining Gizmo to the scene of her crime— Exactly! Let the guilty party stand justly accused. High time, My Mistress sees the "Real Gizmo!"

Turning to go back to the pantry closet, I heard Chinese.

Buggers! Foiled again!

The Givers of Good Food must have heard the commotion. Emerging from their quarters, the woman came forward chatting away excitedly while her man closed himself inside the pantry.

HEY!

Noting my distress and always the gracious hostess, the woman brought out an evening snack. I was so touched. She had saved the best entrail for me!

Xiè xie xie.➶➶

Snack time over and the contents of the pantry re-arranged, The Givers of Good Food closed themselves back downstairs. The door lock clicked.

Yippee! FULL RUN OF THE HOUSE!

We had a blast! Even Gizmo found good humor and joined us! Some nosing about, playing hide-and-seek, and even a few games of vicious dog, before I heard My Mistress' car approach.

Cuing the other two into place, we sat at the front door waiting for it to open.

I opened the front door and was greeted by three dogs sitting in a line, their tails swishing back and forth. Strange, I remembered leaving the happy trio in the game room.✧

➶➶ By this time, my Chinese was fluent. But most likely yours is not, so the rest of my conversation with the woman will unfortunately remain unrecorded.

✧ A little fuzzy now. It's always that last shot of tequila.

Wordlessly, I closed the door behind me and checked out the house. Finding everything in its place, I went back into the foyer where the happy trio were still waiting patiently. What good little puppies!

One "Hello!" and they started jumping about. We all played for a while. I was surprised that even Gizmo joined in the fun.

After that evening, Clea did not come over so often. Her parents were having personal problems, making it difficult to arrange anything, and Niki needed to be on a lead until she was trained to the invisible fence.

None of the dogs were happy with the new electronic collars and, in true form, Nikita the least of all. Her mood darker and darker as the training progressed, she vacillated between brooding and throwing temper tantrums. Once again, she was spending more and more time on her back with her scruff pinned to the floor.

Despite Nikita's opposition, I diligently complied with invisible fencing training method. And, knowing Niki's wanderlust, I spent one week longer than suggested before allowing her off leash. Somehow, I found the time and patience every day, twice a day, for three weeks of drills.

Drills drills drills. I had had it! My Mistress was out of control, again! This time, obviously doubtful of her own fortitude, she enlisted the aid of strangers!

First, a couple of men spent an entire day burying a wire. I wanted to say "hello," maybe even help a bit.[8] But, no such luck. My Mistress refused to introduce me AND kept me locked up!

Humphhh!

All I could do was watch. Hour after hour, more and more wire, until it formed a ring around the house. Then, little flags were placed marking the buried wire.

Huh? T-a-c-k-y, Tacky with a capital "T!" I hope that they paid you for this hillbilly-lawn-ornament-redneck-landscaping joke!

Finished with the "architectural masterpiece," one of the men came over to introduce himself to me. He stroked my head, reminded me how pretty I was and offered me a present— Yes, score!

---

[8] I had already been of great assistance throughout the neighborhood. Earlier that week, I came to the aid of our elderly neighbor. When she was working in her garden, she had mistakenly planted the flowers before removing the critters living underneath. Imagine her delight, when I yanked up the marigolds and the voles with one simple movement! Presto!

Graciously, I bowed my head and allowed him to put on the new collar. It wasn't very attractive or stylish, but I did appreciate the gesture. With a little luck, My Mistress would have enough good sense to remove the monstrosity after he left.

Please leave. Please leave soon. This ugly thing is h e a v y!

But, the man did not leave right away. Instead, he took me for a walk.

Oohhh, a present and a walk! I am liking this man more and more.

Ever the over-protective, intrusive chaperone, My Mistress tagged along— Ughhhh. At least, she kept a respectful distance.

We strolled around the property, the man speaking very little. Eventually, we came close to where they buried the wire. The closer we came to the flags, the slower his pace.[•]

Then, I heard it.

BEEP! BEEP!

The new collar was making noise.

Hey! Get this party favor OFF of me!

I pulled forward to get away— ZAP!

AACKKKK! That does not tickle! What the— BEEP! BEEP!

This time the man rescued me, pulling me back away from the flags. Out of the danger zone, my collar now silent, I tried to make sense of what just happened. Of course, it did not take very long for me to put the puzzle together— Warning: The picture's none too pretty.

Obviously, My Mistress was sooooooo bored with her pathetic life that she now had to resort to strangers peddling wearable tasers just to get her jollies! But, why pick on me?!

[•] In retrospect, I should've interpreted his reluctance as a warning. But, it was such a beautiful day and I was enjoying our walk. I never suspected that My Mistress had persuaded him to be an accomplice in one of her diabolical schemes.

Hadn't I been good? Learned all the commands? Obeying when I heard them? Staying home most nights? Offering presents from my travels? It made absolutely zero sense.

Worse still, I was put back on lock down. Yep, that's right. NO more free time. NO more visiting. NO more fun. My days were once again filled with excruciating boredom.

Every day My Mistress took me to the flags, reminding me of the location of the fence. Yes, every single day the same exact routine! I could not decide which was worse: once again being literally house-bound OR the twice daily, 60minute insult to my intelligence!

Hello! I do not need to be reminded where the wire of torture is buried! I saw them install it— Duh! Are you testing the product personally? Or are you just that clucky?!

My only consolation was that Gizmo was also forced to participate in the drills. With any luck, the electroshock-aversion therapy would do her good! More times than not, My Mistress would "accidentally" leave the special collar on Giz. So, as munchy-crunchy-motor-mouth waddled past the TV on her way into the kitchen— ZzzAP!

Bonus! There was a TV in every room and Giz was always on her way to the kitchen!

ZAP out of your funk! ZAP out of your chunk! ZAP! ZAP! ZAP! Your frown turned upside-down? Your waddle a wiggle yet?! Hah!

*

Another day, yet another drill, My Mistress walked me into the middle of the backyard. This was ridiculous. She was unrealistic if she thought that I would ever be so easily subdued or deterred. I needed my freedom. Fact was everything I wanted to do, everyone I wanted to visit was on the other side of that invisible fence— Humphhh.

Double-checking that the electronic collar was securely around my neck, she untethered me! WooHoo! F-r-e-e, FREE— However, I carefully kept my pleasure under wraps. Absolutely zero need to let her know!

With an apathetic sigh, a shoulder shrug, I turned back moping towards the house. My Mistress hollered after me, wondering if I wanted to play.

Yeah! But, not with you or that stupid, ridiculously pink-colored squeaky toy!

I turned back to face her, took a deep breath, and went for it. Whizzing past her, I heard the "BEEP! BEEP!" No stopping now!

Soaring into the air and over the wooden fence—
ZAAAPP!

As the current pulsed through my muscles I let out a "yippee" to release the energy. Landing on all fours, narrowly missing a mudpie,[note] I shook my fur back into place. When I turned to wink goodbye, the look of awe, of reverence on her face = Priceless!

The cows were still in the barn from the morning milking, so I wandered along the stream sniffing out new trophies. With nothing particularly interesting to be found, I made my way deeper into the woods. On my way back, I passed by the pond to see if the geese were back. No luck there, either.

Disappointed that my first time out in weeks was such a bust, I returned to The Farm early.

Starting from the base, I charged up the driveway open throttle like My Mistress always did in her roadster. I heard

---

[note] Note to self: I must speak with the cows regarding this bad habit of pooping everywhere. It's dangerous! Somebody might get hurt.

the "BEEP! BEEP!" But with my speed so fast, I easily cleared the "danger zone" before the shock.

Yes, SCORE![†]

Slowing my pace back to a trot, I continued directly towards the house. Sitting down in the middle of the driveway by the fountain, in clear view from the kitchen window, I waited for her to see me.

One. Two. Three— The door flung open, My Mistress running out, tears of joy and mascara streaming down her face. Any questions as to where Giz got all her drama?!

Wrapping her arms around me, she carried me inside and kept me close to her for the rest of the evening. Thankfully, not too close.

*

My Mistress was never pleased. She was always wanting something more. More rules, more attention, more perfection, more More MORE! And, since Gizmo had been tapped out a long, long time ago, her resources dried up along with her sanity, it was only demanded from ME— Exactly! After watching me clear the invisible fence with simple grace, she just had to raise "the bar."

Once again, requiring the aid of others, My Mistress called the man back to our house. This time he came with an ugly harness.

No, no thank you. No more "presents" from you! Now, Go Away!

The new monstrosity had two blunt electrodes in the chest, one in each armpit, and two in the belly. Even worse, she made him increase the "danger zone" and the voltage!

[†] Another one for Ni-Ki-Ta! Who's the winner? Who's the champion? Yeah, baby that's right! Me-Me-ME!

AAACKKKK! Please, someone help me! This is no joke! Call the Animal Rights Protection League immediately! I am positive that this medieval-looking torture contraption and usage thereof is in violation of the Geneva Conventions as it pertains to non-combatant canine prisoners! 110% Positive!

No one came to my aid. Grrrrr.

Once again on lock down, I had to endure more drills now with the new harness! But, not Gizmo. As always, she was exempt— Not fair! If hungry enough, that little piggy might just waddle off to the Pittstown Market!

On rainy days, fully aware that she would melt, My Mistress suspended all outdoor training. Yea! Free Day = Play Day! Unfortunately, this particular rainy afternoon, play was not an option. My Mistress discovered a 40+ page illustrated addition to her list of rules A.K.A. a book of dog tricks. These "tricks" were supposed to be performed after a cued phrase to impress her and her guests!

Excuse me, what guests?! No one visits here anymore! You've scared them ALL away!

As if this new pastime was not arduous enough, for today's trick, she insisted to teach us how to "pray."

PL-ease. I know how to pray. But, my prayers are never answered— Exactly! I prayed for freedom and look where I am. I prayed for friendship and look with whom I am playing!

Gizmo on the other hand? She loved it! With every successful "prayer," Giz got another liver treat or a little head massage. Obviously, her prayers answered, Gizzy just prayed for the wrong things— Exactly! She should've asked for things like a higher metabolism, a kinder disposition, and world peace! Hah!

After hours of forcing my head to touch crossed paws, My Mistress tired of this whim and went to off busy herself with some new preoccupation.

Yes! HALELUIAH!

But, that celebration was extraordinarily short lived. Believe it or not, she came back with her treat bag re-filled and armed with a new book!

What? More? My prayers so faaarrrrrr from being answered, Heaven must be on strike!

I shot a commiserative glance sideways towards Gizmo, but she was already in position "praying" for a fresh treat.

Grrreat! If no one else dares, then I'll do it! That's right, time to cut the strings. No more puppeteering! I am not her plaything!

Before I could even work up a real growl and fully express my best fangs-bared-I-am-the-big-bad-alpha-wolf, she flipped me on my back. My neck pinned to the floor, her face in mine. Our eyes locked.

I am NOT caving first! Not this time.

Not again, Nikita. I'm tired of this behavior…

Her behavior is unacceptable! I'm going to fix it!

I'm going to fix her. As much as I want her puppies, maybe that will solve the problem…

She is the problem! As much as I enjoy her eggs-over-easy, she has got to learn her lesson! I am Alpha!

When will she learn that I am Alpha? She's a dog. I'm her owner She must respect me.

Me! Respect ME! That's all I ask!

All I ask is that you are a sweet, well-behaved puppy.

I am not a puppy! STOP treating me like one!

One minute and counting with no sign of caving in. Her determination was tiring me, frightening me…

She was trying to frighten me, to break me. ABSOLUTELY RIDICULOUS!

Absolutely ridiculous. This is not what I bargained for. I want a dog not a willful beast…

My will cannot be shattered like a sheet of ice!

Her ice-blue eyes kept their determination. Void of any emotion. Void of any submission…

Any sign of submission, any sign of weakness—

Please Nikita, just let it go…

Let me go! I am not yours to manipulate! I AM NOT A TOY!

I am not toying around Nikita. The rules are the rules!

Too many rules! Too many expectations! I cannot be your everything! I have had it! ENOUGH!

Enough…

Niki was shaking uncontrollably. I expected her to start convulsing at any moment. Placing my free hand over her eyes, I kept it there waiting for her body to be calm. Only once her heartbeat returned to normal and the spasms stopped, did I release both hands.

Nikita remained motionless on the floor. Her clear blue eyes now expressing a vacant sadness, which I had never seen before.

Regret and doubt clouded my thoughts. Maybe, I had been too strict with her. Maybe, I lacked the temperament to handle such a strong-willed creature. In any case, the situation could not continue. I needed some time and space. Leaving the Chinese housekeepers in charge of the house and the dogs, I left that very evening.

By the time I came back from my little getaway, there was something different about Nikita. She was still independent and determined, but she stayed closer to the house, challenged me less, and was even friendlier with Gizmo. The Chinese housekeepers refused to tell me anything, but I had reasons behind my suspicions.

Like Nikita, the couple were now uncharacteristically nice and agreeable, performing all their duties without a fuss. And, they had taken the extraordinary initiative to bathe all the dogs while I was gone.

Odder still, since my return, Nikita feigned complete disinterest in the cows.

The cows are not my friends. Not at all! While My Mistress took her "break" from reality, I persuaded The Givers of Good Food to free me— just to run around the backyard. After all, a little exercise is always a good idea!

Despite my say-so to the contrary, they insisted that I wear the new harness.

Fine. What-ever! Just let me be free!

I played around the backyard for a bit, but then the cows came out. It had been soooo long since our last visit which had not ended so nicely, I do recall.

Ohhh, forget it! The past is the past. Let's make up for lost time!

Starting from my mark in the middle of the yard, I easily cleared the wooden fence— But, not the electric one. In my excitement, I forgot to calculate the added range and intensity— Oopsy!

With the electric shock-induced muscle spasms continuing longer than I anticipated, my legs buckled underneath me when my paws touched the ground. As soon as I regained muscle control, I tried to stand up. But the field was soupy, making it difficult to find sound footing.

Plunk into the mud— Plunk SPLAT!

The New Bessie was closest to me. She saw me struggling and kindly made her way over to help!   Hey, thanks! Not going to cause a fuss this time? Come to aid of your new friend? Want to give your good neighbor a helping hoof? So very pleased to see you've gotten yourself some higher education and better manners!

She came right up alongside of me, but did not offer any help. Instead, she started to laugh, calling out to the other cows, "Hey, watch this!"

Huh?

Though mud caked eyes, I saw a leg wind up in dramatic preparation to kick me!

You BOVINE!

Quickly tumbling away out of her striking range, I rolled out of the mud straight into a mud-pie!

Ewww! Disgusting!

Worse, Meddling Bessie was still walking in my direction, calling for everyone to watch again! This heifer was freaking demented! Obviously, too many hormones and not enough mooooo-d stabilizers in her feed!

I just kept rolling away, away from that maniacal— BEEP! BEEP!

Buggers! I forgot about—

ZAAAAPP!

In my efforts to distance myself, I had rolled back towards The Farm, under the wooden fence right above the— BEEP! BEEP!

My muscles still not recovered from the last—

ZAAAAPP!

As everything started to fade to black, I heard Gizmo sounding the alarm.

Too late, but thanks anyways Giz— **BEEP! BEEP!**

- Fade to black -

The first thing that came back was my hearing. The Chinese couple was arguing louder than usual. If I translated correctly, the man was insisting that I was a goner and debating between soup or roast— Holy Buggers! I always thought that canine carnivores were just a scary story told to frighten naughty puppies. No wonder they fed Gizmo so well! Hah!

Then, my sense of smell returned— Whoa! Stinky Kitty's here!

My eyes flew open.

The woman was holding smelling salts by my nose. As she moved the vial away, an overwhelming odor of manure and burnt fur sent waves of nausea rushing over me. It was all coming back to me now. The cows, the fence, and Gizmo to the rescue— What an embarrassing fiasco!

And then, it got worse.

The couple had finally stopped arguing and came to an agreement on how to handle "the situation."

No shower room A.K.A. No privacy. That's right— Chinese Water Torture!

With everyone watching, they unrolled the garden hose and bathed me like a common mutt! But that's not the end of it. Believe it or not, it got even worse— Exactly! They whipped out not my floral scented, herbal shampoo, but rather some generic bottle with a Collie on it!

Ahhhhh! Please, someone help me before I morph into a "Lassie-hybrid" like Clea!

Later that evening, as I snuggled in my bed the woman came to me with a small plate of rice and kibble. I appreciated her thoughtfulness. My stomach was still a little queasy.

She stroked my head a few times. Before leaving, she promised that she would never share with My Mistress today's events. However, she added, if I even thought to bamboozle her again, she would let the man have his dinner request— Ughhhh.

*

A return to the sad status quo. My Mistress back from her vacation, the training routine was re-established. Gizmo was, well, gizmotic— Yep, life was predictable again.

Just when I thought good times and fun were lost forever, I heard a car coming up the driveway—WooHoo! Visitors! This totally explained why My Mistress was stuck in the bathroom entrenched in her "private routine" and The Givers of Good Food were upstairs prepping the table for a feast!

When the Chinese man opened the front door, I rushed him from behind and slipped out. Running towards the car, I chased it until it stopped.

Hello friends!

A woman opened the door. New to me, she seemed very nice greeting me with "how pretty" and the usual pleasantries. From inside the SUV, I heard a little, squeaky voice. The back door opened and a little person came out. Not my little person, but another one. Older and bigger— Sweet!

He took one look at me, screamed, "Ahhh! It's a Vicious Dog!" and took off running.

Cool! You know the game! Let's play! WooHoo!

Despite his little legs, he was much, much faster than My Mistress and his little lungs screamed frightfully the entire time— How sublime! Method acting, he was a natural. And just like the "Energizer Bunny," he kept going and going and going and— SPLAATTT!

He tripped.

Pouncing on the little person and keeping him pinned down to the ground, I stared at him.

He pleaded to be freed.

I kept staring. Never taking my eyes off him, I lowered my nose to his.

Acting completely terrified, he froze.

The tension between us high, time stood still until— Licking one ear and then the other, I showered his face with kisses! Hah gotcha!

Giggling at first, before long he was laughing hysterically. Back on his feet, he asked "again?" I nosed him a "yes" and we were off. This time he screamed less, but ran just as fast!

We had fun all day long! When his little legs got too tired to run, we watched some cartoons. Not really my thing, but he was a guest.

Finding us in the game room in front of the big TV, The Givers of Good Food served up a special platter. Naturally, I stayed close by to make sure that there were no unfortunate reprisals of The Gizminator.

Cartoons over, plate licked clean, he rested his head on my belly and took a nap. Life was grand— Until, as usual My Mistress interfered with my happiness. She woke up the new little person and made them ALL go home!

Oh, buggers. Back to my ho-hum existence.

I went out onto the deck to be by myself. As happy as I was to entertain her guests, I missed mine. It had been forever since I saw My Little Person. And, there was my BFF Clea and Stinky Kitty who had both completely disappeared!

Now that I was thinking about it, the real problem was I never went "out." No one took me or invited me anywhere. Even the cows did not want me visiting anymore. I always had to wait for friends to come to me— Not fair!

Returning to my bed, I double-checked that no one was around to disturb me. Crossing my paws, I tucked my nose in-between and closed my eyes. Before I fell into my world of dreams, I said a prayer.

I had just drifted off, when it began to thunder and lightning. My Mistress, obviously afraid to be alone, came running outside and glued herself to my side. From the shelter of the covered deck, we watched lightning dance across the horizon as the violent storm passed.

Shaking like a little scaredy-cat, with every crack of thunder she pressed herself against me as the lightning strikes came closer striking down one after another in the field. It was good to know that she recognized my fortitude.

Now IF ONLY she could afford a little more space and appreciate me from afar! Still, I humored her by allowing her to hold me until the storm passed and she felt safe again.

The next morning, I was woken up by the sound of Clea's car.

HALLELUJAH! Finally, my prayers are being heard! My BFF is here to play!

She had gotten bigger, but naturally I was still taller and prettier! We played and played just like before, but something was off. Clea was not her usual chatty, carefree self. She flatly refused to share where she'd been, what she'd been doing, and why she had not visited me. Every time I asked, she would change the subject or start a new game.

I was confused. It was frustrating.

If we were really BFF's, she would talk. But, she would not even share what she had had for breakfast! If we were really BFF's, I would have an open invitation to Clea's house. But, she never invited me. In fact, I did not even know where she lived!

This is ridiculous! No more pussy footing around.

Cornering Clea in the side yard where we could talk privately, I nicely inquired about the drive over. That way, I could drop by and visit on my own A.K.A. Zero reason to wait so long between play dates!

She got a little funny and said she did not remember anything, mumbling that the car always put her to sleep.

Huh? I've seen you with your nose out the window! Don't you dare lie to me. We're Best Friends!

She looked away.

Not to be so easily deterred, I moved so she could see me.

As nicely as possible, I asked for any details about what she'd been doing. New friends? New adventures?

Her dopey eyes stared blankly. This time, she did not even bother to lie— Exactly! She said absolutely nothing.

Grrrrrrr— Completely un-acceptable. I want to know, now!

Knocking her feet out from underneath and pinning her to the ground, I insisted that she tell me everything!

Clea started to cry.

Don't be such a baby. Just tell me!

She whimpered that I wasn't acting too friendly.

Ugh! Friendship?! You have the nerve to speak the word when you're lying through your canines! What are you afraid of you little sissy?

Still, no answers only whimpers.

Fine. Enough. You disgust me.

I let go of her and walked over to a shady spot underneath the grove of white birch. I needed some time and space to re-evaluate our relationship. Maybe this friendship stuff wasn't what it was cracked up to be. I'd rather be alone than lied to. R- E- S- P- E- C- T, RESPECT! That's what it was all about, my friends!

Clea found me a short time later. Her crocodile tears had dried, but her head was still hanging low. She sat beside me and keeping her head down, looking at the grass, she showed me the marks on her neck. Finally, in a raspy, tear-choked whisper she confided. Life at her house was not a party, not anymore. Not even close.

Things were perfect in the beginning. Everybody was always so happy, laughing and playing. But then, one day her parents began arguing, slamming doors, and her daddy left.

Since then, her mommy completely ignored her, keeping Clea chained to a tree day and night.

No more walks. No more playtime. Some days, no dinnertime! More and more often, she would fall asleep to the sound of her growling stomach.

Clea started to whimper again.

When her mommy got angry, she would leave Clea outside with no water, no food, no blankie!

The few times her daddy returned home, he would free her. They would laugh and play just like before, until the fighting started again. Her daddy always leaving in such a huff that he forgot her.

No matter how good she was, no matter how many promises to stay that way— Once her daddy slammed the door behind him, her mommy would drag her back to the tree.

She had once tried a Niki-Houdini, but without success.

Even worse, after the failed attempt to escape, her mommy took away the pretty, new collar her daddy had given her and replaced it with her old choke collar. Now, left on in permanence. The red welts on her neck were from the puppy-sized choke chain digging deeper into her skin every time she strayed a little too far from the tree.

Just yesterday, Clea had accidentally gotten the lead wrapped up around the tree, a post, and herself. The lead now so short, Clea was forced to remain standing still in one spot or be strangled to death!

Crying for help, a neighbor finally heard and rescued her.

Her mommy was furious that Clea had made such a fuss and bothered the neighbor. She yelled at Clea. She spanked Clea. Then, as "real punishment" and to "teach her a lesson," she chained Clea back to the tree in the pouring rain! Even when it started to thunder and lightning, Clea's mommy refused to let her inside.

A single tear escaped my eyes. How could I have been so blind to my friend's misfortune?

Moving closer to her, I wrapped my head across her back nuzzling Clea until her crying stopped and breath was slow and calm.

Finally, I broke the silence. My Mistress had to know. She could fix this. She would fix this.

Clea shook her head no. She was afraid that her mommy might get mad again.

Not a problem, I assured her.

Coaching Clea on how to gain My Mistress' attention to the marks without tattling, I made sure she was ready.

Dinner's ready! There was no need to actually call out. All the dogs were eagerly waiting on the deck. I slid open the screen door to let them inside and almost got knocked over by Niki and Giz. Clea, however, stayed on the porch scratching herself.

"Fleas? You got fleas?" Clea ignored me and just kept scratching.✧

Oh, great! The guest dog came with guest fleas.

When I parted her fur to get a closer look, I noticed that she was wearing a choke chain. It was way too small and not an appropriate collar to be left on a dog. When I removed it, I saw crimson red, welt marks.

OMG! I tried not to imagine the worst, but in the very least Clea was being neglected.

She charged inside to eat with the others. I called her father. After a short discussion, we came to a solution. Then, calling his ex, I asked her if I could watch Clea for a few extra days. She was more than

---

✧ All of my dogs have been trained to this phrase. If they stop scratching, it's just an itch. If they continue, I flip them and check for fleas and ticks. No one likes to be flipped, deticked/defleaed, and dipped.

agreeable, adding that I could keep Clea as long as I pleased. Perfect!

Over the next couple of weeks, Nikita and Clea had a ball, playing all day and night. For me, it was bittersweet to watch them. Soon, they would be separated forever. All the arrangements had been finalized for Clea to fly to West Palm Beach, Florida.

Florida? Really?! Why so faaaaarrrr? You do know, it's very, very, very hot. Your Sibercollie coat will molt.

Unfazed, Clea giggled, "Only birds molt. We tuft and shed."

She added that she was certain that her daddy had air-conditioning and would only take her for long walks in the early morning and late evenings.

Since moving into The Farm, Clea was back to her happy-go-lucky self. I was proud that My Mistress had swiftly intervened, but wished that we could've kept Clea. Of course, I understood that her place was with family— But, we could be distant cousins! Never know until the DNA results come back!

Seriously though, I was happy for her. It was most fantastic news that her daddy was settled in his new home and wanted her to live with him— But Florida? Land of the alligator, mascot and menace?

"Yes, Nikita. My dad has a super cool condo right at the beach! Long walks and the ocean breeze every day!"

Ok fine. If you must leave, then please make sure that you say "hello" to the geese and let them know their absence has been sadly noted. They never sent a single word after their unannounced and rather swift departure to that sunshine swampland.

On my last trip to Kodakland,✧ I dropped by a breeder to pick out a stud for Nikita. From the very moment I laid eyes on Snow Prince, I was enchanted. He was stunning. All white, blue eyes, and at 10 months old, he was already larger than Niki. I knew that she would approve. After all, he was the canine version of Mr. February!

Unfortunately, right before Nikita's third heat, the kennel had a fire. All the dogs were safe, but the kennel buildings were destroyed. There was no place for any "romantic interludes." I'd have to wait at least

✧ Rochester, NY. Home to the photography giant and the Lilac Festival.

another cycle until they rebuilt or I found a replacement stud. No problem, except I had puppies on the brain.

One evening, I came across a listing for a local breeder who had Yorkshire Terrier puppies available. Not my type of dog, but Gizmo's friend in NYC had been a Yorkie. She had been so depressed since Seamus moved away with his fathers. Maybe, a new "Seamus" would fill the gap and mend her broken heart. I made an appointment to meet the litter.

The puppies were absolutely precious, so cute and little. I especially liked the one the breeder named "Frank."✧✧ A clone of the original Seamus, he was the perfect replacement. The temptation too great, I signed a check and returned to The Farm with a lap-sized bundle of joy.

✧✧ The breeder insisted that the puppy be called Frank because he was long like a hot dog. If she had only known that he'd be living at a house with Chinese housekeepers.

A bundle of fury was charging at me full steam— Yip-Yip-Yip!

You have got to be kidding me. Things your size are just an amuse bouche![3]

Before I could mount any real protest, My Mistress reminded me that there was no "blood-letting" in the house.

Bummer.

Then, she insisted that I lie down on my side. Otherwise I'd be too intimating.

Huh? This makes me less than puppy size! Never was I so teeny tiny.

Bouncing from one side to another, the little puppy sniffed me all over. Since he was never in one place long enough for me to get a good whiff, My Mistress made the introductions.

"This is your new brother, Shamus."

Hello! Excuse me? There is No Way that that little rat dog is going to grow up to look anything like me! He is not my— Ahhhhhh.

This was cute. Pressing his back against my tummy, the little puppy cuddled up into a ball and fell asleep. Cuter still was the look of agony on Gizmo's face.

Hey, we all know that you got a biGGer beLLy. But, what can I say? He prefers mine!

Finally settled in one spot, I was able to check out the new addition.

Mmmmmm— puppy scent, so sweet, so fresh. He had an extra-fine coat, more like hair than fur, with a black body, chestnut head and white roots. His pads were all pink and soft. Even his lips had a touch of pink as if he'd been kissed by a lipstick-wearing angel.

---

[3] My Mistress had added French lessons to my schedule. Ooh là là!

Cute as he was, I would've preferred that Clea stayed. No "brothers" needed here, just friends please! I could already tell he was going to be trouble and not the type of trouble I like.

*

Even before the first winter snow, my prediction proved more than true. The little whippersnapper was Big Trouble!

Supposedly, My Mistress bought him for Giz. She was hoping that the little one would fall madly in love with Gizmo and he probably would have— But naturally, he preferred me!

PL-ease. What did My Mistress expect? Between "Beauty and the Beast," there is no choice! Youth and Beauty? That's right, I got it ALL!

Unfortunately, "all" also included the puppy.

Everywhere I went there was this little shadow yip-yip-yipping alongside. My "brother" was making my life impossible! Under normal circumstances, it was difficult enough to slip under My Mistress' radar. But with the little one in tow, she saw me every single time!

The few times that I had been able to ditch him, I had to come running right back to his rescue. He was always getting into some sort of situation. The little squirt did not realize that he was miniscule— Exactly! Absolutely zero concept of his lack of matter! He got stuck on the steps, hung up on fallen tree limbs, lost in a pile of leaves— Oh Jeeps! The near-death scenarios were endless!

Even worse, totally oblivious to his impending mortal danger, Shamus would continue completely engrossed in the middle of doing "his thing." Luckily, I was always there to intervene on his behalf.

Once I caught him trying to challenge King.

Silently, I maneuvered myself behind Shamus and showed King my pearly whites. Naturally, King immediately backed down. However, it never occurred to Sparky that I was behind him. The 5 lbs.-when-wet runt actually thought he was so freaking fierce that he had just barked down his 95 lbs.-before-breakfast adversary! Simply ludicrous— Obviously, he was farrrr from the brightest bulb on the tree!

What he lacked for in size and intelligence, Shamus did have in enthusiasm. He was always happy, always bouncing around, always willing to do whatever I asked. He made Clea look as amicable as the "Wicked Witch of Whatever." But, quite unfortunately, this eagerness had a HUGE downside— Exactly! He would get too excited, charge forward, yip-yip-yip, and bungle everything!

For weeks now, I had been stalking the wild turkeys. Usually, when they passed in plain view, My Mistress was there or I was confined. This morning, I was neither watched nor tethered. As the turkeys were on their sunrise pilgrimage across the backyard, I was watching them from downwind, waiting for my—

YIP! YIP! YIP!

BUGGERS! He was awake and she let him out!

His mouth discharged faster than his brain could think. The turkeys took flight and disappeared into the woods. Spotting me in my lookout, Shamus swaggered over so proud that he had scared away the turkeys.

Yeah, come over here you little twit.

Once he was close enough, I swapped him with my paw. Flipping him over and keeping him pinned to the ground, I dutifully gave Shamus his first lesson.

"Ok-Ok-Ok", is all he could say. And then, he kissed me!

Arghhhh. Not a single word penetrated that puppy brain. If he wasn't so adorable, I would've smacked him completely senseless.

Despite his obvious shortcomings, I took Shamus on as my apprentice.[*]

Every day, once My Mistress had finished with his obedience lessons, I would give him the more practical lessons of canine life. With the attention span of a gnat, his education proved to be quite challenging— his progress extremely slow. But, I had my hopes.

My hopes that Gizmo and Shamus would bond were in vain. She actually seemed upset that I brought home a puppy and wanted nothing to do with him. Nikita, on the other hand, had taken a keen interest. Very protective, she was always close by watching him, cleaning him, correcting his behavior, and making sure that all the other dogs were nice towards him. As for

[*] Look, I was bored, not a lot "to do" in the country. And, no one else was going to teach him how to dig, the art of the hunt, protocol, blah blah blah.

Shamus, he idolized her. Whatever Niki did, Shamus would copy. It made his training a breeze.✧

Not fulfilling his original purpose, Shamus did prove immensely helpful with Nikita. Since Shamus had joined the pack, she stayed closer to home. Still escaping the "invisible fence" as she pleased, Niki now came back sooner and pulled no more all-nighters.

For the first few months, everything was perfect. Then, Nikita went into heat. And, Shamus decided that he wanted to be "more" than just her brother. The situation bordered between ridiculous and pitiful.

Niki had found a quiet place upstairs where she would spend most of the day curled up in a corner. Shamus posted himself at the top of the staircase. No one was allowed to bother "His Nikita." Anytime anyone passed, he would bark a warning. Oddly though, there were a few times I went past and he did not bother to bark.

Tiptoeing up the stairs, I would peak into the room to find that Shamus was "busy." He did not know where the ocean lay, but he understood the

---

✧ The only command he had difficulty with was "sit." Too excited for a treat or too anxious for the next command, his butt floated in the air like a hovercraft.

motion. Niki always with the look, "Please get this thing off of me."

Please get Sparky OFF OF ME! Do not laugh and leave to get your camera! This is so not funny. And, this is so definitely not a "Facebook Moment!" Two weeks and counting already! I'm bloated, achy, tired— And FYI, I refuse to be held responsible for any mutant puppies!

Every time I fell asleep, I was woken up by Jacked-up-on-Testosterone Terrier humping me. My back, my stomach, my tail— Thank heavens, everywhere but "there!"

I would have smacked him senseless, but I lacked the strength and most of the time he was acting quite the little man, making sure that I was comfortable and that no one bothered me. But, don't be confused. By no means, did I want his puppies— No Way! I was not about to lose my girlish figure.

Later that week, My Mistress removed Macho Mutt from my sight and took him out for a car ride. When they came back, he was wearing a lampshade.

Grrrrrr. You went to a party without me?!

I went over to give him a good lashing. But after closer inspection, I realized that he had exchanged his "package" for the lampshade. What a dumb cluck! Absolutely ZERO sense of value.

Even worse, now we had a very, very serious problem. Everyone knows a "sparkless" Sparky cannot be a protégé. Out of the question! And, aside from his obvious lack of cunning and wits, Shamus also seemed to have reached a growth plateau. Unless he had a miraculous spurt, he would always be a little squirt.

That evening, I had a long talk with Shamus reviewing his lack of significant progress and qualifications. As was my solemn responsibility, I informed him that he would never rise to my greatness nor achieve my prowess. However, despite his lack of natural talent, his vertical challenge, and his missing parts, I would continue his education in the hopes that one day he could function as well as a "normal" dog. Furthermore, if he insisted to shadow me, he would have to settle for the title of "sidekick."

"OkOkOk-OK!" And then, he kissed me!

Arghhhhh. Puppy brain.

*

Over the next few days, we were all confined to the house. A late season blizzard dumped so much snow that My Mistress allowed no one out. We played and watched movies and played and ate. Not as bad as I feared, but outside was The Place to be. With fresh snow, the tracks were easier to follow, the scents sharper.

Of little surprise, Mistress Raise-The-Bar-Higher-And-Higher added a new rule to hide-and-seek. ONLY the first dog to find her would win a chunk of cheese. Given my hunting expertise, it was a no brainer that I would be victorious every time. However, much to my dismay, Shamus turned into a little cheat!

First, he would not touch his butt to the floor and sit.

She'd push it down. He'd let it rise up.

She'd push it down. It would rise up, again!

Ahh, come on. Sit already! I want to play!

Even worse, he refused to "stay." As soon as My Mistress turned the corner, he'd get up and follow her without waiting for the signal! If she'd pop her head back to look, he'd plop his butt down wherever he was. As if My Mistress would not realize that he had moved from the original spot!

Not to be so easily fooled, My Mistress would pick up the little scoundrel, plunk him back down next to Giz and I, and start from the beginning again— Ridiculous!

Whine-cry-whine, Shamus insisted that he needed to get a head start because he was so small and Giz and I were so quick.

Huh? True about me, but the waddler's no real threat, even with a cheese treat up for grabs!

I went to smack him, but he showered me with I'm sorries and puppy kisses. Arghhh. Simply impossible to penetrate that puppy brain!

Fine, my little sidekick. We'll tag team it.

Now, as soon as My Mistress left the room, BOTH Shamus and I would scoot forward. If she turned quickly to look, we'd BOTH plop back down!

And, it worked! My Mistress was none the wiser to our little scheme. Shamus and I would arrive at the same time to her "hiding spot," splitting the treat between the two of us. Gizmo? She was back on a sorely needed cheese-free diet!

*

None too soon, My Mistress finally let me play in the winter wonderland! WooHoo! So much snow still on the ground, no one could come to visit. Not even the snowplow man— That's right! NO tire tracks! Just mouse tracks, deer tracks, bird tracks— So many tracks, like Gizmo on a smorgasbord table, I couldn't decide where to start! Hah!

Digging nose holes here and there, I sniffed out the newest marks. After setting up a perimeter, I waited for my prey to resurface. Unfortunately, she let "him" out.

Ughhhh.

Not wanting Sidekick Shamus to botch everything up again, I sent him on his own search and kill mission. Dutifully, he marched over to his own post. Happily, I settled back into my watch. However, I could no longer concentrate with the circus act only a few yards away.

Shamus was digging tiny holes for his teeny nose. Instead of sniffing, he was chasing the snow pebbles as they flew from his own paws. Pouncing on the "prey," he chomped down and acted surprised when they melted in his mouth!

Please Lord God, give me strength.

I turned away to focus on my own task. Still no movement, I double-checked the sniff holes in case I had missed something when I was distracted by— Puppy chirps? Not again! Seriously, how am I ever going to get anything accomplished?!

Sidekick Sparky had got himself into another one of his "situations" and was crying. His pleas for help too pitiful to ignore, I looked over to see what the problem was and saw nothing— Not even him!

Oh buggers! I'd have to go personally to investigate.

The spot where Shamus had been standing was now a sinkhole. It seemed as though he pounced his way through the snow, falling 4 feet into a window well. I looked down at Snow-Tunnel Terrier.

"Please Niki, please help me. I was only following your—"

ENOUGH, Shamus. I do not want to hear it. Absolutely none of it!

Careful not to fall through myself, I started digging. But the surrounding snow was iced solid, making it a mission impossible. The little munchkin might freeze before I got to him. We would need her help.

Peering in through the kitchen windows, there was no sign of My Mistress. However, I did spy Gizmo circling the table looking for a way up— Tsk, tsk! When was she going to learn that food was not the friend it pretended to be?

Contrary to my pedigreed breeding, I knocked once on the window with my paw.

And, then again.

And, then again.

And, then AGAIN!

At long last, I heard Mistress Absentee Parent coming. I returned to the sinkhole and told Shamus he'd better cry like he was going to die or I'd kill him.

Hearing the puppykins-in-distress, My Mistress came outside and yelled at ME!

Huh?! Use your special eyes, please— We have a situation here!

Quickly, she swallowed her admonishments when she looked down to see Shamus was in quite a pickle. After thanking me profusely for my assistance, she plucked the little one out and carried him into the house.

Yea! Puppykins Free!

Once again the lone wolf, I scouted the rest of the property looking for some action. Luckily, I was downwind when I picked up the heavenly scent of deer. Positioning myself on top of Snowdrift Mountain, I waited for the herd to get closer before I made my move.

Closer.

Closer still.

Now, they were within striking distance.

MmmMmm. I could hardly wait any longer to sink my teeth into— "DINNER!"

Screaming at the top of her lungs, My Mistress came bustling out of the house.

BLAST IT ALL!!! If it wasn't one, it was the other!

I swiveled my head to look at her, and then back to the deer.

Immediately, she stopped screaming, frozen in place just like the herd.

Too late.

With the alarm already sounded, the deer were on guard. The very moment I jumped to my feet, they bolted. Now I stood still, watching in disbelief as ALL my hard work, ALL my expertise, disappeared into the woods.

GRRrrrrr.

In no mood to deal with ANY of them, I walked the long way around the house and back to my bed.

My Mistress found me there some time later and coaxed me into the house with the promise of eggs-over-easy on a bed of kibble and rice.

*

As the snow began to melt, so did My Mistress's loose grip on reality. There were already 5 of us living at the house. Now, she had to go off and invite another— Unbelievable!

The latest addition to our pack called himself Jake. He was no spring chicken and about the size of an elephant! Bumbling out of the car, he clomped his way over to Gizmo. Giz embarrassingly twitterpated that someone finally noticed her, the two engrossed in some sort of painfully awkward, tail-wagging, butt-jiggling hello.

What-ever! Obviously, he was saving the BEST for last! But without even a simple nod in my direction, he continued into the house!

Unacceptable! I am The Woman of this House! Decorum is de rigueur![33]

It was painfully evident that Jake would require a basic course in protocol. As if I was not already busy enough with my own agenda and sidekick. Oh well, as they always say, a woman's work is never done— Humph!

Following everybody inside for lunch, I sat down in front the TV waiting for my plate to be served. Jake lumbered over to say hello. He apologized for his earlier rudeness, explaining it had been so long since he saw Gizmo that he got carried away.

Are you joking? It would take a heavy-duty forklift to carry your tonnage anywhere!

Ignoring my witty commentary, he continued to share the story of how "they" met with Gizmo chiming in from time to time.

Please be quiet. I have zero interest in You or Your History!

None too soon, My Mistress served lunch. After inhaling her own food, Giz went over to Jake. Nudging him over, she stuck her trap in his bowl! Such appalling behavior towards a guest! Immediately, I stepped over to correct Giz. But, Jake intervened between me and the little piglet, saying that a car ride always leaves his tummy a bit queasy and that he could do without finishing the meal.

My eyes rolled back in disbelief. "Tweedle-Dumb" protecting "Tweedle-Dumber and Fatter!" I did not know how much I could take. Hopefully, Jake wouldn't be staying too long.

*

Jake's first days at The Farm were mostly spent lazing around and catching up with Gizmo. My Mistress placed a bed

---

[33] Obviously, I had already mastered basic French.

on the deck for him— right next to MINE! Way, way too close for MY comfort. I told Shamus that it was his and he should mark it.

Dumbfounded as usual, Simple Shamus shook his head, "Why do I need a bed when yours is just the right size?"

And then, he kissed me.

Arghhh. Puppy brain.

Eventually, Jake came outside and plopped his bulk on the cedar cushion which was way too small for his oversized physique. When he stretched out, his head fell off thunking onto the deck with such force drool came flying out everywhere— But wait! It gets even worse! The drool splashed onto My Bed!

EWWWW! Get your wooly-mammoth-mastiff slobber away from me!

Shamus, always the faithful sidekick, cleaned the offending dribble off my bed and then went to the source. What happened next defies all logic— Exactly! Shamus tried to rid Jake of ALL his drool!

Sticking his midget muzzle into the giant's, he suctioned off as much as he could before Jake pushed him away because it tickled! Ughhh, boys!

Not able to take anymore, I escaped to my favorite quiet place under the white birch and prayed that Jake would leave soon.

*

Once again, the Nikita-to-Heaven line was experiencing technical difficulties. My Mistress announced that Jake would be staying, "Indefinitely!"

Huh? You've got to be joking. We do not need to adopt this gimpy giant!

That's right! Jake was an old clod and soft in the head especially when it came to Gizmo. With Jake always ambling to her defense, Giz was no longer applying herself to the rules of etiquette OR her diet. If Jake was staying, he would have to understand the "chain of command" and the concept of "zero contestation" or everything would fall apart!

I sashayed over to where Jake and Gizmo were engrossed in their afternoon chitchat session. Mustering all the sweetness inside of me, I asked Jake to accompany me over to the side-yard. There was something I needed to show him. Privately.

The elephantine simpleton nodded in agreement and excused himself from Gizmo's presence

Oh, *pl*-ease!

I led the way, with the supersized half-wit traipsing behind me. As soon as we were around the corner and out of accusation view from the house, I asked Jake if he knew who was the boss.

"Huh? Where?"

This was going to be more difficult than I expected.

At The Farm you blockhead! Who is Alpha?

"King?"

No, don't be such a chauvinist.

"Gizmo?"

No, don't be so asinine.

"I dunno."

No problem. Let me show you!

Lunging forward, I bit Jake's ear. Even though he screamed like a little girl at the movies, I kept the cartilage clamped between my teeth. Appling more pressure, I demanded, "Who's the boss? Who is The Bosss?"

"You?"

Who?

"You are?!"

Who? Say it again!

"You are the boss."

Again! Like you MEAN IT!

"Nikita is Alpha! Nikita is Top Dog! N I K I T A IS THE B O S S !!!"

Crunching down hard once more for emphasis, my canine finally pierced his ear. And once again, the little wuss was howling for mercy.

Lesson Learned = Lesson Over. I left him there.

With all the girly fuss that Jake had made, My Mistress was outside frantically calling, insisting that Jake and I come immediately— What-ever! There's no problem here. Just a little old-fashioned schooling. Lucky for Jake, he's a quick learner.

Trotting off in the general direction of her voice, I rounded the corner of the house. The moment she laid eyes on me, she seemed relieved.

I was so relieved when I saw Nikita. At least one of the dogs survived. From inside the house I had heard a terrible commotion. All the barking, all the yelping. With no idea where they were on the property, there was no way that I could break up the fight. I was terrified of what I'd eventually find.

Causally, Niki strolled over to me. Innocent eyes suggested nothing had happened. However, the fresh blood on her bib indicated otherwise.

Checking her all over to make sure that she was okay, she seemed amused; and, with good reason. The blood wasn't hers. Oh Nikita, what have you done now?

As proud as I was that she had survived and obviously won the rumble with a 130 lb. adversary, I hoped that there would not be too much to explain. The Farm was supposed to be a safe haven for Jake until his mother settled into her new house and job.

Again, relief washed over me when Jake came happily loping around the corner a minute later. He was the funniest Rottweiler I had ever met. Standing waist high, Jake was terrifically sweet natured 6-year-old dog with a "puppy brain." He had no concept of his size or intimidation factor. Unfortunately, hip dysplasia and arthritis were already limiting his movement.

Niki and Jake, the two of them were now "best buddies" standing side-by-side on the driveway.

Everything seemed okay. Then, I saw the blood dripping from Jake's ear.

Thankfully, all I found was one clean puncture wound through the bottom tip of his ear. Not that bad considering what I had heard and what I had feared. A little hydrogen peroxide and Jake was as good as new.

That evening, as a special treat for Jake, I brought out the flashlight. He liked to chase the bright, shiny light. If you were a little clever about it, he would get so carried away chasing the light that he'd thunk himself into the kitchen walls and cabinets! Hahaha!

Ha-ha! Never had I seen anything so stupid in all my years! Nothing more than a lame-brained attempt at slapstick canine humor. The stupidity factor rising exponentially by the "THUNK!"

Funny thing was, I could not tell if he was doing it for the entertainment of Mistress Bored-into-Further-Insanity or if he was seriously attacking the bouncing ball of light. For a brief

moment, Shamus thought to join in the chase, but one swift thwap to the head and he abandoned that particular idea.

Happily, I did not have to endure too much. My Mistress escorted me outside, kept the others in, and let me stay there the whole night!

Ahhhhh, peace is mine. I must remember to leave a thank you message on the God-line.

HONKHONKHONK!

Huh? Morning already?! And, according to that almost forgotten sound, it seems as though Clea sent the geese flying straight up from Florida— WooHoo! Good girl, Clea!

Instead of charging straight over, I reigned in my enthusiasm. Best I let them settle in a little bit before my "Welcome back to New Jersey" housewarming call.

*

The heavens were smiling on me! My Mistress began preparing for a party. She was running around the house, rearranging tables and chairs, and bathing the little ones. Even The Givers of Good Food were busy, cooking up a feast since this morning. With the guards preoccupied, my window of opportunity was open— Exactly! Time to go say "hello" to my long-lost friends!

Just to be on the safe side, I used the extensive labyrinth under the bushes as camouflage until I was on the far side of the house. Taking a deep breath, I charged towards the fence.

BEEP! BEEP!

Charging straight through the "danger zone," I was in the clear and on my way to the pond!

Believe it or not, after all my hard work and effort to be neighborly, even risking death by electrocution just to say, "Hello there my fine feathered friends. Welcome back!" The geese did not seem that happy to see me. In fact, not in the least! I was so disheartened.

Without even bothering to return my simple "hello," they started hissing feverishly. The closer I came, the more insulting they became.

Ridiculous! I expected a much better reception and display of manners especially after such a long and, quite frankly, inexcusable absence. Hmmmm. Perhaps, I had arrived at an inconvenient time.

With the understanding that I would return later, I excused myself and waited for them to separate, hoping that they would be more reasonable individually. It was such a beautiful day that I almost missed the male flying off— on his own!

Slinking through the tall grasses, I slowly approached the female who had stayed at home on the new nest. Once I was close enough for a little tête-à-tête, I said "hello."

Taken by surprise, she pulled back startled and started hissing.

"Hello!" I said again, this time adding, "Welcome back! How was your trip to Florida?"

The silly goose just kept hissing. How disappointing! All that time away and nothing learned.

Solidly, I stood my ground, letting the goose hiss and hiss and hiss. Until, she was less frenetic.

Done? Good! Now, let's begin our first lesson in politesse, as it applies to neighborly interaction.

Springing forward, I grabbed Goosie Girl by the neck and literally tried to shake some sense into her. Unfortunately, she passed out cold with her body left dangling from my mouth. Not 100% certain that I could handle two "difficult" students at once, I decided it best to continue our lesson privately. The best place for private instruction was the grove of white birch by the house A.K.A. my favorite place. Unfortunately, that also meant having to cross the electric fence.

Starting from my mark at the foot of the driveway, I charged. With the extra weight and the limp body thumping against me as I ran, I couldn't clear the— ZAAAAPPP!

The current passed through me into the goose.

Reanimated from the jolt, her eyes opened. But, only for a moment. With the realization that she was far, far from home and that my grip remained firm around her neck, Goosie passed out cold again. This time, without a single honk.

Acting as nonchalant as possible, I continued to walk across the backyard as my student's lifeless body swung back-and-forth like the bell that tolls. Since all her guests had arrived, I had hoped that My Mistress would be too busy to notice me and the sophomore swinging from my muzzle.

No such luck.

It seems that everyone had been waiting eagerly for my arrival.☯ As soon as they saw me, they began chanting my name.

"Niki! Nikita! Niki! Nikita!"

With all my admirers calling for me, begging for my presence, how could I refuse? This is the reception that I had expected from my long-lost feathered friends! If only Goosie Girl was awake, we'd be one lesson closer to her graduation.

I turned to walk towards the house. With every step I took, the crazier the crowd became! Clapping, hooting, howling, screaming— Whoa! These fans are wild! Somebody get me a bodyguard!

☯ That's right! Tales of my great beauty had reached as far as China making me renowned worldwide! Suck it up, Gizmo!

Somebody get me a body bag!

Of all the days, Niki had to choose this one to bring home a souvenir. My employer was entertaining a delegation of Chinese ministry officials. It was their first trip to the states. Already taken by the expansive views of the rolling countryside from a "dream home" that included an indoor pool, they were also intrigued by the "pet dogs."

Most of them had only known dogs from American movies or TV and as zoo animals. They were charmed by the real "Lassies," the astonishingly huge, and the perfectly lap-sized and lovable dogs. Now, the curiosity factor was directed toward Nikita. After being regaled with tall tales of her adventures on the long ride from the airport, they were most anxious to meet the "wolf dog." Unfortunately, with all the chaos that morning getting everything in order, I had lost track of her.

The guests were the first to spot Niki playfully romping around the backyard with a toy. Everyone chiming in, "What a fantastic show! Bravo! Look at her prance and play!"

And then, a blood-curdling scream as one of the American wives at the party realized that Nikita's "toy" was a Canada goose. Unfazed, the Chinese kept cheering, thinking that Nikita had killed and brought the main course!

Yes, her newest trophy was quite impressive. However, I was now in a predicament having to explain the juxtaposition of why she killed an innocent and "protected animal" and why the only meat choices offered at the banquet would still be pork and chicken.

*

By mid-summer, all the dogs had established their hierarchy and were settled into the new routines. It was such a blessing to have them getting along. Even Jake was playing and running with the pack.[✧]

✧ Since his arrival, Jake had lost about 10 lbs. With extra weight off, he was moving better and enjoying his new lease on life.

However, he flatly refused to run inside and did not like it when the others did.

Whenever Shamus was chasing Niki around the house, Jake would wisely move out of the way to let Niki pass. Once she was clear, he would move back into position and wait for Shamus to arrive.

As Shamus would come flying around the corner, Jake would let out one warning bark. Then lowering his head, he would open his mouth. Unable to stop, Shamus would run inside!

Realizing that something happened to Shamus, Nikita would come back to find a Rottweiler slobbered Yorkie running figure 8s around Jake and nipping at his ankles.

Never a barker, Niki would talk to Shamus.✧

Upon hearing her, Shamus forgot about the offending dog-in-jaws-of-death incident and set off trying to catch Niki again. The three of them would play for hours like this. Gizmo, not so much so. Despite an increasingly restricted diet, she was still

✧ If she was in the mood, Nikita would have an entire conversation with you sounding something like "Chewbacca."

gaining weight. And the bigger she got, the less she played.

*

A summer thunderstorm rolled in one evening. Niki and I sat together on the deck to watch the lightning strikes come down one after the other. The house was situated on the top of a hill with the deck facing the valley below. A magnificent view of the passing storm.

Of no great surprise, we lost electricity. And as usual, the "automatic" generator did not kick-on, so I had to go inside to manually flip the switch.

All of a sudden, I heard too much barking and yelping.

Running over to the back windows, I saw Niki and Queen fighting. The Chinese housekeepers who had also heard the ruckus popped out of their quarters and together the three of us pulled the dogs apart.

Queen seemed okay, but Niki was bleeding profusely from her muzzle. Somehow, Queen had gotten the better of Niki and tore open a gaping hole in Niki's nose almost through her muzzle.

I was surprised by their scuffle; Queen had never shown any signs of aggression. Maybe, she was freaked out by the intensity of the storm. Earlier this summer, she had charged through a screen door moments before a downpour.

In any case, I was now driving in the middle of the night, through increasingly violent weather, to the emergency vet.

I hoped that there would be no permanent damage or scarring.

I prayed that Nikita would be able to forgive and forget.

Forgive and forget? Really? Come on! How can I forget when I am now wearing a crazy lampshade?! And, it's not even a pretty one— AAACKKK!

I looked so hideous that my very own reflection in the plate glass at the emergency vet nearly scared ME to death!

Sadly, the next day proved that this was no drug induced hallucination. Nope. No such luck. The night-shift doctor transformed me into a stitched-together, plastic-collared freak— Just think, never in my entire life had I passed even as

much as an "awkward phase." And now? I had a "Frankensteined" nose!

Grrrrr.

Queen was going to pay for this. That crazy collie jumped me for NO good reason!

When My Mistress got too spooked from the storm and went inside, I went downstairs to "relieve" myself. Queen was skulking in the shadows, weaving back and forth like a tree about to "TIMBER!"

When I nicely asked how much she'd been drinking this evening, she lunged at me! Ridiculous!

She could've simply said, "Niki, please that's not nice. I've been on the wagon for hours now." Or, "Only half a bottle of scotch. And, a small bottle at that!"

But no! She just snapped like a rubber band at my nose! What a kook!

My Mistress insisted that I wear the Elizabethan collar for several days after the incident and kept me under close surveillance. Honestly? I didn't mind too much. It gave me time to prepare my lesson plan for Queen— But before I had a chance to schedule a single session, My Mistress informed us that Queen was leaving, that very day!

Huh? Not fair! I have the entire course program already outlined!

All teary eyed, Queen said good-bye to everyone and then, turned to me and smirked.

Grrrrr. Wipe that Mona Lisa grin off your muzzle. This is not over. I know what you smell like and I will find you. Until then, make certain that you get your affairs in order.

*

By the next full moon, the collar was off and I was ready for the hunt. As was my discipline, I stopped eating a few days prior to work up a good hunger. My senses were always keener with my stomach empty. I spent the entire day resting, drinking lots of water, and waiting for my window of opportunity.

Sure enough, before sunset My Mistress was occupied in the kitchen preparing dinner and with all the other dogs clamoring for scraps— TAK! I was outta there!

It had been so long since I had last been in the woods. Ohhhh, it felt so good to have the mossy floor under my paws and there were so many baby critters to catch— How I do love Summertime!

Then, I caught whiff of a familiar scent. It was her— Queen Nutjob!

Hey! She's pretty close, too. How could My Mistress be so freaking stupid? Queen was not exiled, not institutionalized, she was in my backyard!

I followed the scent through the woods to a house. Staying outside of the wooden fence, I crouched down into the un-mowed grass and waited.

At daybreak, I could hear a chorus of little dogs barking inside. A silver-goateed man opened the sliding glass door and three miniature collies came tumbling out one after the other. The man stayed in the doorway, looking behind him, calling back. And then, she appeared.

Staying crouched down so that the others could not see me, I moved up-wind.

Queen stepped out onto the grass and froze in place. She had caught my scent.

Now, she understood. I would always be close by.

Watching.

Waiting.

Never-Ending Fear = The Sweetest Revenge.

After everybody went back inside the house, I jumped the fence and quickly marked some grass a few steps outside the glass door before disappearing back into the woods.

Taking my time, I waded in and out of the stream up and down both sides of the bank looking for a new prize. A little rabbit scampered by— TAK!

I was in close pursuit, chasing the little white tail bobbing in-and-out of the dense underbrush. Closer. And, closer still. The little white hairs almost ticking my— SNAP!

OUCH! Wild Turkey Farts?!

I looked down at my paw. There was a trap. I was caught.

One hard yank and I went tumbling down the hill into the stream. The trap still closed on my paw.

Buggers! Either I'd need her help or I'd have to chew my foot off— Hmmm. Decisions, decisions.

Considering that I had such pretty paws, I sulked all the way back to The Farm. I was only halfway across the backyard when My Mistress came flying out of the house. Standing in the doorway, was a silver-bearded man— Déjà vu!

I shook my head. Maybe, I had a concussion from the tumble. Then, his scent reached me.

Oh yeah. The contractor who's soft in the head for Gizmo and fattens her up with bagels. So, that's Queen's new father. Humph. With any luck, he'll take Gizmo, too!

The two of them came and started fussing over me. The man had to use all his might and his full weight on the spring to release the trap. As soon as my paw was freed, My Mistress left blabbering something about a telephone call.

Once she disappeared inside the house, the man bent down to whisper in my ear.

Instead of "you're so beautiful" and other sweet nothings, he told me that he had seen me peeing on his lawn earlier this morning.

Oopsy! You weren't supposed to see that. That was a little something for "The Queen."

As long-winded as My Mistress, the silver-bearded man was far, far from being finished. First, he spoke to me about protocol! That "guests" are invited and ring the front door when they arrive! Blah blah blah— That "Queenie" was under his protection now! Blah blah blah— That the "next time" I pulled a stunt like that he would treat me like a common intruder! Blah blah blah— That from a distance and without his spectacles, I could easily be mistaken for a wolf! Blah blah blah—

Pausing for a brief moment, he took hold of my chin. And, after taking his glasses off with a flourish, he brought his face close to mine. Way, way too close— Now, we were eyeball to eyeball!

In a low, demonic, raspy tone, he confided that he had a gun and promised it was fully loaded.

Ughuhhh.

My Mistress came skipping back just in the nick of time! She scooped me up in her arms and, after an embarrassing display of affection, we drove off to the vet to get x-rays. Of zero surprise, as photogenic as I am, everything was picture perfect!

Home in time for dinner and with my hunting days temporarily put on hold, I fully indulged myself even asking for seconds!

*

My Mistress decided that she needed another break from reality. This time, a more extended one. So, ALL of us took a vacation! Springing the big bucks, My Mistress booked two suites at Club Canine Pet Resort, where the New Jersey elite go to play— WooHoo! Let the party begin!

Sidekick Shamus got to bunk with me, and poor Jake was stuck with The Giz. Since our compounds were adjoining, we could play together all day! Running up and down the fencing, lounging in the sun, and even special playtime on the obstacle course! NO boring training, NO stupid rules— The ONLY thing on our schedule was fun-fun-fun! But, not for Grumblini.

Catering to the individual needs of every guest, Club Canine placed the butterball on a bona fide restricted diet. Her new regime consisted of only two meals per day and mandatory daily exercise. No more snacking. No more begging. Her caloric intake was so closely monitored, there was also no more swiping food from Jake. Paws crossed, Gizmo would lose a little weight AND a lot of attitude! Hah! Until that long-awaited event, the embittered potbellied wretch sat in the corner brooding, muttering to herself.

Within only a short couple of hours, withdrawal overtook Gizmo. Completely obsessed with finding something to eat, she sampled every pebble, every twig, even the aluminum water bowl! Becoming more and more desperate, before the end of the very 1st day, she sided up next to Jake and started licking his foot— AACKKKK!

Just moments away from Jake losing an appendage, the CCPR staff appeared and without hesitation moved Gizmo into solitary confinement. Phhhewww!

Bonus! With The Giz out of the way, we could now easily play practical jokes on the dopey dog!

Having Shamus create a diversion, I was able to inconspicuously dig a sidekick-sized hole in the corner formally occupied by Gizmo. Once the perfect pass-through was completed, I gave Shamus his assignment.

Every time Jake snoozed-off, Shamus was to crawl through the hole being very careful not to wake the sleeping giant. Then, he was supposed to sneak over to Jake's ankle, nose, ear, and— CRUNCH!

Aside from scaring Jake which let's face it was easy enough, the idea was that Jake would try to catch Shamus. As Shamus slipped out, Jake would continue to charge forward— THWAP! Smacking his head into the fence! Ha-Ha!

Unfortunately, for the most part, once my scatter-brained sidekick reached the other side, he lost all focus. Either, he'd get too excited and start yip-yip-yipping or he'd get too distracted by all Jake's drool and start slurping— Ughhh!

Still, the few times Side-kick Shamus managed to be successful, it was soooo, soooo funny!

Every evening at lights out, Shamus insisted to cuddle. He liked the warmth and said that it made him feel safe at night, especially in the new place. Crawling up on my back, he would sit for a moment to take in the view. Then, he would lie down stretching himself out over my shoulders, and fall fast asleep. Ahhhh, puppies. Gotta love 'em.

We all knew that vacation was over when they took us to the spa treatment room for "the works." As sad as I was to be leaving, I always enjoy being pampered. In the middle of my brush-out, I was pleasantly surprised to catch a glimpse of a slimmer Gizmo. When I commended her loss of blubber, she snapped and had to be restrained by 2 members of the CCPR staff!

Oh my! Poor Gizzy, still suffering from caloric withdrawal. Not much of a dreamcation for her, but she looked good!

*

Back at the farm, My Mistress was very occupied bossing around the workmen instead of me! With the additional free time on my hands, I was able to focus more attention on Shamus' training. Although he was far, far away from mastering any one skill, his sniffing technique and digging skills had shown tremendous progress. With no one around to interfere, it was a good time to practice.

Lifting him by his scruff, I dropped him into one of the planters.

ZRRROOM! A fury of paws in motion, off to work he went! Digging his way to the bottom, dirt and flowers flying through the air— So very impressive! Better yet, with the rugrat now stuck deep inside the planter, I was free to explore on my own!

WooHoo! I am Brilliant!

As I began my rounds, I spied a critter in a cage on the concrete platform outside the housekeepers' quarters. Jaunting over to investigate, I found inside my old crate a little rabbit A.K.A. My Favorite! Obviously, the ever-thoughtful Givers of Good Food had left me a gift! Xiè xie xie.

My new playmate was so animated! Jumping from one side of the cage to the other, the bunny could hardly wait to play with me! Hopefully, somebody would open the cage soon.

The kitchen door flew open— YES! Let the games begin!

Screaming in almost indecipherable Chinese, the man told me to leave his dinner alone!

Huh?! What-ever! The gift must be from his ever-gracious wife.

He disappeared back into the house and reappeared only moments later wielding a broom like a nun-chuck!

Seriously?! Is this some sort of joke? You do know that IF you have to announce a joke, it's NOT funny! And, FYI? You're no Bruce Lee! So *pl*-ease, go back to your Tai Chi Chuan.

Not seeing the need to watch any more of the raging dragon farce and knowing that no bunny is worth getting swatted with any end of that mad Chinaman's broom, I walked away to continue my rounds, double-checking my marks towards the front of the house.

Buggers. Somebody had freed Shamus. But instead of bouncing up to me and planting kisses, all his attention was focused on a tree. No yipping, just squinting very hard.

Hmmmm.

As I came closer, he shushed ME!

One quick swap to the head, and he apologized profusely.

Shifting my gaze upwards, I saw what had captured his attention. A baby squirrel! Ooh, my second favorite! This was turning out to be a most excellent day!

Keeping my eye on the target, I pulled Shamus off to the side and gave him his instructions. Nodding in agreement, Shamus went back to the base of the tree and started yip yip yipping up a storm. Of course, Shamus improvised the dialogue quite a bit. Telling the squirrel that he was going to run up the tree, bite him on the tail, drag him back down to the ground where he would offer him to the big, bad wolf— After all, I am not a wolf!

Luckily, the baby squirrel was not so clever. It believed Shamus' spiel hook, line, and sinker!

Scared witless, he ran farther up the tree and out on a branch. Reaching the end, he just kept going and *FLEW* to the next tree!

Wow! This was no ordinary critter— It was a FLYING SQUIRREL!!!

Most excellent spot, my sidekick!

As Shamus kept barking threats and running along with the squirrel, I ran back and forth, side-to-side covering every angle. Further improvising, Shamus told the squirrel not to worry about falling. The big bad wolf would be waiting below with jaws wide open to catch him.

Nice touch, Shamus.

The baby flying squirrel looked down. Becoming slightly disorientated by my lupine image circling underneath, he panicked and missed the next— SPLAATTT!

It worked!

Stunned from the fall, the baby squirrel stayed sprawled out on the grass.

I took a moment to appreciate our achievement.

Moment over, time for the— Smootches?!

Shamus had bounced in-between me and our score and was showering me with congratulatory kisses— Grrrr. Puppy brain.

By the time I swatted him off, the squirrel had already recovered and scampered away.

Gizmo came over to see what all the fuss had been about. Shamus tried to fill her in on the details. But before he could properly finish, she snickered and walked away.

Sighhh. All that weight lost and yet none of the attitude.

Hearing the workmen hanging out in the driveway on another coffee break, I went over to say hello. Shamus decided to stay behind and look for more flying squirrels.

Before I finished rounding the corner, Gizmo was already center stage performing her give-me-food-because-they-starve-me dance routine. Tsk-tsk! How disappointing! After weeks of "comprehensive" counseling from the Club Canine Pet Resort therapist and emerging a new-and-improved version, at that first temptation Giz slipped right back into her old habits.

The silver-bearded man now joined the spectacle dangling a piece of bagel just out of the little oinker's reach— We interrupt your normally scheduled program for a Childish Entertainment special presentation: "The Goateed Puppeteer and His Not-so-Mini Schnauzer Marionette."

The more it dangled, the crazier her dance.

Finally, he dropped the bagel. She caught it and tried to swallow it whole! The human-sized piece wedged in her throat— Gizmo was choking to death!

Ni-Ki-Ta to the rescue!

Grabbing Giz by her scruff, I swiftly removed her from the scene so that the innocent bystanders would not be injured when the projectile was dislodged.

Safely off to the side, I shook Gizmo until the bagel came flying out of her mouth.

Thanks to my quick reaction time and EMT training, disaster was averted. I placed her back on the ground. Obviously in shock, the thankless glutton started screaming for help!

Giz, calm down. You're safe now. If you can scream, you are no longer choking— Duh!

Ignoring my reassurances, she continued to screech now claiming that I stole her food!

You paranoid pudgy piglet! I would never, ever waste calories on a regurgitated lump of dough!

But, she just would not listen. And, as always, the responsibility fell upon my broad but weary shoulders.

Grabbing Gizmo once more by her scruff, I tried to shake some sense into her. Unfortunately, before I could fully calm her down and conduct an emergency counseling session, Mistress Unnecessary Interference was there.

None too happy to see Gizmo swinging from my mouth, she demanded that I drop her.

Fine. Not like it's that easy to hold 10,017lbs of lard by the neck!

PLOPP!

Gizmo back on the grass, I turned and walked away.

Completely unaware of my good deed and honorable intentions, My Mistress yelled for me to come back, insisting that I account for my behavior.

No Way! I am in no mood to suffer through another unnecessary, longwinded lecture from you!

I continued walking around the house until I came to a spot of shade. Not one of my usual places, but I needed some quiet time alone. Unfortunately, my quiet time was not quite long enough— Exactly! Before I could even properly collect my thoughts, My Mistress was now on the porch screeching for me.

Ridiculous! Not a moment's peace. Not an ounce of trust.

I seriously needed to re-evaluate my situation. I needed another vacation. Oh jeeps, I needed a life.

As soon as she turned back, I ran off and disappeared into the woods. This time, more careful about where I placed my paws. Before evening fell, I found a long-abandoned hunting cabin. There were cobwebs everywhere and any left-over food had already been scavenged.

Going over to the far corner to keep a clear view of the door and glassless windows, I curled up into a ball and drifted off into a sound, dream-filled sleep.

That morning, I woke up to the creaking of the front door being pushed open. No, "hello." No, "Anybody there?" In fact, no words at all— Somebody was sneaking in! My heart skipped a beat.

THUMP! THUMP!

My breath caught in my throat.

THUMP! THUMP!

I played dead hoping that the black bear stories were only rumors.

THUMP! THUMP!

About halfway into the room, the intruder stopped.

I could hear the labored breathing. I kept holding mine.

Silence.

Finally, a familiar voice boomed through the cabin, "You can cut it out. I know you're awake. Open your eyes, Ni-Ki-Ta."

Jake?

Somehow, he had tracked me through the woods. I was really impressed by the old boy. Not only by the skill set which I never suspected he possessed, but also that he obviously cared about me.

Without missing another beat, the questions started. "What's with the disappearing act? Running away from home? No word. No note. Everyone's worried. The entire household spent hours searching for you no one slept last night. Shamus blames himself. Your mistress jumped at the slightest noise, hoping it was you returning. This morning, at first light, she was back in her car to canvass the neighborhood for the 100th time! What are you thinking? Are you even thinking??"

Looking away, afraid to make eye contact and lose my resolve, I confided to Jake how Gizmo's constant grumbling, lying, and just generally miserable behavior upset me. Her latest display was the last straw in a barn full of hay. And, I was deeply offended that while My Mistress forced me to "tow the line," she turned a blind eye to Gizmo's shenanigans. I could no longer accept the double standard.

He said nothing.

Nothing.

My voice low and soft, choking back my emotions, I shared how lonely I was. No friends. No love. No one understood me. Absolutely no one! I was completely alone. There was no choice, no viable options left— Except for one: To simply walk away and leave behind the misery, the mistreatment, and the constant death threats.

Jake let out a long sigh, "Okay, enough. Now, I want you to listen to me closely.

"Nikita, you are not like the others. You are special. That's why she expects more. That's why we all do."

I opened my mouth to make a quip, but Jake lifted his paw imploring me to stay silent. Curious to see if he had had any insightful observations to add to the obvious, I indulged him.

"Everyone thinks about running away, Nikita. Even I've considered it."

Seriously?! I could hardly believe what Jake was saying. He was such a homefry!

He confided that when he was a puppy, life was not ideal. Every time his mommy left the house, his daddy would beat him and threaten to sell him and his brother as "bait" for a dogfight or to a Chinese restaurant, whoever was the highest bidder.

Then, one morning Jake woke up to find himself chained to the radiator, his brother already missing! Luckily, his mommy came back home early before he, himself, disappeared!

"Now, Nikita listen closely. Before I continue, you must promise me to never breathe a word of the next part our conversation to anyone."

Anxious to get the scoop, I eagerly nodded my head in agreement.

He confirmed that all rumors were true. The first time that he met Gizmo, she was completely different. Friendly, playful, cheerful, and even fearless! Always up for an adventure, she had already traveled throughout the entire United States by plane, train, and automobile! Gizmo truly enjoyed a charmed life sharing it with friends, including her Seamus.

"But Niki, things drastically changed for Gizmo when Seamus moved away with his daddys. Her first, and true love gone. Forever. Never to come back to Manhattan. That loss ripped her world apart. Sadness took her broken heart hostage, bitterness creeping into the rifts created fear paralyzing her free spirit— To be happy meant to love. To love meant her hopes and her dreams could be shattered again."

Jake admitted that when he first arrived at The Farm, he was shocked to find Gizmo so "resigned." After reminiscing about the good old days and many heart-to-heart talks, he was saddened that even he could not sway her mind, reach her heart. Gizmo had been miserable for so long that it was now a "reflex emotion."

"There's no magic pill. No magic words. In the end, Nikita, it's a choice. And, Gizmo chooses every day to continue her suffering.

"We all have difficulties in life. On their own, the experiences are not negative or positive. We hold that power. It's our personal choice. Our perception determines whether an experience has a positive or a negative effect on our life. Our perception creates our reality."

Wow! I never had any idea that he was such a philosopher. I'd have to start calling the big buffoon, Professor J!

He added that he had overheard My Mistress talking about a change of scenery for Gizmo. Ever the optimistic problem solver, My Mistress hoped that a new environment would shine a little light into Gizmo's heart. She reasoned that Giz might thrive in a "one dog" household where she would have undivided attention. But, there were no definitive plans yet.

This did not surprise me in the very least— Exactly! Even though Gizmo was well-trained and outwardly normal, My Mistress was obviously having difficulty finding someone who would take a "special needs" dog. Hah!

Jake raised his paw again, "I'm not finished yet, Niki. No wise cracks! Please, just listen."

When I was finished rolling my eyes and settled back down, Jake continued.

"As a personal favor to me, cut Giz some slack. Don't be so rough with her. When she gets difficult, take a deep breath. Create some distance between you, her, and your emotions. Focus on the good."

Then, after making me double-triple-swear to never, never, ever tell Gizmo, he whispered, "It was her who sent me into the woods to find you and bring you home. She even told me precisely where to look for you."

I could hardly believe it!

Supposedly, she had intended to come herself, but was sporting her electronic collar. Not fast enough to escape the perimeter and not brave enough to suffer the shock, she had passed the torch to Jake— Now, that, I could believe!

Drowning out my witty commentary, Jake bellowed, "And, there's Shamus. Do you have any concept of how much he idolizes you? He'd be sadder than an only available on TV, special edition, 2 cd collection of country love songs, if you ran away."

Well, naturally. What is a sidekick without his super-heroine?!

Still not impressed by my comical asides, this time Professor J cleared his throat with annoyance. So, I resumed practicing my passive listening skills as Jake continued to plead his case.

"Living here, isolated on The Farm, you have no concept of how good your life really is, Nikita. And, I wager that you have no clue as to how much your mistress loves you. I hear her talking about you... All The Time! Niki this. Nikita that. She loves you so very much. Why do you constantly fight with her?

Ignore her love and attention? If you're not careful you're going to end up just like Gizmo, habitually dissatisfied with a beautiful life."

Ooohhh, I never thought of it like that.

We continued to discuss the dynamics of canine life and its social responsibilities. The morning hours passed quickly and not because I was napping, but because what we spoke about made sense. His words and the concepts resonated with me.

On his way out the door, Jake turned and emphasized, "It's your choice, but I expect to see you back at the house by dinnertime."

Leaving the cabin, I followed the stream. Wading in-and-out of the running water as it rippled over the rocks and through the woods, I considered our conversation. Jake had really given me a lot to think about. Honestly, I had never expected so many golden nuggets of knowledge from someone I assumed was just a big dopey-doo.

The bottom line: he was right. My place was back home. I was needed there. Not like I was really going to run away forever, I just wanted some privacy. And, practically speaking, the closer it got to dinnertime, the more I realized that I was hungry. Super hungry.

The stream led me close to the pond where I waited in the un-mowed grasses listening for My Mistress's car. Finally, I heard it revving up the road. Leaving my resting place, I sat in the center of the driveway to surprise her.

VRRROOM! She zipped into the driveway.

YIKES!

The car stopped just a whisker length short of hitting me! Thankfully, the little red convertible still had good brakes despite her aggressively fast and dangerous driving habits.

She jumped out and ran towards me with her arms outstretched, a smile across her tear stained face. Before she

was close enough to grab and harness me, I turned and walked away. Up the driveway, towards the house, towards the invisible fence. Right before the warning beeps, I looked back, caught her eye, and winked.

She winked.

After yet another great disappearing act, leaving me worried, frantically calling the neighbors and police, wondering where she was and if she was still alive, she winked at me and then w-a-l-k-e-d through the electronic fence. Not a twitch, not a single yelp when the current passed through her. Nothing. Once she was on the other side of the fence, Niki looked over her shoulder and winked one more time before continuing towards the house.

Nikita made it perfectly clear that it was her choice to leave; and, her choice to come home. That evening, I lit a candle and said a prayer that Niki would choose to stay more often than leave.

*

With the holidays still a couple of months away, I decided to be proactive this year and start the holiday card photo shoot production. That meant, all the dogs had to be groomed before any photographs could be taken.

I started the bathing process early in the morning and by lunchtime everyone was ready. Luckily, they were all getting along. Even Gizmo was behaving herself. But, getting the 4 of them to sit still and pose was no easy task.

The first photo shoot was shot "au naturel" and for the second, there were costumes. Shamus and Gizmo dressed up as elves wearing red and green velvet collars decorated with little bells. Nikita and Jake alternated costumes. One would dress up in a Santa Claus suit while the other wore reindeer antlers. It was so cute! Unfortunately, only Jake and Shamus seemed to enjoy their costumes as much as I did.

I could hardly wait to get the film processed and choose the photo which would grace everyone's bookshelves that holiday season. Imagine my surprise when I opened the photo envelope and discovered that every picture was black![✧]

Imagine the dogs surprise when they went through the entire bathing ritual for the second time in a week. Most of the new photos came out looking like North Pole Police Department mug shots.

Shoot me NOW! Unless, of course, you plan to hang and fill a super-sized stocking this year!

Obviously sipping the 151 spiked eggnog a bit earlier than usual this season, My Mistress decided that it would be "fun" to dress up and take pictures— Fun for whom, pray-tell? Not like she was wearing a costume, other than her daily "fashion statement!" Hah!

The shampoo, brush, and blowout were fine. The cheese treats in-between shots were yummy. And as naturally photogenic as I am, it was a pleasure to flirt with the camera. However, let's set the record straight— I am beautiful "à poil."[√] No costumes or accessories required. And, a Santa suit? Let's be

---

[✧] No blond jokes, please! The camera lens cap was off. There must have been a problem with the film. Now, I've switched to digital.

[√] French for naked. Let's face it, some things just sound better in French. And, there is the most brilliant play on words. Google it.

realistic, I might have the twinkling blue eyes, but any similarity ends right there!

When she made me switch costumes with Jake, I almost passed out.

Antlers? FELT ANTLERS?! Ooohhh, now that's convincing! Why don't you let me outside with these and see if the deer will mistake me for an albino, pigmy one of them— Ughhhh!

But wait, it gets even worse! A few days later, she forced all of us to repeat the WHOLE THING including the costume changes— Absolutely Ridiculous! *PL*-ease do not make it My Problem that you miscalculated the angles and shot from Gizmo's fat side. Just airbrush her pudginess out!

Whoa! Brake lights! Wait a second, please. Here's an idea: While you're at it, photoshop me a white beard and an extra 200lbs so that I look more realistic!

Before going to bed that night, I made my Christmas wish list. I had been a very, very good girl this year and with all the glamour shots, I expected truckloads of gifts from ALL my admirers— WooHoo!

*

The weather was finally getting colder. Every morning, I hoped that the frost would be snow. This year, before the fountain could freeze over My Mistress decided to drain it.⦸

Walking around the slate coping, I was inspecting the work and checking the bottom for "stranded" critters. As usual, My Mistress was there, nagging me to be careful.

Yeah, yeah, whatever you say— AAACKKKK!

⦸ Last winter, Shamus was working on his skating skills, mostly practicing figure-eight variations. The ice was too thin and he fell through. Luckily, I was there to rescue him.

Shamus jumped out directly in front of me! Afraid that I would pulverize his puny, little skull into marble dust, I side-stepped and lost my balance falling into the empty fountain.

BUGGERS!

My Mistress came over and looked down, "I told you so." And then, walked away.

DOUBLE BUGGERS!

The fountain was 8 feet deep and not wide enough for me to get a running start to jump out. Shamus looked down and smirked, "Hey, looks like you're in a Niki-sized planter!"

Ha-ha. Be funny while you can, my little sidekick. You might get "cancelled" before the season finale!

Shamus started whining, begging forgiveness with "I'm sorry"s and "Gizmo made me say it"s, but I ignored him. All the regrets and the excuses in the world were not going to help me outta here!

I needed a plan. I needed a ladder. I needed a quiet moment to think.

Taking a quiet moment to think, I sat down on the grass in the backyard. It was a beautiful late autumn day. The leaves had already changed creating an orange, yellow, and red hued landscape. With the sun beginning to set, the colors were surreal.

Jake was close by, enjoying the last few rays of afternoon sun. Gizmo was anxiously waiting up at the house for dinner. And, Shamus had just come over and began pestering me for some reason known only to him.

Pushing him away, I closed my eyes and relaxed listening to the sound of the countryside. Crickets chirping, birds singing, a horse galloping… Horses? I opened my eyes to see Niki's body soaring over my head.

She landed a few feet in front of me and then proudly came back to say "hello."

How she ever got out of that fountain, I'll never know. But, I was truly impressed. After a, "Good girl, Nikita! I love you!" I invited everyone up to the house for dinner.

Later that evening, my mother called to say that she was driving down to visit. She planned to spend a long weekend with me before leaving with Gizmo and all her paraphernalia.

With the kids living away from home, she and her man-friend shared a 4-bedroom house with only

Pickles-the-cat. After a long discussion, the two of them agreed to take Gizmo on a "trial basis." Fingers crossed, Giz would be happy and behave herself at least until the trial period ended.

Hard to say which was more exciting, my Mom's visit or a finding new home for Gizmo. Either way, Christmas was coming early this year!

Christmas came early this year! But this year instead of Santa and his "ho-ho-ho" coming down the chimney, The Hummer and her "hum-hum-hum" was ringing our front door!

AAACKKKK! Whatever you do— DO NOT let her in!

Honestly, this rapid character devolvement from humming to stalking was most alarming. Just as I was about to alert the local authorities, My Mistress finally introduced us— This was my Grandma!

Which became more than evident the very moment she opened her suitcase! All sorts of goodies and toys and treats came tumbling out and most of them were for me-Me-ME! She must have really liked the photos!

Later that evening, My Mistress and Grandma sat down with all of us and announced that Gizmo was moving out. I could barely contain my excitement, but Jake kept giving me side-ways glances. My poor Grandma was runny-nosed and

teary-eyed as she said that she, herself, would be adopting Gizmo. I moved closer, cuddling up, and tried to console her.

Oh, Granny don't be upset. I'm sure she won't eat you if you feed her well enough! Just be careful not to give her too much or her cells might go through overnight mitosis!

Again, Jake glanced over at me. This time his eyebrows raised NOT in disapproval, but with the disturbing visual of two identically miserable porkpies in the world— Scary, right?!

Ignoring me and bouncing all over the room, Gizmo was the happiest I'd ever seen her! And with her butt joining in the celebration, wiggling away frantically at the news, she was burning more calories in these happy moments than she had in the past three years!

However, please don't be fooled. Gizmo was not elated to be moving out and living with Grandma, but with Grandma's man-friend. Giz had a fierce crush on the tall gentleman. And supposedly, he thought that Gizmo was the smartest dog he'd ever met! Ha-ha!

I wondered out loud how long she'd be able to maintain that illusion and started placing bets.

Gizmo looked over and snarled at me.

Taking Jake's advice, I took a deep breath, ignored her feeble, last-minute attempts to rile me, and focused on the happy Gizmo-free times to come— WooHoo!

In all seriousness though, I did worry for the safety of her new family. Over the years, Gizmo's delusions of grandeur had become more and more developed. And, there were the health and safety issues surrounding her incessant eating— Exactly! I prayed that the cupboards were fully stocked and both new parents slept with one eye opened. After all, if Giz got hungry enough and devoured Grandma, who would spoil me?!

After the announcement and for the rest of her visit, Grandma's eyes were red and puffy from crying. I tried to comfort her every chance I got, but it was of no use— Obviously, she had come to the realization that she had been bamboozled into switching sweet, adorable Me for The Gizminator!

Let me tell you, that everyone let out a sigh of relief once Grandma drove off with Gizmo in the car. Before going back inside the house, My Mistress even performed her version of the happy dance!⌘ Then, the four of us celebrated Gizmo's departure ALL DAY LONG!

Finally, we could play games without having to wait for her, run around the house without having bypass her, eat dinner without having to lookout for her— This was The Life!

The very next morning My Mistress began decorating the house for Christmas. There was a huge tree, twinkling multicolored lights everywhere, and the finishing touch on the fireplace mantle hung with care— Stockings!

Hummphhh. Mine appeared to be the same size as last year— Absolutely Ridiculous! There was NO WAY everything from my list would fit in there!

Jake tried to reason with me, but I was in no mood. It was plainly obvious that My Mistress simply did not care about me. Doubting that she even glanced at my list, I moped off to a quiet corner in the spare bedroom.

My Mistress found me later and coaxed me out of my funk with a couple games of vicious dog followed by a pig ear. Trying to create a more festive spirit, she dimmed the lights and lit the logs in the fireplace.

With the Christmas tree twinkling and the fire crackling, I was lost in my own thoughts until Jake plopped himself beside me on the flagstone hearth. I moved over giving him more

---

⌘ I'll spare you the gruesome details, but this embarrassing arms-flailing, unrhythmic display was the reason she started taking dance lessons.

space. Aside from the obvious desire to avoid his drool bombs, I knew that he enjoyed the radiant warmth.✍

*

Christmas morning, my stocking overflowed to the point that there were presents on the hearth and even placed under the tree! Everything from my list was there and much, much more! But wait! Believe it or not, it gets even better— Exactly! The Givers of Good Food cooked up a feast, My Mistress served cookies and other little treats, AND my admirers started arriving with even more gifts!

Wow! I L-O-V-E Christmastime!

Even Jake's Christmas wish came true— His mommy came to visit!

It was an awkward reunion. It had been such a long time, since the last time that we all thought she'd left him behind forever. But, Jake seemed happy enough as he excitedly clomped around showing off his new body and range of movement while his mommy clapped and hooted with delight. Thankfully, there were no additional disgusting, overemotional PDAs.

Jake's mommy stayed at The Farm for a few days— Yet another present! With My Mistress and her friend too busy talking to each other to bother with us, we were free-Free-FREE!

Outside, there was a winter wonderland. Fresh snow, fresh tracks, and freshly frozen critters!

Mmmmmm.

✍ Just what the VMD prescribed. With the weight loss and added movement, Jake no longer suffered from severe joint pain. And, the extra heat prevented his joints from stiffening overnight allowing him to play as soon as he woke up in the morning!

Inside, The Givers of Good Food were piling ALL the holiday leftovers onto our plates!

Mmmm-Mmmmmm.

Then one morning, I woke up to find My Mistress already in the kitchen drinking coffee and Jake's mommy packing up Jake's toys and food. This could only mean one thing! There was absolutely no time to waste!

Backing up out of the room before they noticed me, I ran directly to the guest bedroom where Jake was still sleeping— Ridiculous! This was no time to hibernate!

Seeing as how this was a dire emergency, I pounced on top of him, jumping up and down.

Again, and again.

Jake finally opened his eyes none too happy to be woken up so unceremoniously.

What-ever. You need to get over it, my friend— We have to leave now! You are about to be dognapped!

"No such thing, Nikita." Jake said letting out a sigh. Sitting back on his haunches, he looked at me with sleepy eyes and explained.

"Late last night, once I was tucked in, my mommy told me the best bedtime story ever! It was about a new house and a really nice man who lives there. Then, she confided that it's not 'just a story,' but for realz! This morning as soon as the bags are packed, we're on our way to our new home and new family!"

I was not reassured in the least. How could he trust the new daddy? The last thing I wanted to see on my takeout menu was "Chef Delight - Jake Surprise."

Shaking his head, Jake dismissed my concern. "Nikita, that is highly unlikely. My new daddy is also a state trooper. It's his solemn duty to protect the innocent. Look, I never thought that I would stay so long at The Farm. It was supposed to be a short vacation. 3 weeks tops, nothing more. But, I'm so happy to say that this vacation destination became a place called 'home.' Of course, if I recall correctly, there was a rather dubious beginning."

Oopsy. I guess the ear-piercing incident might be forgiven, but not quite forgotten.

Jake waved his paw, signaling that he'd let it go. "I've enjoyed being here, our adventures, our quiet times, I've loved my time at The Farm with all of you! On a more personal note, I am touched that you finally took someone into your confidence. And, that that someone is me. That said, my true home is with my mommy."

In a whisper, he confided, "I'm not sure what to expect at the new place, but I am 112% positive that I can always trust my mommy. After all, didn't she bring me here?"

I lacked his faith in the whole situation. But Jake firmly reminded me, "That's your choice, Nikita, based on your perception. Not mine. This is my life. Leaving with my mommy is the best decision for me. End of discussion."

Jake's mommy burst into the room with an "Ohh, look at the two of you."

Whipping her camera out of nowhere, she started snapping pictures.

Oh fantastic! Intimate bedhead photos. What are you, paparazzi-in-training?!

I sulked back into the kitchen where My Mistress was putting the finishing touches on my breakfast. Even though this morning's offering was fresh hamburger and kibble, I had no appetite. All I could think about was Jake's imminent departure. Naturally, both of the boys wolfed down their plates as if nothing was happening.

Leaving my bowl untouched, I went into the family room and sat in front of the tree. My Mistress had already taken down my stocking. Humph. It's probably too late for another Christmas wish.

Jake came and sat beside me.

After a few moments of silence, Jake broke out with "good news."

Overnight, a blizzard had swept through the downstate area. With the roads impassable, they were going to stay one more day.

Good news? Are you kidding? It's only ONE day and you're still fixed on leaving us!

I got up and started to leave the room.

"Wait! Niki, there's more."

Pausing at the threshold, I waited to hear the rest. Surprisingly, Jake actually had very good news.

He had overheard "them" talking. It seems as though he was only moving a few hours away and their house was on the way to Grandma's— My Mistress was already fixing dates for our first visit!

WooHoo! I do not have to wait until next Christmas for more presents! On the way to Grandma's house via Jake's, I come!

Sure enough, by the next afternoon the roads were cleared. Jake and his mommy said their goodbyes and drove off. Most of our last day together we spent quietly listening to our mommys talk, hoping to glean some more information. If I had known that that was the last time that I would see him, instead of eavesdropping, I would've been visiting with Jake.[Ω]

[Ω] Before the first Spring flower bloomed, Jake had a relapse. The pain in his hip was so excruciating that he could barely stand, much less walk. His bones and joints deteriorated beyond repair, his mommy was left with no choice but to end his suffering. A moment of silence, please, in remembrance of Jake Augustus who brought happiness into the lives around him, especially mine.

*

No more Queen slinking away from a well-intended intervention. No more Gizmo waddling around on a search-and-eat mission. No more Jake thumping around on peacekeeping duty. Life at The Farm had become very quiet. Too quiet.

Of course, Sidekick Shamus was faithfully tagging along. And as always, King was oogling from afar. His drooling still too close for my physiological comfort.

Then, one day it was dead silent.

My Mistress had disappeared— WITH Shamus!

I was concerned that something dreadful had happened to the two of them. It was so unlike either one to leave without the minimal courtesy of a good-bye. In fact, My Mistress always told me when she was leaving for any period of time including the details ad nauseum! Anxiously, I kept watch waiting for any sign of life.

Finally, after TWO whole days, Shamus came happily bouncing through the door.

Immediately, I pounced on the deadbeat terrier. He smelled different— like other dogs and his hair was funny, his bangs tied with a blue silk ribbon. Grrrrrr.

Furious that he had obviously had fun without me, I demanded to know exactly where he'd been, who he played with, and why he left without me.

He tried to kiss me.

No-No-No! No kisses! No excuses! No stories! That is NOT going to work this time, Don Puppy-Juan!

Growling with displeasure, I bared my fangs. I meant business.

Immediately, rolling on his back and begging my forgiveness, he swore that it was all My Mistress' idea. That she dragged him away to this horrible, horrible place. It was busy and noisy, dogs and people everywhere. And then, she left him with strangers who bathed him, cut his hair, and fluffed it with a dryer and brush. He said the worst part was that the bow in his hair did not match his sweater.

Sweater?

"Oh yes. It's very nautical looking, red-and-white stripes with blue trim. It makes me look just like a sailor on leave. In fact, all the little dogs in the city wear cashmere sweaters and matching boots!" Boots?! Unbelievable!

Even after threats of a slow and painful death, he still insisted that the intricate tale was not a fabrication. Leaving Pinocchio Puppy sprawled out on his back, I walked away.

A few days later, My Mistress was packing up the car again. I jumped in— Exactly! It's My Turn to see the Land of Make Believe!

She giggled and said, "Okay, Nikita."

WooHoo! Road-trip!

The entire ride, she talked and talked and talked. In-between her non-sensical chattering was "singing." Ughhhh. I had forgotten what it was like to be confined in a car with her.

None too soon, the ride and side-show stopped.

When she opened her car door, I was slightly lightheaded from all the scents and sounds that came rushing towards me. Shamus had been telling the truth! Everywhere there were people, dogs, dogs dressed like people and more, much more! He neglected to mention the city critters and the cats and the food and the garbage!

Taking a moment for my head to stop spinning, I pretended to wait for her invitation out of the car.

Door opened, leash in her hand, a little stretch, and we were off! So intrigued by all the new things to absorb and note,

I could hardly appreciate the attention from all my new admirers.

Slowing the pace, I searched high and low for some territory to claim. It had been such a long car ride and with the vibration amplified from her excessive speed, I just had to relieve myself! But every single square inch of concrete had already been marked— even by humans! AAACKKKK!

I can hold it I can hold it I can hold it!

She held it. The entire day that we spent in New York, Nikita refused to go to the bathroom. I walked her all over the neighborhood, even taking her to the grassy spots, but she insisted to "hold it" until we arrived back at The Farm. I'm surprised that her beautiful blues didn't turn green.

I was thinking to move back to New York and wanted to see if Nikita could adapt. Aside from the bathroom issue, she behaved herself exceptionally. Nikita immediately heeled, following my every lead. She was pleasantly curious towards the neighborhood dogs. And, most importantly, she seemed to take the energy and the buzz of city life in stride. The only snafu was that every few feet someone would stop us to talk to her, to pet her, to take her photo. What should have been half hour power walks, turned into 90 minute "meet and greets."

Assuming that with time the novelty would wear off and she'd learn "to use" the sidewalk, I went forward with my plans to move back to Manhattan.

*

I could hardly wait. In a couple of days, Nikita, Shamus, and I would be living in a newly renovated brownstone apartment on Spring Street. Just to be on the safe side, ever since I had finalized the move date, I kept Nikita on leash 24/7, no exceptions. The last thing I needed was another disappearing act from my little Houdini. There was one more party planned at The Farm. And then, we'd be gone.

That morning I took the two out for their walk. Because he never strayed far from Niki or me, Shamus was off-leash. As we walked through the backyard, a little groundhog tottered out in front of us. Niki let out one "wookie word" and Shamus took off.

Completely ignoring my pleas to stop and come back, Shamus chased the groundhog across the backyard and then, around and around one of the pine trees.

By the time I reached them, Shamus had the groundhog pinned to the ground. Straddling the little beast, he was chomping at the air above it. The ground hog, which I now realized was only a baby, was also chomping at the air.

Absolutely hilarious! But at that particular moment, I was far from laughing.

Niki was now almost impossible to handle as she wanted in on the action. Thankfully, the Chinese housekeeper heard the commotion and came out.

Handing Nikita's leash to her, she held Nikita at bay as I plucked Shamus off his "adversary." He was so lucky that it was not an adult or he would have been chomped in two instead of the little puncture wound on his nose.

Enough drama for the day, I confined both dogs to the game room with the family's new chauffer as a babysitter. Leaving him with strict instructions to keep the dogs inside, I left to attend to the final preparations and welcome guests.

Everyone had arrived and the pre-banquet cocktail reception was flowing as smoothly as the liquor. Suddenly, the chauffer appeared in the kitchen wide-eyed and out of breath. In between gasps came blurting out, "Niki's gone."

Running into the game room, I saw a screen-less window. As I leaned through the opening and stared incredulously at the broken screen now laying in the flowerbed, the chauffer found his breath and a few more words.

He had been sitting watching TV. Nikita was on the adjacent couch, looking out the window. Everything was quiet. Then all of a sudden, she became "alert" and "POOF!"

My stomach dropped.

Knowing Niki, I was certain that she had seen the baby groundhog from this morning and went to settle the score. Before returning to the guests, I said a little prayer that it was the baby she spied, not the parent, and that please, please she would not cause any murderous scenes.

Back at the reception, all the guests were clamoring outside on the deck alongside the railing. I made my way through to find Nikita pouncing on and sticking her nose into the Juniper bushes.

Not too well versed in canine behavior, they all assumed that she was playing. Proudly, my employer began to educate everyone with tales of the merciless hunting habits of "our" wolf dog, culminating with the gift Nikita presented at the last party.✧

Making my excuses, I scooted down the stairs to round up Nikita. When my feet touched the grass at the landing, she looked up and took off towards the pond. Softly, I cursed under my breath. I was dressed for a party, not a recovery mission.

Hiking up my skirt to above knee length I chased her as fast as I could, running tiptoed to keep my stilettos from sinking into the soft ground. Now if only I had my golden magic lasso handy, I could catch her.

✧ Fantastic. Now this Chinese delegation thought that Nikita was supplying the meat course.

Catch me if you can! Ha-Ha-HA!

Such a ridiculous spectacle to see My Mistress running through the field in her high-heeled boots. Unless we were in an alternate reality or on a late 70's SciFi TV drama, there was no way that she would ever catch me!

She was still in hot pursuit when I made it to the edge of the pond. Sticking close to the reeds, I paddled to the other side and sat down on the bank waiting for her. When she saw me already at the other side, she swore fiercely.

Too prissy to swim, but not about to give up and let me go, My Mistress circled on foot. While she walked around the pond, I noiselessly swam back to the opposite bank and sat down waiting for her.

After an endless eternity had passed, My Mistress finally appeared looking none too happy or too pretty. Drenched in sweat with her hair matted and makeup smeared, her party clothes were torn from the brambles and blood was trickling from the scrapes on her arms and legs. Once her eyes focused and she saw that I was safely back on the other side, her jaw dropped.

SURPRISE!

I winked and took off before a single expletive could pass her lips.

Just because I was moving out of the sticks was no reason to disregard proper etiquette. I needed a little time to say goodbye to and, if asked, leave my forwarding address with all my friends and neighbors!

The Canada geese were the first ones checked off my list. Their family no longer summered at the pond as they decided to permanently retire in South Florida. Carefully I made my way to the barn, keeping one eye peeled for that crazy woman and her bovine spy.

Mmmm- Mmmm— I was soooo lucky today. The bucket was full and the milk still warm!

Leaving the barn before setting off any alarms, I passed by the mule's pen and paid my respects from the safety of the wooden fence. With a disposition that flashed between nasty and just plain evil, he was far too unpredictable to share a more intimate good-bye.*

Last on my list was the elderly woman who I helped planting flowers. She wasn't home. Bummer. Of course, I still checked her garden for any superfluous critters— leaving the ones that I found on her front step. Naturally, with their squeakers removed.

Finished with my goodbyes, I hightailed it home not wanting to miss my ride and be left behind all alone in the boondocks with the caninivorous Chinese housekeepers.

WooHoo! NYC here I come! Let's face it— I might have had a simple country girl upbringing, but I craved for more and more and more Big City adventures. Even on our shortest walk, there had been something, someone new around each and every single corner.

Of little surprise, My Mistress was nowhere to be found. But, her car was outside with the top down. I jumped in and waited for the Miata Express to take me back to the Land of Make Believe.

---

* On our last visit, I had to make a mad dash out of the pen before an unnecessary, uncalled for head butt! Luckily instead of me, he cracked the wood with his thick skull.

New York City

The entire ride into New York City, I sat quietly in the passenger seat watching my mundane country existence fly past at speeds that faaar exceeded the legal limit. As soon as I saw the light at the end of the Holland Tunnel, I turned to My Mistress.

Staring at her.

Absolutely no blinking.

Focusing my thoughts.

Hoping she would get the hint.

No such luck. She insisted to keep her focus on the cars around us and would not even glance in my direction!

Hello! Excuse me! As much as I'd hate to interrupt your long-anticipated moment of concentration, *pl*-ease lower the pane of glass separating me from My Future!

Although a serious infringement of my lifelong boycott on "the encouragement of any physical contact with My Mistress," I reached my paw out to touch her hand. Ever so gently, I curled my claws into her palm pulling her hand off the gear stick.

At first, she ignored me.

Grrrrr.

Returning her hand, she went back to playing around with the car's transmission. Upshift, downshift, My Mistress always had to make things difficult!

DOUBLE Grrrrr!

Naturally, I persisted now digging my claws into her wrist.

As delusional as ever, she reached over and started rubbing my chest and belly.

Huh? You certifiable cuckoo head! Did you forget your meds today?! I want the window down, not by tummy rubbed!

I stared at her in utter disbelief.

She looked over, smiled, and cooed, "I love you, too!"

AAACKKKK! Increasingly delusional and city driving?! This simple request was escalating into a most dangerous situation. Time to employ more blatant tactics.

With one long "Gizmo sighhhhh," I turned my head towards the window and then solicitously back towards her. Once. Twice. Thr— WooHoo! It worked!✍

But, not that well. She only opened the window a crack, just enough space for me to stick my nose out! Funny— Never heard of the existence of a blond scrooge. Somebody better contact "National Geographic" to document and photograph this rare sighting!

Too much? Fine, just fine— Bottom line: This window won't separate me from my new world for much longer.

Bracing myself against the door for stability as the car wizzzzed through the city streets indifferent to potholes and yellow lights, I pushed my nose out as far as it would go. This time knowing better what to expect, I was not overwhelmed by the assault of odors on my highly developed nasal passageways.

Immediately, I began sorting through the notes unique to every city block. There were so many scents yet to be identified, teasing me of the adventures that lay ahead. The people to adore me, the dogs to obey me, the critters to catch, the delicacies to sample— Endless opportunities!

✍ Note to self: Must remember to thank The Giz next time I see her.

Keeping one eye pealed towards My Mistress, to make sure she was not watching, I stuck my tongue out.[*] Mmmm-mmmm! There was food, everywhere! I bet you could get fat just tasting the air. No wonder Gizmo morphed from a trim-and-fit terrier into a chunky monkey!

Yikes! With that sobering realization, I quickly zipped my lips shut. There was no way that I was going suffer the same fate and lose my girlish figure over empty calories.

By the time the car screeched to a halt inside the parking garage, I was more ready to explore by paw. However, I checked my excitement and remained nonchalantly poised in my seat waiting-waiting-waiting for My Mistress to open my door and kindly invite me out.

As soon as my paws hit the painted concrete, a hush fell over the garage. All the men stopped what they had been doing to take turns admiring me, praising my beauty. One even dared to come close. Too, too close!

Right before his dirty, grimy mitts could touch my pristine, well-brushed head My Mistress intervened, handing him her keys— Phhewww!

Disaster narrowly avoided, I turned and led the way. Tail held high, only the tip swishing, and nose in the air I carried myself down the sidewalk with the poise and grace my youth and beauty allowed.

Nikita had arrived!

---

[*] Admittedly, a backwards, hickish thing to do, but it was the best way to quickly absorb and record all the new scents.

From the moment we had arrived in the city, Nikita was trying to bust out of the car. Every few blocks, I kept checking that the doors stayed locked and that the window remained open just a few inches so that she could not wiggle out. Quite honestly, I was surprised to see her so tongue-sticking-out happy to be returning to New York.

Telling her to wait, I emptied the trunk before allowing her out of the car. Half an "okay" and she flew from the passenger seat, scrambling for the exit. A sharp yank on her leash, I gave the command for heel which she did. Not that she was exactly listening or obeying, but the new and correctly attached prong collar gave her an added incentive.

Now remaining more or less by my side, as we continued to the new apartment, Niki insisted on sniffing everything and was diligently marking her way. Normally, I would not have indulged her dawdling, but I was relieved to see Niki emptying her bladder on the sidewalk instead of holding it for a return trip that was not planned for quite a few weeks.

Once we were inside, Niki made the rounds of the floor-through, two-bedroom apartment until she finally settled in the living room, on my Kreiss chaise.✧ Not to be left behind, Shamus jumped up and desperately tried to snuggle in next to her. After she eyed him, along with a little rumble from the back of her throat, he changed his mind nestling instead on the top of the seat back cushion.

I finished unpacking, ordered some delivery and collapsed into the only "non-accessible to dogs" piece of furniture, my rocking chair.

A long day, but phase one of the move was complete. Now, I had to work with my little country bumpkins and help them transition into big city dogs.

*

Handling 5 pairs of feet on the crowded city sidewalks and negotiating them around garbage and puddles of unidentifiable goo was much more difficult than I anticipated. But after Niki's first experience with

---

✧ I was not thrilled that she claimed for herself my 1st piece of "real" furniture and my favorite place to unwind.

chewing gum stuck in the fur between her pads, at least she learned to maneuver the hazards of city sidewalks without breaking her stride. Now our biggest challenge was her "fan club."

Originally, I thought that the attention Niki received was a novelty that would wear off with time. And it did, with our actual neighbors. What I neglected to calculate was the number of tourists flocking to New York. And, thanks to a few movies and TV shows, our once quiet, family-oriented, mostly Italian neighborhood was becoming trendier by the minute.

Regardless of the time of day, "curious" and "friendly" tourists would stop and stand in front of us, forcing us to stop and visit. With zero concept of the notion of privacy or tact, they snapped photos and doled out uninvited opinions on the inadequacies of city life for dogs.

On the weekends, there were streets that I had to avoid or they'd swarm around us like bees to honey. There were times that I'd feel more like an attraction listed on "Trip Advisor" than a NYC resident.

Ironically while everyone doted on Nikita, almost no one bothered to even notice the cute little Yorkie standing by her side. Completely unfazed by all the attention and praise lavished on Niki, Shamus would stand back a discreet distance while keeping a watchful eye on the people and the environs as if he was her bodyguard. It was so adorable!

The very few who tried to engage him, were rebuffed as he'd turn his head and feign indifference keeping his focus. Once they were finished with Niki, he'd swagger right alongside of her until the next audience appeared. Then, he'd reassume his protective, observatory stance until that "show" was over.

Show's over, you little terrier widget. Right now! This is not the "Terriers On Parade" hour— Cut the pretense and walk like a d-o-g, DOG!

Ever since we came to New York City that little boy beast to my right insisted to walk paw-to-paw with me. But, these past few days he was actually s-t-r-u-t-t-i-n-g, STRUTTING! Ridiculous!

Earth to Shamus. This might be the Land of Make Believe, but your reality in every world is as my sidekick, my minion, my

groupie, NOT my equal! And, what precisely do you have to strut about? If it was not for me parting the crowds, people would trip right over you!

He grunted and continued his peacock parade ignoring me— Grrrrr.

Not wanting to cause a scene in public and while attached by a prong collar to My Mistress, I waited until we were home to interrogate the insolent little bugger.

Cornering Shamus in the guest bedroom away from her prying eyes, I asked him again what he thought he was doing strutting down the sidewalk next to me. After all, no one gave the half-stack a promotion.

"Hey. Be careful, girlfriend," the impudent runt asserted.

"Don't give me your attitude. Sidekick Shamus is gone. Over. Done with. Left the building. Got it? I am the M-A-N, MAN! And that makes you my H-O, H—"

THWAP!

One swift smack to the head brought Shamus spinning back into his reality.

He started whimpering. "Niki, now that we live New York City and now with Jake gone and now I'm only male in the house, I just thought that—"

THWAP!

Rolling over onto his belly, he pleaded for mercy, "Please Niki, please. Don't be upset. It's not my fault. My Mistress told me—"

THWAP SWAP!

Enough! Let me set you straight you dipwit twit! You gave your package away. You are no man. No how. No way. No LONGER! And, she is MY Mistress— I am yours! Got it?!

"But—"

Lifting my paw in warning, I informed the addlebrained pipsqueak that there was no such word in his vocabulary.

"Yeah b-b-b-b*t Niki, I'm just so proud to be with you. You're so beautiful. You're canine perfection. Sky blue eyes, a luxurious, pristine coat, perfect symmetry, all in one package cruising the city streets with a supermodel runway walk. Everyone looks at you. Everyone wants to say hello to you! Everyone wants to be friends with you!"

Hmmmm. My little minion did have a point.

Timidly standing up on all fours, his bashful eyes seeking approval, "I just feel so lucky to be here, so honored to share a water bowl. I love you, Nikita."

And then, came the puppy kisses. Arghhhh.

*

I wish that I could say that the days flew by and melded into weeks in a whirlwind of adventure and discovery, but that would be a lie. Why? Because I counted every single step, every single time I went out, with me attached to My Mistress by a barbaric, clunky prong collar.

That's right! While all the other New York City dogs had studded-leather collars or fancy patterned harnesses,[*] I had a stainless-steel girdle around my neck.

Even more motion restricting, no extend-a-leash! Oh Heavens, no! I was tethered to her royal highness by an ordinary 3-foot nylon lead, which she wrapped around her wrist to shorten at whim!

Can you spell control freak with co-dependent separation anxiety? Let me help you, M-y-M-i-s-t-r-e-s-s— Exactly! My Mistress!

---

[*] Of course, Shamus was no exception to this rule and he even wore fruity-tutti outfits on occasion. But, that's another story and an image you cannot unsee.

Let's be realistic— within those first few walks, I had the entire neighborhood grid in place. Partially, because that's just the type of girl I am. Mostly because I was concerned that Mistress Broken Compass would lose her way. And needless to say, I quickly grasped the importance of looking both ways before jaywalking. After all, you never, never cross in front of a bike messenger or city bus or taxi because they never, never stop! The undeniable facts now stated— I simply could not fathom what she was waiting for!

Hello! I'm a Siberian Husky, remember?! My people are extremely adaptable to any environment. So please, why don't you do us both a favor and make a hard copy of the long, long list of breed attributes and post it to the fridge, so that you can reference it as often as necessary A.K.A. hourly!

Some days, she would take me for a walk along the Westside River Park and just to rub my nose in her lack of faith, directly to the dog park where all the other dogs were off-leash— Grrrrr.

There I was reduced to a canine voyeur, only allowed to watch the careless freedom of the other dogs as they ran and played together.[√√] One by one, the lucky mutts would come up to the chain-link fence separating us, taunting me because I was not allowed in— DOUBLE Grrrr!

Then, like fingernails on a chalkboard, I would overhear My Mistress yakking away to the other owners that she'd "love" to let me in to play, but that she was "so afraid" that I'd jump the fence. Hello, again! Remember "Siberian Husky," not a "goat!" And please, I have a much nicer coat, even than a cashmere goat or, at least, I used to— Exactly! My Mistress had not taken me for a proper and promised grooming! I was

---

[√√] I could add a snarky double entendre about my "mounting desire" as I watched the other dogs, but I am not so crass and prefer to keep this story rated PG.

beginning to smell a little mangy despite my daily brushing and nightly footbath.

Hey! Don't get me wrong. For the most part, I was enjoying my time in Manhattan. But, the stress from constantly being under surveillance— and constantly being with her— and constantly shadowed by the terrier widget, was beginning to wear thin. Even the continuous, unsolicited attention from strangers was not always comforting. Believe it or not, some of them had sticky, dirty hands, which they refused to have licked clean!

I wanted some alone time.

I wanted some playtime.

I wanted some Nikita time.

I missed the days at The Farm. The freedom of being off leash— the solitude of a lazy day spent under the shady grove of white birch— the adventure of charging through the electronic fence to explore the wilds of Hunterdon County— Exactly! I missed My Space.

Since we moved to New York, my living quarters had been severely downgraded. I now had to sleep in the same bed with both of them and even shower time was reduced from a 10x10ft shower room to being hosed down in a fiberglass tub!

Of course, now that we lived in the big city, there were other possibilities— a spa day would be easy enough to arrange and would go a long, long way to make up for all the smothering.☎

Closing my eyes, I tried to fall back asleep so at least I could dream about—

BLONK! BLONK! BLONK!

☎ Nothing too extravagant. Perhaps, just a simple shampoo, paw trim and blowout. And if you schedule a mani/pedi, please remember to bring my OPI "Princesses Rule" polish.

Ugghhhh— Simply ridiculous! My morning reverie shattered by her alarm clock and for zero good reason! Not like she ever went anywhere, anyhow, with anyone! Ohhhh no! Since we left The Farm, Mistress Co-Dependent-Separation-Anxiety worked from home. She told people it was to help "us" adjust, but I knew better. The 24/7 surveillance was just another manifestation of her inability to trust me.

As we began our walk, I knew her routine too, too well to expect any "morning at the spa" surprise from her today. Coffee at Balthazar's, looking in store windows along Elizabeth Street before the shops opened, and walking right past— Zoom! Zoom! Zoom! —The dog boutique and salon without hesitation. Ahhh, come on. Not even a looksy? That's what store windows are for— Humphh!

Yes, the normal routine. Even strutting off to my right was the crop-legged, package and care-free wonderboy wearing his fancy patterned harness, naturally with a matching leash.

We rounded the corner onto Cleveland Place and about halfway down the block— PRESTO! My BFF popped out from a shadowed doorway!

WooHoo! Clea!

But, wait one second— You're NOT Clea!

Holy Moly! Another Sibercollie? Only in New York do these things happen!

We stopped to say hello and visit. As it turned out, the Clea impersonator was just as friendly as the original! Precisely, what I needed— A girlfriend in the city! Maybe, we could go shopping or meet at the spa or play at the dog park!

I was so caught up with thinking of all the possibilities that it took a moment for me to fully grasp the situation. Clea-Clone was lacking a collar and her owner was nowhere in sight. She was a runaway A.K.A. My canine idol!

Here she was living The Life in The Big City! No owner, no responsibilities, no more tasteless kibble, no silly rules, no restrictive neck gear— Oh my! The possibilities were ENDLESS!

I wanted to ask her how she did it, how she ran away, how she managed— But, before I could get in a single why, what, how, she started pumping me for 411 about my life and my good fortune!

Huh?

Clea-Clone explained that she had seen me the past few weeks walking around the neighborhood, with my "happy family." She wanted to know how she could get a "sweet deal" like mine

Huh??

"You know, a nice place to live with a family, just like yours!"

HUH?!

Quickly, I set the record straight telling her that I considered myself much more an orphan with a pigmy tag-a-long and a human taskmaster and that the two-bedroom, marbled kitchen and bath, city apartment was cramped quarters compared to the sprawling countryside estate that until recently I called home.

"Marble! Fan-cee! And, two whole bedrooms! Whoa, that's super sweeeet! I bet your place is soooo freaking big that you even have room for one more!"

Huh? Didn't you hear me?!

But obviously not, because Ears-on-Strike Clea-Clone continued, "Awww, come on. Tell your Mom that I'm 97.5% housebroken[ii] and that I promise to not chew anything as long as she plays with me at least once a day. Please, please, please.

[ii] In case you're curious, the other 2.5% is when she has a full bladder and is tickled "too hard." Honestly, if I cared even just a little bit, I would've instructed her on Kegel exercises.

You have soooo much space. All I need is a corner for a comfy bed and a small bowl of kibble."

This was going beyond the ridiculous. I did not know her, not even her name for that matter, and here she was already inviting herself into my home! I had zero need, zero desire, for another clingy, intrusive addition to my life. Two straitjacket companions were absolutely all that I could handle!

"If you like, you can call me Clea-Two, even though my name is Bridget." She added with an ingratiating smirk.

I was alarmed. Not only had Clea-Wanabee not processed a single word about the dismal situation A.K.A my life, she was obviously delusional! What dog in their right mind would offer to be called "Clea-Two?"

Finally realizing herself that Clea-Wanabee was lacking an owner and a collar, but came with a full set of fleas and untreatable psychosis, My Mistress stopped trying to befriend her. We did a prompt 180 and continued our walk.

But, not alone— ACKKKK!

Keeping a constant distance of half a city block behind us, we had a Sibercollie shadow!

Static-cling Clea-Clone was not a runaway, not a stray, not even abandoned— Exactly! She was a Psycho-Stalker Puppy! Like I said, ONLY in New York do these things happen!

Scarier still, Mistress Lacking Common Sense encouraged her to follow us all the way home and into our building! Even holding the door open for our unwelcomed shadow.

Hello? Newsflash! We don't know this flea ridden, garbage-scented, street canine. Maybe, someone ditched crazy stalker pup for a reason and FYI this is not a Sibercollie rescue home. *PL*-ease, the apartment is already way, way, way too small for the 2½ of us!

Before Shamus could fully process the insult, I shot him the look of shut up or death by Chinatown. And as usual, he feigned indifference surveying the area for "danger" which considering his diminutive size could mean a baby New York City rat! Ha-ha!

As much as this next part pains me to admit, it seems as though My Mistress was perhaps slightly more clever than I had originally thought.

She led Stalker Pup straight past our stairwell, into the courtyard and introduced her to the contractor working on the carriage house. An odd character in need of medication-under-doctor's-supervision himself, he and Psycho Stalker Pup bonded instantly— like crazy and suuuper crazy glue!

In a voice, which thundered through our courtyard and to the next, he proclaimed that Stalker Pup was a sign from the heavens above— A direct manifestation of HIS recent two-way conversation on the God-line. Falling to his knees, arms outstretched to the sky, he thanked the heavens above for the four-legged gift bestowed to him.

After an all-too-short silent invocation, he rose to his feet and ordained that from this moment on the flea-ridden-stalker-puppy would be known as "Spring." The honor, his alone to shelter this heavenly manifestation.

Hallelujah! Now, that was an answer to my prayers!

As the contractor continued to evangelize to anyone within unavoidable listening distance, basically the entire freaking neighborhood, Spring sidled up and thanked me for all my help.

Not a problem. Trust me, really not a problem.

Regrettably, my efforts to assure her were in vain because, much like her new Daddy, she continued oblivious to my utter, complete, total lack of interest.

"I knew that you and your little bother would be the answer. But, I never thought I'd get this lucky! A cool name and a Daddy who's going to make me a pivotal part of his quest to restore the Archangel Michael to his rightful place! Whoa! Hold the Horseman of the Apocalypse! This is way cool!"

My ears were starting to bleed.

Reality check, please! First, Shamus is most certainly not my "brother." He's nothing like me. There is no way in this world that we are of a similar pedigree! Second, you are named after our street. There was no divination! And third but no less important, Pa-pa is just a siren away from the closest, secure, public mental health facility!

"BTW, we can still be BFFs! Since Daddy works here, we'll get to see each other every Monday through Friday, and maybe even some Saturdays! Unless, of course, our calling takes us to new and exotic places like Indonesia or Vermont or—"

OMG! Would this ever end?

At the first opportunity, I pulled My Mistress away. I had had enough. This morning's ordeal had been emotionally draining, far beyond my pre-breakfast capacity. I could not wait to get upstairs and inside.

Inside the apartment, I was happy to see Niki adjusting well to the smaller space. Lazing around most of the day in the chaise, she saved her energy for our long walks, a.k.a. adventures on the city sidewalks. On the occasions that she wanted some privacy, she'd disappear for a while into the guest bedroom.

True to her Siberian nature, she had yet to bark instead keeping an alert silence when there were people in the hallway or at the door. Niki'd simply lift her head, turn it towards the noise and listen and watch and wait. The few times Shamus had started to yap-yap-yap at the door or a window, she'd go over to investigate. If there was nothing, she'd smack him silent and walk away.

The biggest apartment living issue was that she was a night owl and liked to start playing after midnight. Although her footsteps fell as softly on the hardwood floor as they did on the grass at The Farm, Shamus was another matter. He sounded like an entire herd of baby elephants as he thumped his way around. And, there was the racket from the toys. So far, hiding all the noisy toys and confining playtime to the living room after 10pm kept my downstairs neighbors happy and their baby sleeping.

On a much more personal note, there was one other adjustment: Fur. Everywhere there was fur. Tufts of white all over my otherwise pristine apartment. Daily vacuuming and brushing helped, but by the next morning the white wisps gathered along the baseboards and in the corners.✧ Although the rational side of me understood that this was a drawback to owning a Siberian, the clean freak side of me was about to have a nervous breakdown.

The only thing that seemed to have any effect on the sheer volume of fur that she shed was a bath, offering 3-to-5 days of relief. But at $100, plus tip, for a shampoo, dry, and brush-out, Nikita saw the grooming salon much less frequently than the inside of my tub.

Since we moved to the city, I mostly worked from home which allowed me to spend more time with my gruesome twosome, taking more frequent walks and spontaneous procrastination breaks for a few rounds of hide-and-go-seek. And, the times I was busy on the computer or the phone, the dogs entertained themselves creating games of their own. By far, "kamikaze puppy" was the most entertaining.

✧ What suffered the worst was my chaise. No matter how many times I pushed her off and vacuumed the chair, it now had a fur slipcover. Anytime anyone with two legs sat there, they walked away looking like they got hit by a one-way blizzard. I was seriously considering buying stock in those sticky roller tape people.

It would always begin with Niki relaxing on the floor, lying on her side all stretched out. Shamus would nonchalantly begin searching for a hiding place under a piece of furniture or simply around a corner and wait.✧✧

Then, that crazy little dog would burst forward with puppy bounces and dive bomb her legs, paws, head, ears, whatever he dared to chomp at. Before his luck expired, he'd scoot back to his hiding place and wait, again.

Acting totally surprised before carelessly shooing him away, sometimes pretending to chomp at his little legs as they scuttled around her, Niki allowed Shamus these small victories.

Shamus would go back and forth and back and forth until— BOOM!

Niki would spring into the air, landing on all fours, and pounce on him. Now, sprawled on his back and pinned to the floor, Shamus would beg for mercy and shower Niki with kisses until she was satisfied with his display of contrition.

✧✧ No. I have no idea what he was exactly waiting for and I am not sure that he did either.

Of course, equally fun was our new game, "Who loves Shamus more," which we discovered quite by accident. One evening, I picked up Shamus and held him in the air. He looked so cute dangling there that, in a sweetly pitched voice, I told him, "I love you, Shamus. I love you, my little boo-boo."

Twitterpated by the extra attention, he started wiggling about and straining his little neck forward, trying to get close enough for a kiss.

Hearing the fuss and wondering what was going on, Niki came over. With the easy pickings at the perfect height, she playfully nipped at one of his legs. Nothing more than a little love bite. However, taken completely off-guard, Shamus freaked out.

The conditioning was instantaneous and permanent. From that moment on whenever I held Shamus mid-air and sweetly cooed those three magic words, he'd go completely berserk, looking behind him, growling and frantically trying to escape. A little cruel, but a hoot to watch! Hahaha!

Ha-Ha-HA! It was hilarious to hear the tourists scream! The most entertaining were always the easily rattled Japanese women, but the Italians with their flourish and passionate use of words came a very close second. It probably would have better if we understood all the terrified screams and expletives, but the manic quick-step routine that always followed made up for the lack of translation— That's right! Shamus and I had a new game.[✋]

Look before making any rash judgement, the simple fact is that when you are reduced to the daily monotony of being walked on leash throughout the most alive, exciting, stimulating city in The World, you must devise ways to cope and "make the best" out of the situation. And isn't it true that all's fair in Love and Tourism?

Some days, the sidewalks and streets in our neighborhood were super crowded with tourists. Usually the tourist sea would part at my appearance. First admiring my beauty and poise from afar, I'd catch words whispered amongst them like "wolf dog," "White Fang," "Little Red Ridinghood," "Thunder." If they worked up enough courage to approach, My Mistress would be assaulted by an onslaught of questions as hands touched me and shutters snapped like paparazzi.

However, there were a very, very few tourists, usually female, who were so enamored by the store fronts and window shopping, that they failed to immediately notice my presence

---

[✋] Stop. I know what you're thinking, but "I love Shamus" was not a game. It was, however, yet another sick perversion resulting from My Mistress' boredom. And as far as I was concerned, she could have the drool collecting end anytime she wanted!

making them ideal targets— Exactly! Rolling a baby blue in Shamus' direction A.K.A. "the sign," Rat Dog was on the prowl.

WooHoo! Let the games begin!

First, I would pull ahead and say "hello." Taken by surprise at my linguistic capabilities and mesmerized by my stunning beauty, the women would begin to coo. This was Shamus' cue to action.

As the women came over to talk with me and admire my well-groomed coat, Shamus would slide forward, rubbing his hairy little body against their ankles. The relay time between rubbing and reaction depended on the skittish nature of the target, but the result was always the same Rub-Rrrub-Rrrrub—

WHOOSH!

Straight up into the air, screaming— "AHH! Rats! Rabies! I'm going to die! ECCO! Ratti giganti! Per amore di Dio, la prossima volta a Miami Beach! EEEK! Kirāratto! Battoman herupu! Herupu!"

Once the victims' feet landed on the ground, an awkward side-stepping ensued as everyone tried to avoid trampling Shamus while looking for the offending creature.

Sometimes, Shamus would add his own flourish to the game by licking well-pedicured toes instead of the body brush.[✓] This was a brilliant adaptation as the results were equally guaranteed for tourists and locals! In my honest and humble opinion, this worked best in crowded elevators where the victim had no place to escape the doggie slobber on Manolos and could not visibly identify the offending party. Either way, they always blamed My Mistress which always doubled my pleasure!

✓ Yes, only the well-pedicured ones. I did not mind to indulge Shamus' fetish, but there were issues of hygiene to be considered.

In cherished moments like these, I could almost forget how much I missed The Farm, my adventures there, my old friends, The Givers of Good Food and the delicacies that they supplied. Just as things loomed hopelessly bland on the culinary horizon, the city of New York stepped up offering up a more than satisfactory substitution for that particular loss— Exactly! Believe it or not, we lived only 1-2-3-4-5-6-7 short blocks away from an entire neighborhood of them!

There, the sidewalks were always littered with food— the windows filled with glazed ducks, plucked then boiled chickens, unidentifiable cuts of charred meat all hanging from hooks just waiting to be tasted— fish and herbs and vegetables and nuts tumbled out of baskets lining the storefronts— It was amazing everything that one neighborhood had to offer! Luckily, My Mistress only went there in the early mornings allowing me to inspect the newly delivered products before the afternoon crush of people.

Without question, absolutely every time we went into Chinatown, I kept a watchful eye on Shamus while sticking closer than I preferred to My Mistress. I saw the hungry look in some of the shopkeepers' eyes and understood their intent from the almost inaudible mutterings in Mandarin.[⊖] My destiny, my life's mission was most certainly NOT to be placed on a rack alongside a duck or a chicken or a little Gizmo-piggy!

Our latest excursion into Chinatown was super early on Friday morning. Most of the delivery trucks had already left, but sidewalks were still a maze of crates staked upon crates, twice as high as My Mistress.[††] And, with the obvious

---

[⊖] Of course, not ALL of them spoke proper Chinese. And honestly, it was the ones uncivilized even in language that worried me the most.

[††] And just to clarify, that would be 1,000,000 times taller than Shamus!

exception of one stack filled with durian, everything smelled so mmmm-GOOD!

Shamus lifted his leg to diligently mark a crate filled with bibb lettuce when— BOOM!

Popping out from under a truck, this scrawny little, black cat blocked our path.

"Eh! Waat yoo doooo whittle daawg?"

Panic-stricken, Shamus froze. His leg still hoisted in mid-pee position. Even I was stunned into speechlessness at the brazen display from this Chinatown kitty that reeked of rancid produce. In dire need of a bath and a long lesson on the necessity of hygiene, he was obviously a distant cousin of Stinky Kitty.

Recovering my poise, I made an attempt to be courteous. Smiling my sweetest smile, I kindly informed our new stinky-kitty neighbor in my very best Mandarin that I enjoyed eating Chinese as much as speaking it.

He squinted at me completely perplexed.

"Waat? Smartie paawzzz — Hahh — I Kung-Foo Kit-tay — I talk only Kung Fooooo — Tell yoo whittle chiii-waa-wa — NO pee-pee — Dis MY dynaastee — Wahahh-haaaa!"

Finding both the crassness of this new neighbor and his delusions of ownership unacceptable, I took a step forward.

"Ho! Yoo stop dere boo eyez OR I chop-chop yoo in toooo-twoooo — Dis NO jokie! I Numba One student of great Chinatown mastaaa — Yoo are warnnn. Come any closah preetay woofie, I make you tumm-yumm-yummm doggie-dinnah. I very hungree dis morning — Whoo-waaaa!"

Hah! I hadn't laughed so hard since last week when those Japanese tourists jumped so high in the air that they almost entered the earth's orbit! Obviously, this was not Kung Fu Kitty, but Slapstick-Comedy-Cat! Let's face it, no pint-sized, underfed, Chinatown-schooled kitten was a match for me!

"Prepare four crouching ti-ga — Whoo-ee-yaaaa!"

In acknowledgement of his outstanding farce, I rolled my eyes back as far as they would go mimicking the sheer absurdity of the situation.

Yeah. OK. Whatever. Now you listen here, no squatting kitty is going to— O! M! G!

All THREE of us now stood dumbfounded on the sidewalk as Kung Fu kitty contorted his scrawny body and balanced it into a striking position.

Perhaps, it was the insult to his pedigree— Perhaps, it was illusions from "Mighty Dog" dog food heroics— Perhaps, it was simply the calling of every side-kick— But, Shamus was the first to react. Lunging forward, the lucky puppy was spared as he stopped inches short of reaching his impending doom.[〃] Within that same moment, Kung-Fu Kitty's arm extended itself THREE TIMES beyond its normal reach!

Shamus was still in the safety zone— BUT THEN Kung Fu Kitty's paw continued the forward motion literally flying through the air! The in-flight paw smacking Shamus silly while somehow simultaneously knocking his legs out from underneath him.

WOW! This was some C-A-T!

As I stepped forward just to get a better look at Kung Fu Kitty's technique, his other arm disengaged and swiped my nose with double-extended claws!

Hey! Try that again you tricky little kitty and I'll— GASSSSP!

Before I could finish my promise, My Mistress yanked my choke collar cutting off my air supply. As she forcibly escorted me down the street, Kung-Fu Kitty taunted, "I like yoo

---

[〃] His lead more tightly wrapped around My Mistress' hand than I had originally suspected. In this unique instance, her control-freak issue served to be a useful vice.

pre-tay woofie — that why I NO hurt yoooo — Only whittle teekle-teekle — Hah-haaaa — Yoo come veeseet ANY time, boo eyezz — Yoo on very short leeesh — I likee — Boo-ee-yaaa — Wahahh-haaaa!"

GRRRR— Even though, I am being dragged down the street, THIS is NOT over! Let me tell you, you stinky little— GASP CHOKE GASP!

Stop pulling me, you OCD freak! Once, that's one single time, is enough! I'm coming already. I've got ZERO choice, at this moment.

*

Shamus and I needed to have yet another "talk" and let's face it I am not the type of girl who likes to "talk." True, I was able to convince him to limit the strutting and surveillance gig to our evening walks. However, to fill the void, he had developed new AND disturbing habits.

Annoying habit #1: He stared at me constantly.

This was no joke, but was getting to the point of a lunatical farce! As much as I could understand his wanting to appreciate my stunning beauty inside the apartment, he continued this obsession outside! We'd be walking down the street, he'd be staring all starry eyed and— BOOM! Into a signpost and— BOOM! Into a fire hydrant and— BOOM! Into a garbage can. Ugghhhh.

As usual, My Mistress was of no help. With her sick and twisted sense of humor, instead of protecting him she let him plunk into things and then snicker away while telling him to be more careful. Aside from the sheer embarrassment, I was concerned that the self-inflicted blunt head traumas were doing irreparable damage to his already limited cognitive and motor abilities.

Annoying habit #2: He was always interrupting my quiet times.

In the cramped quarters that we now called home, his piddly, little terriersaurus brain confused the smaller space and constant access to me as a welcome to bug me with unwelcomed puppy slobber and awkward attempts to play. I'd quietly be relaxing, recalibrating my spine on the hardwood floor, when thump-thump-chomp-thump-thump would come along. Eventually, I'd have to get up, pin him to the ground, keeping him there until he apologized.

Annoying habit #3: Talk Talk Talk Talk TALK!

Since we moved into the city, Shamus discovered the sound of his own voice. He just could not zip his puppy lips! He'd sound "the alarm" at nothing, forcing me to get up, investigate, and then whack him silent. That blessed silence would only last a few moments.

Confusing my appearance as interested company, he'd start to pontificate on X, Y, Z. The constant verbal drone of inane subjects was beginning to wear down my intellect![⇆]

Annoying habit #4: Poetry.

Oh yeah, believe it or not, City Slicker Shamus loved applying his limited vocabulary to rhyming verse. This latest aberration was 1001 times more grating on my nerves than ALL the puppy drool and stupid games and constant staring and yakking put together!

Just today, my mid-morning snooze was interrupted by this little ditty:

[⇆] If you really must know, the pressing issues to the terrier widget ranged from the importance of the pig ear tree and the preservation of its forests for future generations to the dire need to escalate the movement to rid the Yorkie-verse of the malevolent skateboard. You asked!

ONCE THERE WAS A BEAUTY NAMED NIKITA
AS INTOXICATING AS TEQUILA
WITH EYES SKY BLUE AND THOSE PEARLY WHITE SMILES
SHE STOPPED THEM IN THEIR TRACKS FOR MILES AND MILES
BY FAR THE FAIREST CANINE OF THEM ALL
MY HONOR TO ANSWER HER EVERY CALL
EVERY SUNRISE GREETING HER WITH KISSES
ALL DAY LONG MY GOAL TO GRANT HER WISHES
IN THE EVENING CUDDLING NEXT TO HER
MY BODY CLOSE ENOUGH TO FEEL HER PURR
NIKITA IS MY ONE AND ONLY LOVE
SHE REIGNS OVER MY HEART FROM HIGH ABOVE
HER HEAVENLY PERCH TOO HIGH FOR MY TOUCH
MY HOPE THAT SHE CARES FOR ME HALF AS MUCH

A sonnet? Really?? When was he going to learn he was a Yorkshire Terrier and not an English poet! Her idea of discipline discretionary to stifling Siberian nature, My Mistress turned a blind eye to Shamus' growing eccentricities. So, once again it was time for me to step in. It was beyond frustrating that the responsibility of Yorkie Education 101 was always placed upon my shoulders. Worse, after every single lesson, all he had to say

was "okokokokok." And then, came the puppy kisses— Ugggghhhh!

I was just about to start today's class when My Mistress burst into the room announcing that she was taking the pipsqueak out for the entire afternoon— WooHoo! Nikita time!✍

Peace and quiet were exactly what I needed and absolutely perfect once the music that My Mistress left playing for "my entertainment" was finally finished. ♪

The sun had long ago set and I was pleasantly napping when the key turned in the door. The terrier poet bounced over to announce their arrival and say hello with puppy kisses. That was his downfall. They were ribeye flavored— Grrrrr!

Promptly flipping the bugger on his back, I inspected him and was NOT pleased in the least! This was not the first time that I had smelled other dogs on him. But tonight, he reeked of the contractor's house, mini-collies, and Queen!

TRAITOR!

"Niki, Niki please-please-please-please. You saw how she harnessed and dragged me out of here. It wasn't my idea. Please-please-please don't be so angry."

You brainless, no good, two-timing rug-RAT! What in blazes were you thinking of?!

"Nothing, Niki. Nothing. She put me in the car and I took a nap. You know how the car's motion zonks me straight out every time. Next thing I knew, I was at a house. All the other dogs were out and they came over to me. Of course, my 1st

---

✍ Note to self: Must remember to place a "Thank you!" call on the God-line.

♪ Today's musical selection was a playlist of Bach's organ works including my favorite, Toccata and Fugue in D Minor. Not bad, but better suited for moonlight drives through the countryside with the top down.

thought was of you. I wanted nothing to do with them. Absolutely nothing! Promise on my Yorkie honor! The barbeque was—"

THWAP SWAP!

I had heard enough.

Do you want a slow and painful death or a quick and excruciatingly painful one?

"Please Niki-please Niki-please Niki." Shamus continued to plead his highly doubtful innocence, "She made me do it. You know how she can be. I had no choice but to play and eat the food they offered me. You've always lecture on the importance of politesse. It's so, sooo rude to refuse good food. Please-please-please-please, Niki-Niki-Niki! I love you-I love you-I love you!"

"Nikita! Cut it out and come here." My Mistress' voice temporarily interrupting the sniveling scamp's pleads.

I peeled one eye off the groveling terrier to see that My Mistress had brought back some charcoal-grilled steak and a slice of buttermilk bundt cake as a peace offering— Mmmmm.

Easing my grip off the boy bugger, I let him apologize a little more and then went into the kitchen. In good humor after my time alone, I was willing to overlook this particular indiscretion as it was the 2nd offence. But, next time's MY turn to go on a road-trip!

A road-trip was definitely on the agenda. Spring was in full bloom and I had cabin fever. After making a few arrangements, we were on our first adventure... Savannah!

As soon as we crossed the border into North Carolina, we switched to the local highways and back roads. All of us happy to be out of the city and breathing the fresh country air. My gruesome twosome proved to be excellent travelers, even taking turns between who rode shotgun and who napped in the back seat.

The B&B I had reserved was impressive and worth every pretty penny. Well-chosen antique furnishings and period-themed furnishings gave the impression of arriving at a mansion from the "Gone With The Wind" days or the pages of "Southern Hospitality." I was really looking forward to their famous pecan-crusted French toast in the morning.

The owner was gracious, but not too pleased to see Nikita and Shamus. They were a dog friendly property, just not for the room that I had been assigned. After some negotiation, mostly promising not to let either dog on any furniture, we went to our room.

The minute the door was closed, Niki soared into the air, landing on the antique-looking four-poster bed. From her 3-foot-high perch, she smugly observed Shamus as he whimpered unable to jump much higher than the box spring. Ignoring their drama, I unpacked before going out to explore.

With the azaleas in bloom and the magnolia trees just beginning to flower, Savannah was the perfect getaway. Acting like locals, we strolled the streets, passed time with a sweet tea or mint julep at the sidewalk cafes, and lazed away the days in the shade.

Our spring break passed too quickly. In the blink of an eye, we were back in New York, back to our routine racing down the sidewalks at breakneck speeds.

*

All in all, I was pleased with my four-legged children. Nikita was such a civilized dog in the city that it was hard to believe that in the not so distant past, she was a wild beast stalking the New Jersey countryside. On our walks, Niki accepted her leash boundary adjusting her stride to my lead. Even when going down the stairs, she would not advance until she saw my foot land on the first step. Whenever we passed the neighborhood delis, she'd insist to pause and smell the flowers for sale outside. She loved looking in store windows and once inside, Nikita behaved extraordinarily well either shopping like a pro or hanging out with the staff.✧ Always patient with the attention from strangers, she was best with children allowing them to pull her fur and poke her wherever their sticky fingers landed. Amicable with the neighborhood dogs, Nikita had even forged a bizarre relationship with a cute, little Chinatown kitten that would pop out to say "hello" every time we passed its hangout on Delancey.

Of course, not everything was so perfect all the time. There were a few dogs in the neighborhood that she wanted to "even the score" with. She had almost caught a few rats and remembered the spots where she saw them. And, there were times when she'd stop walking and sit in the middle of the sidewalk because

---

✧ She even had her favorite places to visit which thankfully included my favorite shoe store and clothing boutique. Less surprisingly, Ciao Bella also ranked high on her list.

she wanted a longer walk or a different itinerary. But thankfully, long gone were Niki's wild ways of The Farm. Or, so I had assumed.

One lazy, summer afternoon, we were walking past the Italian bakery on Elizabeth. With the ovens off and the workers gone for the day, any unsold bread was piled into the dumpsters. Scavengers that they are, the pigeons were clamoring about trying to get what they could until the alarm sounded at the proximity of Niki and Shamus.

I smirked at the flock's hasty departure. After all, there was no real danger. My two beasts were lawfully on-leash for the safety of fellow New Yorkers including any "wildlife."

A few of the birds ignored the alarm and were still gobbling up whatever they could cram in their beaks until that last possible departure. Niki had been mindfully watching the flock. I could feel her body tense, her attention focus, as we approached the stragglers. She watched as they took off, one by one.

Pausing momentarily in her tracks, she leaned into her haunches.

BOOM!

She plucked one unlucky pigeon mid-flight, mid-air!

Simply amazing, like watching "animal planet" live! And yet, completely revolting as she held a filthy, winged rat captive in her mouth.✧

I pulled sharply on her leash commanding, "Drop it!"

The moment she did, Shamus picked it up and started shaking it like a squeaky toy. I pulled his leash, "Drop it!"

Reluctantly, he did. And, Niki took it back.

"Drop it! Drop it! Drop it! DROP IT!"

Back and forth they went with their newest trophy.

Eventually finding a window of opportunity between big and little jaws of death, the masticated pigeon escaped and hobbled into the street waiting for the next available taxi to run it over and finish its miserable little life.

✧ For those of you who are unaware of the reality of NYC pigeons, trust me they are disgustingly dirty creatures. I once had the misfortune of being grazed by a pigeon that mis-negotiated the height of my head. The stench was so foul that people backed away from me on a packed rush hour train; and moments after arriving at work, I was asked to go home and shower.

As I stood there proud, disgusted, and musing the pigeon's current fate, I became aware of a woman screaming at the top of her lungs, her boyfriend trying to calm her. Quickly, I gathered my senses and escaped the scene of the crime before the police came to inquire and take Nikita away from me.

Someone take me away from her. *PL*-ease! Do you have any concept the level of applied physics needed, the concentration required, just how hard it is to pluck a pigeon out of mid-air WHILE attached to an OCD freak by a prong collar and a ZERO foot lead?! Well, of course, I could do it with my eyes closed. But for the average canine— It's beyond impossible!

And then, to force me to drop my newest trophy AND allow Shamus to get his puppy slobber all over it! But wait— It gets even worse! With a prime opportunity presented rather than to go for the kill, Boo-Boo Head chose to play with it like a squeaky toy gone wild! Clearly, city slicker life and poetry writing had further dulled his already stunted senses.

I was completely fed-up with the TWO of them! She insisted to control my every movement, curb my every instinct with that barbaric prong collar— And him?! Well, his "intelligence-not-included" brain could only retain, collate, and employ only droplets of information at any given time.

Just as I was about to lose my temper, we rounded the corner and scooted into "The Pet Stop." As an unexpected apology for her un-welcomed, un-appreciated, un-necessary intervention, My Mistress allowed each of us to choose a treat. Which, I deemed an agreeable substitute— After all, today I wasn't really in the mood to pick feathers out of my teeth. Unable to decide between a flossie and a bully stick, she got me both! Score![6]

*

My life at The Farm was slowly slipping into fond and distant memories as New York obviously had so much more of EVERYTHING! And, let's be honest— From the very moment that my paws hit the pavement, I knew that I was a city girl which was confirmed 110% when My Mistress introduced me to the very, very best part of New York living— Exactly! The pleasures of s-h-o-p-p-i-n-g, shopping!

By far it was better than all the pigeon catching, rat chasing, new territory marking— Paws down, my absolute favorite big city pastime, especially on a "girls' day out." True, girly-time meant having to be alone with My Mistress— However, it also meant time away from the little boy bugger and his constant-cuddling, drool-collecting, sneak-attacking, and endless-kissing routine.

Sometimes we'd begin our excursion with an espresso or a drink with her "friends," but it always meant canvassing for hours-on-end different city neighborhoods for new boutiques

---

[6] Please. Always mindful of my figure, I had absolutely no intention of eating them both at the same time. One was for now; the other, I would slowly savor, nibbling on it for hours on hours A.K.A. Torturing Shamus, for days! Revenge is best served as a everlasting bully stick. Muah-ha-haaa.

and lots of purchase power— Cha-CHING! Store after store, an endless parade of clothing and shoes and accessories for humans and canines.

On our last shopping excursion, she even acquiesced and bought me a fancy harness with matching leash— WooHoo! Of course, with her incessant need to ruin every happy moment, she only used it to display my custom ordered, hand-cast sterling silver identification tag. But, it was still a baby step in the right direction!

Naturally, all of the places My Mistress preferred to shop were prepped for my arrival. From the moment that my front paws crossed the threshold, the sales associates would fawn over me and without hesitation offer some bottled water and a treat. Usually dried liver or chicken, sometimes even a homemade biscuit! The best shops were the ones in Nolita and on Carmine Street that welcomed me with real biscotti.[FYI] Invariably, wherever we were exercising her platinum card muscles, as My Mistress perused the racks, I was liberated from her by a salesperson insisting to adopt me, even if only for the time she shopped— WooHoo!

Unfortunately, there were a few stores, mostly the flagship ones in SoHo, that were not very welcoming nor properly prepared for my visit. The staff would rummage through drawers while apologizing insincerely until they unearthed a stale grocery store biscuit coated with pen marks and eraser bits.

Excuse you? Is there any part of me that resembles a common, undiscriminating canine?! *PL*-ease, immediately remove that offending clump of artificially flavored corn meal

---

[FYI] Just in case you are planning ahead for my visit, pistachio and almond are my favorites. And of course, nothing with chocolate because chocolate can kill even a Siberian Husky like me.

away from my nose and offer me instead a bite of your Balthazar's sandwich or a taste of your soup from Olive's.

Of course, the very best spent girl-time was on spa day! After a short morning walk and coffee, we'd be chauffeured to the salon. Escorted to my own room, I'd be groomed and pampered until evening. Not that it took me so long to become even more beautiful, but they obviously had a whole lot more work to do on Mistress In-Desperate-Need-Of-High-Maintenance before her appointment could be considered "finished!"

All jokes aside, I was beginning to worry about My Mistress. Even though she insisted to pull me closer to her side than a shadow, snapping on my lead if I strayed one freaking inch from the allotted space, no one saw her— Exactly! Without fail, absolutely everyone ignored her. Why? Without question, because absolutely everyone was taken in by my presence!

I was genuinely concerned that the emotional trauma she suffered daily from taking second place to my beauty and charm would affect her and her co-dependency issues adversely, possibly inducing psychotic fits of jealousy or throwing her into the depths of irretrievable Gizmotic depression.

Just this evening, after spending the day at Doggie Doo and stopping at Ciao Bella for a vanilla bean gelato, a man approached us. Bending down to pet me, he was barely able to pry his eyes away from mine and couldn't take his hands off my freshly groomed coat. Now, this particular admirer was a real gentleman— very kind and considerate towards My Mistress asking her little pleasantries and occasionally looking in her direction. However, every time he looked at her, she got a goofy grin on her face and with every question he asked, her face got redder and redder. Her eyelashes fluttering away, she even stammered a few times.

Just fan-tas-tic! I finally meet a good man AND I'm in the company of My Mistress, the smiling mute. Thankfully Shamus wasn't there or the whole situation would have been painfully embarrassing.

Time stood still between the man and my-self. A deep regard, a connection, which becomes that timeless moment of forever. Finally looking at his watch, he was surprised to learn that he was late for an appointment, but added with a smile, "There couldn't be a better reason."

Unable to control herself, Mistress Awkward-is-My-Middle-Name mumbled something ridiculous about, "a pleasure shared."

Reaching inside his coat pocket, he took out a business card and scribbled a few words on the back. As he handed the card to My Mistress, he insisted, "Please call."

At first, I hoped it might be a referral to a psychiatric practice specializing in co-dependency, separation anxiety, name your syndrome-of-the-hour counseling.■ But judging by her reaction, it was something else.

It was something else to be handed a business card for a date with your dog! No, not a joke. After stopping us on the sidewalk and chatting me up for at least 20 minutes, this guy handed me his card. On the

■ Like: 1-800 we help [psychos like] u

back was written, "Anytime Nikita needs to be walked, call me."

Really? A date with my dog?! Obviously, the late summer heat had all the crazies coming out of the woodwork, so I took the dogs and escaped the city.

Driving up the Atlantic coastline, stopping in small towns off the beaten path, we found ourselves a week later in Bar Harbor. Still not ready to go back, we continued our "summer vacation" taking the ferry to Nova Scotia and traveling up to Prince Edward Island.

The dogs were well-received everywhere we went and even cultivated "followings" in the small towns and locales. In Halifax, a couple approached us at dinner one evening. They had first seen Nikita at the ferry in Dig by, then walking around in Yarmouth, and were happy to have the opportunity to finally meet her.✧

It was a great spontaneous adventure and the dogs were perfect little traveling companions. But after 3 weeks on the road, I had run out of dog food, greenies, and chicken treats. It was time to go home.

✧ Ok, so maybe we didn't leave all the crazies behind in New York.

Home-sweet-home! Please do NOT be misled into thinking that I am a homebody, but after a l-o-n-g road-trip with funny accents, foreign languages, too much people food, and unfiltered tap water, it's always nice to snuggle in my own bed that first night back. And let's be honest, it's ZERO vacation for me to be stuck in a car with the TWO of them— Especially when they're singing and bopping along to the polka station!

Even worse, on this last trip My Mistress would leave us in the hotel room with the TV as a babysitter. Never thinking to change it to a different channel, Shamus got hooked on Animal Planet documentaries. Not much of a TV viewer myself, I'd leave him eyes glued to the TV instead of me and enjoy the time alone. But, that was a HUGE mistake— Exactly!

Sitting there un-chaperoned, listening to breed characteristics and afflictions AND unable to tell the difference between a Great Dane, a Lhasa Apso, a Chinese Shar-Pei, and himself, self-accredited Dr. Shamus was certain that he was showing signs of hip dysplasia, developing a pronounced underbite, and sporting a rash from the new fabric softener. I'd let him babble on for a few minutes before smacking his senses back into place, reminding him that he was a Yorkshire Terrier— Ughhh! Either I needed to sit in front of the TV with him and be tortured by watching other animals at play OR he needed to pay better attention to the breed being showcased.

Of course, the very next episode was completely dedicated to Yorkies.

O-M-G! My nightmare A.K.A. His fantasy come true! With hundreds of terrier clones running all over the screen, Shamus could hardly contain himself. Listening attentively to all the positive attributes and history of the breed, Shamus was flying high that he came from such a "distinguished lineage." But then, came the possible hereditary behavioral issues and physical ailments. Surprisingly, NONE of Shamus' real problems were among the ones listed!

"I knew it. I knew it. Didn't I tell you?"

Oh boy, here we go.

"Remember, last week after the hike when my knee was bothering me? Well, I actually had a slipped stifle. See, I told you it hurt. Oh, jeeps. There it is Niki, just plain and simple. From this point on, it's all down, down, downhill for me! I'm getting old. Really, really old. Plain as day, my body just isn't what it used to be when I was a puppy. Nope, not at all. Before you know it, youth disappears. Poof! Who knows how many more walks I have left before my tendon stretches out completely or snaps! I'll need emergency surgery. Did you see that part where only 39% fully recover? There's no guarantee. I might just wake up crippled for life! Minimally speaking, post-surgery, I'll be hobbling around in agony. They'll place me on pain meds which my stomach can't tolerate making me sick from both ends. She'll feed me anything I want just to keep some calories in me. But, mostly the sugary stuff. You know my sweet tooth. Then, the cataracts will form, my retina will begin to degenerate. I won't be able to see or—"

WHACK!

Forced into a momentary break from his useless tirade, I informed Dr. Catastrophize that I did not want to hear ANY of it. I knew that My Mistress has laid out the "Big Bucks" for him. Certainly, she double-checked his lineage for problems.[•]

"But the teeth, Niki. She never brushes my teeth! And you heard what they said about dental hygiene as a precursor to

[•] Obviously, just not the right ones!

general health and how Yorkies are especially prone to tooth decay and rotting gum lines!"

Well then, stick to plain kibble. And yes, that means stop eating Chinese food and cheese!

Faced with the most torturous existence imaginable A.K.A. a fate of culinary Hell-on-Earth, his jaw dropped to the floor. I slipped away before he got started again, hoping that the silence would clear his mind. No such luck. Unfortunately, the idea festered in his piddly, pea-sized brain taking on a life of its own.

With every passing day that My Mistress had not brushed his teeth, the potentially-toothless terrier became increasingly neurotic. I was hopeful that at the border, he'd be forced to leave his slothitis① behind or thrown into quarantine until cured. However, customs let this one slip past. By the time we were back in New York, his dental hygiene obsession morphed into— Annoying habit #1,000,005: Tooth cleaning! And not his, but MINE!

Oh yeah! That first morning back in New York, my mid-morning snooze was disrupted by Shamus' tongue probing the inside of my mouth!

What? Wwwwhat the?!

"Niki, please just relax. I'm almost finished."

You are finished, you little Freak Show!

"Niki, Niki. Just let me get this last piece of kibble and egg."

Shamus, I have had it with you. Ça suffit!● This time, you have pushed too far the boundaries of acceptable, respectable, explainable obsession. There is ZERO reason—

"But, there is. There absolutely is!"

I could hardly wait to hear his latest mental diuretics.

---

① Fear of having no front teeth, in case you didn't know.

● Again, some things sound better in French. Et voilà!

"Cleanliness is next to Godliness. And you? You are My Goddess. I love you. I worship you. I would do anything for you, anything!"

Go away! Go set up your very own booth at the Diminutive Canine Fetish Convention!

Too absorbed in his line of reasoning to even consider my suggestion, half-deck continued. "A clean and healthy mouth equals a clean and healthy body and I want you to live forever and ever. So, if she's not going to clean my teeth, at least, I'm going to clean yours! See. It makes perfect sense."

Oh, yeah. Sure. I see it now. Perfect sense. A dream, I must be having a freaking nightmare!

I tried to pinch myself awake, but to My Mistress's untrained eye it looked like scratching. With her screaming "Fleas? Fleas?" and Shamus all doe-eyed pleased with his conclusion, I placed an emergency call praying them both away.

The God-line connection in good working order, My Mistress marched me straight to the new salon in our neighborhood and left me there for the entire day.

- Amen -

My Mistress came to pick me up without the terrier turned dentist fetishist AND took the l-o-n-g way home, even stopping at one of my favorite restaurants for take-away! WooHoo!

Just as we were rounding the last corner before the apartment, a familiar voice called out, "O, Boo eyez! I miist yooo!!"

It had been ages since I saw my long, lost friend who I feared in his absence had met the same fate as most Chinatown kittens— a master and his protégé, a carnivore and his dinner. Ha-ha!

"O, yoo smell so boo-ti-ful tooday — Haaa, like freshly chop-chop melon flowas — Mmmmm!"

Turning around to welcome back my friend, I was completely taken off-guard.

Already suspended mid-air, in-flight was a much larger, better fed, faster, stronger Kung-Fu Kitty!

"Whoo-ee-ya — Ha-haaa!"

I blinked once in disbelief.

His paw extended. Claws suddenly spiked were now grazing my nose!

Ouch! Not fair!! I was not properly—

I blinked once again in disbelief.

Kung-Fu Kitty was already resting in a seated position on the sidewalk, head cocked to one side. "Very diis-pointing, pre-tay woofie — Yoo learn na-ting and so, soo sloooowwa —"

All too aware which end of the prong collar I was on, I maintained my cool and chose to stare my adversary into submission.

"O, no look so saaad — No boo-boo. I no hurt yooo — Neva wheel — Yoo toooo pre-tay!"

GRRRrrrrr! This cat was out of his martial art mind!

"Maybee, next time yoo bring leetle creeket — He more fun — Boo-ee-yaaa!"

That is it! YOU ARE F— GASP CHOKE GASP!

My Mistress just had ZERO sense of timing always cutting me off mid-threat!

Now being marched away with determination by Mistress Hungry Tummy, I heard his ingratiating voice ringing out behind me, "O-kay bye-bye, boo eyez — I be waiting four yooo — MUAAHH — Wahahh-haaaa!"

Ha-ha, to you too! Nice try, but there's NO WAY that this time I'm going to turn around to see a levitating feline above my eye level. No, no thank you. Once is enough!

Back at the apartment before the food got too cold, Shamus did not greet me at the door. Humph. Typical, typical, never where he should be, when he should be, doing what he should be doing.

I tiptoed inside and found him in the usual place— Asleep in the bedroom. His little button-nose pressed to the baseboard with his legs flailing through the air like a sad little sock puppet. Obviously in the middle of a dream, he was either fantasizing that he was finally a "real dog" or chasing after one of the mice.

Mice. At least four of them had taken up residence in the apartment walls while we were gone on vacation. How do I know? Because that's how many I found masticated, lying next to my garbage pail… Ugh.

Although I never saw them actually catch one, I'd watch the gruesome twosome mobilize for "mouse patrol" as soon as one of them heard the pitter-patter of little feet between the drywall. Setting up posts on either side of the wall shared by the two bedrooms, at regular intervals they'd consult at the doorjamb. Back and forth, back and forth, sometimes tag-teaming each other switching rooms.

If there was no action within a few minutes, Niki would determine that it was a false alarm and walk away. But Shamus, whose terrier lineage made him much more tenacious, would continue to run reconnaissance on his own running back and forth between the two rooms sniffing the outlets, windowsills, and baseboards. He'd occupy himself for hours until falling asleep usually with his nose kissing the wall.

That Autumn, I began traveling a lot more, sometimes with the dogs, sometimes without. But even with the time now divided among hotel rooms, Club Canine, and home, the dogs had settled into the daily routine of city life. Of course, Nikita still had her difficult moments, but they were becoming more the exception than the rule. Shamus was a breeze even if a little kooky with his Nikita obsession and his newest habit of running into the bathroom and whining every time I brushed my teeth.

Before I realized, it was already December and time for my grandfather's 90th birthday party. A day-long affair was planned with all his friends, colleagues, fellow Rotarians, and family. It would also be my only chance to visit until after the holiday season was over.

♫ Over the potholes and through the tolls, to Grandma's house we go!
The GPS knows the way, but My Mistress may stray—
I can't wait to play in real snow! OH!
Over the potholes and through the tolls, oh how fast she does drive!
I'll pretend to be asleep, pray that Shamus makes not a peep—
Until we arrive in one piece and alive! ♫

Woohoo! Grandma C here we come!

It had been faaar too long since her last visit and opportunity to spoil me! But, there was yet another very good reason for our visit— NOT to be mistaken for a "softie," I was genuinely concerned for her well-being. After all, I still remembered Grandma C's tears at the adoption. I just hoped we weren't too late and that the poster child for "Voracious

---

♫ Excuse me, but as everyone very well knows, Huskies are excellent vocalists and I am NO exception to that particular rule!

Terriers" hadn't chomped off all Grandma's bits and parts by the time we arrived!

By the time we arrived at our exit on the turnpike, my seasoned traveling companions woke up from their snooze. Niki sat straight up in the passenger seat, becoming more and more excited the closer we got to my mom's.

We were all welcomed to visit, but Niki could not stay inside the condo. My mother was still allergic, and it was always shedding season for Niki's coat. So, to accommodate her grand-dog, my mom transformed her entire garage into a dog-friendly room. There was a bed with blankets and towels, a couple of space heaters, new toys, water, a soup pot full of dog food with a giant-sized, gourmet dog biscuit placed on top.✧ And just in case Niki-Houdini got any ideas, the

---

✧ Yes, there was more kibble and treats available than she should eat in weeks, but Nikita was a self-feeder and never over-indulged.

automatic garage door was disengaged to prevent any impromptu exit.

It was a perfect solution and an excellent idea to keep Niki and Gizmo separated since from the moment they locked eyes, the hateful stares proved that time had not softened their feelings towards each other. I just hoped that Gizmo would keep her distance and Nikita her cool, as we passed through the house on our way in and out the front door.

The next day, my mom was at work and I was alone in the house with the dogs. I took Shamus and Gizmo out first; and then, Niki. As I marched Nikita through the living room, smart little Gizmo kept a very safe distance watching us through the railing from her perch on the staircase.

When we returned from the walk, Gizmo was no longer on the staircase. Not wanting to run into her on our way through, I called out her name a few times. But when she didn't answer, I figured she was sleeping in the bed upstairs.

Then, I saw that I left the garage door to the house open. Oh my...

O-M-G! That little oinker was back to her old tricks. But, this time My Mistress finally caught her mid-scarf— Gotcha Gizster! Lips-locked and mouth-FULLY-loaded!

Please, allow me to set the scene.

Loving me the way she does, Grandma C understood my need for privacy and set up an adjoining, yet private suite for me— Double-Triple BONUS! Because it had been sooooo long since our last visit and she loved and missed me sooooo much, she tricked out my room with all sorts of toys and treats just for me-Me-ME!

With attention paid to every detail, my room had dimmed mood lighting, freshly-drawn chilled spring water, and enough food and treats for a P-A-R-T-Y! My only grievance was, with the space heaters jacked up to high, it felt like the tropics. However not wanting to seem ungrateful after ALL Grandma C's efforts, I pretended that I liked Caribbean beach vacations.

Bottom line: I was pampered and spoiled and ALONE![*]

I ♥ Grandma C!

With her typically lazy start to every day, that very 1st morning when My Mistress finally came to walk me, she mindlessly left the door open to my room— Exactly! An EPIC mistake!

Counting the rawhide chews, pig ears, high protein kibble, and sugar plums as she watched us leave, our little butterball's eyes glazed with the vision of an endless parade of treats within easy chomping distance.

Back from our walk none too soon, we caught the chunky monkey mid-scarf, crumbs falling out both sides of her

---

[*] Super-Duper-Quadruple Bonus?! Gizmo was miserable at all the extra TLC towards me!

mouth— Ewww! Such disgusting table manners at her age and with her pedigree!

More than happy to teach the Gizmatic Gorger a reminder lesson in etiquette, I stepped forward. But, as expected, My Mistress kept me reined in at her side under the illusion that she could do better.

"Gizmo, Gizmo! Stop, Stop it! N-o-w, Now! GIZZZ!" The walls shook with the force of My Mistress's words.

Her gluttonous rapture having reached an untimely, unceremonious end, Gizmo turned the suction power to high, inhaling more and more and more— Holy MOLY! There was no time to waste! I placed an "emergency call" on the God-line. One more piece of kibble and SPLAATBOOM! She'd be deader than a duck from Toulouse!

With the divine intervention now on her side, My Mistress possessed enough physical strength to pry Gizmo away from the pot. Not to be so easily thwarted, Gizmo jammed a couple of rawhide bones in her craw as she waddled her retreat! Unbelievable!

Only a few pieces of kibble and assorted crumbs were left. Maybe enough for a snack, but certainly not lunch. Even the Colossal Great Dane sized biscuit treats had been gobble-gobbled up!

Mad as a hornet, My Mistress left me in the remnants of my once cushy room to take out her frustration on Gizmo— Ridiculous! She never had any sense of priority! Throwing a conniption fit when she should've been on her knees praying that Grandma C wouldn't turn back into The Hummer and "grin" at the path of devastation left by a now abnormally puffy schnauzer.

What-ever! No matter who The Hummer's wrath was directed at made ZERO difference to the pleasure I now saw on the horizon— Precisely! My Shopportunity!

Closing my eyes and shutting out the din continuing inside the house, I began my list of ALL the things for Grandma C to buy on our trip to Pet Supermarket later that evening. List finished, I put in a little, extra nudge on the God-line. The most sincere requests always granted, I intended to enjoy the rest of my visit at Grandma C's Gizmo-drama, Mistress-hovering, and Hummer-smile FREE!

*

Super early the next morning, my door opened and standing at the top of the stairs, was not My Mistress, not Grandma C, but My Uncle! I didn't even know that I had an uncle! But, there he was all geared up to brave the cold and take me jogging— WooHoo! •

Around and around, weaving between the freshly plowed streets and shoveled sidewalks, this uncle of mine had stamina, even if a little slow in comparison to my natural stride— Oh well, let's be honest. At this point, any outdoor activity was better than stuck in my toasty confines!

However, when he turned to the path up towards the canal, I immediately hit the brakes.

STOP! That's far enough, uncle of mine!

Tempting as it was to sink my paws into the salt-free, trodden-not-plowed snow, I was NO fool when it came to "the" haunted towpath. Unfortunately, my uncle mistook my healthy caution as fatigue and we returned to Grandma C's house— Bahhhh.

Grandma C was at the front door when we arrived. Instead of being shooed straight into my room, she toweled me

• Originally, he had planned to take Gizmo; however, she was still bloated from the "incident" and grounded indefinitely. And let's be honest, he wanted to go for a jog, not a lug-a-long!

off and offered me breakfast. Most excellent! Nice that someone remembered my favorite post-workout meal— Hot oatmeal with kibble, mmmmm-good!

Even more impressive, considering her ever-expanding size, Gizmo was nowhere to be seen. Of course, Morning Sunshine Shamus was bouncing all-around, asking me about my run, chattering away, and showering me with kisses. With the constant interference and, "Hurry up-hurry up! Let me clean your teeth-let me clean your teeth!" it was almost impossible to enjoy my meal.

DING-DONG!

Neglecting the last few pieces of kibble that remained, I looked up towards the door to see what this new interruption was all about. Maybe, I had another uncle who liked to play in the snow!

Humph. No such luck. A red-headed woman opened the screen door and— Wait one second! Who's that trying to push through?

No way! This is farrrrrr better than any uncle— That's right! My Little Person had come to visit me-Me-ME!

He tore free from the red-headed woman, past Grandma C, through the living room and threw his arms around me!

Wow! Look at you! You've gotten so BIG! Now, we can play hide-and-seek and run around the yard, contraption-chaperone FREE! WooHoo!

First, showing him my room and all my new toys, we played and played and played— But, wait! It gets even better! With The Gizminator securely locked in the upstairs bedroom, MLP and I had total run of the whole townhouse!

Left behind as the third, the smallest, and obviously non-essential wheel, Shamus watched the happy reunion. Eventually, Mr. Paralyzed-By-So-Easily-Replaced-Angst sulked away into the back corner of the coat closet. Finally Yorkie-voyeur-free, the two of us snuggled on the floor, MLP using my chest for a pillow— Ahhhhh.

Equally touched by the connection between a little person and his dog, Grandma C made a call arranging for MLP to stay the entire weekend! Someone sure did L - O - V - E her favorite grand-dog!*

I was in such high spirits by the time we left, not even the long, long ride back to New York City with Christmas carol sing-a-long torture rankled me. Besides, I was on my way back home for my 1st Christmas in the big city.

The transformation in just a few short days was amazing! More people, more lights, more food, more shopping— and the very best surprise? Trees everywhere, from everywhere! Douglas Fir from a nursery in Upstate New York, Leyland from South Carolina, Balsam Fir and Virginia Pine from Dutch Pennsylvania, and even a few White Spruce from Maine— Exactly! A virtual olfactory album of my travels! Ahhhh, such sweet memories.

Holiday BONUS! With boxes arriving every single day, just like Mt. Everest, Endless Presents Mountain kept growing higher and higher! Stacks upon stacks of gifts for ALL 3 of us— But wait! It gets even better! Grandma C contributed to Holiday Booty Butte mailing the biggest, the heaviest boxes ever! Perhaps, it was just another senior moment forgetting about all the toys she had just given me, but I now had more gifts AND even a personalized stocking already stuffed— just in case Santa didn't get our change of address!

Have I mentioned before? I ♥ Grandma C and Christmas is paws-down my favorite time of year!

---

* Me-Me-ME!!! Just in case there was any doubt!

Christmas is hands-down my favorite time of year in New York City. With the lights twinkling from windows, balconies, and streets, the store windows decorated for the holidays, freshly-cut trees sold at every corner, mailboxes filled with cards, and gifts from all corners of the globe... everyone seems happier, the city seems happier, even my dogs seemed happier. But, for me, the real magic of Christmas happens with the candlelight, incense, and music at midnight mass.

This year, I decided to attend St. Thomas Episcopal Cathedral, on 5th Avenue. Even though I arrived 2 hours before the service, all the seats in the nave were already taken and there was only one seat left available in the galleries.

Climbing up the stairs, I was thrilled to have a perfect bird's eye view on the entire service from my aisle seat at the railing. What I didn't realize was how much hotter it was up in the rafters; and as the church began to fill, it got warmer and warmer. Dressed in cashmere for the chilly winter weather, it wasn't long before I began to feel uncomfortably warm.

The service began, the choir sang, the clergy entered, the heavily perfumed incense rose, and before the first hymn was finished, I started to swoon. Not wanting to make the headlines in the Christmas morning papers with a premature end on the flagstone floor below, I excused myself from the pew.

As I tried to walk, my legs buckled underneath me. An usher rushed to my aid holding and guiding me towards a doorway. By the time, we reached the upper vestibule I was in a fog. Someone asked me to sit. I remember saying, "No, thank you." before collapsing on the floor.

Everything went completely white.

I have no idea how long I was unconscious; but when I came to, I was aware of a couple of shadowy figures and muffled, masculine voices speaking French. At first, I thought that I had died and these were my angels come to take me to heaven.

As it turned out, I was rescued by a French-Canadian usher and a Swiss tourist. The Swiss man stayed with me for the rest of the service, making certain that I was okay. Before leaving the church, he asked for my phone number.

Thank you, God, for the best Christmas present, ever!

Thank you, God, for the best Christmas present, EVER! Aside from the usual treats and toys, My Mistress surprised us with a man— That's right! And, a Swiss one! Oh-di-lay-ee, lay-ee, lay-ee-ooo!!♬

I don't know where she found him or how she managed it, but at our front door, ringing the bell on Christmas morning, was a good-smelling, always smiling, fun to be with, French-German-English speaking man! Wow Wow Wow! He was absolutely perfect! Merry Christmas, Ni-Ki-Ta!

Every time he came over, which was every single day, he was super cool and nice paying attention to ALL THREE of us. No one felt left out— not even Mistress Forlorn!

With some positive attention finally directed her way, My Mistress was beginning to loosen up a bit laughing and having fun instead of the usual nag-n-cling routine. And Little Boo was

---

♬ I was already practicing my yodeling for the alpine adventures to come.

showing signs of growing a new pair, now that there was a masculine presence in the house. We made a perfect family.

Sometimes he would come over and hangout, sometimes we'd go for uber long walks— One perfect snowy winter's day, even across the Brooklyn Bridge and back! He loved to cook, preparing dinner, and cuddling ALL night long before making us breakfast in the morning! I ♥ Basel Switzerland!

Everything thing was picture perfect— Until, one afternoon. He arrived at our home with his luggage and announced he was on his way to the airport!

Absolutely ridiculous! There's not enough time to pack my bag OR find where she hides my passport— Grrrrrr!

All I could do was sit down and watch as he walked away.

Nikita sat down on the sidewalk and watched as my Swiss friend hailed a cab to the airport. Even after the taxi drove off, she refused to budge. I don't know which was worse, saying good-bye to one of the nicest guys I'd ever met or watching Nikita pine after him.

For a few weeks after my friend's departure, every single time we passed a man on the street Niki'd turn her head to take a sniff. It was a little sad, but funny as the guys spooked by the sudden movement, half-jokingly asked, "Does your dog bite?"

"Not usually," was typically my sighed response. But on those off-days, I'd reply through a forced grin, "No, but I do."

It was only a couple of weeks after the holidays when my telephone rang in the middle of the night. Hoping that it was my Swiss friend forgetting to calculate the time difference, I was surprised to hear my father's voice on the other end. My grandfather had just passed away.

No more hugs, no more jokes, no more laughter, no more stories, no more anything. The person who meant the world to me was gone. It was by far the worst news of my life.

It was by far her worst point ever. Once she hung up the phone, she totally stopped breathing. Just when I was about to come to the rescue with CPR,[*] her sobbing gasps began. The rest of that night, she laid sleepless in bed, tears flowing down her face.

---

[*] Canine Pulmonary Resuscitation. And, of course, I'm certified.

The next few days, didn't get any better either. Sitting in her rocking chair, chain-smoking and comatose most of the day, she took us out for only the bare minimum. Sure on our abbreviated walks, she'd visit and laugh with our neighbors, the flow of tears held at bay with a smile— However, once the key turned in the lock and we were inside, she went back to the rocking chair, back to the empty stares, back to endless tears. Sad. So, so very sad.

Look, I could totally sympathize. I knew exactly what she was going through. After all, I had witnessed death plenty of times. All those ill-fated critters at The Farm croaking from playing too rough. And, there was the loss of my friend, Jake.

I loved Great Gramps, too— But, this was over the top. She was beyond inconsolable, ignoring all my attempts to play and hardly cracking a grin at my slap-stick comic farces.[☺] Still, I tried my best and kept Shamus in-check. I even put in a few dedicated calls on the God-line.

None too soon, she loaded us into the beamer and started driving out of the city. Road-trip, heated seats, and Grandma C's?! Good times, pig ears and bully sticks, here I come— WooHoo!

BUT, we arrived to find Grandma C equally cheerless. Ugh. Even Gizmo was more miserable than usual. Although in her case completely understandable considering the long, long, looong list of people who had already left her!

Ok-okay, fine. No more deadpan humor. All jokes respectfully now pushed aside, I had zero desire to stay with the red-eyed, red-nosed lot of them. I had already been swimming

---

[☺] Please, there's absolutely no other reason for my paws slipping out from underneath me or my doing a tummy-flop into the chaise! Trust me here, it was all done to lift her spirits up.

for days in mistress tears and was utterly tapped making it beyond even my capacity to handle the angoisse times 3! ☞

My prayers always answered in the order in which they were received, I wasn't staying at Melancholy Manor— That's right! Even in mourning, ever thoughtful towards her favorite grand-dog, knowing that my usual suite would not be insulated enough from the drama AND rightfully concerned that Gizmo might seek solace in my kibble bowl, Grandma C arranged for me to have a private run at Add-En-On Kennels with hikes, camper time, and even bonfire story-times scheduled— Simply perfect! Some Nikita-time would give me the chance to recharge my batteries and mourn my loss in quiet reflection.

Amen.

*

By the time we returned to New York her mood had lightened, but NOT her grip on my lead.

I had had high hopes that within the prolonged bereavement period, she would learn a much needed "How to live and let go" lesson— But, no. Oh, NO! Time and time and time again, pulling me closer and closer and closer— Simply ridiculous!

This time, we were casually walking around the East Village Shamus-free glancing in store windows and— YANK!

OUCH! What is your problem, now? Give me my s p a c e!

Losing my forward focus to glare at her, I missed seeing the giants that had turned onto 3rd Ave headed our way. Of course, I had seen Colossal Great Danes on those programs

---

☞ Stop. In case you thought there'd be a half-pint joke, forget about it. Shamus was oblivious to My Mistress's condition and the deteriorating situation. If by accident he happened into a room with a crying female, he'd silently retrace his steps. Typical, typical male.

Shamus watched— but, they looked much, much, much smaller on TV. Even at 2 blocks away, they were bigger than our television, bigger than the word "colossal." They were freaking HUGE![9]

Now, I understood her problem-du-jour. She was afraid of these lumbering clods and required my protection. As flattering as that might seem, it was really just another responsibility to fall upon my already heavily-burdened shoulders— Sighhh.

Pressing my torso against her leg in reassurance, I sized up my approaching opponents. Fact was, the pair were too, too big to challenge directly. I'd have to employ more subtle tactics.

Now only ½ block away I took in deep, deep breath puffing my chest up-and-out to appear at least one size larger. Keeping my focus determinedly forward, tail held high yet casually in the air, I looked larger, super tough yet with a cool confidence. With a little luck, the list of breed characteristics accurate, the dimwitted duo would be hoodwinked by my clever illusion.

We passed through the beasts like a river flows through a gorge. Out of the danger zone and able to resume normal breathing, I exhaled exhausted from all my efforts.

Thankful to have cleared the sizable opponents and now only steps from Veselka's, My Mistress stopped in for a quart of celebratory borsht. Mmmmmm— There's nothing quite like a good bowl of hot borsht and kibble to show genuine appreciation on a cold winter's day.

Moments like these, made me happy to live with her and in New York City. She was still suffering more than her fair share of post-traumatic, grief-stricken moments— But, let's be realistic! With the sale season in full swing, her spirits were easily buoyed with a new pair of shoes from Sigerson Morrison reduced 75%! So now, my only tangible obstacle to that warm

[9] They were soooo big, I bet even their poops were bigger than Shamus!

fuzzy feeling of complete satisfaction was a rather small, but insanely annoying one— Exactly! S - h - a - m - u - s, Shamus!

Always "under paw," staring ad nauseam, finding pleasure in the sound of his own bark, reciting his poetry, blinded by delusions of grandeur, suffering from bouts of acute hypochondria, and cleaning my teeth— ALL in no particular order of annoyance, the fly in my happiness ointment was up to his old shenanigans. That's right! As if it couldn't get any worse, Shamus added "philosophy" to his ever-growing list of annoying habits.

One evening, acting as if he had scaled Mount Sinai instead of a mound of snow, King of the Yorkieverse decided to share with the entire neighborhood his latest brain aberration.

"Life is not always as you perceive it. Is a paper bag really a paper bag? Or, is it in truth, a cat cloaking device?"

Please do not ask which was worse, listening to his mental diuretics echo throughout Nolita into Chinatown OR knowing that with one gust, I'd be resurrecting Pompous Puppy splat!

Hey! Get down n-o-w, now! There's no lifesaving, mouth-to-mouth on the agenda in your entire lifetime which by the way is getting shorter exponentially!

"Ok Niki, ok Niki, ok Niki. No worries! I'm coming, I'm coming."

None too soon, my existential sidekick. Zero patience is my phrase of the day. There's a lot of ground to cover before the salt's out.

"You know, Niki, even if did I slip, she's here."

Really? Do you honestly think that Mistress Laughs-Out-Loud-Every-Time-You-Smack-Head-First-Into-A-Sign-Post cares?

"Well, I am the one with the growing collection of multi-colored harnesses and matching accessories."

Really?! A segue from life-saving to cross-dressing? Wrap your philosophical insight around this little nugget, Nietzsche Widget: I am in no mood to tango to your metaphysical milonga!

And as usual, yap-a-matic ignored all my warnings.

"Anyway, if there was a choice, I wouldn't mind her brushed minimally 3-times-a-day cinnamon and fennel breath to—"

TWACK! SPLAT!

"Niki-Niki-Niki, please-please-please don't be angry. It was a joke, a funny one. Ha-ha. Okay? I was only joking. I love your wolf breath. I love you! I love everything about you!"

And then, again, came the puppy kisses— Ughhhh. Impossible.

Ever vigilant, even through the slobbering, I discerned a faint mewing sound.

Hmmm. Perhaps Kung-Fu Kitty was in need of help— Ni-Ki-Ta to the rescue!

Pushing Four-Legged Fabio to the curb, I did a 180 and headed in the general direction of the distress call. However, getting to the source was not as easy as all that— Exactly! Despite my strong lead, My Mistress was still not trusting and once we reached the Old Police Building, she flat out refused to walk down the back alley! Absolutely ridiculous!

Wake up to Reality! I am here to protect both of you clowns while saving the sacrificial kitten![*]

The meow for help distinctly echoing between the buildings on Center Market Place, intensified during our stand-off. With the cry now at decibels loud enough to reach her deaf ears, My

[*] It should be duly noted that by this point, I already knew that it was not Kung Fu Kitty who required assistance. Equally to be marked upon, knowing the helpless party never has and never will preclude any heroic efforts on my part.

Mistress overtook my lead moving swiftly towards the heart-wrenching mewling.

Peering 10ft down into a window well, two sad, lonely, scared little eyes were staring 9½ feet back up— Awwww.

Awwww… Poor little kitten. Having fallen down into a window casement, the sweet little thing must have been there for at least a few days because someone had dropped in a couple cans of food. Far too deep to reach on my own and assuming that a late night 911 call for a "kitten rescue" would not be looked upon kindly, I dragged the dogs around to the front of the building and spoke with the doorman. He did not look that pleased with or interested in our feline altruism. However, when we checked the next morning, the kitten was gone.

*

It's a little cliché, but after my grandfather's death I began to seriously re-evaluate my life. As much as I loved being in New York, I was lacking a certain quality of life. My job consumed my time, my rent consumed my paycheck, and the only "meaningful relationship" I had was with my dogs. With my apartment lease up for renewal in a couple of months and a substantial rent increase proposed, I had already started to search for a new place. But in order to rent a new apartment, I needed references for myself, separate references for the dogs, and up to 10 months security.

My grandfather was gone, my mother just announced that she was moving to Florida, and I flat out refused to pay 12 months of rent for a set of keys. Nothing was keeping me in New York City anymore. It was definitely time for a change.

The big question was where.

**♬ Where oh where has my Grandma C gone
Oh, where oh where could she be?**

It's been far too long since our last visit
Oh, please come back, spoil me ♫

Excuse me did I hear you correctly? Grandma C moved? To Florida? Already?! No "good-bye?" No "I love you?" No, "I'll miss you, my sweet Nikita?!" Ridiculous!

My Mistress, she always cut me out of the Vital Information Loop! When was she going to learn that the "privacy act" is highly applicable, and in fact strongly encouraged, when discussing her boyfriends, NOT family! This was MY Grandma! She denied me the opportunity to say good-bye or to maybe hitch a ride down to Florida. I could hang with my BFF, Clea, and visit the Canada Geese, Eh![*]

It was high time for her to trust me and to discuss with me important family issues rather than the usual inane drone and shuffling me off every single time it was "inconvenient"— Exactly! My case-in-point? I just came back from a weekend getaway at Club Canine to find the entire freaking apartment cluttered with boxes and nowhere to sit! Yet even more disturbing? She was carrying Shamus zipped into a bag like a furry wallet!

Excuse me, Mistress Conclave of One, where is all our furniture? Why would you give away my air-conditioner AND my chaise? What in blazes are you doing treating Shamus like an accessory? And exactly why are you insisting we speak "en français?" This is completely unacceptable!

Standing in-between her and the boxes stacked in the living room, I gave her my very best "I am of an appropriate age

---

[*] And, what about Gizmo? No "good-bye" from her, either? I might never, ever, ever see the black butterball again. Living on a lakefront property, she might be eaten by an alligator which in her case would take two chomp-chomps!

and maturity level I wanna know now" incensed beyond belief stare— Grrrrrr.

As usual, misunderstanding my exasperation for "behavioral issues," My Mistress turned to a new accomplice for help— That's right! Pharmaceuticals!

What I had thought this morning was a routine vet visit, was actually a run for mind-numbing, veterinarian-prescribed narcotics. Even worse, for her perverse entertainment,[⚐] she snuck a full dose into my afternoon cheese snack— And then, took me out for a walk!

Not expecting that her sense of propriety had fallen below rock bottom, nor to be bushwacked by family, I was completely taken off-guard. Before we turned the last corner, my entire world began swimming before my eyes. Every single sense distorted! Somehow, I finally made it back to the safety of home-sweet-home.

Was I allowed to relax on the floor? To watch the tin-type tiles spin overhead? Oh, no! Mistress I-Googled-Husky-Torture locked me in the ugliest, the stinkiest, blue plastic crate with ZERO windows!

Hey! Little Hummer, let me out now-Now-NOW!

As usual, hearing impaired to my cries for help, she faced the wire gate towards the TV and tuned it to a "Home Alone" marathon! The sheer irony of it! Obviously, yet another aberration in her good judgment, I was over th— Zzzzzzzzz.

[⚐] Please excuse the redundancy intentionally used for theatrical effect.

Asleep. She was finally asleep. Just a little over an hour for the sedatives to kick in. Now, I had to time the duration and watch to make sure she had no adverse reaction.

Not that I was a fan of drugging dogs for flights. I understood that the tranquilizers impaired the dog's ability to react to pressure changes and sudden movements which in turn could prove fatal. However, I sincerely doubted that Nikita would be able to contain her displeasure for the entire 6-hour flight and feared she might hurt herself trying to escape. The days of being allowed down into the plane's cargo hold were long, long gone, so this was the best solution to help her handle traveling alone.

Thankfully, Shamus was a much easier matter. He fit into a pet carrier and actually liked being toted around.

The contents of my apartment in boxes and ready to ship, given away, or placed in storage, most of the arrangements made and all the paperwork done. By this time next week, we'd be sipping "un café" at our local bistro and strolling down the sidewalks of Paris!

Paris?! Are my cognitive facilities compromised by a drug-induced hallucinogenic state or did she say Paris— as in Paris, France?! Ooh là là! 3,622 miles closer to Basel, Switzerland![*] Huh. Maybe, just maybe, her cognitive facilities are in a better sh— Zzzzz.

Zzzz-zzz-zzzz

"Good morning! Good morning! Good morning, my most beautiful sunshine! Wakey, wakey!"

PL-ease! Get off of me, Spunky Monkey— Ugghhhh!

Very, very difficult to choose which was worse— A.) Waking up after a drug-induced coma with a blinding, cluster headache— Or B.) Being woken up by a bouncy, kissy terrier. Of course, thanks to Mistress Ever Thoughtful, I did not have to choose— Grrrrr.

Now, it might seem to you that I was "living the life" and acting a bit spoiled or pretentious, but this certainly was not the "Siberian Dream." Yeah, yeah, I know I was somewhat pampered with intermittent spa days and the occasional culinary treat— And sure, moving to Paris was kinda cool— But, these things were my only compensation for the carefree life that I left behind at The Farm. After all, there was still that one huge impediment to my life anywhere— Exactly! Canine

---

[*] Or 5,833 km, if you're metrically inclined.

Bondage! Even with the new harness that sent her back beaucoup bucks, My Mistress still insisted to attach the prong collar Every Single Stinking Walk!

In my humble, most honest opinion, Paris seemed as good of a place as any to start fresh and with a little luck that clunky contraption would not clear customs. Of course, with a little more luck the bag-fitting, neurosis-suffering terrier midget might be detained by customs— Indefinitely!

Allow me a private moment to indulge my post-narcotic hallucinatory fantasies— Sighhh.

Ok, enough of that! If my years of co-habitation misery have taught me one single thing, I'm certain Mistress Micro-Management has covered every angle and I've got a zillion things to do before the flight!

Number One: Remove Yorkshire Terrier from my person.

Number Two: Schedule spa appointment for "The Works."

Number Three: Say goodbye to my friends.

Number Four— Well, I'm sure by now you have the idea.

Á bientôt!

Paris

How I'd love to recount the pleasures of traveling in Air France business class. The personalized welcome, the cushy pre-flight lounge, the flowing rosé champagne, the chef-inspired cuisine, the extra-wide leather seat that reclines into a bed, BUT this was not my experience. Oh, no-No-NO!

Resorting once again to her stash of pharmaceuticals, My Mistress laced my pre-flight snack and shoved me back into that ugly, stinky, blue plastic crate— actually waving as the skycap wheeled me away! Absolutely ridiculous!

With her obsessive fixation on all the preparations for our voyage, you'd think that she'd have made me her certified "emotional support animal" instead of bestowing that particular honor to Shamus.* When was she going to learn that "real love" and "emotional stability" does not fit into a carry-on?!

Luckily, the sedatives had mostly worn off by the time we landed at Charles-de-Gaulle and my French speaking skills were regaining fluency because the entire flight crew surrounded my crate, lamenting the fact that My Mistress did not have the foresight to take me on board.

---

* If you ask, I'm sure he would love to share the luxurious flight experience along with how to design, finance and build an Airbus 380. Hope you've got a comfy seat, a pair of silicone ear plugs, and a very, very long shot of Don Julio Anejo!

As she was nowhere to be found, they soon began debating on whether or not to let me out. I was hoping that one of them, preferably the handsome in a euro-chic way pilot, would adopt me— But with her sense of timing always finely tuned to spoiling my fun, she appeared.

ACKKK! What a sight!

Looking none too fresh or too pretty considering her A+++ ride, My Mistress stood there finger-raking her hair and pulling at her clothes in a futile attempt to approach something more visually appealing. Even worse, obviously flustered by her lack of conversational-with-other-people French, Mistress Fluent-Only-When-Talking-To-The-Mirror started sputtering in Franglais! This was way beyond embarrassing!

Unfazed by yet another rude and ugly American monoglot, the flight crew ignored her lingual surgery and opened my crate— WooHoo! Liberté!

Still a little woozy from the drugs, I had some difficulty negotiating my steps on the freshly polished floor. Thankfully, my Air France escorts remained by my side, keeping me safe and steady. After loading the blue plastic monstrosity onto a trolley, they all escorted me through customs to the taxi stand where Yorkie-in-a-bag and the rest of our luggage were waiting with Grandma C— Whoa! Wait one second. That cannot be right— This must be a post-narcotic induced hallucination since NO ONE cc'd me on any memo about her moving to Paris with US!

My Sky Team escorts guided me straight past the grandma mirage to the passenger door of a silver-grey minivan. However, before I could snuggle into my front-row leather seat, Mistress Impeccable Timing found her voice and French language abilities long enough to instruct them to shove me and that crate into the rear hatch— Grrrrrr.

Rather than make a big fuss, I maintained my composure. After all, a little snooze would help mitigate the residual sedatives in my delicate system. There were first impressions to take into consideration. Not like I wanted my new neighbors to think that I was just another hazy-eyed, self-medicating American! And, let's be honest— One of us had to keep up appearances— One of us had to be well-rested and looking beautiful— One of us had to be able to communicate en français! After all, we were in Paris!

We were really in Paris! From the moment I saw the dome of Sacre Coeur rise into view from the autoroute, I knew that I made the right decision. This was home.

It was just before 7am by the time we arrived in Montmartre. Our new neighborhood was still silent save for the sounds of coffee brewing, breakfast dishes clinking, and the occasional Vespa zooming off. What a difference from New York.

After I lugged the suitcases and Nikita's crate up 2 flights of stairs, the 4 of us✧ went for a coffee. At Place d'Abbesses, our path to the Bistro St. Jean was blocked by a flock of pigeons.

My ferocious little Shamus bounced forward barking, startling the sleepy-eyed beasts into flight. But Nikita, still a little stoned from the tranquilizers, reacted moments after the last bird safely landed halfway across the square. Hard to say which was funnier, Niki's delayed response or the confused look on her face as she chomped down on nothing more than Parisian air.

A café au lait and pain au chocolat later, we returned to the apartment where my mom would wait for the mattress delivery as I waited at France Telecom trying to open an account. By late afternoon with the bed delivered and made, the telephone and Internet promised to be turned on before the end of the week, we were out exploring our neighborhood.

At the top of Rue Ravignan, we found a terrace restaurant with an open table. The ideal spot to

---

✧ My mother had met us at JFK. I needed an extra pair of hands and eyes at the airport with the dogs and luggage. She liked the idea of a one-week vacation in Paris.

spend our first evening watching the setting sun cast rose-colored rays over the rooftops of Paris. It was magical.

Once I finally managed to get and settle the check, we went directly home. I was completely exhausted after a sleepless night in the air and a long first day negotiating with rusty French. My only thought was to a solid and sound 1st night's sleep.

What seemed like only moments after I dozed off, my mother shook me awake. With my eyes half opened, she began pleading "Look at your dog. Look at her. Look!"

Look, I was quite pleased that someone was here to play back up and chaperone My Mistress, holding her hand throughout the move. It was a great burden lifted off my already heavily weighted shoulders. However, if Grandma C thought that that small favor gave her the right to sleep on my side of my new bed, she was sadly mistaken.

True, I was partially responsible. I should have never allowed her head to touch my pillow in the first place. But, while I was busy finishing my evening snack, which Grandma C had

offered me, she snuck into my place— Just think about it! Such outrageous trickery from my very own grandmother!

My-self, supposedly her favorite grand-dog, snookered by an extra Greenie, into spending my 1st night in Paris sleeping on the floor! Completely UN-acceptable— Grrrrrr.

With steadfast patience, I waited for my spot to be liberated knowing I wouldn't be inconvenienced for too long. Let's be honest, at her advanced age she'd obviously have to get up to tinkle at some point during the night— Especially with all that wine she and My Mistress guzzled down at dinner! Ha-ha!

Sure enough, just before the midnight hour Grandma C's bladder could hold it no more. As soon as she disappeared into the bathroom, I claimed my proper place spreading out over my half of the bed.

Ah, heaven. What a perfectly firm mattress these French artisans make. Worth every single franc!

My-self now snuggled into bed slipping off into a restful slumber, Grandma C returned from her bathroom trip and insisted that I move.

No! You sleep on the floor. I understand that it's good for your back. Sweet hard-wood floor dreams and bonne nuit.

She asked again, this time nudging me.

Of course, I refused to budge a single inch. This was my place and the absolute bare minimum as compensation for the horrible suffering, the sheer indignity of my 1st Trans-Atlantic flight spent drugged and locked in the cargo hold like some wild animal. Grandma C needed to show some compassion, some well-deserved consideration towards her "favorite" grand-dog.

Persistent in her pointless endeavor, without any further verbal warning she tried to pull me off the mattress— Redonkulous! I had already dismissed her claim with the pleasantry of, "good night." Clearly, the combination of jetlag and Petit Chablis had adverse effects on someone of advanced age causing this spiraling decline to the physical abuse of loved ones.

With my own pearly white-toothed smile and nothing more than a little grrrrumble from the back of my throat, I let her know that this was My Place. Period. I spent last night in that off-gassing, blue plastic monstrosity. No more concessions from this girl! Good night and sweet dreams!

Undaunted, Grandma C made her way around to the other side and started pushing My Mistress!

AACKKK! There was no way My Mistress would move— No Way she would even care!

Sighhh— Yet another sign of Grandma C's fading grasp on reality. So sad, to have my 1st night in Paris marred by the disturbing antics of her withering mind.

Hovering at the foot of the bed, Grandma C pled her case to sleepy ears.

True to form, My Mistress opened one eye, smiled at me, and before nodding back to her fantasyland dreams informed Grandma C that this had nothing to do with her, "It's between the two of you."

Ha-ha! Told ya so!

Instead of coming back over, asking me nicely with promises of a small, yet terribly expensive, gift for my sacrifice, Grandma C sunk to the floor, tears swelling in her already puffy, blood-shot, jet-lagged eyes.

Ugghhh! This had rapidly deteriorated from a misunderstanding, a simply remedied inconvenience, to an uncomfortably awkward, coyote ugly situation.

Perhaps my-self suffering from jetlag— Perhaps my remembering of all her nice gestures over the years— Perhaps my knowing that eventually she'd leave and return home to an uncertain future with The Gizminator, I succumbed to my true, benevolent nature and moved over enough to allow Grandma C to snuggle into bed with the three of us.

*

I'll save all the boring, tedious, minute, insignificant detail recitation for My Mistress. Let's face it, I have much better things to talk about than furniture delivery, apartment decorating, and her usual blah blah blah— Exactly! I live in P-a-r-i-s, Paris! I now reside in a most civilized society where canines are treated as individuals! Welcomed in all stores, all restaurants, all hotels— And, are NOT spayed, NOT neutered— And, definitely NOT leashed!

However, this last particular detail somehow escaped My Mistress' conscious perception of my cultural adaptation. Believe it or not, Mistress I-Double-Dot-Every-i missed the entire "I trust my faithful companion" thing!

Excuse me? How do you expect me to ever assimilate tethered to you like an unruly toddler at Disneyworld? Might as well wrap me up in an American flag and toss me into the Seine!

Of course, never thwarted by her attempts of hapless interference for very long, with my good looks, American charm, and French language capabilities, within the first few hours of our arrival, I was "The Talk" of Montmartre.

Unleashed and free to approach, there was no hesitation from my aspiring four-legged boyfriends— That's right! No mistress, no daddy, no amateur dog walker pulling them back, insisting that there was "no time" or "maybe, at a later date." Nope. In France, it was about freedom. That particular romance that comes from living in the moment— Fully appreciating every single opportunity as it presented! Have I mentioned yet that I ♥ Paris?!

Politesse essential to every proper social interaction meant charming conversation! Most of my admirers spoke sweetly, welcoming me to the neighborhood, complimenting my American good looks, remarking on my natural poise and grace. Those very, very few who were obviously street mongrels and showed no courtesy or who were complete players whispering inappropriately explicit "possibilities" in my ear as if I was a casual tourist, never got another sniff!

My suitors from Old European lineages, whom were without question formally educated, used eloquent words and intricate verb tenses that Mistress Franglais neglected to teach me. Oddly enough, that's where my underfoot hindrance finally found a "raison d'être."

Forced to pack and carry at all times the English-French-Terrier Reference Dictionary because he could never retain any information, Petit Shamus proved valuable in this singular instance— But, pardonnez-moi for the digression as I have something much more important occupying my thoughts than the Once-In-His-Lifetime-Helpful Terrier— Exactly! Bones!

Oh, s'il vous plaît. Before jumping to any conclusions, immediately drop the misconception of me so easily seduced into a gluttonous rapture by French cuisine and take notice of the capital "B." No way, no how, did I turn gizmodic with a simple continent change and the higher latitude.

That's right! I am not talking about the type of gourmet treat offered by the local butcher, but capital "B," Bones! The super cute, French-English-Spanish-Arabic speaking, testosterone-charged neighbor on four legs AND my 1st Parisian boyfriend— GrrrGrrrGrrrrrr!

The majority of his days were spent in the downstairs bar with his owner. Day after day, walk after walk, his hopeful eyes watched my grace and beauty through the single pane window as we passed. Finally one afternoon, by the time we finished our walk, Bones had liberated himself and was waiting for me at our front door.

He was exactly my type— Young, Blond, Bold, Energetic, and totally into me-Me-ME!

Completely absorbed in the magic of love-at-first-sight, I blissfully forgot my pigmy tag-a-long. That was, until it started jumping up-and-down between me and Prince Charming. A farcical attempt to steal back my attention, My Mistress thankfully had enough good sense to pick up Pogo-Stick Puppy before he sprained something more than just his dignity.

From that day on, every single time that we passed the bar, Bones would find a way out to be with me— Either finding us a block later, saving me from the tedium of walking alone with the gruesome twosome OR waiting for my return at our front door. Of course, not by any means my only boyfriend, he was by far the cutest, the youngest, and my very, first Parisian— My Bones Bones Bones!

Boxes, boxes, boxes. Strewn all over the sidewalk, a few spilling into the street. The movers that I had hired in NYC, sub-contracted to a French company. My quote was written from "door-to-door." The man standing in front of me, now, was telling me that there was nothing mentioned about two flights of stairs and the door to my building was the only door that he saw from where he stood.

When I offered him extra money, his only response was a snarky grin. Then, turning back to his crew, already waiting in the truck with their cigarettes lit, he joined them and drove away.

One-by-one, I began to move the boxes into the hallway and stack them waist-to-shoulder high along the wall to get them safely inside before carrying them up the narrow, spiral staircase.

At no time throughout the enfolding drama and solo-move did my neighbors come to my aid. Rather, they had kept an apathetic distance, chain-smoking cigarettes from across the cobblestone street.

Just as I began the climb to my apartment with the very last box, the grocery owner came over and kindly offered me a crowbar with the "suggestion" that I open and empty the furniture crate immediately.

Wedged in-between two cars, it was blocking the orderly flow of parked traffic. The city of Paris had been notified and was on the way to remove "the obstruction."

This was my official introduction to the particularities of Parisian life. According to Parisian standards, my neighbors were quite helpful keeping a watchful eye on my belongings. And by warning me of the officials coming, they went above and beyond their neighborly duties by saving my pockets from a substantial fine.

I wasn't completely sold on that concept. After all, who called the city in the first place? But then in Manhattan, my boxes would've disappeared from the sidewalk in a New York minute, the crate opened and emptied like a piñata at a kindergarten party.

Goodbye New York. Bienvenue à Paris.

*

With our belongings more or less arranged in the apartment and no 9-5 job to occupy my time, I was free to explore. Paris is a city best experienced by foot and dogs are welcomed almost everywhere, especially well-behaved, good-looking ones like Nikita and Shamus. When our feet got tired or we wanted a speedy journey to our destination, we hopped on a subway train.✧

Being new to and enamored with Paris, I wanted to absorb everything… the magnificent architecture, the street signs, the people, discover hidden courtyards, peek into apartment windows, follow the aromas wafting through the air, decipher restaurant menus and hours of service… absolutely everything about Paris. Unfortunately, more often than not, I found myself looking down at the sidewalk to avoid a slippery, stinky mis-step.

Even though there's a law to remasser,✧✧ it's rarely enforced. Partially because Parisian dogs are typically unleashed and have learned to do "their business" in the gutter, between parked cars and far from the view of the owner. The other reason is a little more obscure, a little more French.

There's a municipal job to scoot around on a moped tricked-out with a vacuum and suck up any

---

✧ A taxi would've been first choice, but was next to impossible. First, the challenge was to locate a taxi stand with taxis available. Second, was to find a taxi driver who would agree to a large [by European standards], white-furred, wolf-like passenger.

✧✧ To pick-up dog poops. Some things just sound better in French offending matter. By the socialistic or, more commonly referred to as, noble-minded Parisian rationale, to pick up dog droppings is denying someone the right to work.

Needless to say, the 3 of us quickly learned and became adept at the "Paris Poop Side-Step," which is a Level 3 dance when coordinating five pairs of feet.

Aside from being off-leash and "gutter-trained," the other distinction from the majority of their American counterparts is that Parisian dogs are calm, taking everything in stride. Maybe it's the water, maybe it's the promise of fresh bread, paté, and Camembert at home, but you'll never find a Parisian dog running around, barking madly, or just in general behaving in an uncivilized manner.

In a heartbeat, Nikita embraced the Parisian nonchalance. Leaving her ugly American ways behind her, she no longer paid attention to pigeons, feigned indifference towards admirers, and sat poised, statuesque at bistros. Her integration was so fast, so seamless that within that very 1st week, she had a boyfriend!✧

As for poor, little Shamus, most people and dogs never bothered with him. He was just another drop in the Parisian Sea of Yorkshire Terriers. Every time a dog approached Niki he'd jump up and down between them trying to get some attention. Nikita would usually ignore the desperate attempts. But if he persisted, she'd shoo him away like a pesky fly.

The very few times a dog would befriend Shamus directly, he'd start hyperventilating. Without hesitation, I'd squat down, grab him by the head with one hand and block his nostrils with my free fingers, forcing him to breathe through his mouth until he calmed down and regained his breath.

A simple remedy, it worked like a charm every time, but looked a little peculiar and I'd have to do this while calmly explaining in French to anxious owners that nothing was wrong with Shamus… or at least nothing contagious. O-M-G.

✧ An adorable, little 9-month-old Golden Retriever named "Bon-ze." It was the sweetest thing to find him at our doorstep and ready to play after almost every walk. I hadn't seen Nikita so playful and happy since her playdates with Clea.

Oh Mon Dieu! I sincerely hoped that the God-line still worked from France. I'd even pay the International charges! I had a problem. A 10lbs when fed and wet p-r-o-b-l-e-m, problem— Exactly!
S-h-a-m-u-s, Shamus!

Once we arrived on French soil, he had transformed into a Woody Allen Impersonator! Look, I understand that all French are mega Woody-buffs, but this was no way to win attention or assimilate! Trust me on the street and in the form of a terrier widget, his skit was completely out of cinemagraphic context.

Every time a Parisian purse-sized dog approached the little fruit-loop and said a simple "bonjour," he'd have a full-blown panic-attack— Wide-eyed, gasping for air in-between choked words while looking left-and-right, up-and-down like a bobble head for his dictionary which he routinely now left at home because it made him look fat.

PL-ease, it was not the dictionary that was making him a paunchy pup. No-no-no. Sugar bloat was his "new condition" and *pl*-ease— Do NOT mention sugar! That particular cue would shift the sputtering of nonsensical French syllables to an equally unintelligible ad nauseam monologue on addiction and how he simply could not help himself— The sugary cravings overrode any cognitive abilities AND any day now he'd be diagnosed with early onset diabetes— The most aggressive type AND because Yorkies are already dispositioned to macular degeneration

A.K.A. progressive retinal atrophy— Of course, with the sugar induced cataracts, any day now he'd most certainly go blind which would mean a certain, albeit untimely, death while crossing the street because he couldn't see the scooter zoom-zoom-zooming from around the corner— AAAACK! Someone *pl*-ease deport this overbred, purebred back to the U-S-A!

Only ONE thing could halt his wheezing, delirious rant— My Mistress shoving her fingers up his nose like two human epi shots!

Oh, Ugly Buggers! Where did you learn that?! You do know that not everything you read about on the Internet is a Good Idea!

Ok, perhaps it did stop the hyperventilating four-legged embarrassment and the possibility of seizure, but is suffocation the only alternative? Come on— If he loses any more brain cells, for his next impersonation The Most Amazing Neurotic Terrier will demonstrate his impression of a Brussels Sprout!

Whenever, this happened I tried to keep my distance. Unfortunately, forever conjoined to My Mistress by a multicolored leash and stainless-steel prong collar, this was at best 4-foot max. But with an I-don't-belong-with-them attitude, I created the perception of a multiverse between us— Let's be honest. Not like I wanted to be associated with a "Saturday Night Live" visits Paris skit gone rogue. No, no thank you.

Somehow fused with this daily embarrassment A.K.A. annoying habit #1,042,453, 54— Oh Jeeps! Too, too, too many to count— Believe it or not, there was yet another personality hiccup with my brother-from-another-planet!

We are well aware that Shamus always had his insecurities, but more-or-less he managed to keep them under-wraps, hiding in the closet or under the bedcovers brooding them away. Maybe it was the water, maybe it was the French bread, the Camembert, and the charcuterie, but his ability to cope vanished into Parisian air— Exactly! What I had hoped was a singular incidence that first time I met Bones, became Jealous Habit #1.

A fellow canine would come over and naturally pay attention to me. Now if I did not like the dog, say that it was Flirt-the-Pervert or Otis the Drooling-Freight-Elevator-of-Montmartre, then of course Follow-the-Bouncing-Yorkie-Fluff-Ball was certainly welcomed. However, this appreciation did not extend universally!

Let's be honest, when it was the likes of Bones or Luc-Marcus, the Fire-Water Rescue Golden Retriever Hottie in all his Seine River Police uniformed glory, the last thing I wanted was you-should've-been-institutionalized family interference AND realistically, a terrier marionette will never be this season's "must-have"— even in the 16th arrondissement!

Back in New York, a few swift thwacks to the head would route his return to the gravitational pull of his Planet-Earth-Reality. In Paris? No such luck. Leaving me with no choice— I'd have to verbally puncture his jealousy balloon. Best case scenario, well-chosen terse words of discouragement would ground him permanently. Worst case, I'd convince him to resume his refreshingly silent, invisible bodyguard stint.

Hey, Hey! Bounce House Pooch, settle down and listen up!

I waited and waited and waited until he had all four paws simultaneously planted firmly on Parisian asphalt, his full un-bouncing attention.

Allow me to explain something to you.

"Yes, my Niki-love?"

Your inability to "parler français" and make friends is classified under "Not My Problem." Pas de Tout! Now, please stop popcorning like a guinea pig and hop back into the Hervé Chapelier tote where you belong!

"Okay, but Niki, I'm a Yorkshire Terrier not a guin—"

THWAP!

"Sorry-sorry-sorry. Anything for you, my Nikita. Anyway, I really don't mind so much. It's a super comfy ride. And, the views of you from those heights is simply breathtaking. Just like a Yann Arthus-Bertrand movie."

Oh, please. Make it stop.

"And, Nikita? My love, my life, my one-and-only, my beloved, I must tell you—"

No, no you don't. I really, seriously could not care any less. You may stop right there.

But, he continued.

"I'm not interested in learning French. Nope. Never have. Never will be. I only want to speak Siberian!"

And then, came the puppy kisses— Ugghhhh.

Diffusion of the issue. Sappy excuses. Showered with puppy slobber. Yep, despite my most ardent prayers and most sincere, heartfelt request, Pogo-Stick Puppy was here to stay. Sadly, making this newest aberration, his daily contribution to our Paris routine.

Our Paris routine was beginning to take shape. During the week, in the mornings I was either in French class or exploring Paris museum by museum. The afternoons were time spent exploring parks and the different arrondissements with the dogs. Depending on the place, day, mood, and weather would determine on which dog or if both would tag along.

On Sundays, Montmartre's closed to vehicular traffic. So, there's lots of people watching, street entertainment and typically some sort of art or antiques street market. After a stroll through the vendors, we'd take the metro down to Concord and pop out to walk along the riverboats. Following the Seine, we'd cross the river on the pedestrian bridge by the Louvre to Ile de la Cité to peruse the weekend animal and flower market. After visiting with the bunnies and birds and checking out new flowers for the window planter, we'd sit in front of Notre Dame before crossing the footbridge to Ile de St. Louis to watch the street performers.

No matter how long the line, we'd indulge in a frozen gastronomic indulgence, a Parisian tradition, ice-cream from Berthillon. At the take-away window, I would order 2 cones. Invariably, the server would snicker at the single American ordering more than she should consume. That sneer quickly turned to horror as I offered one of the pricey treats to my dogs.

At times like this, it surprised me the camaraderie between Niki and Shamus. Sharing a scoop of vanilla, the one flavor we could all agree on, they'd take turns licking at the single scoop. Once it disappeared into the cone, Niki would nibble at the cone and whatever fell to the pavement would be for Shamus. My very own version of "Lady and The Tramp."

Speaking of which as I was looking down at Shamus, he was seriously beginning to look like a little street mongrel. It'd been far too long since his last grooming in Manhattan. The question was where to go. A bad haircut for Shamus couldn't be covered with a hat or a sweater and boots.

In our neighborhood, slightly off the beaten path, I discovered this really cute little boutique, with an equally cute name: Aux Quat' Pats. Nikita and I always enjoyed looking in the windows at the puppies and I had noticed well-heeled owners with well-groomed dogs walking in-and-out. It was a little intimidating. Finally working up the nerve to open the door and venture inside, we found well-chosen toys, treats, premium kibble, and a few kittens, too.

Both ladies in the shop were surprisingly friendly and one even spoke a little bit of English with me. They were usually booked weeks in advance, but had just had a cancellation for the following day. Serendipity!

Unlike Nikita, Shamus was not a huge fan of being groomed and barely tolerated babies, human or canine. So, when we went inside the next day and he realized that it was not for more treats, but to leave him there for the next few hours, his whole body began to tremble.

The groomer, who only spoke French, asked me how I wanted Shamus groomed. I replied in French, "He usually gets a puppy-cut."

Her smile turned to concern as she asked again.

With a big, reassuring full-toothed American smile, I replied again in French, "A puppy-cut, just like a puppy."

Something was wrong.

Her brow furrowed, her lips pursed in that disapproving Parisian way. Even worse, already not happy about our return to the puppy filled store, with his delicate constitution sensing the increasing tension, Shamus was almost in convulsions.

In an attempt to make myself understood, I motioned to the puppies in store speaking louder in over-enunciated French, "Like a puppy. Like the puppies over there, like the puppies over there."

Now, there was fire in her eyes, smoke coming out of her ears. The groomer was seriously angry. Struggling to keep her dignified, Parisian manner, through tightly pursed lips came out, "How?"

Completely lost as to what her problem was, I replied again in French, "Like a baby dog, Madame. A baby dog."

Her facial muscles relaxed just enough to say, "Fine. Come back in a couple of hours."

With a "merci," I handed her Shamus' leash. And, she dragged him away into the back room as he scrambled wildly on the tile floor in a futile attempt to escape.

How bizarre.

As Nikita and I continued our morning walk around the neighborhood, I replayed the scenario in my head trying to figure out what went wrong.

Wrong, wrong, wrong. So very, very wrong. When was either one of them going to learn the beautiful cadence, the precise pronunciation, the official language of the country we now called "home?"

My Mistress, she consistently butchered the romance language with her American tongue. Much to my horror, she had just asked the groomer to give Shamus a crappy haircut— Requesting that he look just as crappy as ALL the other dogs in the boutique! AND, as if that wasn't enough, she continued her lingual butchery by comparing the entire store, puppies and all, to a communal toilet in India!

AAACKKKK!

For once in his life, Shamus had good reason to be panicking wildly at the idea of a grooming, flopping all over the cold stone floor like a hippy-haired fish out-of-water. With so many problems already, the very last thing that Shamus needed was a bad haircut.

After her latest faux-pas, My Mistress roamed aimlessly around the neighborhood muttering to herself. Finally popping onto our favorite boulangerie on the back of the hill, she picked up a ham and cheese baguette sandwich and a cookie which we shared on the steps at Sacre Coeur.

Distancing myself from her to prevent any possible interference, I hoped that the God-line was working. Placing a mini-prayer that the pipsqueak would not be hacked to unrecognizably ugly by that angry groomer— Wait a second!

Rewind please for a prayer refinement.

How about the groomer works a little "Ooh-la-la" magic and Voila! Frenchify Fido's style! Oh yes! That single possibility would be the answer to several of my outstanding A.K.A. lost-in-the-queue prayers— Exactly! With a French haircut and French food and French water, Easy-to-Bamboozle-Terrier would think he was French, start speaking French and assimilate A.K.A. Leave-Me-Alone!

Hallelujah! Praise to the Powers that BE!

And God, by the way while we're still connected, I'd like to request a little something for my sweet, adorable self— a nice shampoo and brush out, with a paw and nail trim. Please. Pretty please? Please God, can you hear me? Give me a sign that you still care.

On one of the highest points in Paris, I assumed that the connection would be excellent and it was— Unfortunately, I miscalculated the effects of the higher elevation AND the amplifying power of a church that conducts "Silent Nights of Adoration." Yep, that's right. I suffered a Gizmodic Episode A.K.A. I prayed for the wrong thing in a BIG way— Precisely! The response swift, but horrifically skewed!

Instead of a chic salon in the 15th arrondissement, I was marched straight back home! But wait— that's only the beginning!

Asking me to "sit-stay," I had a most undesirable front-row seat to Terrorism Theater as she slowly, meticulously took off all her clothes and jewelry while bopping through the apartment in varying states of naked to a French pop station. In a mind-numbing blur of un-erasable images, I watched her putting stuff away, taking beach towels out. A tragic interlude on this otherwise beautiful early winter afternoon in Paris.

Finally acknowledging my captive, but not captivated presence— wearing nothing more than a smile, Mistress

Naked-Is-Not-A-Good-Look-For-Everyone dragged me into the bathroom.

WAIT! I'm still NOT finished! It gets EVEN WORSE— Mais oui, it's possible!

Shoving me into the only big enough for 1 European-sized-person shower, she squeezed her way in to join me— AAACKKKK!

Don't laugh! Trust me, NOT amusing, NOT entertaining, in the very least! This is exactly the type of blunt emotional trauma that fractures personalities and creates the need for hospitalized psychotherapy and mind-numbing intravenous medications!

Look, I could handle the change of country and language. It was culture relief, not culture shock— And, I was willing to accept the much smaller living quarters as an exchange for my European-living experience and the refined, French cuisine— However, being bathed in a 2 x 2 plexi-glass cubicle by Her Holy Nakedness went beyond my threshold of tolerance.

Even with NO possibility of escape once the glass doors clicked shut, she insisted to straddle me securing my already captive body between her Thunder Thighs!

Please, please God make this nightmare end or just put the IV needle in my vein already!

Reverting back to The Hummer days I closed my eyes, trying to manifest a different realty. An alternate world where the shower was in-far-fetched-fact a well-disguised travel pod.

Yes! Ok, whenever you're ready. Beam Me Up to the Swiss-German Alps! Danke schoen.

Too, too far away from the cathedral steps for a 911 intervention from Heaven, instead of being transported to a well-manicured, a pampered jet-set life with Basel, the cold water running down my back brought me straight back to my current reality— Baaahhhhhh.

I had hoped that living in Paris, the mecca of culture and social refinement would have some influence on My Mistress. But so far, her total immersion to include new clothes, new shoes, and a stylish Parisian cut-and-color, had little impact—Exactly! No friends. No life. No clue as to how unhappy I was!

Long gone were the good, old times in New York City. The spa days becoming a distant, quickly fading memory. Now reduced to a homespun beauty regime, my spirits suffered greatly from this depressing, humbling downturn from my once glamorous, well-maintained life.

Of course, I did not require a makeover like either one of my unfortunate companions A.K.A. the gruesome twosome. My natural beauty shined through regardless of my Cinderella circumstances. However, a professional shampoo, blow-out, and brushing would do wonders to lift my spirits.

Sighhhh. My one and only consolation was that she remembered to import my favorite shampoo♦ At least, I smelled good, my hair silky smooth.

Towel-dried and brushed, I curled up on my cedar-filled bed. Nose tucked under my tail, I prayed for the right things.

*

Ding! Da-Ding! Ding!

No. Not Tibetan bells.

No. Not a call to prayer.

Certainly NOT a surprise visit from one of her non-existent friends!

Those were chimes blinging away wildly in the kitchen. The multi-pitched tings interspersed with Shamus's freshly trimmed

♦ Finesse, shampoo with conditioner, original scent. Just in case, you have room in your check-in luggage.

nails scuttling on the floor. Of no great surprise, My Mistress encouraging the ruckus.

Reluctantly, I left my hidden-from-their-reality corner nook to witness the current shenanigans.

I walked in just in time to see Shamus on his hind-legs like a circus bear, ringing a set of chimes with his nose. All that was missing was a fuchsia tutu and a little accordion music.

Shrieking with delight, hands clapping enthusiastically, Mistress Ringmaster cheered, "What a good boy!" and tossed him a treat.

Looking up to see me in the doorway, she invited, "Niki?"

No. Absolutely n-o-t, NOT! I am a Siberian HUSKY, not some circus tutu'd Siberian BEAR! Most certainly not some errant Pavlovian experiment— And, unlike bowling-ball-belly boy, I wish to keep my sleek, elegant figure. You may keep your chimes, your treats, and your sideshow theatrics to your indulgent self. BUT before I walk away, *pl*-ease explain WHY are you teaching him bell ringing when the BOTH of you should be reviewing French pronunciation rules and exceptions. Must I be responsible for absolutely everything?!

Hanging my head down low full of ennui, I returned to the living room and my cushion. At this rate with their antics I'd be in meditative prayer for the rest of my life. Change my name already to Sister Nikita Azure!

There must have been quite a disturbance on the God-line, because a Nietzsche-turned-Buddhist-widget emigrated to France and was living in our home! Oh yeah, chimes now cast aside, belly bulging with liver treats, the soggy-noodle, yoga-brained terrier was back to his philosophy AND completely oblivious to the fact that one single yoga video and a swollen Buddha-belly does not make you a reincarnated prophet— Exactly! My God-line meditation-connection was interrupted by

this Facebook philosophy nugget meme: "Change is inevitable. Suffering is optional."

TWACK!

"Niki that hurts."

Well, you chose to share with me your idiosyncratic rhetoric A.K.A. You chose to suffer.

"You know Niki, the Marquis de Sade was French."

Listen up here 50 Shades of Yorkie, the marquis inflicted pain— not received it.

And that pseudo-factual nugget gained me precious moments of silence as Marquis de Rien pondered his fate.

Not fate, but a dream come true to be an American living in Paris. So lucky to be living here... Or, that's what I reminded myself every morning, day, and night. So far, Parisian life was not the fairytale that I expected.

The city itself was amazing. Parks everywhere, daily markets, museums for every interest and curiosity, food to tempt the most finicky palette, and boutiques to suit every budget, every whim. And, with each arrondissement offering up its own distinct neighborhood vibe, simply crossing the street from one into the other could take you into a completely different cultural experience. Enter one passageway in the 5th arrondissement, and you'll discover it opens up to children playing soccer on the grassy ruins of a Roman amphitheater. Enter yet another in the 9th, and you'll be transported to an Egyptian souk!

I was busy busy busy, distracted all day long. But, at night I felt painfully alone. It seemed impossible to connect with people. Make acquaintances, yes. Make friends, no.

The French make friends through introduction. And, the only souls I knew in Paris were attached to me by a leash. People would stop and talk to Nikita and Shamus, perhaps ask me a question, and then continue on their way.

As far as it being the "city of romance," it was incredibly romantic. At night, the city lights cast a golden hue illuminating the centuries old buildings. The Seine sparkles as if kissed by fireflies. But, I only had my canine companions to stroll the quai with me. On those walks, the few men who approached us and struck up conversations were either players hoping to score a blonde, American tourist or interested in a French visa for Green Card exchange.

About 3 weeks into classes at the Alliance Française, I finally met a fellow American. A tall, Texan beauty with pitch-black hair and piercing blue eyes, she was the type of woman whose presence makes both men and women take a second look.

She had moved to Paris to be with "the love of her life." As it turns out, he happened to still be married... Or, as she explained, "separated," but still living at home with his wife and 2 children. Consumed with her relationship drama, she had little energy left for other pursuits including friendships. Still, we managed an occasional afternoon movie or coffee after class.

One day, in a completely out of character burst of friendly chit-chat, the owner of the laundromat downstairs introduced me to an American who I had mistaken as a Parisian. A Harvard student working on her doctorates in French literature, she lived just down the street.

We hung out as often as her schedule and grad student budget allowed. Helping me negotiate French culture and insisting to speak only in French, her friendship and guidance helped me survive my transition into Paris-life.

Even with the two new friends, I was still a little blue. My comfort zone, my family, my friends, everything I knew, was far, far away. Most nights, I would lean against the radiator in the kitchen and sink to the floor in tears. As holidays approached, I began to seriously question whether or not to stay. That's when my "roommates" coaxed me out of my funk.

Never before the cuddly puppy, as the temperature outside dropped, Nikita began to warm my side of the bed every night. When I was ready to get into bed, Niki would skootch over. With her pressing against my back, the warmth was like a half-body heating pad.

Then, lifting the covers high, I'd call out, "Snuggalert!" Hearing this, Shamus would leave whatever he was up to and jump up into bed slamming his little body against mine where he'd stay until I fell asleep.

It was Heaven.

No, not Heaven. This was Living Hell.

As if leash walking, cubicle-showering, and lingual surgery were not enough— she now stole my space every single freaking night, forcing me to sleep on the WRONG side of the bed! Even worse, she wanted to "spoon" with me!

Pardonnez-moi, but you are aware that we relocated to Paris, "The City of Lights," most certainly not ever, ever, ever referred to as the "City of Canine Love!" S'il vous plaît, go find yourself a boy-friend, a man-friend, a species-appropriate-friend! Stop using me as a surrogate!

As for the boo-boo boy he was more than happy to snuggle up under the covers— BUT to what effect?! Already receiving human-finger-nose-plugs at least once-a day, he certainly didn't need to lose any more brain cells from an oxygen deprivation chamber A.K.A. under-blanket-all-night snuggling.

Look, I am aware that there are twists and turns in every story— but I am 110% ready for My Fairytale Ending! Living with an addled-brained terrier and a woman who cries herself to sleep every freaking night is enough of a story arc for me! Just call Basel already or buy me a one-way ticket to the Swiss Alps— We can end this farce right now!

It would go something like this: After yet another perfect day spent with Basel, she curled up next to him on the Italian leather sofa. The fire crackling, the fondue bubbling, a Keith Jarret album playing in the background, they enjoyed a quiet evening in their mountain-side chalet. And yes, they lived happily ever— ZzZZZggGGwWWzzzAAARPPHHHZzzzzzz!

Seriously?! A discordant sonata resonating from the under-blanket cuddle bug disturbed my sweet, sweet reverie.

I looked over my shoulder at my gruesome twosome snuggled up like two peas in a cashmere blanket pod. If only the pod worked, they'd be teleported back to their home planet or to the U-S-A! It really made ZERO difference considering current politics! Ha-ha!

Ok-ok. I know that they weren't going anywhere and neither was I without them— Truth be told? What would they do without me?! She needed emotional support. He needed protection from himself. I was the only one who could, who would do it!

Look, sometimes I was a little blue, too. I missed The Farm— The freedom, the wide-open spaces, and my friends. And of course, I missed New York— The energy, that constant buzz of excitement, the shopping, the spa days, the take-away from Mexican Radio and Veselka.

But wakey-wakey and smell the French Press! This is Paris, baby cakes— The Cultural, The Fashion, The Culinary Meccas of The Civilized World! And, it also happens to be the perfect launching point to explore the rest of Europe— Including, Switzerland! By the way, have I mentioned in the past 5 minutes that Basel is only a short train ride away A.K.A. 3-hour-snooze away A.K.A. enough time for you to work some Chantecaille-magic-on-your-face away! Hint-HINT! Allons-y!

Of course, there was one other consideration to staying put in Paris. The colder temperatures meant one thing— Exactly! My most favorite time of year! Christmas time!

I was super looking forward to finding out how the French celebrate, what Grandma C would send, and whether Santa or Pere Noel or BOTH would bring presents! Just in case, I was leaving absolutely nothing to chance— Precisely! I'm making TWO lists this year! One in English and the other en français!

Now, for my real dilemma of the evening— How does one say "spa day" in French?

*

Bonjour! Bonjour! HeLLoooo! Pardons-moi! What in blazes are you doing? Not only are you awake and out of bed THREE whole hours earlier than usual, you're making a HUGE racket sorting through your helter-skelter "filing system." Did you forget, yet again, where you hid the chocolate from yourself?!

Ignoring me, Mistress My-OCD-Does-Not-Apply-to-Paperwork continued rummaging through her growing disaster area, gathering up OUR travel documents!

No-No-NO! No Way! No How! I flat-out refuse to go anywhere before the holidays! I've already sent out my letters with the rue des Trois-Frères address! *PL*-ease, do not dare to interfere with my Christmas cheer!

Still ignoring me, Mistress Gypsy Spirit harnessed up the happy-to travel-in-a-Tumi-tote-bag terrier and my unwilling self, marching us straight out the door and down the street at a breakneck pace. Jaywalking across the boulevard, she bulldozed us through a neighborhood we had yet to explore.

Bonjour-bonjour-bonjour! Pardons-moi encore une fois! Do you think that you could you *s l o o o w* it down a little Mistress Three-Espressos-Before-9? There are "practical needs" to attend to after being locked up all night long— And, it would be civil behavior, the correct thing to do A.K.A. The Parisian Way to stop and smell the roses, the fire hydrants, the light poles, the open boulangerie doors, and to greet and exchange pleasantries with our fellow citoyens.

Zoom-Zoom-Zoom! From one arrondissement into the next, until— BAP!

We stopped at a door. Mostly, because it was locked to prevent her from entering.

Finally, somewhere long enough to get a whiff.

Ugghhhh. The stench of sick dogs and cat vomit was unmistakable!

This was NO store. This was NO canine spa. This was a Veterinarian's Office!

Hello. Hello? HeLLooooo! That door is locked for a reason. We do NOT need to go in. This was the BIG hurry? Seriously?! My morning dreamscape disrupted, my morning constitution rushed for an unnecessary, unwelcomed, unwarranted poke-and-probe appointment?! *PL*-ease.

Ring-Ring-RRRing!

The buzzer sounded, the latch freed, and Mistress Button-Pusher-Extraordinaire dragged us in.

Ugghhhh— Really? This is ridiculous! This is a perfectly good waste of a beautiful morning. I do not need to see any doctor. There's nothing wrong with me! And, please scratch off your list any memo on French pharmaceuticals. I am 100% certain that the French do not believe in, do not need to sedate their travel companions— Pas de tout! And, all my vaccinations are up-to date— Precisely! I am in perfect health! Now, as for the cockeyed-lopsided-3-legged-stool-of-health terrier, the chances are extremely high that he'll require more specialized attention than this office— Ohhhh. Oh my!

Is that a French Veterinarian?

Ahemmm— Mmmmmmm.

Suddenly, it was hot, really hot, inside the small examination room. But, there were chills— Yes, tingly sensations running up-and-down my body. My breath rapid and shallow, difficult to catch, making me a little light-headed. I struggled to keep my composure.

Ohhh, oh my! I feel a little feverous. In the mad rush to make our appointment, I was mouth-breathing. You know, it is flu-season and airborne viruses are very contagious. Perhaps, I caught "la grippe." Since we're already here, why not let this good doctor check my temperature and lymph nodes. Yes, definitely— Wait! Maybe, it's my throat. Yeah, yeah, it's feeling dry and scratchy. Very, very dry and scratchy my throat is— AND, my heart seems to be beating slightly irregularly, maybe even a little faster than usual.

Actually, now that I'm thinking about it after our Trans-Atlantic move, just to on the safe side, I would agree to a full-physical examination. Please, allow me to hop up on the examination table, first. As Alpha Dog, it's my responsibility to set a good example for the omega terrier widget.

The veterinarian smiled at me and the compliments flowed as he began my check-up.

Oh, yes. This is one of those rare moments that I'm happy to be her dog.

This is one of those rare moments that I wish I was my dog.

The veterinarian came highly recommended. Best veterinary school, a clean and modern office, excellent with the animals, and charged reasonable fees, he was exactly what you look for in a veterinarian. However, no one mentioned how handsome, how charming, how sent from heaven perfect he was. Tall, perfectly proportioned body with the muscle tone of someone athletically inclined, thick and shiny dark-chestnut hair with a little wave just short of a curl, clear blue eyes, sun-kissed skin, and a huge friendly smile... Oh my, I was taken completely off-guard.

By the time his deep-baritone voice spoke in beautifully articulated French with the occasional English word throw in, I had completely tranced out. Thankfully, he already knew that we were there on a "well-visit" to pick up the dogs' French passports,[✧] allowing me to day-dream as he fussed over Niki and Shamus.

By the second time he asked, I realized he was now talking to me. A little embarrassed to be caught in the middle of an "inappropriate thought," I mutely smiled through the blush and handed him the dogs' American vaccination records.

As he filled out the EU document booklets, he chattered away about how both dogs were healthy,

---

[✧] A booklet for companion animals with their photo, physical description, complete medical history, vaccinations records, and chip/tattoo location. It's recommended for easy traveling within the EU and requested at boarding facilities.

well-groomed, and well-behaved, "A pleasure for him to spend time with us this morning."

That was definitely a pleasure shared. Throughout the appointment, Niki was voguing and Shamus was super cool instead of his usual vet-visit jittery self. Both dogs even allowed the doctor to insert an identification chip beneath the skin on the neck without a fuss.

As we walked out and back up the hill to Montmartre, I was searching for any excuse to make another appointment.

Grabbing a coffee at the St. Jean, my thoughts of an impromptu veterinarian visit were put on hold as I watched Shamus scrounge the un-swept floor. It'd be pointless to interrupt. No one could dissuade him from his mission. Nothing could break his 110% focus.

A few weeks after arriving in Paris, one of the regulars at the bistro was mindlessly unwrapping a cube when he saw he'd captured Shamus's attention.

After a mind-numbing soliloquy about how sugar is horrible for dogs, causing them to go blind and die early, the man flashed a toothless smile and dropped half a cube to the floor. Shamus snatched it up with alligator jaws.

After that first crunch, he was never the same.

Now every time we went for coffee, Shamus needed to establish that all the wrappers on the ground were empty. Only after that, he'd relax either perched on my lap or on an empty chair where he'd snooze until he heard the promising sound of a sugar cube being unwrapped.

Today, there was no treasure to be found. Feeling sorry for my little boo, we headed home via Shamus's favorite route. A hidden passageway I liked to call, "Allée des chats."

The entrance was through an arch which opened into a flag-stone paved courtyard. It was "the hangout" for all the neighborhood cats and secret parking for those in the know.

At the far end of the square, next to the staircase, just inside a gated interior garden courtyard, la custodienne left treats and bowls of fresh water for her feline friends.

Shamus would walk past the deli cat without a sideways glance, sit calmly at the bistro as dogs passed by, but mention "Allée des chats" and like a compass he'd pull in that direction.

In the square, he'd search under every car, scooter, or whatever was suspicious. If he found a cat, he'd stare it down intensively, fearsomely.

As soon as the cat twitched a whisker, he'd lunge forward giving chase as far as his 6-foot leash would allow.

Masters of The Art of The Tease, once the felines became acquainted with Shamus and his restriction, they would stop and sit just beyond his reach.

Niki never showed interest, but just to be on the safe side I kept a firm grip on her lead while I let Shamus have some harmless fun.

All it took to get Shamus to threat level RED was a simple Manchurian Candidate cue, "Le chat. Où est le chat?"

Cat? Seriously?! Out of ALL French words in the dictionary the first one he chose to learn is c-a-t, cat? As proud as I might be of this minor lingual accomplishment, his rudimentary hunting skills never made the flight across the pond. Pouncing on pieces of paper and empty plastic bags, Short-Sighted Shamus missed ALL the cats perched on car hoods and roofs watching his lack-of-prowess A.K.A. comedic-hunt-for-nothing!

If only she would let me off-leash, I would happily remind him, show him the way it's done. But no, oh no. Mistress The-Only-Thing-I-Have-A-Tight-Grip-On-Is-This-Lead reigned me in protecting the feral felines!

PL-ease, like I would want Eau-de-Sewer fur between my teeth!

Today, as we left the alley Otis the Drooling-Elevator-of-Montmartre was waiting at the top of the stairs.

Drip-pant—*drool*—pant-drip.

Ugghhhhh. Please, go away. Vas-y!

So out of breath from walking down the street all he could manage was, "Bahhh oui."

Get your bull-dog tonnage out of the way!

"Bahhh oui."

What on Parisian cobblestone streets made him think that he had a moment's chance?

Drool-pant-drip— "Bahhh oui."

Drool a little more, pant a little more— "Bahhh oui."

Drool like old, faulty plumbing, pant like a late-season hurricane— "Bahhh oui."

Incapable of taking a breath deep enough to form a coherent sentence, thankfully he was able to move his flabby mass enough to the side so that we could negotiate our way around him without getting slobbered.

Not finished with our morning walk, My Mistress marched us past the over-sized, over-salivating neighbor, diagonally across the street, and up the next staircase.

Otis followed us, f a a a r r r r behind us, leaving a trail of drool in his waddling wake. The outta shape monstrosity in his futile pursuit, pant-drool step by pant-drool step.

Seriously?! Full moon rising or not THIS —*whatever you're thinking*— will never happen. Mais que jamais! You and your cheap red wine slobber and stale cigarette breath has less than zero chance with Moi!

Now standing at the foot of the stairs, the lovesick drooler was gazing longingly up at— AACKKK!

Reflexively, I tucked my tail— But NOT before his intrusive eyes got a full view of my coochie!

Inspired by the stolen view, Peeping Pervert Otis started the climb one drool-pant-drip at a time. By the time we reached the top he was still only 5 drools from the bottom

Bye-bye, soggy-froggy! Á jamais, s'il te plaît.

"S'il vous plaît, madame. 'ave you seen my dogue?"

The vintage clothing store owner who had never acknowledged my presence much less spoken to me, approached while keeping his distance and his arms folded across his chest.

"Oui. But, it was about 30 minutes ago. He was following us up the stairs to Rue Berthe."

"No, no. Dis ist not my dogue. 'E does't do stairs."

I wanted to say, by the looks of him he doesn't do much, period. But, I wasn't sure that the humor would translate or the truth appreciated. So instead, I looked up 4 flights to the top of the staircase where a drooling, panting, bull-dog's pudgy little face was peering down. Then shrugging my shoulders Parisian-style, I made my best "je ne sais pas de quoi"✧ smirk, and continued home.

Before going in our building, I popped into the grocer to pick up some water. Niki heeled perfectly at my side, but Shamus was sniffing around. I snapped his lead and told him to sit-stay.

The grocer asked, what did you call your dog?

Raising one eyebrow, I responded, "Shamus?"

"Oh, the way you said his name it sounded like the word for sunshine in Arabic. That's a funny name for a dog."

✧ Loosely translated as, "Whatever!" Some things definitely sound more elegant in French.

"Perhaps. But, his name is Shamus." I replied motioning towards the little one on my right.

"Shay-moooose."

"Sham-us. It's an Old Irish name, Gallic, for James."

"James. Oh, you mean like Jim. Jimmy. Jimmy Carter."

Chuckling to himself, he bent down towards Shamus. "Bonjour. A pleasure to make your acquaintance, Monsieur Le President."

"President. Mr. President! Niki did you hear that? How fantastic! And, that would make you The First—"

One sideways glance stopped that subversive thought before it passed his puppy lips.

"Huh. I wonder which party I identify with best. I'm old-school Republican at heart, but that really doesn't exist anymore. In fact, I might just be the last living Lincoln Republican! So, maybe a New School Republican, like a Libertarian? I believe in minimal government and I eat meat, so there's no way that I can be a Democrat. And then, it's true that I like the outdoors, appreciate wide-open spaces, and prefer

more natural, untamed and ungroomed habitats, so maybe a grass-roots party affiliation? What do you think?"

I think that NO ONE elected you president, nor do you play one on TV.

"Oh TV, maybe I could be the 'Unexpected Survivor!'"

Sighhhh. Yes, very unexpected indeed that you live through this conversation. Listen up Bumbling Bureaucratic Buttercup, if you don't practice your 5th Amendment rights immediately, the only ticket you'll find your name on, is a one-way ticket to Death Valley.

"Wow! That sounds like a real adventure! Thanks, Nikita! You're always so thoughtful and full of surprises. I've never been to a valley before. Niki, when do we go? I need to pack. Good thing we have our French travel passports ready. It'll make border crossings so much easier. Is it anything like the Valley of the Kings? I've always wanted to go Egypt and eat pigeon pie, but caftans make me look fat and the sand gets super-hot and my belly dancing looks more like Flamenco— "

Sometimes, you've just got to walk away— which I happily did UNTIL she pulled me back into her gravitational pull with that multi-color braided umbilical cord.

Ughhh. Can we go home already? Too much drama for one day. My head aches from the both of you and your shenanigans.

*

Negotiations. This has never been one of my vocabulary words. Not because I am in any way dis-agreeable or egoistic or stubborn, but because there is no finesse to the word. None at all. It doesn't roll off the tongue as easily as a "No." And, in my current reality, the multisyllabic lingual abomination implies compromise at my expense and that. my dear friends, is nothing more than a mistress-administered-narcotics-induced concept!

Let's be completely honest— Time and time again, the evidence has proven that My Way is The Best Way! There is absolutely nothing, nada, rien, for me to negotiate!

When we moved to Paris, I was agreeable to the smaller, one-bedroom apartment, learning how to deal with more together-time and how to cope with no more spa days— However, I drew the line at the sharing of the kibble bowl.

At first, I thought that she neglected to pack the second bowl or that it somehow got lost in the move. Then, I was certain that on one of her numerous trips to BHV or Galleries Lafayette or Hermes that she would return with a new one for me— But, no such luck!

Too easily distracted by "en solde" and "nouveauté" signs, she'd walk out with another pair of black pumps or a cashmere sweater in this season's heather blue-green or yet another rose lip balm for the collection at the bottom of her purse— forgetting about my porcelain, or crystal, kibble dish every single time! At this point, even an English stoneware saucer or a stainless-steel bowl with a rubberized bottom would be acceptable.

Look, there were caloric considerations to sharing an ice cream with the little boo boy. And, he was more than welcomed to crunch away on the sugar cone carbs as they fell to the ground— However, there's ZERO nutritional benefit to Shamus slobber on my kibble.

True, every night she prepared fresh meals and served us separately— But still, Mistress Short-Term-Memory-Shopper was completely touched in the head if she thought that I wanted terrier saliva drizzled on my in-between meals kibble.

Today, I was a little hungry after the morning walk and was eating when the Gizmo impersonating terrier stuck his head underneath mine and into the bowl snatching kibble!

No!

"But, Niki?"

No means, NO!

Just before I handled NO-gotiations My Way, Mistress Unwelcomed Interference walked into the kitchen to refresh her coffee cup and empty the ashtray. "Niki? Shamus?"

For the first time ever, assessing the current situation correctly Mistress Momentary-Stroke-Of-Genius placed a little bit of kibble on the floor for Shamus. Clean-Freak Terrier was excited to help tidy-up, I had the bowl to myself.

Hallelujah! Now, for a real miracle— a water bowl filled to the brim with Evian! I'd better place an updated request on the God-line, ASAP!

Finished with my morning snack, I walked into the bedroom to find Shamus already snoozing with his nose in a book.

Hey, wakey-wakey. You know she's going to Freak-The-Blank-Out if she finds you drooling on her books again. Remember the last time?!

"Nikita. Please leave me alone, I'm studying."

No. You were sleeping.

"No. I was absorbing knowledge through osmosis."

Shamus, it doesn't quite work that way.

"Yes, it does. I saw it in a movie."

Sha-musss?

"Look, Niki. This is my one and only chance to educate myself. I'm trying to better myself to impress you!"

Really? Awww. That's kinda sweet, Shamus. Taking the initiative to better your sorry little plight. Out of idle curiosity then, what are you reading today?

"A classic tale of struggle and resolution."

Which classic? *The Iliad and The Odyssey*? *Pride and Prejudice*? *Atlas Shrugged*??

"*The Pokey Little Puppy*."

Somehow, I managed to get myself to my cushion and wrap my tail around my face before breaking out in sobs of uncontrollable laughter. Tears and laughter— Laugh so hard, you cry. Cry so hard, you laugh. There's little difference in this madhouse.

*

"Niki-Niki-Niki-Niki!"

Yes, Shamus.

"Niki, she's making plans to go on a trip and I don't think that she's taking us!"

Well, that's not necessarily a bad thing Shamus.

"No, Niki. You don't understand. In Paris, it is a well-known fact that people leave their dogs behind when they go on vacation."

Again, I do not see the problem.

"Niki! There's a huge ad campaign about it in the metro stations. Haven't you seen the photos of the starved, the emaciated dogs who were left out on the street to fend for themselves while their owners took a 4-week holiday?! That could very well be us!"

I glanced over at Catastrophizing Terrier who was barely tolerable on most days, but on a cold and rainy, stuck inside the apartment day like today— It was a migraine in the making. Wisely, he had placed his annoying little self just out of swiping reach.

Right before I got up to permanently end his latest rant, I had an epiphany— Exactly! He was working himself up into a

Colossal Fit! His breathing shallow. His heart rate rapid. If he collapsed, she'd have to take us BOTH to the veterinarian! Him, for the obvious medical reasons. Me, for the emotional support. Brilliant!

You know—

Letting my voice trail off, looking away from him as if contemplating whether or not to share.

"What, Niki? WHAT?!"

Well, now that you've mentioned it, perhaps you have a reason for concern. There is an arrondissement here in Paris which is only Chinese— Chinese stores, Chinese grocers, Chinese movie theaters— and the restaurants? Well, they serve all the specialties from back home— ALL made with local ingredients, including the local "wildlife."

"No! That's not true!"

Ah yes, it's very, very true my sweet-tasting, little friend. But what's more concerning, is that once shaved, seared, and baked it's almost impossible to tell the difference between the head of a baby baa-baa sheep and a Yorkshire Terrier. Even the little, white teeth look the same—

"No, Niki! No! Stop! She wouldn't do that! I'm her boo-boo-boy! I'm her snuggle-bug! I'm her petit ti-ti. I'm her—"

Hyperventilating and in Full-Freak-Out Mode, Shamus was quite the sight. Mistress Finally-with-Perfect-Timing came into the room to give us our after-dinner treats.

Squinting her blind-to-reality eyes at the almost-in-convulsions terrier, she asked him to sit. His belly swollen from his latest anxiety attack, he rolled on the floor like a bowling ball.

BRRRING! BRRRRING! Docteur Pays-Basque? We have a canine emergency, a life-or-death situation. We need to see you immediately!

Perrrrfect.

Perfect. 5 minutes before I need to be out the door and Shamus is having some sort of medical crisis. The day was without incident. Healthy appetite, lots of playtime, long walks, everything was fine. But now, his tummy was so bloated that when he sat for his treat, he rolled over like a beached whale.

At this hour, we'd have to see the emergency vet and I'd have to cancel the evening with my new friend. Of course, if we waited until tomorrow, we'd see our veterinarian and I could go out as planned.

Rolling the dice with Shamus's well-being, I decided to wait until the morning. It was a fairly safe bet. He was a sensitive little thing and had been watching me pack.

The next day, I was taking off to London for a Sci-fi literature convention hosted by one of my favorite British far-fetched fiction authors. My gruesome twosome were heading off to the northern suburbs of Paris thanks to Association Millepats.✧

Mine was a hard request. Not only because it was last minute, but it also required a home with no dogs, no cats, and no other miscellaneous pets like bunnies, ferrets or rats. After a few passes through the database, the coordinator found a home in the suburbs of Paris.

In the morning, Shamus was back to "normal," so we hopped on the RER to St Denis. The neighborhood was a little rougher than I expected, but it was too early in the day for any hoodlums to be out and about. Still to be on the safe side as we navigated through litter strewn streets past graffiti covered storefronts, I put on my "New York face" and kept Niki close like a ferocious wolf-dog prone to attack.

Arriving at the building, a woman answered the door with a huge, welcoming smile and gestured us inside. Contrary to the neglected environment, her home was well-maintained and nicely appointed.

✧ For a nominal, yearly membership fee, Millepats finds loving homes for pets while the owners are away. The rates are fixed and caretakers are thoroughly screened by the association making it easy and safe.

Niki and Shamus disappeared checking out their new digs as the woman and I sat down to sip an orange juice and discuss the care for the next few days.

Our conversation was interrupted by a large, furry, black blurrrr flying through the living room with both dogs in hot pursuit. Strange. I understood that this was a pet-free zone.

Leaping from the couch to the kitchen table, the cat found momentary refuge. The dogs, on full reconnaissance, were circling the table looking for a chair askew enough to use as a way up. Sensing this was not the safest place and that time was of the essence, the cat decided to bolt again. From the table to the counter-top, one final leap to the refrigerator.

A miscalculated leap.

Hanging by its claws at the top of the door, its hind legs were scrambling wildly on the stainless steel surface. Finding nothing to propel it in any direction, the cat was slipping off towards Niki and Shamus eagerly chomping below.

Not a moment too soon, the woman swooped in grabbed the cat and threw it in a spare room slamming the door shut. Nikita and Shamus quickly posted themselves outside, taking turns placing an inquisitive nose underneath the door. Switching places, after getting swiped by angry claws.

The woman insisted, "This is not a problem. Not at all. It'll be just fine. I've hosted many dogs in my home. Eventually, they forget about Tabi-ta."

Before she changed her mind, before she knew better, I left.

Left in a questionable neighborhood with a strange people and an unsocial feline was most certainly not my idea of a weekend get-away. I would've much preferred a little Basel-time A.K.A. a one-way ticket to Switzerland— However, as soon as Mistress Romantic-Vacation-For-One abandoned us, the woman opened the refrigerator to display all sorts of French and Tunisian delicacies— Mmmmmmm!

Our first dinner was freshly-caught, lake fish steamed with chickpeas, raisins, and lemon wedges in coriander leaves, served on a bed of basmati garnished with a toasted melody of garlic shavings, rosemary, and pignolias, and finished with an olive oil drizzle. Wisely, she kept the American-sized salad for herself and her son— Have I mentioned yet that I ♥ French-North African Cuisine and Hospitality?! Good thing that we

were only staying the weekend otherwise I'd be in the market for a happy-happy-hippo sized collar!

After dinner, her son paraded me into the center of town, displaying me like some trophy. It was OK, but a little awkward. Let's be honest— We were only using each other. He was using me to raise his social standing with people who didn't like him to begin with— I was only interested in working off the tagine-cuisine calories consumed.

Sure, for a few days it was convenient— However, there was absolutely no future scope for a cosmopolitan girl like me. *PL*-ease, be realistic— Do you really see me settling into the French provincial life, walking around this banlieue posing as a "Suburban Husky?" I didn't think so.

Of no great surprise, Couch Potato Terrier happily stayed behind watching TV. He promised to be on surveillance, watching for the cat's exit. Yet again, of NO great surprise, in-between snoozes and snores, he only watched the Arts Channel— Exactly! He missed the whole feline déplacement!

Believe it or not, Unsocial Kitty relocated to the apartment right next door in order to avoid any contact with the two American dogs! Go figure! After all the, "S'il te plaît, be nice to tourists!" campaign propaganda and metro posters with smiley faces, there was still lots and lots of unwarranted anti-American sentiment which now extended to their leashed canine companions— Beyond Ridiculous! Imagine to be classified as "undesirable by co-habitation." If only I could gain a private moment, I would more than happily further the Chat de Maison's multi-cultural awareness education.

Yet another sign that this was not to be mistaken as a forever home— Sighhhh.

By the time that My Mistress returned, I was happy to see her. Oh, *PL*-ease, do not be so easily swayed, allow your emotions to be influenced by sappy, hopelessly optimistic and romantic Hallmark Channel movies— There's absolutely sentimental between her and me! Not ever, ever, everrrrr!

I have something much better occupying my thoughts— Exactly! My 1st Christmas in Paris!

In our short absence, Paris had transformed itself into a Christmas Wonderland. Christmas markets magically appeared on every square with vendors offering stocking AND tummy stuffers! The store windows on rue St. Honore displayed the best gifts for people with platinum card purchasing power— AND, Ding-Ding-Ding! The post arrived with cards and prrrrrresents!

Have I mentioned in the past 5 minutes that J'♥dore PARIS?!

But wait, this gets even better! There's a Christmas-in-Paris BONUS— Exactly! With all her clown-sized shoes and fancy cigarettes, there had been zero extra-space in her luggage. The Santa suit, felt antlers, and jingle bell elven collars were safely locked away in a storage unit back in the good ol' U-S-A! WooHoo!

But wait— It gets even better! Since the French do not dress their dogs like four-legged-people-pageant-freaks, NO last-minute substitutions were purchasable! Finally her cultural cluelessness working to my benefit, all of our holiday photos had to be taken à poil!

Joyeuse Nikita = Joyeux Noel!

Unfortunately, my happiness was short-lived as non-sensical gibberish gushed loudly from the kitchen ruining my reverie. Ughhhh. She was at it, again!

When would she speak proper French or English with Shamus? Even worse, the syllabically challenged terrier thought that the current word-mash was "Yorkenese"— Redonkulous!

To my highly-trained ears, it sounded a lot more like a lingual bridge of English and French over troubled Mandarin water A.K.A. My Mistress can't remember which country this is after the 2nd fishbowl glass of Côtes du Rhône!

Seriously though, her insistent usage of smashed up words like "snuggalert" which meant Absolutely Nothing to anyone who lived outside the walls of this 34sq meter flat A.K.A. The Entire Freaking World was NOT helping the terrier widget to assimilate A.K.A. Leave Me Alone!

"Niki, don't be a hater."

Pardon me, was I speaking out-loud? In any case, good to know you still speak a proper language!

"Niki, her vocabulary and pronunciation have improved dramatically. Snuggalert is very close to snuggabuggawuggawannaalarm which is formal Yorkenese for—"

That's IT! Choose your method of death wisely smarty pants puppy— TAK!

A yorkie bullet shot through the room right past my raised-and-ready paw to lodge itself under the bed.

Humph. Impressive.

With the new under-bed storage boxes hiding her shoe and sweater addiction, which by the way had grown exponentially since we moved 3,000 miles closer to Italy— I'm surprised that the putting-on-the-holiday-pounds pup could wedge himself into any leftover space. Well, nature may hate a vacuum, but I love the solitude! Au revoir and s'il te plaît, take your sweet time wiggling out!

"Niki-Niki-Nikita."

Ugghhhh. That was NOT enough time! When would I learn that there was no such thing as having the last word with the loquacious terrier.

"Niki, you know solitude is not a very healthy idea."

Really? Come a little closer, so I can educate you about healthy boundaries.

"No Niki, I'm serious. When it comes to mental health, the preponderance of evidence show—"

Preponderance? *PL*-ease that word is biGGer than you, even after a full meal or with a fresh shampoo and blow-out! Have you been at the dictionary again? Can you even spell that?

"t-h-a-t."

Shamus, I'm warning you.

"y-o-u."

TWACK! SPLAT!

"Niki please-Niki please-Niki please, you just don't understand. I'll never be as big as you as strong as you as adroit as you, but maybe I can become smart like you!"

Big words do not make you a Real Dog!

"But, iloveyouiloveyouiloveyou— Hey, I've got an idea!"

Really? Please, don't share.

But, ears-on-strike terrier just kept on talking.

"How about a game of cache-cache before bedtime?"

Nice touch with the français, Terrier Beret. Sure, why not? Let's play! Why don't you hide first and stay hidden!

"But Niki, wouldn't you miss me?"

Let me think about that.

"Ok. No worries. You can take all the time you need, my most beautiful, most wonderful Nikita. I'm not going anywhere."

And then, came the puppy kisses.

"Snuggle—Snuggle—Snugglalert!" chimed through the apartment from the bedroom.

Arrghhh— Impossible to escape the mental diuretics of either one. And, pardon me, but where were her sense of priorities, tonight? Had she left them behind at British customs? I wasn't even in bed yet and she was inviting him?! Absolutely un-acceptable! Ça suffit— That's right! This housemate has had enough of their bedside-stealing, undercover-snuggling routine!

Pushing Smootchy Puppy off to the side, I walked over to the bed, jumped up, and slammed my body against hers.

OK, let's see how you like it.

AAACKKKK! She liked it!

She liked it sooooo much that she purred in my ear something about, "I love you, too."

Hello-Hello-HELLO! Is this your attempt at dry, bone dry English humor?? Let me explain something to you Mistress Toast-With-Crust— If you have to explain that it's a joke, it's NOT funny. And, just in case you cannot see with your special eyes, I am not smiling, not even a little smirk!

But, this story of woe was faaarrrrr from over.

Having lost complete control of her senses, Mistress Rational-Is-Not-My-Middle-Name wrapped me up in the covers with her!

Stop it! After all these years of close quarters co-habitation, haven't you noticed that I already have a plush coat and an internal furnace set to 1000 Degrees! There's absolutely no need for further insulation!

Wait one second! By any chance, is this just another quirky manifestation of your jealousy, your incapability to accept playing second fiddle or perhaps just some sort of misguided pre-emptive payback? Well, NewsFLASH— Revenge is best served c-o-l-d, cold!

So, listen up closely Mistress Unsolicited Warmfuzzies— Release me at once, this very moment, before you roast us like a couple of marshmallows at a harvest moon bonfire!

But then, believe it or not, it got even worse— Exactly! Not knowing where to go, where to sleep, unable to be too far away from me, for too long, Shamus climbed up Cashmere Mountain. The bungee-cord dwarf found his way underneath the covers burrowing further and further and further until his pint-sized body was crammed between us!

Within minutes, the yorkie wedge was snoring. Not sleeping— s-n-o-r-i-n-g, snoring!

Tightly lodged between myself and Mistress-I-Think-This-Is-So-Adorable, there was zero space for his lungs to expand A.K.A. Bugger Boy couldn't breathe A.K.A. accelerating his devolvement to total vapidity!

True. Perhaps, not my barrel of monkeys— However, tonight I find myself in the blanket barrel, faced with yet another dilemma— Exactly! Not one to give up, I was also not fond of a sleepless night in a makeshift sweat lodge entertained by the vibrations of a compressed larynx— AND, my party schedule did not accommodate for any extra naptime— AND, absolutely no way was I going to spend the holidays with my fur singed— AND, a zombie terrier is so totally not on my wish list at any time of year!

So, I moved.

Not wanting Mistress Misconception-of-Canine-Motivations to confuse my choice with retreat or surrender, I went directly into the kitchen. At this late hour, she had no choice, but to listen as I crunched biscuits and drank water as enthusiastically as possible A.K.A. she'd fall for the pretense of a late-night munchies fix.

Gizmo-full, but hydrated, I returned to bed, making certain to leave lots and lots of distance between myself and the snoring snuggle bugs.

Welcome to my Parisian life.

Parisian life was still proving to be more challenging than my romantic notion of it. Every day was a new linguistic hurdle as both my French and my English were subject to corrections. Sometimes helpful and appreciated, but as I was interrupted with the "correct" pronunciation and usage for the umpteenth time in any given conversation, I wondered the point of speaking at all.

Aside from the language barrier, there were cultural ones too. So many intricacies to interpersonal relations, some were obvious, like exchanging pleasantries. Others less so and particular to Parisians, like how many times you kiss someone on the cheek or which side to start.

My downstairs neighbor, an elderly widow, had become accustomed to the peace and quiet of living at home alone and, since my apartment had been vacant for several months before our arrival, with no upstairs neighbor. The few times I had passed her in the stairwell, we had exchanged a nod and simple greeting. Then one day, she saw me with Shamus and stopped me full of questions about my "petit toutou."

A few days later, she saw me with Nikita. Her eyes popped and she asked me what happened to "le petit." Smiling, I quipped, "He grew!" Unfortunately, the humor did not translate, not in the least.

One of the reasons I decided to move to Paris is that it's illegal to deny occupancy to someone who has a pet.✧ What I didn't know is that a tenant can be voted out of a building by the owners. At the next co-op meeting, she tried to get us evicted. Luckily, a couple of my neighbors liked me well enough to vouch for me and my two well-behaved dogs.

This latest layer of the Parisian cultural onion was explained by my upstairs neighbor. The dogs and I were walking through the square at Abbesses, when she called out to us from her bistro seat. A delicate, little thing, I had much respect for this woman as she was well into her 60s and still climbed the stairs to her apartment on the 5th floor of our building. My respect grew as I learned that she was our main defender at the board meeting when the downstairs neighbor complained that my dogs were yappers.

✧ This rule applies cat, dogs, birds, rabbits, ferrets, and rats. If you have a reptile, you can be denied.

We chatted for a few minutes, catching up on building gossip, before she asked if we wanted to join her for a coffee. I said, "thank you," but declined.

Time, we had. But, the only things in my pockets that afternoon were keys and plastic bags. If anything, I owed her a coffee, not the other way around.

We said our goodbyes and when I went to continue our walk, Nikita planted her tush on the ground and refused to budge.

Chuckling away, the neighbor informed me, "Nikita would like to stay."

"Perhaps, but we need to go."

I tried to move again, tugging gently at Niki's leash. Still refusing to move, Nikita looked the other way.

Now, the woman was laughing. The other patrons nearby were starting to snicker. Not wanting to be overrun by my four-legged companion, I did the only thing I could.

I could NOT believe it! She picked me up and started to carry me down the street— Whoa, Instant Flashback! Taking me right back to the humiliation of our very 1st walk! What was wrong with her that she now felt the need to embarrass me in Paris? This is No Way to express the holiday spirit AND a little FYI— Only fitness-freak Americans training for Iron Man Alaska carry their dogs!

Luckily, not in training for anything other than a double-handed, pinot noir burgundy press, Mistress Zero Stamina returned me to Parisian cobblestones after half a block— Still, the very worst moment of my Parisian experience to date.

But wait! The day was not over yet— Exactly! She stopped the "big rush home" to talk some more to yet another poor unsuspecting neighbor. Thankfully, this Parisienne was a professional translator and spoke beautifully articulated English A.K.A. No one had to suffer Mistress Still-Can't-Pronounce-Croissant's verbal calisthenics. In-tow, was her equally bilingual French-Irish rugrat whose dirty, sticky hands were reaching for my freshly brushed coat.

Always more than happy to help with the cleanliness crusade, as I started to remove the cookie crumbs and ice cream from his fingers, he squealed with delight! Finished with one hand, he offered the other— What a pro!

Unable to assess the simplest of actions, Mistress Obtuse Observations squatted down to inform my petite Parisian-via-Dublin friend that dogs licks are really kisses and that I must really, really like him, before returning to her conversation with his mother.

What happened next is exactly what happens when you put bad ideas and misinformation into the heads of perfectly good children.

Leaning into me, he whispered, "Thank you, merci beaucoup. I like you too, je tiens à toi." Then, he started licking my head— AAACKKKK!

Every single day, I am subject to the terrier tooth cleaning fetish and intermittent bursts of puppy slobberfest— And Every Single Day, I have to be vigilant for presents left by ardent admirers A.K.A. Otis drool puddles— *PL*-ease, do not tell me that I now have to suffer 3-year-old lollypop licks!

Ignoring my current state-of-trauma, My Mistress and his mother Laughed Out Loud, even allowing him to linger before pulling Misguided Affection Toddler off of me!

My fur now plastered to his lips and lining the inside of his mouth, his mother wisely decided to march him straight home. But, not before a few more giggles and hushed comments.

PL-ease, I can hear you and I can understand what you're saying! This is not cute, not sweet, and certainly not adorable! Oh Bones, where are you? Please come back from vacation early and rescue me.

BUT with the luck of the French-Irish now slobbered all over my head, only Flirt-the-Pervert was in ear-shot and came over.

"Oui, Mademoiselle. You 'r in need of assistan-ce?"

No, not from the likes of you. I refuse to associate with a canine who is foul-mouthed figuratively and literally!

"Bu-t I em 'ere for you, Belle. All of meee, for all of you. Jouste like da song"

S'il te plaît, no more talking and absolutely no singing! Just turn around and go back to your yellow curtain installation on the gallery's wall.

"Belle, Mademoiselle Belle-de-Jour, Belle-de-Nuit, per-aps, a leetle art will 'elp to relax you. Whee can collaborate toget-er! Looook, your leetle friend is alreadee signing da bottom corner. "

Please, I'm in NO mood for your potty art. Leave me ALONE!

Pushing him back into his latest creation on the bricks behind us, he smiled and said through tobacco stained canines, "Ah, oui. I like eet, ruff-rrrruff."

Seriously? You enjoy being slammed into urine soaked walls? My head is about to explode. Please stop. Just STOP!

"Stop! Staaa-pah!"

From down the street, Flirt's father was rushing towards us. I couldn't tell if he was screaming at me or his dog, but at least he was coming over. Flirt was a sweet, older Rhodesian Ridgeback who belonged to the grumpiest man in the neighborhood.

Arriving in a huff and immediately pulling his unleashed canine off to the side, Flirt's owner gave me a dirty look. I guess Nikita's playful roughhousing appeared a little too aggressive for his Parisian sensibilities.

Before I lost my temper, with a wide-grinned American smile I thanked him for gaining control of his dog and turned away without waiting for a response. No reason to muddle my afternoon with more French idiosyncrasies.

*

Christmas Eve, I attended midnight mass with my Harvard friend. On our walk up to the butte, the streets were practically empty. Almost like a ghost town. So when we arrived at Sacre Coeur, I was surprised at how many people were there. It was busting at the seams with visitors trailing down the steps outside. My friend and I maneuvered our way inside and we found a couple of seats at the very back of the cathedral.

Decked out in holly and flowers with incense filling the nave and the boys' choir singing, it was Christmas magic. And, a fantastic spectacle with all the people watching and listening to the multiple languages spoken in the service and by the congregation. However, it quickly became a sensory overload. We left after a short hour in search of an open restaurant on the butte for a celebratory glass of mulled wine.

Most of the bistros and restaurants were already closed in observance of the holiday, but we finally found one that still had a few lingering patrons and agreed to let us sit for a glass.

As we were sipping the hot and spicy Christmas cheer, they began to close down the restaurant. Or, that's what we assumed. But, this is Paris and things are rarely as they appear. There are many layers to a French onion.

Once the blinds were rolled down and the door locked, they began to move the tables off to the side and rolled out a piano. The restaurant owner stood up on a chair, clinked a glass a few times before introducing an older couple. They were celebrating their wedding and had invited everyone for champagne. We stayed until the wee hours of the morning singing and dancing. A magical Christmas moment where, even in Paris, strangers become friends!

Paris really is a different place at Christmas. Not just the holiday markets and decorations, but the Parisians themselves are smiling and laughing more than usual, even a little friendlier. Maybe infused with the holiday spirit, maybe relaxed with a few days off… Whatever the reason, it was a relief, a welcomed change as my social connections grew and calendar exploded.

I was so exhausted by the time that New Year's Eve came around that I considered cancelling my plans. But then, I am not one to refuse a home-cooked meal, especially when duck confit, gâteau au chocolat, and champagne will be on the table. After the decadent meal with a couple of friends near the Bois de Vincennes, we hopped in their car to go back to Montmartre figuring it was the best view of the fireworks at the Eiffel Tower. Traffic was hideous as everyone was repositioning before the countdown.

We finally arrived at the bottom of the hill minutes before midnight, only to find all the roads up were blocked off by police. The car was stuck in a complete bottleneck, not able move forwards or backwards a single inch.

My friends wanted to stay with their car. I wanted to experience my 1st New Years in Paris watching fireworks, not taillights. Leaving them with best wishes for the New Year, I dashed up the stairs to catch the firework display.

The butte was packed with people like sardines in a can, but the camaraderie festive and friendly. I was able to wiggle my way through the crowd and secure a place along the fence at the Arènes de Montmartre.

At the stroke of midnight, fireworks lit up the sky. Champagne corks were popping and flying all around me. At the very end of the show, the Eiffel Tower lit up like a Christmas tree. It was amazing!

I felt a slight tug at my sleeve and turned to the man standing next to me. Our eyes locked. He smiled. I smiled. He pulled me towards him and kissed me.

My first kiss from a French man who, by the end of the week, officially became my first boyfriend in Paris!

Finally! HAL-LE-LU-JAH!

No need for the typical segue here! We're starting the New Year right, indeed! Her very 1st French boyfriend! Sure, it took

her all freaking night and a few bottles of champagne to convince him to take her number— But, she returned in the wee hours of the morning, happy and smelling like a Frenchman!

Looks to me like ALL those extra prayers at Sacre Coeur— ALL that time spent in deep, deep meditation finally worked! Answered prayers = A most excellent omen for the New Year ahead!

She took the next few days alternating between cleaning the house and hashing out the details of her New Year's Eve to whoever would pick up the phone. Judging that this morning, Shamus and I were subject to "à la maison" baths and that now she was spending countless hours in the bathroom A.K.A. her "beauty" routine, I had a sneaky suspicion that the first date was tonight.

Not completely amused by her antics, I was thankful that she was taking the time and making an effort— Let's face it, she needed ALL the help she could get if there was any hope for a second rendez-vous!

Everything was well within the realm of good 1st date prep acceptable until out of the closet, she pulled out a new purse the size of a carry-on— When Terriers Fly?!?

Pardons-moi, may I offer some advice? Do NOT bring your luggage on the 1st date!

DING-DONG!

Woken up from his snooze, insecure terrier ran to the door barking like a snugglebug about to lose his snuggle.

One shift thwap stopped him cold.

Hey, look here Bozo Barker, she needs this to go well. We need this to go well. You be on your very best behavior, or else!

"Or else, what?"

Seriously, do I have to explain absolutely everything to you?!

"Well, sometimes yes. Look Nikita, I've never heard anyone ring the bell before. And, I was having a very, very bad dream, a veritable nightmare, about the evil skateboards taking over the entire world! When the bell rang, I thought that they were already here— At our very own door! Anyway Niki, why can't you just be a little bit nice to me? Don't you remember your resolution? 'New year, new attitude.'"

Please not everything has to do with you. In fact, nothing does. Now, stay focused and behave. We need him to like her!

Dawdling precious minutes away in the bathroom, if she took much longer answering the door there'd be NO ONE there! After one more overly optimistic smile to herself in the mirror, she finally unlocked and opened the door.

There he was— an age-appropriate, species-appropriate, freshly-showered, dark-haired, good-looking Frenchman from Burgundy!

Without a moment's hesitation, he bent the knee to greet me first. Already, I felt a very strong connection to this one.

After lavishing me with the usual French flattery, he patted Shamus on the head, and then greeted My Mistress with a simple "bonsoir." There was an awkward moment at the threshold. Then, as an obvious after-thought, he hurriedly kissed her on both cheeks.

Welcoming him inside, she fussed around the apartment giving him the grand 2-minute tour of our tiny flat before they left. Sad to see him go, but hoping to see M. Dijon again, I placed an emergency call on the God-line that she would not screw it up!

Unfortunately, this meant that I was now left alone with the verbally challenged terrier for the entire evening and a very unwilling participant in his quest to fulfill his New Year's resolution to speak French![⊘]

Let me tell you— there is absolutely nothing worse than a Yorkie born in New Jersey with an Irish name and an English heritage speaking French unless you're trying to communicate with "une vache espagnol!"

The very moment that we heard the door downstairs close, he started.

"Nikita, Niki-Niki-Niki."

Yes. I am right here. No need to repeat my name ad nauseam.

"Right. Niki, did you see my Christmas present? It's sooooo beautiful. It's the very best present ever! J'adore ma poule!"

Huh? No one gave you a chicken!

"No, please listen carefully. I said MA POULE!"

I know what you said and no matter HOW LOUD you say it, No one gave you a chicken for Christmas, not even the good rotisserie people on rue d'Abbesses!

"No, Niki. My pool. You know, the one she gave me for Christmas. Come on, don't you remember?"

Unfortunately, my soon to be unfriended and blocked friend, I remember everything! No one gave you a swimming "pool" OR an invitation to a private "pool" OR a season's pass to a public "pool!"

"Oh jeeps, Niki, when are you going to learn French?"

Watch it, Sanctimonious Puppy, you are treading on very thin ice.

"Niki, I am trying to talk to you about my new cashmere sweater."

[⊘] Of course, he also committed himself to losing weight and growing taller, but out of the 3 resolutions learning French was certainly the most realistic! LOL

Right. Gotcha. Listen up closely, Terrier Franglais. That's "un pull"!

"Yes. Excellent. You do remember! It's super soft and the color compliments my eyes. Since it's so cold tonight and she left, I was hoping to wear it. But since we can't find it, I guess I'll just have to snuggle up with you!"

Before I could protest, before I could place another emergency call on the God-line, came Velcro Puppy with his puppy kisses— Ugghhhhh.

*

The next morning, she was chatting up her friends in the states, bragging about her new French beau.

Ummmm, reality check please for Mistress Blurred Lines! You are aware that one, single, solitary date does not a relationship make, no matter How Much you talk about it! And by the by, best you put down the phone and pay some attention to your four-legged beast A.K.A. Treat Withdrawal Terrier who is having a breakdown in the kitchen right this very moment!

"Niki-Niki-Niki. I can hardly take this anymore. I've been ringing and ringing and ringing for treats, but no special delivery! I think that I might drop dead from starvation, if she doesn't feed me soon!"

Seriously?! Take a look at your reflection, paunchy pup. You could easily go a week without meals before you hit your pre-holiday weight.

"Nikita, I'm super serious. My blood sugar is dropping fast. I feel so weak and dizzy. I might just fall over."

Well, at least you don't have far to go!

"Niki!"

Fine. I will control my sharp wit in your time of distress. Anyway, you should know better by now. She cannot hear you when she's on the phone and smoking cigarettes— TWO things at once, that's her multi-tasking safety limit especially when she's holding fire between her fingers.

Hey, wait-a-second! Here's an idea for you— Why not get her attention with a present?

Of course, I was thinking puppy slobber would be an appropriate cadeau for Mistress Allergic-To-Dog-Saliva— Nothing like a red-hot itchy skin rash to shift her focus and fast! Unfortunately, what happened next is EXACTLY what happens when you put perfectly good ideas into the heads of addled-brained terriers.

Instead of running over to Mistress Too-Preoccupied-To-Care and showering her with those puppy kisses, he scooted back into the kitchen and banged the chimes with such force that they crashed to the ground.

Of no great surprise, that still failed to gain her attention— So, he pulled everything off the fridge!

Standing in the middle of his chaos, surveilling the wreckage, he chose her prized duck magnet to re-gift and brought it Terrier Express into the living room!

AACKKK! Are you nuts? Have you completely lost your mind?

"No. I am Shamus. And, I have hunger. GREAT HUNGER!"

Well, what-ever, who-ever you are had better put that back in the kitchen before she slaughters you. You know very well, that is her souvenir Toulouse Duck, not some rotisserie Christmas Goose.

Fully possessed by his Pavlovian treat cravings, his gaze as vacant as his mind, there was nothing that I could do— except watch. So, I strategically navigated myself out of the way of the ensuing Mistress Monsoon.

He walked over to her and placed the ill-gotten trophy at her feet. Caught up in the umpteenth recitation of her evening, she continued to ignore him. Not about to give up, the tenacious terrier began to throw the felt duck up into the air sometimes catching it, sometimes letting the masticated mascot plunk down on the floor over and over again in a classic terrier tantrum until, "Shamus! Drop the duck n-o-w, NOW!"

True to the forecasted path of impact, she whipped Shamus up off the floor by the scruff of his neck and delivered him straight into the kitchen. There, she discovered the disaster conniption-fit terrier created— God, help him now!

Although not an exact request, there must have been a portal open to heaven in our apartment because the God-line was open with miracles on tap— Exactly! Instead of obliterating bad, bad puppy as predicted in her tsunami of rage, she inhaled deeply and plopped him down on the floor. With a long sigh she asked, "Did you do this, Shamus?"

Guiltier than charged, Shameful Shamus hung his head low.

"Are you sorry, really sorry?"

Shamus tilted his head to one side as if thinking about it. His eyes rolled back as if looking for an answer. Oh please— This was worse than watching some cheesy Telemundo telenovela.

Come on Señor Shamus, much more heartfelt than that. Your life depends on it!

He must have heard my thoughts willing him towards an Emmy nomination worthy performance. With his very best "Gizmo sighhhhhh," he turned his head back towards his disaster area before slowly raising his big, sad puppy eyes.

Good boy! Keep looking as pitiful as possible. You know, your usual sappy self— Perfect! That should do it. Just hold it. Hold it steady. She's falling for it, hook, line and stinker!

"Then, come here and tell me how sorry you are."

Responding with more and more and even more puppy kisses, Energizer-powered love terrier kept at it until she was laughing! The puppy slobber must have absorbed into her body and passed the blood brain barrier acting as a hallucinogenic!

Why?! Because what happened next defies simple logic and every good training principle— Exactly! Replacing the chimes back on the fridge at Shamus level, she opened up the chicken tender jar and she asked him to ring one more time!

Are you mental? Listen here Mistress Terrier Enabler, the very last thing treat addict terrier needs is more negative re-enforcement— And, with just 1 millimeter more on his pudgy belly, he'll mutate into a certified Gizmo 2.1! *PL*-ease, this apartment is already too small without a roly-poly puppy to accommodate!

Ignoring my plea for common sense, she turned and offered me a piece.

Rolling my eyes at the weak bribe, she offered a second.

And then, when I refused to even blink an eye, a third.

Sure, why not? If you can't beat them, join them— But then, make certain to drag them on an uber long walk! After all, Valentine's Day is coming up and we need to look boudoir good!

*

Our French Beau was turning out to be quite serious. Every single weekend was dedicated to spending time with us! This weekend was no exception to the new rule.

Now, I had placed several requests on the God-line that M. Bourgogne would come and only take me. But, forever the gentleman, he resisted the temptation offering the backseat of his car to our gruesome twosome— Sighhhh.

At least, with the window down, the white noise blissfully blocked any attempts at conversation from our backseat drivers. It was such a pleasure to be in the Parisian countryside breathing the crisp air. It reminded me of The Farm, but more French— However, there always seems to be a terrier wrench in my happiness A.K.A. Life is never a simple walk with a high-maintenance terrier in-tow!

The very moment we arrived at Parc de la Muette, adventure-less terrier was allowed off-leash! But, me?! Oh, no-no-no! Never able to extend any trust in My Direction, Mistress Forever Jaded insisted that I remain on leash, switching out my prong collar with a color-coordinated, but pickle-ugly, harness. Absolutely ridiculous!

My only consolation was that although puppykins was free, he went nowhere— Precisely! While French Basel and I went off into the woods blazing new paths, Mistress I-Don't-Move-That-Fast and Size-Restricted Shamus puttered the paved trail around the lake.

Always hoping that he'd forget about them and run away with me, after an hour or so his mobile would ring. A technological leash reminding him of our humdrum companions.

Today, we went a little farther outside of Paris to a new park. Hooray! I was soooooo excited to run through unexplored territory leaving "Hansel-and-Gretel" farrrrrr behind with their grumble-crumbs! But, the entire ride there, Mistress Clingy Needy whined until he agreed that we all walk together— Oh buggers! Foiled Again!

Neither one of us happy to share our private time, French Basel whispered in my ear before we left the car, "Demain, tomorrow. Jouste us, nous-deux. I promeese."

Have I mentioned in the past 5 minutes how much I ♥ the sensibilities of this Frenchman?!

Forever considerate towards our feeble-bodied, tag-team tag-a-longs, once we arrived at the water's edge after only a few kilometers walk, he insisted to take a break. While those civilized in our tenue were appreciating the view across the sizable reservoir, Shamus was up to his typical country bumkin' antics— Exactly! A lackluster impersonation of "Baloo the Bear," to include singing while wiggling on his back in the red dirt! Ughhhhh.

Can you spell embarrassing? Allow me to help you. It's S-h-a-m-u-s, Shamus!

Mistress Love Goggles took a moment's break from her romantic-view notions and told him to stop which he did— Until, she looked away! Then, tone-deaf terrier started it up, again!

Ridiculous! I would never, never ever be allowed to get away with something like that!

Hey, Naughty Little Doggie! She asked you nicely to behave. Now stop acting like an American on Spring break crack and Cut-It-Out! If you embarrass us any further, he may never see us again A.K.A. No more weekend get-a-ways!

"Niki, relax a bit. It's the whole reason to leave the hustle-and-bustle of the city. Just like the song says, 'Enjoy the bare necessities— The simple bare necessities. Forget about your worries and your strife! Bada-badap-baaaa.'"

Shamussss—

"Come on, Niki. At least let me finish the refrain, otherwise I'll get song burn. Besides, this feels soooo freaking good! You should give it a try. All the pebbles on the ground are accessing my pressure points. It's like outdoor shiatsu!"

Shamus, I am personally going to simultaneously manipulate ALL your pressure points, if you don't stop right n-o-w, NOW!

Lacking any form of self-control, he just could not stop. Wiggling to the left. Wiggling to the right. He was moving farther and farther away.

"Ah come on Nikita, don't be such a fussbudget. Just a little more. I could do this all the way hoooo—"

SPLATSPLASH!

Holy Buggers!

The three of peered over the edge to see if Shamus survived the 4ft fall.

Much to my surprise, we found the 3-lives-left terrier already treading water. His head swiveling back-and-forth, bobble-head terrier was in Full-Freak-Out mode. And for once, with good reason! A sheer drop from the embankment to the water, there was nowhere to go— Absolutely none!

What happened next proved that he fallen headfirst knocking out the last two fully-functioning brain cells— Exactly! Spotting the opposite side of the lake AND with zero concept of distance, near-sighted and navigationally-challenged Shamus began to doggie-paddle in that direction!

SHAMUUUSSSSS!!!

My Mistress and I screamed in unison at broken compass puppy.

For the very 1st time ever, we were of a like mind! Neither one of us wanted to go for a 1km swim this afternoon! Of course, that meeting of the minds was very short lived.

With not many more functional brain cells than concussion puppy, Mistress Rash Reaction threw her body to the ground dangling it over the edge almost falling off herself— AACKKKK!

Quick to action, French Basel grabbed her by the ankles saving us from the second splash into the icy water. I looked down at the drowning puppy and my suspended mistress, and then back at our French man.

Softly, I nudged him to let go.

Please, just loosen your grip a little. Let her slip off to join him. We'd be so, so, so much happier just the two of us. You know it's true. We could even go for a jog this afternoon while they contribute to the cycle of life as fish food.

"NeeKee, no." But then, he smiled.

Sighhhh. He was right. Far too many witnesses in a public park, on a weekend. Our time would have to wait a little longer.

A little farther and I'd be able to grab the little bugger.

One minute, Shamus was rolling around on the ground. The next, he'd fallen into the lake. Reaching over the ledge, I was too vertically challenged to rescue him. Thankfully, my friend had longer arms and was able to pluck Shamus out of the water. And thankfully, he also had towels and blankets in his car.

Heading back to Paris earlier than planned with a wet, shivering puppy, at least we escaped the traffic and the day's excitement gave us a good excuse to settle in for a quiet night at home.

Things were moving along smoothly with my new boyfriend. We'd been spending more and more time together. Whether at one of his favorite hangouts in-and-around Paris or going to the movies, or even just cooking at home, I felt more "Parisian" being with him. And, the cliché proved true. My French was getting much better with a French boyfriend!

This was the Paris that I had dreamed of… the fairytale come true. A kiss from a stranger who becomes so much more. Still, I was surprised when he invited me to come with him to his sister's home outside of Annecy for his nephew's baptism. Family affairs were special occasions and usually kept private. When he also mentioned spending time in Mâcon, his hometown, I got a little skittish.

Not only was this a big step forward in our relationship, I was also overwhelmed at the thought of meeting his family because as little English as he spoke, his family spoke even less.

My friends back home insisted that I was on a good relationship track and that it was a great opportunity, exploring social customs and a new region of France. Following their advice, I pushed my anxiety aside and agreed to the road-trip.

Although the dogs were invited to come, I decided it would be easier for me without them. So, I contacted

Association Millepats to see if they could locate a home in Paris for Nikita and Shamus.

This time with more notice, I insisted on an updated dossier with confirmation that there were absolutely no other animals in the home. Finally, the coordinator located an Italian woman and her daughter who met all my requirements. When I saw their address, I was pleasantly surprised. They lived in the 9th arrondissement, within walking distance and not too far from the veterinarian.

The Veterinarian! Why are we walking past his office? I know that you like him, too. There is nothing else that makes you wake-up early, put-on your Chantecaille magic, and brush-out your own hair. Come on, just stop in for a little, "Bonjour, good Docteur. Would you like to join us for un café?"

Zoom-Zoom-ZOOOOM!

She just kept on going farther down the hill, farther down the street— Even passing her stinky hot yoga studio! Without slowing down, she took an unexpected left wizzzzing past the corner bistro without a single, longing glance for our good docteur— BOOM!

Full brakes on, she stopped at a door across the cobblestone street from a chapel.

Ummmm, pardon me. Just to clarify, you are aware that it's French Basel's nephew who wants to be baptized not me! I much rather prefer to be spritzed with Moroccan orange blossom water after a day at The Spa— Hint-Hint!

As usual, ignoring me and my most sincere heartfelt desires, she dragged us into the building and up 4 flights of steep stairs before Mistress Need-To-Catch-My-Breath stopped again.

Knock-Knock-KNOCK!

Pasta and coffee and charcuterie and bread and grilled vegetables— Before the door even opened, my head was swooning from the aromas filling the hallway. Did we just climb the stairway to Italian Heaven?!

A little woman with wild, Lucy-red hair appeared at the doorway instead of Archangel Raphael. From behind her, a smaller, younger, black-haired version squealed with delight at our arrival.

Humph. Not exactly whom I was expecting, but I am certainly willing to make allowances when prosciutto is involved.

Myself blessed with the grace of an angel, I waited for my invitation to enter— However, Possessed Puppy Paws was a different story. Somehow, Demon Dog broke-free and charged-in jumping on the squealer showering her with puppy slobber! Sweeping him up, she held him at arms-length, but that did not deter Italophile Terrier from his embarrassing display of affection.

Ahhhh— Come on, show some restraint! We haven't even been properly introduced yet!

But, no such luck. Almost impossible to sway once in the throes of his current obsession, whenever Shamus heard Italian all bets were off! Not that the linguistically challenged terrier understood a single freaking word, but he did have a fondness for pizza, pasta, biscotti, antipasto, gelato, well you get the idea— Exactly! Anything off an Italian menu!

Inside and with the door closed and bolted, Mistress Control Freak finally allowed me to roam around the apartment.

WoW! It was HUGE! If my calculations were correct, it encompassed the entire floor! Sadly, the bedroom door was closed to inquiring canines-who-want-to-know. However, the kitchen was open for business— Mmmmmmmm!

Ginger Nonna came behind me like a lightning bolt with a resounding, "No!"

Hummphhhhh. Looks like she'd need some breaking in, if this was going to work out!

Sitting down, I looked up at her with doleful eyes.

Refusing to blink.

Mesmerized by my baby blues, she couldn't help but smile.

"Ok, Ni-Ki-Taaa! Voilà!"

And with that she tossed me a slice of chorizo. Not exactly the Prosciutto di Parma or aged provolone that I was hoping for, but Ginger Nonna was showing potential. Breaking my steadfast rule on outwardly displays of affection only to keep the forward momentum with positive reinforcement, I gave her a quick thank-you kiss.

Her smile and head tilt said it all— Lesson #1 = A Complete Success!

Ba-da-bing, ba-da-BOOM!

Before we could commence with Lesson #2, My Mistress came in the kitchen looking for scraps herself! True to her Italian hospitality, within minutes Ginger Nonna had espresso brewed and whipped up a plate of treats for everyone!

Have I mentioned in the past 5 minutes how much I ♥ Italian nonnas who live in Paris?!

As soon as Mistress Excruciating-Detail was finished giving instructions for our care, they ushered her out the door— About time! Ciao-Ciao!

Better yet, The Little One also left and took the little pipsqueak with her!

Hallelujah! A real vacation at last!

Unfortunately, this blessing was short-lived— Exactly! She lived in the flat directly above, so I still had to spend every single afternoon with Intermittent Snooze Puppy.

But wait! Believe it or not, it gets even worse!

Every single night, discordant elephant stomping entertainment was provided by Tutu Puppy as he performed his circus routines on a continuous loop— Ugghhhhh.

My saving grace was that after only a couple of days, Ginger Nonna couldn't stand the ruckus either. So, early one morning before the sun rose and long, long. long before the night owls regained consciousness, Ginger Stealth and I slipped out of the building. With only the essentials packed, we hopped in her car and drove away— Never looking even once in the rear-view mirror!

A vacation within a vacation? What great fortune! Have I mentioned in the past 5 minutes how much I ♥ My Nonna?!

Driving farther than we ever, ever went with French Basel, Circuito del Garda Nonna drove full-throttle into the French countryside keeping the windows down so that I could navigate our way as she bopped along to the radio.

Now, this is a real vacation!

Only slowing down once we were off the autoroute, we puttered along on the backcountry roads until we finally arrived at a stone-hewn farmhouse on the outskirts of a small village.

As soon as she found the hidden key, she opened the door and unhooked my leash.

Then, the most unprecedented, unbelievable thing happened— She asked for my help!

How cool is that? Finally, someone who appreciates my expertise.

Honored, I immediately set about investigating the home, making certain that there were no stray critters! One intruder found-and-captured, I left the motionless body-of-evidence on the hearth in the kitchen. Although I was fairly certain that one offering was enough for compensation, I kept my radar on auto-alert while taking a break, to savor my good fortune, in front of the cast-iron fireplace.

The next few days were the very best of my entire life! Spending time with Ginger Nonna was such a treat! We understood each other. I gave her her space and she gave me mine. There was NO fussing, NO cajoling— just uber long walks and homemade Italian food! Even my desire, my need to connect more deeply with my true nature was within her grasp— Precisely! She and her man-friend took me hunting for rabbits and wild boars in a real Medieval forest! A perfect vacation until— DING! DONG!

The door opened and Powerball Puppy bounced in.

"Niki-Niki-Niki! We found you!"

So, it seems. You may go back to Paris now.

"Seriously Nikita, I looked everywhere for you! There was no note. Your kibble bowl was left full of biscuits. I was afraid that you had been dognapped! I thought that I would never, ever see you again!"

I had hoped for much the same.

"Niki. That's not very nice. I was really worried. I could hardly sleep. All I could think about was you. You define me. My life is completely meaningless, an empty shell of time-consuming activities without my Nikita, my love, my one and only, my beloved, my firewood—"

And once Don Juan Doggie could find no more terms of adoration, came the puppy kisses—Ugghhhhh.

*

With Shamus back in residence, the meal-sharing plan stopped abruptly!

What?! You have got to be kidding me! There is zero humor in this joke! Let me assure you, not funny in the very least! It is bad enough that I have to share paradise with the boy blunder, but to be reduced to a diet of bland dog food? No, not happening.

"Niki. When are we going to eat? The smell of food cooking is driving me crazy."

Tell me about it.

"Nikita, I just did. Why do you have to be so difficult sometimes? I'm going to go ask Nonna for a snack."

Don't bother. It's all kibble, all the way.

But of course, he did. And, as expected, she placed a bowl of kibble of the floor.

"Niki. It's not so bad. It's the same thing that we eat at home."

Just before I whacked some sense into Mr. Happy-Go-Lucky, I had an epiphany— Exactly! A hunger-strike! Absolutely Brilliant! No Nonna could bear letting her guests, especially her loved ones, go hungry! The main hiccup was convincing the Veracious Terrier of my plan.

Shamus?

"Yes, my Nikita love?"

Do NOT touch that kibble. Do you understand?

"But—"

No buts! You have to trust me on this.

"B-bb-bbb—"

Shamus, I mean it. Hey! Let's play a game of cache-cache instead!

"Really? You want to play with me?"

Always, my little twitter-bug. Why don't you go hide first. I'll come find you when dinner's ready.

"Niki, that doesn't sound right."

Well, those are the rules today. Do you want to play or not?

"Okay-okay! Give me at least until the count of ten."

Smiling, I thought to myself, "I'll give you until the count of 10 MILLION!"

Once he left the room, I curled up on the couch and counted the moments of quiet reprieve. When Ginger Nonna walked in to find me looking wistfully out the window, forever accommodating, she took me outside for some much-appreciated fresh air. Unfortunately, the fly-in-my-happiness puppy found me the moment we returned.

"Niki-Niki-Niki! What happened? I hid and you never came. That's not right."

Shamus, I told you I'd find you once dinner's ready and it's not.

"But, I'm hungry."

Just wait.

"Niki, did you hear that?"

Yes. Unfortunately, I do not have my ear plugs in today. I hear absolutely everything.

"Huh? Ohhh, ha-ha. Very funny, Nikita. Well then, you must've heard my tummy saying, 'Feed me. Feed me. Feed me, now!' It's soooooo empty and won't stop complaining. I can't stand it any longer!"

Ginger Nonna came into the kitchen and placed two bowls of kibble on the floor.

Quickly, I shot Shamus a warning look.

He sniffed at the biscuits and with a mopey, little gizmoesque sigh, he sulked out of the room.

Thinking that perhaps he also needed some fresh air, Ginger Nonna let Shamus out and asked me to keep watch.

With pleasure! Always happy to be of service— Oh, Mon Dieu!

I turned around to find Shamus furiously digging away in the garden and eating clumps of dirt!

"Not dirt, buried bones."

Shamus! Stop! Spit it out! She's going to strangle you. That's her biodynamic fertilizer!

"Well, I had to do something! I'm starving to death! Since it's only a matter of time before I die, I figured as long as I'm out here I might as well start digging my own grave. By chance, I un-earthed the bones and figured, 'Why not?'"

Pinocchio Puppy!

"Ok-ok-ok! I watched her bury charred bones in the garden and thought that they might tide me over until the hunger strike has ended. Look, I'll push the dirt back and she'll never be the wiser."

Listen to me, Evidence-Challenged Terrier. You'd better clean up your face up, too, before she—

"Shay-mousse!" Ginger Nonna came flying out of the house looking none too pleased with the garden gravedigger.

"Niki, did you hear that? She called me a moose! I knew it. I must be really, really fat. No wonder, it's only kibble in the bowl. It must be an intervention diet just like they did to Gizmo! Why didn't you say anything? Why didn't you tell me the truth about this 'hunger strike?' You know, we're scheduled to go on a trip! If I'm one ounce overweight, I'll have to ride in cargo! I don't think that I could take it! The noise, the cold, the noise, the cold—"

Shamus fell over semiconscious.

Ginger Nonna swooped him up in her arms freaking out. Her Italian so fast and furious, I could only understand "starve," "the American," "kill" and the final Italian word, "basta."

BEEP! BEEP!

The butcher truck's arrival interrupted the oncoming slew of more colorful Italian phrases. Ginger Nonna went running around to the front to catch him before he left.

Everyone back inside the kitchen, we watched Ginger Nonna prepare dinner. A mix of cubed beef, pork, and lamb, boiled in water, with pasta thrown in the last 10 minutes. Even my tummy was talking now.

Then, a full-fledged miracle happened at Villa Beauchemin— Exactly! Ginger Nonna ladled heaping portions into our kibble bowls and placed them on the floor! She had created the meal just for US!

Holy Moly! This exercise in passive resistance proved much successful than I projected!

Impromptu Picky-Eater Puppy still refused to eat his kibble, picking out the pieces and spitting them out on the stone tile. This simple action completely convinced Ginger Nonna that the dog food was no good.

And then, the 2nd miracle came to pass on this sacred ground— The entire bag of remaining kibble was tossed into the fire!

Hallelujah! Praise be to the Heavens and Saint Nonna! Commission a commemorative grotto to be built on this Blessed Holy Ground— Amen!

*

Early the next morning, Ginger Nonna began cooking up a storm in the kitchen which meant only one thing— Party Time!

Sure enough, stashed inside The Little One's luggage were goodies from the Parisian traiteurs and Ginger Nonna opened up her cellar to expose an impressive stock of aging cheeses and dried sausages from her last trip to Milan. The living room was tidied up. Extra chairs and little tables were brought down from the second floor.

As much as I wanted to help, "someone" gave Ginger Nonna the idea to tie me up to the tree outside. This latest treachery had "My Mistress" written all over it— Bah.

Somehow always excused from mistress-sponsored torture, Shamus was tearing up the house, running room-to-room looking for treats. Constantly underfoot, I watched as he almost tripped Ginger Nonna and The Little One every time they brought platters into the living room— Ridiculous! Had I not proved myself useful when we first arrived? If I was free, I would be able to corral the terrier-gone-wild!

Finally coming back to her senses, Ginger Nonna brought me inside to monitor the problematic puppy. As patiently as possible, I waited for him to return from his current circle-of-frenzy. The very moment that he rounded the corner, I swiped his legs out from underneath him.

"Hey! Niki! Why'd you do that? I could've broken something."

Look at this rate that only thing you are going to break is the record of how many times a terrier runs uselessly around the house.

"Really? Super cool! I had no idea that there was a record for that. Will I get a shiny trophy?"

No. But, you are going to get permanently grounded if you don't shut your front door and sit still. I want to show you something.

"Ok-ok. I only have eyes for you, Nikita. Just please hurry up before the pasta is finished cooking."

Rolling my eyes at the futility of showing an old puppy any new tricks, I nonetheless proceeded with the lesson.

Slowly, I walked around the living room. To the untrained eye, this appeared to be nothing more than a nonchalant stroll in search of the perfect place to rest. In reality, I was checking out the best plate to indulge in— After all a real Parisienne never, ever wastes calories!

Ginger Nonna came out of the kitchen. "Ni-Ki-Ta? Whhhat are you doing?"

Keeping her eyes locked with mine, I causally made my way back towards the coffee table with a plate of chorizo. And with a fatigued sigh, sat down.

Satisfied that I was behaving myself, she returned to the kitchen.

Now Shamus, watch very closely.

Double-checking that I only had my canine witness, I tilted my head towards the plate.

Removing only one slice of chorizo, I quickly swiveled back, right before Ginger Nonna peeked in.

Seeing two idly sitting dogs and seemingly nothing amiss, she returned to her cooking.

"Cool beans! Nikita, show me again!"

With pleasure, my little pupil!

Not the fastest learner, the plate had only a couple of slices left by the time that he was ready to try. Jumping up on the couch, he leaned in for a nibble just when Ginger Nonna appeared in the doorway.

"Shay-mooose! Nooooo!"

Caught in the middle of a botched attempt, Shamus looked at me for support.

Nope, not going to happen. Not now and probably not in this lifetime. You need to learn from your mistakes puppykins, to be accountable even if only for your intentions!

"But, Niki! That's not fair! I didn't even get a single—"

Before he could file an appeal, CSI Nonna removed the perfect scapegoat locking him in the upstairs bedroom. Coming back into the living room, she picked up the plate with a grimace.

Impossible to offer the suspected Shamus slobber sausage slices to her guests. She looked in my direction and with a shrug, offered the last two slices to moi— Score!

With my tummy super full, the terrier thorn-in-my-side removed, and the house beginning to fill with her guests A.K.A. my admirers, it felt like a vacation again!

*

Ginger Nonna was packing and The Little One was going around closing the shutters. This meant only one thing— Vacation's over A.K.A. Time to return to Paris. Bummer.

Ginger Nonna apologized for our hasty departure. My Mistress had called late last night, claiming that she "missed" us and wanted to have us back today.

Seriously?! What's the hurry? Did you botch up the romantic get-away with our boyfriend? Did you embarrass yourself in front of his family?

No telling what kind of Mistress induced drama we were going to be subject to back home. Thankfully, Ginger Nonna had enough time for one last walk through the neighborhood. A parting gift, a little fresh air before breathing in the environmental, and emotional, pollution back in Paris.

At the end of the street, the goat was chomping grass so enthusiastically that it did not hear us approach A.K.A. have time to skedaddle to the barn, as usual.

Reaching out to say, "Hello! Pleasure to finally meet you! I could smell you all the way down the street!" — Well, before I could utter more than the simple "bonjour," our non-social neighbor grazed my nose with her horn!

OUCHHHH! When Turnips Fry! That was not very nice!

About to return the favor with my bared canines, Ginger Nonna yanked me back towards her house. I tried to convince her to let me have a little more time with the nasty ninny, but she insisted to clean me up before My Mistress saw the bloody disaster on my bib— You do know, nose wounds are always the messiest!

Turning back towards ill-tempered chèvre, she had already hoofed it back to her barn— Humphhh.

Our visit might have been interrupted, but no worries! I know where you live and promise to make a house call the very next time that I'm in town. After all, I owe you an educative session and trust me— YOU are at the very top of the scholastic list! Yes, indeed!

Back at the house, Ginger Nonna fussed over me until the wound stopped bleeding. Under her breath a heard her mutter "L'Americaine" and. "une cicatrice." Most excellent! If my filling-in-the-gaps French was correct. My Mistress would be upset by my latest escapade and I had finally earned my second permanent war-wound! I just wish that Sneak-Attack Goat had aimed someplace other than my nose— Let's face it, I already had my very 1st scar there from Queen Nutjob! It would've been nice to accessorize a different part of my body.

All the same, I couldn't wait to see the look on Mistress Perfectionism-Is-My-Flaw's face when she saw me! For once, I could not wait to get home.

Home. Such a pleasure to walk in the door, sit down, and be alone. The trip wasn't horrible, just intense. My boyfriend had decided to cut out our couple time to spend more time with his family. They were welcoming, very gracious and patient with my awkward conversational French. And, I enjoyed a few one-on-one moments spent in the kitchen with his sister who showed me her cooking techniques and shared family recipes.

However, the vacation was akin to cultural immersion boot camp. Ten solid days and eleven nights of 8 adults, 4 kids, 1 dog, 2 cats, with the constant drone of the television or radio in the background. My mind was suffering French overload from sorting through the simultaneous conversations not knowing what they were always talking about and not always aware if they were talking to me or about me. It was a relief to be home, close the door, and have the silence.

I had 24 hours to detox and unwind before Nikita and Shamus were scheduled to come home. Still with the Italian woman, the lucky pups had been invited to her countryside house, so there was no way to get them any earlier. As much as I missed them, I was thankful to have the time to myself.

When I did pick them up the next day, the Italian woman regaled me with stories of her adventures with Nikita in the forest. It seems as though Niki tried to get between a wild boar and her piglets. It took the combined force of both her and her male companion to reign Nikita in.

She was happy with Nikita and already thinking of things to do with her in the country for the next time. That was music to my ears. I already had a trip to the US planned and didn't want to take Nikita in cargo hold. As I was floating the dates past her, Nikita finally sauntered out from the kitchen.

Oh Buggers!

There was a huge slash across the tip of Niki's nose. The Italian woman explained that the neighbor's goat was out and swiped Nikita as they walked past. I shrugged. Nothing to do and nothing that wouldn't have happened on my watch.

She let out a sigh of relief. "Thank goodness. You're American, but not like the others."

Not exactly sure what that was supposed to mean, I smiled and took it as a compliment to be deciphered later.

*

Spring was in the air and with the rising temperatures and longer days, the French began the season of picnics. My boyfriend and I joined the other Parisians, along the Seine, with a blanket laid out over the stones. It was so romantic to sip a little wine and share a few kisses watching the riverboats drift by as the city lights began to illuminate the city.

Tonight, we were going to one of his friend's house close to Chantilly for my 1st French barbeque. I was a little surprised that they embraced the idea of the American barbeque, until I saw the interpretation.

There were no hamburgers or hot dogs on the grill, no macaroni salad or coleslaw, and definitely no soda or beer. Instead, making an American tradition more "French," on the grill were sausages and varied cuts of lamb and beef; and placed on the table; were bowls of couscous, green salad, and roasted vegetables, several baguettes fresh from the bakery, and bottles of red wine and sparkling water. It all smelled really, really good.

The friend's home was a beautiful property, with a stone-walled backyard garden where they set up tables and lanterns. Seeing that the wall was high enough to make it impossible for Nikita to escape, I let both dogs off leash to explore and enjoy the party.

Niki made her way around saying "hello" to everyone and scrounging table scraps. Shamus explored the backyard. Climbing to the top of a pile of wood, he turned around and began to bark at the guests.

Everyone started laughing at the spectacle. And when he would not stop, they asked me what he was doing.

Laughing uncomfortably at his odd behavior, I said, "Obviously the little dog, now on very top of a mountain of wood, has a Napoleon complex."

The entire party fell silent.

Simultaneously, everyone's head turned to me.

I could feel the color rising to my face as I felt the bewildered stares.

Finally, one out of 20 voices popped the unbearable silence. "Comment? How was that? What do you mean to say?"

Not sure exactly what was wrong, I explained my off the cuff comment. "Well, you know… A little dog who's just like a little person thinking that he's something special because all of a sudden he's big."

Silence.

Complete, total silence.

20 angry faces staring at me.

Turning a deeper shade of crimson, I stuttered over French and English words trying to dig myself out. Sensing the need to redirect the conversation, my boyfriend finally came to the rescue with, "Who needs a little more coffee?"

Who needs an idiot box when you've got these TWO? However, let me tell you a TV is faaarrrrr preferable because you can turn it OFF— If only, I could find the remote and press the mute button!

Interrupting the flow of human conversation, Shamus climbed to the top of a pile of leaves from where Raise-Your-Freak-Flag-High Terrier proclaimed, "I am the King of the Soirée! Now, give me your viande hachée!"

Somewhat impressed by his application of correct French and his ability to rhyme in a foreign language, the stupid American dog was asking for hamburger when there was fresh-off-the-grill chorizo available!

Not to be outdone by the little American mutt's crass naïveté, Mistress Poor Judgment contributed to the farce insulting French sensibilities by comparing the terrier widget, a 10lb barking tantrum to a formidable general, a beloved humanitarian who captured the hearts of his countrymen with his encouragement of science and support of the arts, and who was also a revolutionary thinker introducing the Napoleonic Code which transformed the world's political stage by creating room for equality— Seriously? Even I was stunned by her latest faux pas.

Afraid that Mistress Self-Sabotage messed it up for good this time and not wanting to hoof it all the way back to Paris, I nuzzled up to French Basel reminding him that not all Americans are that gauche. Thankfully, he agreed to give us a ride back home— Albeit, a silent one.

Unfortunately, that particular silence lasted many, many days.

Every time that the phone rang, she jumped on it. And every other minute, she was checking her "social media." But judging by her sour puss, the pajama's all-day attire, and the growing number of cigarettes in the ashtray, French Beau had said his final adieu— Oh jeeps! Mistress Loose Lips really botched it up for me this time.

Just when I had given up all hope, the doorbell rang AND he was there! Pushing her out of the way, I let him know how much I missed him and how much I'd prefer for him to take full custody, if he decided to part ways again.

"Ahhhh, Nee-Kee-Ta. Moi aussi, je t'aime."

And, there you have it folks. A declaration of love before she even got a single like! Such is the curse of my charmed existence, to be loved and adored by all!

"Oh, Nikita. Truer words have never been said."

No need to restate the obvious, my redundant terrier.

"But Niki! I can't help myself! In fact, the whole world can't help but love you! You're perrrrrrrfect. Rrrrrrrreally perrrrrrrrrfect!"

Have you developed a new speech impediment?

"No. Don't be silly Nikita! I'm trying to be a cat"

Now I'm certain that I am going to regret this, but why do you want to be a cat?

"Because cats purrrrrrrrrrr."

Continue carefully. You do know, "Curiosity killed the cat."

"Yes, but, 'Satisfaction brought it back.' Anyway, the purr? That particular sound vibrates at up to 150 times per second! And that's how many times per second that I want to say, 'I love you' each and every second, of each and every day!"

And then, came the puppy kisses— Ugghhhh.

*

Flowers in full bloom and lovestruck admirers at every corner— It must be Springtime in Paris! With the scent of lilacs and love in the air, even Mistress Lovelorn was in good spirits taking advantage of the longer daylight hours with even longer walks!

At the top of Rue Chappe, we bumped into a Golden Labrador. Not exactly crossing paths, as it looked like he was setting up his home-base on the dead-end courtyard square. A very wise move for a homeless dog as all the American tourists stopped there completely winded from the adjoining staircase— Exactly! Totally out-of-shape, they'd reach that first landing and argue about whether to go back down the 2 flights and fork over the 2 Euros for the funicular or continue the climb-up, about 300 more steps, to the top. Maybe, one day he'd get more than scraps of leftover crepes and ice cream, like a one-way ticket to Cleveland! Hah!

As locals, we did not need to stop and most certainly did not want to encourage friendships with strays and their migratory fleas— My Mistress and I were for one moment on the same page! Turning a blind eye to the vagabond, we kept chugging up the staircase full-steam.

Hearing someone behind us, hoping French Beau took off work for a mid-day surprise, I glanced back see Goldielocks just a few steps behind!

True, it might've just been a coincidence that he was behind us, closing in fast— And true, the stamina required to overtake Mistress Thunder Thighs was impressive— However, it felt weird. Just plain wrong. Even, Mistress Nonchalant Aires was creeped out. Stopping at the top of the stairs, she shooed the unwanted tag-a-long away.

But, he refused!

Instead, he pushed his way in-between us. Almost shoving her off the landing, he sidled up next to me.

"All-o Belle! Belle-Belle-Belle."

Please go away. I have no interest in monosyllabic mutts.

"Belle-Belle-Belle."

Forcefully prodding him off to the side, My Mistress continued our walk picking up the pace— But, no matter how fast we walked OR how quickly we turned weaving in-and-out through the tourists at Place du Tertre, Goldie Zombie was only a "Belle-Belle-Belle" breath away!

Oh Mon Dieu! Please tell me that the God-line is open! This is an emergency! We have a volatile, high-risk situation— Exactly! This is not just another ardent admirer, not some "springtime fling"— Oh, no! This is a stalker dog! Incroyable! I thought that these things only happened in New York!

This was just crazy! Always 3 steps behind, muttering "Belle-Belle-Belle" on a continuous loop, he followed us through the tourist packed streets, down the backside of the hill, and into the little-known residential part of our neighborhood— Until, we stopped at a red light.

Seeing our law-abiding stop as an invitation, over-excited Goldie Stalker sided right up to us!

The light longer than anticipated, the traffic too fast to jaywalk— We were trapped at the street corner!

Confusing my inability to escape with a solicitation for something more, Incorrectly-Stimulated Goldie-Stalker attempted to mount me— AAACKKKKKKK!

Seeing unwanted mutant, hybrid puppies in the future, My Mistress yanked me away and stepped in-between with a bent knee thrust into the offender's midsection.

WoW! Nicely done, Mistress Swift Intervention!

Without a second's delay, she pivoted on her heeled boots and scampered up the staircase back to our side of the butte, leaving the breathless heap sprawled out on the sidewalk.

Not to be so easily thwarted, Goldie Stalker shadowed us all the way home!

Oh Mon Dieu! Do you not understand the word, "No?" How about, "Non?!"

This must be the sexually-driven male equivalent of the original psycho-stalker-pup, Spring! I didn't particularly care for the first version, no need to suffer though a horny re-make— Even if, it's a French-speaking one!

Rounding the last corner back to the Rue des Trois Frères, I let out a distress cry.

BOOM!

Flirt popped out of the bar.

BA-BOOM!

Otis rolled out of his doorway.

Both were quick to assess the situation.

Blocking Goldie, they corralled him into the alley for a "private talk."

Mistress Security-Threat-Level-Orange took a quick look back, double-checking that our unwanted friend was out of sight before we entered our building.

Of little surprise during this whole escapade, Shamus was of zero help. My Mistress had picked him up, holding him safely in her arms, after Goldielocks, in his ardent quest, almost trampled over the pipsqueak— Just between us? This is the one and only time that I wished she would've picked me up and held me in the Embarrassment Zone!

Back in the sanctuary of our apartment, I felt dirty. Completely slimed. So much so, I actually prayed for a cubicle shower! Unfortunately, the God-line must have been down for maintenance, because the only thing she washed was my feet— Sighhhhh.

Trying to find solace on my cedar cushion, I curled up tight into a ball with my tail wrapped over my eyes in an attempt to elude my current reality A.K.A. Shamus, The Terrier Stalker. The Gateway to Hell must've been open. Why? Because once again today, I had absolutely zero luck.

"Niki-Niki-Niki. Are you okay? That was soooo scary! I thought that we may never escape! Soooo nice of our neighbors to help out. Maybe, we should write them a thank-you note or toss them a bone? Do you think that they'd like a 'Greenie' or is it too American for their French sensibilities. You know, chicken bones are no good because they splinter and can cause severe damage to the intestinal tract. However, the cartilaginous joints are rather chewy and provide an excellent source of calcium. Did you see how big he was? And, soooo persistent? I was soooo thankful that our mistress had my carry tote with her. I felt super-duper safe as the sides hugged me tight. Do you think that I've gained weight and that the tote's perhaps a little too snug? I'm hoping that it's more muscle than fat. With all the stairs and all the walking, it's most likely the case. Perhaps, on our next vet visit they could measure my BMI. Oh jeeps! Enough about me. Would you like a hug? Or, just a little cuddle?"

And before I could respond, before I could move out of its path, came the Warm-Fuzzy Terrier Express powered by puppy kisses—Ughhhhh.

*

Mistress Everything-In-Its-Right-Place was trying to make it look like we didn't live there anymore which meant only ONE thing— Exactly! Company! Most fantastic! I see relief from her constant conversation— Wait! Better yet, I see presents in my future!

When she changed the sheets on our bed, I was concerned that Mistress Questionable-Personal-Boundaries might force the visitor to bunk with us. Fortunately, our already crammed full-of-shoes space was spared this calamity as this was just her "impress-the-guests" routine.

Walking over to the hotel on Rue Ravignan, we met our company in the lobby— Grandma C!

WooHoo!

Before tackling Present Mountain, I gave Grandma C a very thorough sniff-down making certain all her bits-and-parts were still attached. Happy was I to report that not only was she a Voracious Terrier Co-Habitation Survivor— No Giz-molars were attached! Obviously, my well-placed calls to the God-line for her protection from the black-butterball schnauzer had been answered!

As usual, her puffy, jet-lagged eyes welled up with tears. This time, her nose turning Rudolph-red from violent sneezes.

That's right Grandma C, sneeze that Gizmo straight out! You have entered a Guaranteed Gizmo-Free-Zone. No fear of reprisal, no fear of re-infection, no fear of retaliation. Now, how about I give you some extra love— enough for you to take home as a souvenir!

Pressing and rubbing with all my affection against her legs, I was certain that a green-eyed Gizmo would have an epic conniption fit— ♫ Oh Happy Day! ♫

That happiness quadrupled when emerging from the elevator, walking towards us came a tall, most handsome man— Grandma C's man-friend! What a fantabulous surprise!

Decorum pushed aside, I reached up to his lofty heights. Gently placing a paw on each of his broad shoulders, I puckered up for a proper kiss.

To be expected, Mistress Forever Jealous snapped my lead preventing me from laying a big smooch on Big V.

PL-ease! No need for such dramatics— For once, be realistic! There's absolutely No Way, I would compete for male attention with The Reformed Hummer. God only knows what'd happen once his affections naturally gravitated towards my sweet, lovable, irresistible self!

Mistress Unnecessary Intervention's latest antics quickly forgotten, I had a most fantastic reunion with Grandma C and Big V! As expected, lots and lots and lots of presents— And, most unexpectedly, lots of free time, too!

Always thoughtful and gracious, they kept My Mistress and the terrier thorn-in-my-side busy all day long— Precisely!

Falling for their ruse, Mistress Aspiring-Tour-Guide and her totebag terrier happily helped our guests negotiate the Parisian metro, streets, and sights.

After traipsing all around Paris, in-and-out of stores and museums, entertained by Mistress Long-Winded's commentaries comprised of non-sensical facts, Grandma C was in need of a solid break and an entire bottle of Chiroubles!

Always full of pleasant surprises, proving to be ever more thoughtful and more gracious, Grandma C and Big V invited me to join them for dinner A.K.A. My Favorite Culinary Indulgence!

Have a mentioned lately that I ♥ Grandma C AND Her Man?!

One short week later, our company said their goodbyes to return to the emotional chaos and psychological games from the chronically unhappy Gizminator. As I tried to comfort Grandma C lavishing her with as much Love-and-Appreciation as possible, her eyes once again filled up with tears. It was simply heartbreaking to see her in such a state, obviously anxious about the impending doomsday drama in the Gizmo-Occupation Zone.

There was really nothing that could be done, except to offer even more love— Along with my most sincere promises to aid in the recovery-effort by creating a kick-starter page. Ha-ha!

The very moment My Mistress returned from Charles-de Gaulle, she tore our house up in a frenetic cleaning episode, again— Un-precedented!

You never clean like this twice in ONE week! What, pray-tell, is going on? Are you trying to "de-grandmother" our home? She is The Best, The Only, thing to walk in here since French Beau!

Mistress Freaky Sneaky was up to something and post-goodbye trauma, I was in no mood for any surprises! However, do you think that she cared?! Oh, no. Never feeling the need to include me in any scheduling changes, she leashed up the bugger boy and my sweet self, dragging us on a metro ride to the posh side of the 17th arrondissement where we walked a new-to-moi street.

There was something very wrong about this scenario. My antennae were way, way up!

Mistress Information Control stopped at a door and rang the buzzer. A solid premonition washed over me that this was not going to go well.

Wait-Wait-WAIT! That door is locked. I'm thinking that there's an excellent reason for the added security! I smell a lot of small dogs, on the other side— A whole lot! Please, just once in your life, listen to me. *PL*-ease, don't make me beg— Whatever you do next, DO NOT open that door! There are some things that you just can-not un-see!

Refusing to heed my warning, the door swung open to reveal my worst nightmare A.K.A. an endless sea of Shamuses— ACKKKKK!

Wave after wave of pint-sized, animated fur balls came rushing towards us.

Ughhhhh. Nausea swept over me.

Lifting my head in an attempt to clear my field of vision and my head, I saw yet another unprecedented and highly-disturbing sight— Rodent-sized Shamuses frolicking inside a doll house! Proof Positive that we should have never, ever stepped inside this laboratory posing as a storefront which was obviously colonizing a strand of terrier bacteria to infect the entire Parisian canine population!

Without another moment's hesitation, I zipped my lips, refusing to breathe or budge another inch.

No Way was I going to enter the Yorkie Contamination Zone and become Patient Zero of the oncoming Yorkie Epidemic!

Not to be confused with Mistress Catastrophise-Every-Situation, allow me to reassure you that this was not an irrational fear. This was in fact, a valid concern based on solid evidentiary proof— Exactly! Obviously exposed, the salon owner herself already showed signs of metamorphosis!

PL-ease, no other explanation is possible, is plausible, for a French Woman with natural blond hair to have a "well-clipped, terrier hair-do" and to be speaking in high-pitched, staccato tones! None! Absolutely none!

"Niki, did we just open the doorway to Heaven?"

No, not at all. This is more like an earthly version of a lower ring of Hell.

"Are you certain Nikita? This is the first time that I feel at home in Paris."

Please. Eventually, they will start speaking to you and you will start hyperventilating.

"No. Seriously Nikita. This is like a dreamscape. As if, I'm in a mirrored room looking at images of myself, in different aspects of my life's journey. This is far better than one of my yoga meditations. This is truly a lucid dream."

No. This is a wealthy-and-bored human subversion of the natural order of things.

Ignoring me, wandering off into a wave of blond and tan fluff, Shamus disappeared— POOOFFFF!

Under no circumstance was I going to follow. No-No-NO! This was farrrr beyond my "Save-the-Shamus" threshold!

Sticking much closer to My Mistress than preferred, I placed an emergency request on the God-line. We had to leave before I became infected and morphed into a giant version of arghhhhhhh— I dare not utter the words into this skewed reality!

The God-line available 24/7 for requests in this high-rent, high-pledge neighborhood, we left before any transformation took place— Merci-Merci-Merci Dieu!

The connection even more privileged than I thought, my subconscious request was also honored— Exactly! Walking at a breakneck pace out of the exclusion-zone to the contamination-reduction-zone, we hoofed it sans-metro ALL the way back to Montmartre, straight to Quat' Pats!

The staff immediately recognizing my predicament, took me without an appointment. Expert hands massaged my body, working up a specially-formulated shampoo into a thick lather to suffocate any residual Yorkie Fungus. The power jet rinse washed it ALL away into the Parisian sewer. They even cleaned and trimmed my nails!

To be treated like royalty after such a harrowing, near-death experience = one of life's small blessings— Amen.

Unfortunately, that was a rather short-lived blessing as Mistress Chronic-Poor-Choices decided to extract the out-of-my-sight, out-of-his-mind terrier from the contamination zone. Just this once, I wish she'd give me some extra terrier-free time instead of importing the high-on-the-terrier-life junkie back into our idyllic home!

"Niki-Niki-Niki! Look at me! I look Parisian, un vrai Français!"

Perhaps, but your accent gives you away. So, how about you keep silent. Maintain the illusion, Frenchy Fido.

"Ah come on. I look really good. You've got to admit, it's a transformation!"

I do not have to do any-thing!

"Check it out! The lady even gave me a curtain!"

Curtain? Looks more like a mullet, to me!

"You're so funny. It's just a little fringe to keep my privates warm."

Seriously? Reality check please for one eunuch terrier! You do not have a package anymore. You traded your testosterone generator in for a temporary lampshade A.K.A. party favor!

"Well now, no one has to know that!"

Quelling my tongue, I inhaled deeply and looked up. A slight change of perspective, an eye rotation of a single degree upwards and— POOF! No more Shamus!

Unfortunately, this did not apply to his verbiage which traveled all too clearly to my ears sight unseen. Talking-talking-talking. Never saying much of anything, he was always finding new ways to abrade my peaceful, loving nature.

"Nikita, what's wrong? You seemed troubled. Are you upset? Does it bother you that I can't give you puppies?"

Hmmmmm. You know me so well don't you.

Of little surprise, the sarcasm escaped his pea-brained perception.

"Oh yes! I know everything about you! You're my most favorite subject. I've spent my whole life studying you, Nikita. Watching everything, listening to everything, absorbing every single detail!"

Ok, Mr. Honorary-Degree-in-Advanced-Nikita, what are my favorite four letters?

"L-O-V-E?"

No.

"T-A-L-K?"

N-o, No!

"Nikita, that's only 2—"

Shamus!

"Of course, you do know that the word "no" spelled the Irish way—"

S-t-o-p, Stop!

"Wow! Really?! I had no idea! Not a single clue. Thank you, Niki, for sharing something new about you today. I feel so much

closer to you with every layer peeled away, with every aspect that I discover, with every nuance revealed.

"Do you know my favorite 4 letter word? Let me show you!"

Before I could protest, before I could escape, I found myself front row and center to Puppy Slobber Cabaret— Ughhhhhh.

Ughhhhhh. This was embarrassing. With all the excited little Yorkshire Terriers bouncing around the grooming salon, I could not recognize Shamus.

An article that I had read, highlighted this groomer and her salon calling it the "premier location" for Yorkshire Terriers in Paris. Whether it was the truth or the buzz from the article, it took a month before Shamus could get an appointment.

Stepping inside the salon was like entering a taping of "Animal Planet's Dogs 101: The Yorkshire Terrier." Yorkies everywhere. Every surface had a Yorkshire Terrier on it, living, stuffed, porcelain, portrait, or otherwise. There was even a dollhouse full of teacup puppies for sale.

Finally, I identified Shamus by his harness. He was running around the store, playing with his clones. It was the first time I had ever seen him happy at the groomers. He even seemed a bit reluctant to leave.

But, leave we must. I had a friend coming in the morning and had many things to take care of before her plane landed.

Her first visit to Paris after many years, we were going to explore the city a little before heading on a road-trip through France. We had lots of ideas, but no set itinerary. Traveling in Europe isn't the same as in the states. Whether driving from one point to the next or simply checking into a hotel, things always take longer than planned. And, there's always that place that you discover and simply don't want to leave. With a little luck, good signage, and a tank full of petrol, we'd have quite the adventure!

By the next morning, the house was prepped, the dogs groomed, the car rented, and the 1st night's hotel reserved. I made my way to Charles De Gaulle arriving just in time to find my friend coming out of the revolving door.

A revolving door policy now applied to our home! Unbelievable! We had company, again! When would she find middle ground? Mistress Social-Life-Pendulum swung from lonely and forlorn to social butterfly and over-scheduled! However, now all that cleaning and the dishing out the big bucks for grooming made perfect sense!

Waltzing in the door with her friend in-tow, there was something oddly familiar about this woman AND not in a good way! On second sniff, this was no friend! Not in the very least! This was Lumer! The female counterpart to the Keeper of Queen— Treachery! To have such a reminder of darker days invade my Parisian home— Grrrrrrrr!

Right before I went to assert my position, the interloper reached inside her bag and pulled out a dinosaur bone A reminder of the good ol' days, my first hunting days at The Farm.

Sighhh. Perhaps, there is some wisdom to be found in keeping your enemies close. Besides, as I snuggled in with a little "thank-you," what a perfect way to torture Queen— To know I am still alive and waiting for my chance to settle the score! More perfect yet— Mistress Self-Appointed-Cruise-Director had all sorts of activities planned with our guest A. K. A. Out-of-the-house, Out-of-my-hair, All-Day-Long!

*

Waking up from a little snooze, the house was blessedly quiet with one exception— Exactly! Snoring! So loud, Shamus was waking himself up with the racket, muttering unintelligible words, before going back to work on destroying the forest! Ridiculous!

In our miniscule flat, it didn't take much to locate the source of my habitual irritation. Simply looking up from my slumber, I laid eyes on the rhonchus dreamer drooling in our guest's clean
clothes— Unbelievable!

Hey, hey! Wake-up Dryer-Sheet Terrier and get out of her suitcase!

"I can't. It smells so, so good in here."

Move it! Now! I can hear them staggering up the stairs from tonight's escapes.

"But Niki, it smells just like our first home."

Shamus, do not bury your nose in memories. You are not an ostrich!

"Ahhhhh, just like The Farm."

Focus on only the past and you will miss this moment A.K.A. No present A.K.A. No future!

The little terrier twerp shuddered as he began to calculate the trajectory of his current
wayward path.

Wait a second! Epiphany being downloaded— Re-write!

Aaaand, Take 2!

Since you're so freaking unhappy here, why not just bury yourself a little deeper and hitch a ride back to the states?!

"Niki I'm sorry-I'm sorry-I'm sorry-I'm sorry."

Instead of following with the usual spray of puppy kisses, I was most unpleasantly surprised as he hopped out of 3rd class stowage to New Jersey and into my 1st class cedar bed, spooning his furry, little body into mine— Ughhhhh!

"Niki, that was super-duper scary. The simple suggestion, the mere thought of not having you in my day-to-day existence gave me chicken-bumps! Brrrrrrrr."

Huh? You mean "goose bumps."

"No, Niki. Chicken bumps. I'm far too little to have goose bumps."

SNARK!

There are times when you just have to walk away AND I tried but today it was impossible to break free from Industrial Strength Velcro Dog! Even worse, in addition to the full-body-press, he continued with his mind-numbing rhetoric! Why is the God-line always down for maintenance when I need it the most?! Ughhhhh.

"Niki, I absolutely love my life in Paris! Do you know why?

No. Nor, do I care.

"Well, it's very simple logic."

Oh lord, please spare me. Nothing's ever simple with the neurotic nugget. I rolled my eyes up to heaven, once again imploring the God-line to intercede— But, it seems that it was still down for maintenance.

"If, my life in Paris is beautiful. And if, Nikita is beautiful. Then, it logically follows that, Nikita is My Life!"

Oh, Shamus. I sincerely appreciate the sentiment, but your logic is thoroughly bunked.

"No, it's not. I have an advanced understanding of logical matters. In fact, I am working toward my 500-hour certificate in—"

Stop! Sleeping on textbooks does not qualify as hours towards any degree! Now, please listen up to this piece of applied "Shamus-style" logic.

If Shamus is small. And if, an M&M is small. Then, Shamus is a M&M! Now, do you see how flaw—

"Ohhhh, Nikita! You think I'm sweet and little, but something you'd never eat just like a chocolate candy? Thank you! That's the nicest thing that you've ever said to me! My Nikita, My One, My Only, I Love You!"

Right before the shower of puppy slobber reached me, the God-line finally kicked in. My Mistress and Lumer stumbled through the door and the Shamus smooches were bestowed on them.

Hallelujah! Saved from puppy slime and time for my evening constitution = Life is very good, again!

*

Just when I thought that my life couldn't get any better, it actually did! Lumer convinced Mistress Homebody to leave Paris and go on a vacation! Of course, it would've been absolutely perfect if we hadn't of taken Shamus— But, there was always the possibility that we would ditch him somewhere!

Lost in my Shamus-free daydreams, I was jolted awake by the bumper car parallel parking skills of Mistress Valet-Parking-Only. Anxious to stretch my legs after the long and rather bumpy ride, I jumped of the car and almost lost my footing on the sand.

Wait, sand?! No one mentioned that we were going to the beach! You are aware that is not-at-all a vacation destination for a girl who prefers the frozen tundra! Did you take a wrong turn on the way to The Alps?

Then, it dawned on me. This vacation was not for me— Not for Mistress Sunburnt-in-15-Minutes— Not even for Lumer A. K. A. Mrs. Give me an easel, a paintbrush, and a view— Exactly! This sunshine sojourn was for Shamus!

This was made all too clear moments after Mistress Questionable Priorities unleashed him. The new poster child for

"Raise your Freak Flag High" wiggled his paws in the sand before running elliptical circles on the beach nose first!

"Niki, you have got to try this! This sand thing is grrrreat! Just like snow, but it's not cold!"

This is nothing like snow.

"I know, it's hot and sticks to my nose instead of melting! Just look at the design I've created for you! It's the 13 petaled Flower of Loooove! Ahhhhhh. The sun's super, duper hot on my back. It feels soooo good. I think I'm going to catch a few rays. You know, get some color on my belly before we return to Paris. But, no swimming for me. The water looks a little rough and I doubt she remembered to pack my floatie vest. Maybe, I'll just get my feet wet and connect with the sea. The saltwater, it's restorative. Did you know that? Of course, you did. You know everything! Do you think that we'll eat fish for dinner? Of course, not our Mistress because she's allergic. But, perhaps Lumer will order and share. Come to think of it, she doesn't seem to eat very much, so most likely she'll give us her whole plate minus a couple of bites! Maybe, if I was on a diet like hers, I could be skinny like her, too! When she turns sideways, she disappears! Poof! What do you think? Yeah, probably better that I start intermittent fasting after vacation. Oh Nikita, I am so happy to be here and to share this experience with you!"

And then came one BIG crunchy, sand-tumbled kiss before Freak Show Terrier went back to his ocean-side carnival routine. For once, she was quite wise not to let me off-leash! I would have run all the way back to Paris via Switzerland!

Taking in a deep breath to clear my mind of terrier rhetoric, the scent of crêpes filled my nostrils. Mmmm-mmmm. My favorite Normandy specialty, after raw-milk camembert. With a little luck Mistress Munchies smelled it too and we'd leave the beach before I melted.

After all, it was waaaay past my lunch-time!

Time to leave the beach, check into the hotel, and find an open creperie for lunch. Shamus lollygagged behind, having way too much fun to walk with us. High on sand crack, he'd come up to say hello and then go back to running crazy 8s. For once, my healthy appetite terrier was interested in something more than food. Of course, I wasn't sure if he was eating sand. But that, time would tell one way or the other.

According to the signs posted at the entrance, the beach was prohibited to dogs. But, a quick look from one end of the beach to the other said otherwise. Dogs of all sizes were walking, playing fetch, and swimming. I didn't trust Niki off-leash. She'd run all the way to Germany and back before you'd catch her. But I figured, it was safe to let Shamus enjoy some freedom.

It was a good idea and absolutely hilarious watching him play by himself… until he chose to mark the "Interdit aux chiens" sign in front of the beach police station! Oh buggers!

My friend, Niki, and I just kept walking, pretending like he wasn't with us. For a few moments, I even considered leaving him behind. But once we got to the car, I allowed the happy little ball of sand and fur to jump in.

Normandy is a "must do" for Americans and the picturesque town of Honfleur proved to be the perfect launching point for our trip. When we checked into the hotel, the staff fell in-love with Nikita and Shamus and upgraded us to a much larger, dual-level room with an extra bed.

My friend was so excited remarking, "How thoughtful! That sweet little European single bed is perfect for the dogs!"

And it was, but Niki had other ideas. Before our luggage was unpacked, Nikita was already sprawled out over one of the king size beds claiming it as hers.

As it turned out, traveling with dogs was a breeze. In fact, the easiest part of our trip. Immediately viewed as French or European travelers, we bridged the cultural divide. Intrigued by the oddly paired, well-behaved, well-groomed dogs, the curiosity started conversations that resulted in prime dinner reservations in restaurants that were fully booked and special access into historical sites and garden grounds.

Sadly, we couldn't bring either into the Caves of Niaux. However, while my friend and I explored the underground caverns on a small group tour, Nikita and Shamus were invited into the "employee-only" area and spoiled with attention and treats.

My friend had a bucket list of places and towns to visit where famous artists had found inspiration; I was interested exploring restored chateaux and sampling regional culinary dishes. She chose where to go; I chose where to stay and eat. Most hotels accepted dogs. If not, by about the third time you asked nicely, they would either acquiesce or send you to a sister property. And yes, it is very easy to spend more on dinner than on a room. And absolutely yes, there were a few nights where we happily did just that!

My favorite hotel was a medieval castle nestled in the Tarn River Valley. Lovingly restored by a family, the attention to detail was exquisite. Stone walls, wood and stone inlay floors, walk-in fireplaces, luxuriously plush furniture, flags and banners, stepping into the foyer was like stepping back in time to the 15th century. Simply magical.

Our room, located in one of the turrets, had a painted ceiling, tapestries hanging on the walls, and the stone floors covered by woolen rugs. A custom bed, about the size of 2½ Californian Kings, provided enough room for my friend, myself, and Nikita to spread out comfortably. Shamus invariably took turns throughout the night cuddling amongst "his women."

The hotel's restaurant was a favorite with the locals and we were fortunate to secure a table for dinner. With a menu solely based on local items, dinner was skillfully prepared and perfectly presented. Worth every single franc and every single calorie.

Leaving the narrow 2-lane county roads clinging to the cliffs in the valley, we hopped on the Autoroute for Lyon where we stayed on the edge of the old city along the Saône River.

Lyon was my destination choice. Not only to explore the antiques district, the textile museums, and its culinary richness, but mostly to visit my favorite indulgence, the "maître chocolatier," Bernachon.

The last evening after dinner, we took the dogs on a walkabout winding through the serpentine streets of the Vieux Ville. Whether it was the late hour, the wine consumed at dinner, or the maze of streets and staircases in a foreign city, after about an hour of meandering we were completely turned around.

With no cell phone reception to pull up Google maps for a location, most businesses closed for the evening and with no "approachable" strangers, I looked at my dogs. They were overdue for their evening treat and whereas Nikita could be finicky, Shamus was never one to forgo his evening ritual. A little crazy, but it was worth a shot.

Stopping in the middle of the sidewalk, I addressed my 4-legged GPS machines. "Nikita. Shamus. Who wants a Greenie? Let's go! On y va!"

Both dogs immediately headed in the same direction, picking up the pace as if racing with each other. It was unbelievable the way that they navigated right back to the hotel, even jaywalking at the same spots! In less than 10 minutes, we were upstairs in our room.

Thankful for the safe and speedy return, they each got two Greenies as a reward.

A reward? A reward would be a day at the spa. A reward would be an unchaperoned trip to see Basel. A reward is something Out Of The Ordinary— Not the same freaking thing, we get every freaking night to clean our teeth, freshen our breath, and tide us over until the next meal!

Of little surprise, this simple concept escaped Mistress Lost-In-More-Ways-Than-One. The only bright side to this scenario, is that Done-in-60-Seconds Terrier finished his "reward" in four bites forcing him to watch as I lingered over mine, savoring the delicious terrier-torture well into the twilight hours.

*

"Niki-Niki-Niki! Wake-up! Wake-up! Wake-up!"

How is it even possible to stay asleep with a terrier alarm clock that's too, too far away to SMACK the snooze button?

"Niki, come on-come on-come on! Wakey, wakey! We're leaving Lyon, the gastronomic capital of France. And, you'll never guess where we're going next!"

Basel?

"Nope. Try again."

The Alps?

"Nope. Try again."

Switzerland?

"Niki, you're so silly in the morning. Try a different country."

I don't feel silly. Fact is, I don't feel like playing a game of Shamus-charades. Why don't you
just tell—

"Ormancey! We're going to Nonna's!"

Seriously?!

"Yes! Isn't it great! Our cultural and culinary odyssey continues!"

Well if it's true that's great news, but—

"Niki-Niki-Niki! Guess what else?"

Ughhhh. I am most certainly going to regret this, but what?

"They are going to teach me how to hunt for truffles! Can you imagine that?! How great will "Truffle Hunter Extraordinaire" look on my resume?"

First thing. That would be the only thing on your resume.

Second thing. You are aware that you cannot eat the truffles that you find.

"Not a problem. They're too rich and give me indigestion. However, I do understand that they are really expensive. I hope to specialize in black truffles. They're the most common in France, so they should be easy enough to find. Even just a few ounces worth, pay out handsomely! Soon, I'll be making beaucoup bucks and can buy all the Greenies I want!"

Perhaps, but it seems a bit odd. Normally, pigs are used.

"Not necessarily, the Italians use highly-trained, much-loved, well-fed dogs!"

Reality check please for one delusional terrier! We live in F-r-a-n-c-e, France! Here, they use hogs not dogs, my little oinker.

"Niki, that's not nice. You know I have image issues and struggle with my weight."

Well, the truth is not always nice.

"That's not my truth!"

Oh well, that my tubby terrier falls into the category of "Not My Problem!"

Impossible to stop a Yorkie Thought Missile once programmed to follow a trajectory, locked-on-target terrier continued.

"My Truth is that I Love You. And no matter how mean, no matter how childish, no matter how spiteful you might act, I still love you. Why? Because I know that inside that protective, snarky shell, you are all soft and cuddly-wuddly."

And then, came the puppy kisses— Ughhhhhh.

*

That very afternoon, Mistress Google It convinced Ginger Nonna to attach me to a truck tire via a 15-foot rope, under the guise that it would give me "more freedom" while keeping me "close by" AND "easier to catch."

PL-ease. The only thing you know how to catch, Mistress New Yorker, is a taxi in the rain!

Still, it was more interesting than being confined to the circumference of the tree— Better yet? The look of disbelief in Ginger Nonna's eyes as she watched me lug the circular monstrosity through her fresh plantings.

Ha-ha! You see? Not everything you read about on the Internet is a good idea.

Minding my own business, sniffing around the garden for stray critters, I heard cackling in the distance. Not quite the same pitch as My Mistress, I looked up to see the goat out of her barn snick-snick-snickering.

What's so funny? Did they put something "extra" in your salt lick?

"No, pas de tout. But, how can one not laugh at a typically gauche Americaine?"

Huh?

"Si te plaît, look at you. Accessoirisée with syn'tetic rubber! Even gypsy dogs know better bling! You're obviously no'ting more than a genetically-modified, typique Americain mutt!"

ENOUGHHH!

TAK!

I was on my way to finally continue Nasty Neighbor's lesson plan!

Somewhere behind me I could hear My Mistress, Lumer, and Ginger Nonna calling my name, pleading for me to stop—No! Absolutely n-o-t, not going to happen!

Ohhhh. My dear Mistress Alternate-Reality and friends, did you really think that a simple 100lb tire would prevent me from My Mission? Ha-ha! My People pull sleds loaded up with gear through the frozen Tundra. I can certainly access enough ancestral DNA to pull a hunk of rubber through a couple of backyard gardens! Nothing, absolutely nothing, will prevent me from confronting Ill-Tempered Chèvre face-to-face! That crass neighbor has bleated her very last insult!

Time to reduce the local heckling shrew population by one!

One minute, we were all in the garden enjoying the beautiful weather and idyllic surroundings far removed from the hustle and bustle of the city. But then, in the blink of an eye, it changed from a picture-perfect day to the surreal.

The Italian woman who had watched Niki and Shamus invited us to her home in Ormancey, a 400-year-old, stone-hewn farmstead. This was such a treat. Taking in a little sunshine, Nikita and Shamus were lazing away stretched out on the grass while we sipped a glass of rosé from a local vigneron. Life was grand... Until, Niki jumped to her feet and took-off running full throttle out of the backyard, taking with her the tire which was supposed to hinder her escape.

Our hostess, the first to react, leapt up out of her chair towards Nikita. She missed her target and landed instead on the tire. Now clinging to the tire, she was going for a ride, flying through the air.

Bounce-bounce-bounce.

Undeterred, Niki was not slowing down at all.

In what looked like an attempt to bridge the gap between herself and Niki, the woman began to climb the rope hand-over-fist.

Boommmphhh!

The tire took a bigger bounce over a low hedge and flipped over. The woman's arms and hands now entangled in the rope. She was caught under the tire as Niki continued still unthwarted.

Once again, I found myself chasing after Nikita, following in her wake, while shouting her name. The neighbors starting to filter out of their homes to witness the spectacle.

Niki finally came to a full-stop, 5 homes down, in front of a pregnant pet goat.

The goat fainted.

Not done yet, Niki seized the goat by the scruff of its neck and began a victory march back with her trophies: the goat, the pallet attached to the goat, our hostess, and the tire.

Oh please, make this be just a bad dream.

The children in the yard began crying and screaming. This was no dream.

The goat's owner charged out of his house swinging a baseball bat. Now the adults joined in the screaming, instructing the man on how to "properly" use the weapon.

Oh please, no-no-no!

Instead of bashing Niki's skull in or beating her into a bloody pulp, he deftly inserted the bat under her harness and twisted it until Niki was forced to release the goat in order to breathe.

With a sigh of relief, I grabbed Niki and pulled her away.

The Italian woman unbound herself. Lots of bruises and scrapes, but nothing was broken. Thankfully, the goat was still alive and not hemorrhaging.

From under his furrowed brow, the goat's owner gave us a look not to be trifled with and growled in French, "Turn around. Go away."

Without hesitation, we left. As we walked away, I thanked my lucky stars and our guardian angels.

Thinking it might be time to return to Paris, we all went into town for a good-bye drink. The local bistro was closed for the afternoon. However, when the owner saw the Italian woman, he let us in.

They were old friends and they had much to talk about especially after the day's excitement. She was already showing him the rope burns and animatedly gesturing the way Italians do when storytelling.

With no other patrons in the bistro, they assured me that it was safe to let Nikita have a little off-leash freedom and wander about. The door would remain closed and locked.

After the goat fiasco I was hesitant to agree, but they insisted.

An espresso was just placed in front of me when a dark grey blurrr streaked across the room into the kitchen… Nikita not far behind.

It seems as though they forgot about their "feline resident."

Running into the kitchen, we found Nikita pacing on the stainless-steel countertop looking for the cat who had found refuge between the wall and the oven.

Lacking humor after hearing about the earlier situation, the owner unceremoniously threw all of us out of the bistro, adding, "Never come back. Never."

Tears in her eyes, the Italian woman was shaking her head as she walked with us back to her house and our car.

After a heavy silence came the apologetic decision.

The dogs would not be able to stay behind with her as planned for the next couple of weeks. The day's escapes had cost her friendships with good neighbors, good people. Perhaps in the future, she'd be more inclined and better equipped to handle Niki's intensity.

What a day…

What a day! To have my escapes go viral through-out town within the hour was The Perfect End to Our Epic Vacation through France!

After recognizing me by the tell-tale scar on my nose, Espresso Cat became a little skittish. Not wanting his only impression to be of my undeserved notoriety, I followed after caffeine-charged kitty to assure him of my good intentions.

Mon petit chaton, my little kitty. No need to worry. The classroom is closed for vacation. I only have a few questions—GASSSSP!

Before I could get the full scoop on the gossip circulating around town, Mistress Needless Interference swooped in, pulling me off my vantage point and back into the restaurant.

What, pray-tell, is wrong with you, now? You have your friend and my Ginger Nonna to keep you company. Why won't you let me make one single friend? You know, someone to visit with my next time here.

"But Niki, I'm here. You always have a friend in me, indeed!"

Oh Shamus, of the many words I could choose to describe what you mean to me, how I would coin our relationship, "friend" is not one.

"Ohhhh, that is so beautiful Nikita. You always find a way to stir my heart. I also find our relationship beyond description, beyond the confines of a simple word. On our ride back to Paris, allow me describe all the things I love about you."

No, no. That's ok. Instead, let's just have a moment of quiet reflection.

And for the first time ever in his existence, the incessant flow of words stopped! The puppy lips zipped into a silly grin. His eyes glassed over with lucid dreams of sugar plum love fairies dancing.

My smoldering eyes set to the horizon, only on the inside did I smile— Hmmmmmm.

*

Back in Paris, Lumer was packing up her bags while Mistress 127-Year-Old-Millennial was on the phone texting and talking.

PL-ease how rude! Act your age, not your dress size! We have a guest! Do you think that you could put the phone down for just a few minutes before you are alone again, forever and ever?

Sidling up to comfort Lumer, she assured me, "Oh sweetheart, don't you worry. She'll find someone to watch you."

Huh? If that's the case, she could've just left me with my Ginger Nonna— Wait! Better yet, I'm certain Basel would love to arrange for his pilot to fetch me.

Never listening to my advice, Mistress Other Ideas hung up the phone with a victory smile.

Uh-ohhh— It was never a good sign for ME when she was that happy.

With little ceremony, we left Lumer at Charles de Gaulle and drove through the countryside in the opposite direction of Le Bourget— AACKKKK!

Once again, she was lost! And, this time with considerable consequences— Exactly! I'd miss my cushy little 1st class ride to Switzerland! How long would the pilot wait before flying back without me? Ridiculous! She'd stop at nothing to sabotage my happiness! She even refused to crack the window open a smidgen!

With my very best Gizmo sigh, I turned my head towards the window just in time to catch the sign for Meaux— Wait a second, as in "Brie de Meaux?" My favorite triple crème indulgence? For the very 1st time ever, I might actually be happy that My Mistress did not listen to me!

Finally stopping the car in front of a stone fortress, there was no button for her to push-push-push. So, Mistress Minimal-Effort was forced to exit the car and lift the cast iron knocker.

One-two — Three-four.

From a hidden side door, a man came out and greeted all three of us before getting into our car.

Wait! Have we learned nothing from all those police dramas you watch on a continuous loop? No matter how good he might smell, how kind his smile might seem, how polished his French might be, inviting a strange man into your car AND driving into a secluded, wooded area is a Very Bad Idea! I do not want my image on a milk carton!

Once again, Mistress Listening-Only-To-The-Voices-In-Her-Head ignored my concerns! When would she ever— What is that?!

On the crest of the hill was a circular enclosure with dogs. Lots and lots and LOTS of barking dogs!

Seriously? No home-stay? Afraid I'll stay and never come home? Why, oh why, would you lock me up like this in a veritable dog prison? How am I ever supposed to get my beauty sleep at Party Barkers Central? Please, tell me that at least you've arranged for me to be in isolation.

"Niki, this place looks pretty nice."

This is no Club Canine.

"Yeah, but look at this! We have our very own suite with an indoor living space and an outdoor run! There's even a deck for me to sun myself! And, I hear they offer recreational activities, like an obstacle course, hiking trails, and even a pool! Of course, I'm not one for swimming, but the obstacle course sounds really cool. I'd like to try something new. You know, shake up the routine. Do you think there's a zip-line too? I'd love to feel the air as I wizzzzz on through the forest canopy. It must be just like flying without a plane or driving really fast without a car!"

My upper lip twitched at the thought of granting him either experience by slingshotting him through the air— Without a parachute!

Shamus, perhaps you'd like to take advantage of our sun deck while you're still alive and breathing.

"Ooohhh. That's a very good idea. Niki, you are always so thoughtful. It makes me happy to see how much you care about my happiness, my well-being. And as always, you're right. Best to catch the evening rays, so I don't get burnt. I'm pretty sure she forgot to pack my sunscreen which is okay because it can also inhibit Vitamin D production. And, I'll need to keep my strength, my stamina up to run the course tomorrow!"

Yes, yes. Off you go! I'll just stay inside. And, remember to rotate yourself frequently like a rotisserie chicken! Ha-ha!

*

Sunny every day and with no one to keep Tanorexic Terrier in check, Mistress Shrug-My- Responsibilities came back from Italy just in the nick of time! Any more direct exposure and Shamus would have a complete meta-Gizmorphosis! His tummy was already blackened like a seasoned and pan-fried catfish fillet— Scary!

Now perhaps you ask, how do I know that she went to Italy? *PL*-ease. My first clue was when the owner of the dog prison drove us back to Paris in La Ferme's "paddy wagon." There's only one possible reason that there would be no room in her car— Exactly! Shoes!

Et voilà! Walking into the apartment, we discovered Mistress Black-Pump-Addict desperately trying to squirrel away shoes in every nook-and-cranny! So many pumps and wedges and sandals and boots, it was impossible to take a single step without walking in her shoes— And that my friends, is not on my bucket list! Pas de Tout!

Seriously though, an intervention was long, long overdue. We'd have to act fast before the reserves were tapped leaving zero funds for our long overdue trip to Basel.

Instead of taking herself to seek long-overdue professional help, she took us to The Veterinarian! Seriously?!

Okay. Truth be told, I wasn't that upset to get a little check-up. It'd been sooooo long since our last visit AND mottled pigmentation terrier might require some salve for that skin damage— However, what transpired was pure treachery! Her devious plot exposed when we returned home. Believe it or not— She snuck French pharmaceuticals into my afternoon Camembert!

What on Earth are you up to, now?! There's no need to drug me. I have zero choice, but to go places with you! Hello! Remember? A short, short lead for every single freaking walk! And why, pray-tell, are you bothering to assemble the blue monstrosity? Basel has a private jet. I have my very own seat! No need f— *Zzzzzzzzz.*

- Total Blackout -

Waking up with a blistering headache, I saw a sparkling-clean, blue cage in the middle of the living room and her luggage in various stages of packing— Ughhhh. Seriously?! I need a vacation from her— Not With Her!

There was nowhere left to hide in this upside-down suitcase frenzy, except under the bed. How my life had sunk to new, unchartered depths. Sad. So terribly sad. Sniff-Sniff.

Maneuvering between the shoes and sweater boxes, I lodged myself underneath. Completely hidden with the exception of my tail. It remained in view, swishing back-and-forth, back-and-forth.

PL-ease, do not be confused. I could've easily fit myself underneath in full stealth mode— Exactly! This was a distress signal!

My plan? Simple. Mistress Easy-to-Dupe would think that I was stuck under the bed. Then, she'd have to call French Beau— Wait! Better yet, she'd overreact, dial 112 and Jean-Luc Marcus along with the rest of the Fluvial Brigade would answer the SOS coming to my rescue!

Before I could relish that happy thought, Mistress Unhappy Endings rather discourteously grabbed me by my hind legs and extracted me.

Buggers! Foiled again!

Drugged and manipulated like a hand puppet, could this day get any worse? And then, believe it or not, it actually did!

Forcing us to look at her, Mistress Excruciating Detail enumerated her upcoming plans. Brown-Nosed Puppy sat on the bed with rapt attention to her mind-numbing soliloquy, even nodding his head as if in agreement.

Where is the God-line when I really, really need it?!

"Niki-Niki-Niki! Isn't this great? New York, New York! And, just in time for the San Gennaro festival in Little Italy. Ooohhh! I hope that we can go at least one day. I'd love to have some funnel cake. Mmmmm. Okay, I know it's not good for my sugar levels or my tummy, but my mouth sure does loooove it! Do you think that we'll be able to stay for Halloween, too?! Wouldn't that be awesome sauce? Last year, I was so bummed missing the 6th Avenue parade being in Paris and all. You know, it's never too early to start planning so just in case, what do you think my costume should be this year? I'm kinda leaning towards 'Chef Shamus.' You know what a foodie I am!"

Finally able to walk away from both auditory thorns, I curled up on my bed and hid under my tail, sulking. Not once in her endless itinerary did she mention "spa day" or "girls' day out" or "Ciao Bella, vanilla gelato!"

Hoping that the God-line was open and taking late night requests, I prayed that she would remember the things that made me happy!

New York City

It felt strange to be back. It had only been a little over a year since we moved to Paris, but I didn't remember New York like this… so noisy and dirty, the sidewalks wide and the parks small, the constant noise from honking horns and people shouting, and every night there were garbage bags stacked shoulder-high lining the curbs. It was reverse culture shock becoming re-acclimated to the place which I had once considered home.

With a little luck and a lot of Internet searching, I found a sublet in our old neighborhood, on Crosby Street. It was a little more than I had wanted to spend, but it was a really cool duplex apartment in what originally was a guesthouse for a mansion that existed in the days when Broadway was still considered "the countryside." On the first two floors was a trendy, farm-to-table restaurant and, as the upstairs neighbor, I had a guaranteed table.

With a little cajoling, lots of promises and an extra cash deposit, the owner accepted both dogs. Since my current project had me in the city for the next 10-12 weeks, it made sense to bring them back with me.

From the moment their paws touched the pavement, the dogs acted like we never left remembering our old haunts and retracing the walking routes. I was happy to have them with me as they always proved to be a good excuse to take a break.

The neighborhood had changed greatly in such a short time. The best find was the restaurant supply store had been repurposed into a swank, high-tech grooming salon with live video feed of the entire facility. After a little impromptu tour, Niki tried to steer me there on every walk after the usual Ciao Bella pass-by.

Of course, that was only on the days we didn't meet up with her new friend, Nanook, a pure white, 2-year-old Samoyed, fluffy in appearance and temperament. Every time they met up, they romped like puppies. Sometimes Nikita was a little rough, mounting him and nipping at his ears. But, Nanook took it in stride and thankfully so did his owner.

Since they lived next door, we bumped into Nanook and his father almost every day and would usually continue our walks through the neighborhood in tandem. When time allowed, we'd wander over to the Hudson River Park enjoying the quieter walkways and pedestrian zones.

This morning, we happened to be flying solo. Daydreaming about the day, I looked down to see Shamus doing a one-legged handstand. How cool! I had a little yogi-dog!

Namaste.

Na-ma-DON'T-stay there!

"But, Niki! I've got to go and I'm trying to mark exactly where Nook did!"

What-*ever*! You will never be a "Canine Illustrated" cover model— More importantly? You forgot the "golden rule!" You're downwind! One gust and—

"Niki, don't worry. I've got this under control. It's ok."

No! It's disgusting. This is not "splash-back Thursday!"

"Well, sometimes we all have accidents."

Pardon you? I am not personally familiar with that particular word.

"Nikita, even if I did miscalculate, she'll throw me in the sink once we're home. And, there's nothing better than a good shampoo to wash away your problems, to cast them away across a sea of scented bubbles."

Oh please, if only—

"Niki. It's a double metaphor."

More like a meta-whatever for!

"Ok-ok-ok. Well, look at me now! I'm in perfect balance, an equilateral triangle, I'm a downward-facing-dog! WOOF!"

Really? You look more to me like a crouching, ball-less terrier. How about a more familiar, more submissive pose like reverse-supine happy-puppy asana?

"Niki, that's not funny."

I know. I'm not laughing. I'm not even smiling.

"This is exactly why you need to practice yoga, rid yourself of your vritti, and attain the 3rd niyama of contentment."

The only ripple in my mind is the one caused by your constant chitchat— And, I am happy, just not at this particular moment with you and your antics!

"Oh Nikita! I knew it! There have been moments where you've been happy with me! This is simply grand! I am totally going to include this reveal as a segue in my book."

Reveal? Segue?? Book???

"Oh yes! An autobiographical piece. My memoirs with photos, of course! The working title is: *Tales of a Continental Yorkie, a world-traveling adventurer extraordinaire.*"

This last verbal siege was proof positive that since Shamus came back to NYC and started practicing yoga daily, he'd shifted and not in a good way! Transcendental Terrier barely existed in this dimension without any lucid dreaming A.K.A.

terrier-themed hallucinations! Let's be honest, a better working title would be: *Couch Potato Terrier Tales, a never-ending soliloquy.*

Before I could share this present world reality nugget, My Mistress turned abruptly into the doorway of the salon— No way! Bada-Boom-Boom-Diggity-BOOM! A shampoo, brush and blow-out, and playtime with the staff ALL Shamus-Free!

My most ardent God-line requests finally answered! Thank you! Thank you! Thank you! Now, let's hope this includes a single scoop of vanilla bean gelato on the way home.

The building's concrete walls must've blocked my affirmations of most sincere gratitude AND my last-minute addendum— Exactly! When she picked me up, Mistress Stiletto-Power-Walker marched me straight home!

This is ridiculous! I look absolutely fantastic! There's zero reason to keep me sequestered in the house until my date tonight.

"Tonight? We have a date? Oh jeeps, Nikita. Forgive me, I totally spaced out and forgot. Give me a minute to get dressed up. What's the weather—"

Tonight, I have a date with Nanook. You have a double date with the TV and a bone.

"Ooohhh! A double date! You're not too jealous, are you?"

No, not in the least. Have fun. Do a little couch yoga, my little echelon of pretzeldom terrier. Balance your derrière on a cushion. Use your rawhide bone as a jaw prop. Spread out in frog pose. See if you're finally limber enough to occupy more than 17.2% of the love seat— Just please, this time, do not drool in savasana.

"Ok, sure. This is simply perfect. The "Dogs 101" marathon is tonight and I've been looking forward to it. Besides, I'd rather stay nice and cozy at home. It's been getting a little chilly at night, but it's far too early in the season for one of my cashmere sweaters and my sweatshirt still needs to be laundered. Anywho, that's a moot point. There's way, way too much commotion for my taste with the festival opening. Did you see all the people already gathering like a flock of drunken seagulls? I hate when my paws are stepped on. It hurts so much worse than my tummy does when she forgets our mid-morning snack. Good thing that you'll have Nanook to help part the wave of tourists. He's such a great neighbor and so much friendlier than Bones or Otis. You know, sometimes they pretend like they don't see me. It hurts my feelings when they do that. But Nook, he always says hello. Did you know that even when you're not there, he'll play with me! That makes me feel so important, so special, like I matter. Oh look! I'm 'using my words!' Are you proud of me? I am! Oh look, again a positive expression of sentiment! Would you like to share your feelings, too? No? Okay. Well, whenever you're ready, I am listening. Yep, ears wide open and permanently tuned into y-o-u, you! The Nikita Station, 24/7, 100% Niki, 0% Everything-Else! Are you going to have a funnel cake with extra sugar? Of course not. You're always so disciplined. That's why you look so good all the time! Although today, you look especially beautiful, truly stunning! And, the scent of that new shampoo is simply exquisite! Have I told you today have much I love you?"

And right before the curtain lifted on The Puppy Slime Show, Mistress Finally-Good-Timing intervened whisking me away from tonight's scheduled performance. However, instead of taking me straight out on my date, she dawdled in the kitchen.

Hurry up! What's wrong with you? We're going to be unfashionably late!

Reaching across the table, she grabbed something wrapped in paper and offered it to me.

Oh, no! No-No-NO! I no longer trust your presents and

accessories are 110% un-necessary! I am perfect just the way— WHOA!

O-M-G!

I looked up at Mistress Full-of-Surprises.

In her hands was the most beautiful thing I'd ever seen! A smooth grain leather collar in the most perfect color red, studded with sky blue turquoise stones and silver beads.

Where? When? How? Why?

As she slipped it over my head, 2 shiny disks captured my attention. Not the cheap aluminum or colored tin ones that get stamped in the store while you wait— but, believe it or not, 2 brand-new, hand-cast and engraved Sterling Silver tags! One for Paris, one for New York! It must've cost her a small fortune!

Holy Buggers! What kind of truffles do you—

"Truffles? Did you say truffles? Is it truffle season already in the Northeast Corridor? Oh wow, Nikita! Look at your new collar! It's stunning. Not as beautiful as you, of course, but wow! The stones, they bring out your eyes. And the silver, it mirrors the luster of your coat. See! I told you that she loves you! I was with her when she picked it out. A special order just for you because you are special! And now, you look like a real princess! Princess Nikita, the Dauphine of my heart, the Tsarina of my world!"

A real spa day, a real present, soon a real date— The whole day was one monumental moment followed by another. So extraordinarily touching, it brought tears to my eyes.

"Niki?! You're not just crying, you're bleeding! There's blood all over the floor!"

Huh? You've got to be kidding! Oh jeeps! If she finds out, my date is cancelled. Do me a favor?

"Anything!"

Clean up the drops on the floor.

"Ummmm. As much as love the SyFy channel, I am not a vampire terrier."

Just do it and say nothing. Don't botch my big date. Do I have any spots on my bib?

"Nope. You're my snow-white Siberian Beauty. As beautiful and as perfect as ever! Are you certain that there's nothing—"

I'm fine. Just a whirlwind of a day. Everything is perfectly fine. Just fine. All I need is a few deep breaths to clear my head.

With my nose in the air, the familiar taste of blood trickled down the back of my throat. It had been quite a while since I tasted my own blood. The flow had just begun to dwindle when I heard her calling for me to come downstairs and leave for my date.

Once. Twice— As a good rule of thumb, I'd wait until the 6th "come here" before stirring in her general direction. After all, I'm not at her disposal. Not like I'm some Yorkshire Terrier that goes scurrying at the first sound!

"Niki! That's unnecessary. Why do you have to be so mean?"

Please. Zip the puppy lips. I am talking "about" you— Not "to" you! And, be honest. How many times have I had to remind you? Never move the first time asked! Always wait. You are a d-o-g, dog. Not some ghost waiting to be summoned!

However, today the imperative show of self-respect through restraint would not be possible.

Why, do you ask?

From the bottom of the stairs came an extraordinarily loud, semi-discordant melody. Mistress In-Full-Form either thought that the Amato Opera's Doors were re-opened for auditions or that it was "Amateur Night at the Apollo"— Exactly! Disastrous either way! Someone had to silence her

IMMEDIATELY before she ruined the appetite of every paying customer eating in the swank restaurant below!

As always, with No One else available, capable, or willing to intervene— that responsibility fell on my already heavily burdened shoulders— Sighhhh.

Trying to keep my cool and not induce another nosebleed, I walked over to the staircase. As soon as she saw me, she began today's anthem from the top. A homespun rendition of the Miss America Song.

♫ Here she comes, my Nikita girl.
Here she comes, her eyes so blue.
Can't you see, why everyone loves her.
Can't you see, why this is true!

Come to me, my Nikita girl.
Come on down, let's go outside.
We'll have fun, Nanook is waiting.
We'll have fun, time spent side-by-side! ♫

Ughhhhh. The rhymes so weak, and that ending verse a sad reflection of her desperate longing to connect. By the time I reached the landing, a few drops of blood fell from my nose. It was of little wonder that my ears weren't bleeding, too!

Keeping my head held high, I hoped that she wouldn't notice.

I noticed. How could I not notice the blood splattered on the hardwood floor? But aside from cleaning it up, there was nothing to do about it tonight. Already scheduled for tomorrow morning was an appointment with a new vet. At some point in the past year, our trusted veterinarian had left her practice. This one came highly recommended and his office was within walking distance.

Niki had been sneezing a little too much the past few days, but this was the first time that her nose bled. There were no other symptoms. Her appetite was good, spirits were high, and she seemed genuinely excited to be going out.

Tonight, she had a "date" with Nanook. And, I was looking forward to sharing time with the other "chaperone." There was no way I was going to cancel.

And, I'm happy that we didn't. What a fantastic time! It was early enough in the festival that Mulberry Street was still walkable and early enough in the evening to avoid the drunken mayhem.

Separately, Niki and Nanook were attention grabbers. Together, they were like a celebrity power couple on the red carpet. Most of our evening was stopping for photos and fielding questions. The best photo of the evening was the one taken by a festival vendor with the two of them lounging in a giant, black pleather chair.

As the festival lights began glowing and the crowd grew more and more dense, it was time to leave. But, none of us were ready to go home. Ice cream always a good idea, we headed over to Niki's favorite haunt.

Her vanilla bean gelato disappeared in record time especially considering the lack of help from Shamus. Obviously, she was feeling fine. Maybe, she had allergies.

The next day at her appointment, she checked out in perfect health. Aside from her symptoms, there was nothing wrong. The vet vetoed the idea that it was allergies. He believed that it was very probable that she simply caught "something" and recommended a course of antibiotics.

I pushed him about further testing. I wasn't a huge fan of medication and wanted to make certain the diagnosis was correct before dosing my dog unnecessarily.

Taking off his glasses to look me straight in the eyes he said, "Yes, of course. However, they are quite expensive and you would not like the results from those types of tests. Not a happy ending there. So, what do you say we try the antibiotics, first?"

With a little gulp, I nodded in tacit agreement. No reason to argue with a pill-pushing pessimist. Besides, a few days of antibiotics might help, give her immune system a little boost. And if not, we'd be back in Paris soon enough with a kinder-on-the-ears, gentler on-the-eyes doctor who actually cared about my dogs.

Rounding the corner back to the apartment, Niki pulled away towards Prince Street. Haha! "Someone" wanted a longer walk… and today, I had the time to humor her.

Letting her lead the way, we passed by where Nanook lived and since he wasn't in sight, she pulled ahead. Crossing Lafayette, I had a pretty good idea where this walk was going. Sure enough, a couple of blocks and a couple of predictable turns later, we arrived at Ciao Bella.

She looked up at me with hopeful eyes. I sighed.

Only yesterday, we were here. It was too soon. But then, when I don't feel well sometimes a scoop or two makes it all better.

Looking at her, I smiled. Who could resist that face? Those eyes?

Okay! Ice cream it is! But, I have a better idea.

A better idea?! You?! IMPOSSIBLE!

She pulled at my lead to continue towards Houston. Seriously? I was in no humor to leave without my gelato fix, but her history of canine abuse had to be taken under serious consideration— Exactly! In no way, shape, or form did I wish to suffer the embarrassment, the ridicule of being carried down the sidewalks of New York City! Definitely NOT something on my bucket list! So, I indulged the "better idea" fantasy letting her take me on a drag into the depths of the lower east side.

Crossing 2nd Ave, we entered some sort of culinary vortex. The scents were so mouth-watering, I could feel the pounds being packed on with every breath. Bagels, knishes, herring, salmon, a diner, an old-world delicatessen, a Lebanese bakery, French cuisine, Indian street food— Mmmmmmm.

Uncharacteristically stopped at a street corner, waiting for a light, my nose detected more delicate notes. Vanilla beans,

cacao, mint, sage, lavender, honey, pistachios, pecans, fresh fruits, sweet-
cream— Believe it or not, the building directly across the street was Gelato Heaven!

The flavors all so wonderful, I was happy that she ordered for me TWO scoops— Lavender-Honey and Sage A.K.A. The Best Medicine ever in disguise as gelato!

For the 1st time in my entire life, I could call her Mistress Good Idea! And, let me tell you— Only in New York do these things happen!

Of course, that particular novelty was short-lived, only lasting until the return home when a reminder of one her many previously poor decisions came bouncing down the stairs— Ughhhh. Why couldn't she have left the turbo-charged terrier in France or sent him down to Florida for semi-retirement?

"Niki-Niki-Niki! Where have you been? How did the doctor's appointment go? Are you okay? Tell me. Tell me everything! I've been so worried. I've been sitting here alone on the couch. She forgot to turn on "Animal Planet" and left it on "The Weather Channel." You know how the news gets me all agitated. Especially, now! There's a late season hurricane moving across Florida. Do you think that Grandma C and Giz are okay? It's a good thing that—"

Everything's fine. Just fine.

That's what I said, but I was so tired from the day. Too much poking and prodding and excitement. All I wanted to do was take a little snooze— but no. Oh, no! Time-to-Talk Terrier was just getting started.

"Niki? Do you like long walks along the Riverside Park?"

Please, I like anything that has nothing to do with you!

"Haha-haha! Oh Nikita, you're sooo funny! The reason that I asked you such a random question—"

Please stop, right there. My head can't handle it today. Oh Shamus, my sweet little Shamus.

"Yes, my Nikita love?"

Has it occurred to you ever in that pea-sized noggin of yours that— #1. Everything you ask seems random to me— And #2. I do not care. Not one single iota!

"Niki. That's not very nice. And even worse, you're still neglecting your New Years' resolution. I am so disappointed. I expected so much more from you. You're nicer than you pretend to be. I just hope that your nice switch doesn't get permanently stuck in off position."

And with that, he walked away!

Like I've told you before— Only in New York do these things happen!

*

From the kitchen came the sounds of Mistress Scared-Of-Her-Own-Shadow shrieking and pans falling to the floor. This could mean only one thing. I sprung to my feet and ran to the doorway— YES! Delivery! And not just any delivery, but happy, fat, lazy little rodents from the farm-to-our-table restaurant downstairs! WooHoo!

When we moved to Paris, there were a few things that I missed about New York— Delivery service was certainly one. Don't get me wrong, I still enjoy a good old-fashioned hunt and scaring the breath out of unsuspecting critters, repeatedly— However, there is something oddly, deliciously decadent about having unsuspecting prey lured into our kitchen by the scent of popcorn— Yes, popcorn!

Tired of the fancy fare downstairs, the aroma from freshly popped kernels would entice our little friends to travel through the walls and into our flat. Once they realized that they had left the safety of the restaurant, they'd panic darting left-and-right before hiding in the windowsill. That's where Shamus finally proved worthy of his plane fare— Exactly! Back to tag-team basics!

Shamus, able to jam his tiny snout into the mouse-sized opening, would snort a few times into the crevice. Hearing the huffing and the puffing, the rodents brainwashed by bedtime tales of wolves would panic. The rational brain reverting to ultimate survival mode, their instincts were to "escape" out the side exit, precisely where I'd be waiting— The Living Lupine image from their very worst nightmares!

TAK! Slamming my paws down in a wall of fury, they'd spin around to find a terrier-sized rodent behind them nostrils flaring, his doggie dragon eyes hungrily fixed on them.

Some would faint at the sight of one of us or the other. As expected, a few were blessed with a little stronger constitution. And as always, those were the ones who were more playful, more fun, putting on a better show running from wolf to dragon to wolf to dragon to wolf— SPLAT!

There was one steadfast rule: Absolutely NO Tasting!

PL-ease a girl has to be careful these days especially in the Big City! Let's be realistic— No clue as to where these new-to-the-city mice have been "snacking" and death-by-dehydration is certainly not on my agenda, period!

This afternoon, we hit the rodent lottery as 1-2-3 Fresh-From-Vermont mice came to investigate— WooHoo! Let the games begin!

Shamus? Shamus?!

Nothing.

Where are you?

Still nothing.

We've got live ones! Hurry up!

Absolutely no sign of the terrier troops.

Typical, just typical. There when I want him the least—absent when I actually have need. Sighhhh.

Leaving Mistress Faaarrrrr-Too-Late putting out her glue traps, I set off to find the no-show terrier. Not like it was a challenge or a mission impossible to find the little deserter. All I had to do was follow the sounds of snoring which were currently rippling down the stairs from her closet A.K.A. the guest bedroom.

Peering in the doorway, I found the snoozer loser pretzeled up in a pile of clothes.

SHAMUS!

"No! No! No! I won't do it! Neverrrrrrrr!"

Shamus! Snap out of it! N-o-w, now!

"WOOF! Oh-oh-oh. Hi, Niki. Jeeps, you scared me."

You missed the last delivery!

"Sorry. I was meditating."

You mean sleeping.

"Well, I might have snoozed off."

Pinocchio Puppy!

"Ok-ok, I fell asleep. But not "sleeping." It was full-moon nightmaring! Have you ever had one of those dreams that was so real that it is real?"

Hmmmmm. Somehow, I feel like I'm in one right now.

"Well, that's what this was and that made it super-duper scary! You see, I was back in the Paris. All alone in the apartment. Next thing I know, this Belgium chocolate bar appears and starts taunting me. You wouldn't believe the things it said— in French, English, and Flemish! Did you know that Flemish is a derivative of Yorkenese? I can understand Flemish, but they struggle to understand the Yorkshire vocabulary. Well, I just walked away. Nothing you can say to someone who doesn't appreciate lingual similarities or French fries! But, it followed me— closely, too closely. So, I picked up my pace, faster and faster, until into a full-run. And, so did the chocolate bar! Can you believe it?! A Belgium milk chocolate bar chased me! And not one of the single bite snack-sized ones, but one of the really giant ones with 15 squares! It was so much faster than you would ever expect! I was so scared, like totally scared out of my wits! I made a mad dash into the kitchen. The floor was still wet from being cleaned. I slipped. A total wipeout! In an instant, the chocolate bar was on top of me, pinning me to the floor. A slowly melting top square hovering above my face. I can still hear its screams, 'Eet mee. Eet mee!' Oh Niki, when you called my name, so did the chocolate bar! It was—"

You know chocolate can kill a dog.

"Yeah, I know. But, death would be a relief! Before then, you're mostly likely to fall on the ground in violent seizures and have severe intestinal cramping."

Oh yeah smarty pants?

"Yes! Absolutely. I was watching this documentary on the 'Animal Channel' which—"

THWAAP!

"Niki, why'd you do that?"

I was trying to change channels. Here let me try again!

Before I could, a piercing whistle sounded through the apartment and— ZIP-ZAG-ZIP! The terrier escape artist maneuvered past me flying down the stairs at record speed for a liver treat!

Oh sure, for a game of hide-n-seek with Mistress Pocket Treats, you skedaddle. Of course, those pricey treats do leave a better taste in the mouth and reduce the possibility of fur struck between the teeth to 0%— Hummphhhh.

No matter, no reason to hurry. He never found her the first time around.

Instead of sniffing her out, Perfunctory Terrier would run straight to the kitchen and work every room from there. Wise to his unsleuthful ways, she would often slip from room-to-room, whistling in short bursts to throw him off.

The moment Inspector Clueless was completely confused and about to give up, she'd sneak up from behind and— BOO!!! Scaring the living daylights out of him.

It was cruel. But for once, brilliant on her part especially because she knew better than to even try and scare me. At the same time, it was sad. The lengths he'd go to for a piece of over-priced, freeze-dried meat.

Slowly coming down the stairs, I waited mid-way for her to circle around. 1-2-3-4-5— Hello!

Not expecting me there, she jumped sky high— Priceless!

Once she regained her footing, placing one finger up to her lips with the other hand she offered me a weak bribe. I stared her down.

Emotionless. Complete Poker Face.

She doubled the bribe.

I took it and she slinked off past the stairs into the living room. Like I said before my friends, New York City delivers!

Shamus came around the corner a heartbeat later.

"Have you seen her?"

I shrugged my shoulders.

"Come on Nikita. I can smell the liver on your breath."

Rolling my eyes, I motioned towards the living room. Best that this particular farce was over early today— Exactly! I had an idea!

Shamus walked into the living room, she jumped out, he acted scared, and we all got treats. Quid pro quo— Now, for my idea!

Turning to face the clueless twosome, I crouched into play pose. Once. Twice. Then with a wink, I shot off like a bullet into the kitchen before stealthily looping back toward the staircase— Precisely! The hunter becomes the hunted A.K.A. My turn to hide!

Of course, it would be ideal if they never found me— But that was a very unlikely scenario. After all, not like there are that many places to hide inside and I certainly can't go to JFK with the door deadbolted!

Once I heard their footsteps behind me, I circled back to the living room and dove into my crate. This should take them quite a while! She'll never suspect that I'd willingly go into the blue monstrosity!

From the cover of darkness, at the back of my crate, I watched them search high-and-low, left-and-right.

Ahhhhh— This brings back memories of her roaming around The Farm calling for me, frantically looking for me when I was right there watching from under the shadow of the white birch trees every single time!

After the 3rd pass by, it was time to scare the bejeezus out of her— However, there was No Way that I wanted her to know where I was hiding. This was farrrrrr too good of a spot to relinquish to Mistress Elephant-Memory!

Waiting for the both of them to round the corner into the kitchen, I exited my crate. In full stealth mode, I slinked my way towards the kitchen. Hearing them rounding back, I pressed myself into the wall shielded from view by the couch. Oh, this was going to be EPIC!

Walking back towards the living room, they were busy discussing the possibility that I escaped out the open window and was on my way to JFK when— GOTCHA!

The vision of the two of them hovering in the air in total fright = Priceless Beyond Words!

Speechless. I couldn't believe that not only did Nikita want to play with Shamus and me, she actually wanted to hide. A miracle on Crosby Street or the antibiotics were really mood stabilizers? Either way, I was asking no questions. It warmed my heart to see a more playful side of Nikita.

She also seemed healthier with fewer sneezing fits. Maybe the pollution levels in the city irritated her nose. We were no longer accustomed to the incessant car traffic and bus fumes. Even I was having trouble breathing and started carrying an inhaler with me.

Taking them out for an afternoon stroll, we bunked around the neighborhood making our way towards Greenwich Village. Since we'd be around for Halloween, I wanted to check out the costumes at a locally-owned pet store. Of course, that was not my only motivation. The "real reason" to hike all the way over there was the puppies in the window. Unlike Quat' Pats which kept the puppies at human eye level, this storefront display began at ground level. A full windowfront of cuteness!

When they saw Niki and Shamus peering in from outside, some of the puppies went completely bonkers. It was simple entertainment and a little tempting, too. Before I got puppy fever, we went inside to check out the costumes.

They still had a wide selection available, but nothing that seemed right for Nikita. Shamus and I had already found his costume in a little boutique in SoHo. Then, hidden behind a dinosaur suit and a three-headed dog costume, I spied a red cape with a bonnet!

Could anything be more perfect?

Perfect viewing from this angle! Shamus, why don't you come over here and check out our new brother?

"Whatever."

Pardon you?

"Nikita, I am not falling for it this time. I know you're both looking with no intention to buy. You know, just 'window

shopping.' She would never get a puppy from a puppy-mill. She's messing with you!"

With that he turned back to face the 6th Avenue traffic.

What a shocker! Shamus not interested in destroying the competition? A show of masculinity from the powder-puff terrier?

Turning towards Suddenly Suave Shamus, I gave his hindquarters a little sniff.

"Niki! What are you doing? That tickles and I thought PDAs were forbidden!"

Yeah, they are. I'm just checking to see if you grew a new pair of royal jewels.

"Niki, that's not very nice."

Well my dearest gelding, I've been accused of many things "being nice" is not one of them!

"Ok Nikita, you can't blame me for hoping. I'm an optimist. It's my nature. My constitution and I hold steadfast the belief that one day you might just succumb to your pleasant side. And, I am so looking forward to that day."

Right before the prohibited puppy PDAs began, she yanked us inside. I was hoping that we'd have some playtime with the little apricot Havanese, but no! Mistress Other Ideas led us directly into the back where they tried to hide the Halloween costumes from her! Before I could establish a connection to the God-line, she placed a rainbow-colored clown wig on my head—ACCKKKK!

No! Absolutely, resolutely not! Anything, but that! I am not an errant circus freak. I just live with TWO!

*

I woke up from my mid-morning snooze and things were quiet, too quiet. That could only mean one thing— Exactly!

Mistress Goosecackler had left me alone! That happy milli-moment was quashed with the annoying sound of pant-pant-panting A.K.A. the little twit terrier.

Slowly, I opened one eye and peered in the direction of the huffing-and-puffing to find Shamus carefully arranging the air above a pig ear. Pushing and pulling imaginary dirt with his nose, taking a step back to survey his "work," and then pushing from the other side making the necessary "adjustments." As hesitant as I was to suffer his delusional diatribe, there was the need to know. And, the curiosity was killing me.

Shamus?

Like a deer in headlights, he froze mid-movement.

Shamus?!

"Oh, hi Niki! I thought that you were napping. What's up?"

No. That's my question for you.

"Oh, this? I'm just working on my muscle memory."

Extrapolate concisely, please.

"Well, just in case we go to New Jersey or for when we return to Ormancey. You see, I need to keep my treat burying and my truffle digging skills honed. The best way is to maintain the muscles necessary is through a similar, repetitive movement. Besides, it was a quiet way to pass the time while you snoozed. You've been having so many headaches lately that I thought that you might need a little extra sleep. And not that you need it, but a little extra beauty rest can turn a frown upside-down!"

As my eyes rolled back into my head, a brilliant idea shone through the terrier muck.

You know, Shamus, the intent way that you moved nothing, it was just like—

"T'ai chi ch'üan?"

No, Tiger Puppy Paws. You showed great potential to be a mime.

"A mime?"

Yes, indeed! A performance artiste who creates a visual image, presents an entire story concept without talking. Absolutely, no words.

"Wow, Niki that's so cool! I could train by performing in Washington Square Park. The New Yorkers would tell me in a minute what was wrong and toss me money for lessons, the tourists would take pity and throw money in my kibble bowl for encouragement! What a fantastic idea! That alone would off-set my income during the non-truffle season. This is just—"

Never wanting to promote physical contact, with great reluctance I lightly placed a paw down to halt the puppy lips.

No words my furry performer, just movement.

And, with that he nodded an "okay" and with a deep bow went back to his current masterpiece.

O-M-G! If only I had known that it was sooooo easy!

Returning back to my bed, I closed my eyes hoping to skip right back to my dreams of—

"Niki-Niki-Niki!"

Oh, Holy Buggers! No matter how often I tried to otherwise occupy the pipsqueak, it was never, ever long enough!

Yes, Shamus, I'm right here. No reason to repeat my name like some arcane incantation to conjure my presence.

"Ok, right, sorry about that. Anyway, I just picked up a disturbance on my radar which could possibly impact our future!"

Have you been watching "The Weather Channel" again? Well, allow me to present an up-to-date forecast—

"Nikita, don't you hear the footsteps on the stairs and the luggage being dragged up? She's bringing people home! We have guests! Who do you think it is?"

Looking at him, I nonchalantly shrugged my shoulders as if I didn't care. But, in all honesty, I was concerned— *PL*-ease, not about the guests. This was about ME!

The dull thud from a headache that rarely went away had hindered my keen perception of my environment. Already, the medication was making me tired and dull. I didn't need any more impediments especially in New York where you always have to have your wits about you.

Not wanting to alert Helicopter Puppy to my situation, I reminded him that we must never look too eager, too willing, too available. Best to— Wait one second!

There was a long-forgotten voice calling my name. Could it be?!

Pushing Underfoot Terrier out of the way, I bolted down the stairs farrrrrr ahead of him!

Now, I could clearly hear little feet running up the stairs.

Meeting me at the landing was My Little Person!

WoW! Just look at how much you've grown— You're My Little Man, now!

Not far behind him, Mistress Photo Burst was capturing our long awaited and totally unanticipated reunion.

Cut it out! And while you're at it, wipe that Cheshire cat grin off your face! What's wrong with you? Did you swallow the Vermont vermin? Go away and work on your selfie-pout with the soon-to-be-jealous, 2nd Place Terrier!

At first, I was concerned that MLM and I would have zero quality time together, but when you're privileged with a direct-link on the God-line, the universe provides— Exactly! He arrived with an entourage of two! One to entertain Mistress Living-Vicariously-Poster-Child— And, a second to coddle the high-maintenance terrier!

Life is soooooo good— Amen!

I had so much to share with him. Washington Square Park, Central Park with the obligatory carriage ride, the old gelato place, the new one, Veselka's, the Belgium frites stand— The possibilities in New York were endless!

Do you want to know best part? Our long walks at night when My Mistress relinquished my lead to him. Here he was all grown up and taking me for an evening stroll on the tree lined streets of Soho and The Village. It was magical. So much so, that the gnawing headache faded away into my periphery.

With My Mistress and his entourage moving heavier than when they arrived suitcases down the stairs, it meant only one thing! — Precisely! An untimely extraction!

It was waaaay too early for his visit to end! I nudged MLM to follow me up the stairs to my special place— A little alcove in the living room where we could pow-wow privately.

He threw his arms around me and buried his head into my shoulders. I wrapped my head around to lightly touch his.

Tilting his head slightly, he whispered into my ear, "I know."

Pulling away, I looked at him.

With tears in his eyes, he smiled and pulled me back to him. Wrapping me in a tighter embrace, he whispered, "I love you, Nikita. You are mine forever."

Burying his face once again into my shoulders, I could feel him sobbing.

My heart ached.

My heart broke. I walked into the living room to find Niki with my nephew tucked into a corner, cuddled up together. Neither one looked up. So, I went over and gently placed a hand on my nephew's back. He looked up at me with fur stuck to his tear streaked face.

Squatting down next to them, I asked my nephew for a hug good-bye. As much as I hated to separate the two of them, my brother and his family had a flight to catch. And, realistically, the sweltering heat and humidity of Miami was not a place for Nikita.

From the moment that my nephew arrived it was as though no time had passed between the two of them. Nikita played like a puppy all-day and cuddled all-night with him. That initial bond was as strong as ever. And all these years later, I was once again impressed with Nikita's patience and gentle nature with my nephew. Even on their walks, she let him lead her not the other way around.

Better yet, throughout the entire visit, there were no more sneezes, no more nose bleeds, and Nikita was full of energy. Whether it was the pharmaceuticals, the tlc, or a synergy of both medicines, the magic worked.

*

Finally! Halloween! The very best holiday for people watching, especially in New York where the imagination and playfulness of otherwise stoic adults is celebrated. Basically, a one-day-pass for your inner-freaky. I could hardly wait for the evening to dress up the dogs. But then, why should I wait? It's Halloween all-day-long, right?

Calling Shamus over, I put on his silver cape and off he went zooming around the apartment. A strange vision of a "Super Dog" and "Captain Tom" hybrid orbited at the speed of light navigating around the furniture and through the doorways.

Finally catching him, I placed on his head a silver beanie with two eyeballs bouncing from coiled pipe cleaners. Et, voilà! My little Space Cadet!

Space Cadet? You spent money on that? That is NOT a costume, but rather a silver lamé

manifestation[*] of his personality! Of course, dressed like that there is the possibility that the Mother Ship will come and beam you BOTH back to your home planet! Seriously though, you could've been slightly more creative and dressed him up as a frog— Rrrrrribit!

"A frog? That's a great idea! You could pucker up and kiss me! Then, I'd turn into your Prince Charming! And, we'd live happily ever after. Mmmmuahhhh!"

No! Back off Terrier Toad. I have Nanook, the centerfold from "Tundra Hotties."

"Well, as long as you're happy. I looooove my costume! The cape makes me look so sleek and slim and fluid as if I'm moving like quicksilver! Zoom-Zzoom-Zzzoommm! The hat feels a little strange though. I'm not sure that I have a head for hats. You know, hats don't look good on everyone. And, I'm afraid that when she takes it off, I'll have helmet-hair. However, I'm loving the extra set of eyes to look at you!"

Side-stepping Lovelorn Terrier, I bunked right into My Mistress who smiled and tied a red cape around my neck and a bonnet on my head— AACKKKKKK!

You cannot be this cliché! And just when I thought it couldn't get any worse, It did— Exactly!

She took us for a walk.

Outside.

Parading us all gussied up in-public!

Why is the God-line connection always down when I need it most?!

From the moment we stepped out of the building, the attention was barely tolerable. People caught sight of my getup, and started howling maniacally with heads tilted up towards the sky. Even Nanook joined in the accolade— Oh, Holy Buggers!

---

[*] Yes. The pun is intended, even if obvious!

New Yorkers have extraordinarily limited reflex filters! What total freaks!

"Niki, don't be such a kill joy. They're just acknowledging your clever ruse. This is so much fun!"

And for him, it was.

Why? Because for the very first time ever, ever, ever people saw him! Of course, they were laughing their patooties off at him— But, Raise-Your-Freak-Flag-HIGHER Terrier was digging the attention no matter how perverse.

My head was beginning to pound from the sheer madness of it all. That was, until I was introduced to the one and only redeeming aspect of Halloween— Exactly! Trick-or-Treat! And in New York for this Little Red Ridinghood, it's ALL treats!

Popping into our favorite stores and restaurants, everyone offered a consolation gift for us being dressed up by Mistress Misplaced-Mothering-Instincts. The day spa loaded us up with treats and gave me a little pedicure. The swank boutique where my collar came from took a couple of candid Polaroid shots before handing us an entire tub of chicken tenders— Mmmmmmm!

On the way back home, Superman and a Lion Wrangler asked us to join the 6th Ave Parade— On the Best-Dressed Canine Float! Of little surprise, Mistress Party-Pooper-Costume said "no" pulling the plug at the height of our evening— Humphhhh.

Let's face it, I wasn't too happy with her high-handed decision to end our Halloweening— But then, the best time to leave the party is when you're still having fun. Good memories are everything. And walking back to the house, Shamus was still flying-high with his silver cape flowing in the wind. Seeing the misfit terrier so happy was very good indeed.

Curled up in my bed for the night, I was having trouble falling asleep. The excitement from the day and the extra sugar from the Halloween treats, was making my heart beat a little faster and my head thump a little louder. Counting sheep wasn't working for me. I don't know how, but I was finally drifting off when— BOOMSMACK!

Woodpecker Tail Feathers?!

Something landed square in my rib section, temporarily cutting off my airflow. Springing to my feet, I heard the THUD of my aggressor smacking into the floor.

Too dark to identify, I wasn't about to wait and allow the sleep disrupter to escape. Biting down on the furry body, I recognized the taste of herbal shampoo— Ughhhhh. Shamus.

"Nikita. I'm sorry-I'm sorry-I'm sorry."

Listen here Bounce House Terrier, your tubby little self almost cracked my ribs!

"But, Niki—"

I don't want to hear your sorry excuses! I only want to hear your deathbed cries.

"Oh, please Niki-please Niki-please Niki. I forgot where we were. I'm not used to sleeping on this side on the bed. It was totally an accident."

Thinking about all the ways his death could be made to look like an accident, I looked up to see Mistress Sleepy Eyes— Bahhhh. A witness, even if half-asleep, is a complication.

And then, the most amazing thing happened.

She got out of bed, placed Shamus in mine, and hoisted me up into traumatized terrier's spot giving me a little massage where he landed.

The look of disbelief on his face was far better than any apology.

*

Finding it more and more difficult to sleep throughout the night, I was snoozing more and more during the day. Not only did Mistress Temporary-Office-Space vacate the premises, but the little boy blunder left me alone— And, honestly? The thudding in my head just seemed a bit duller.

Falling asleep after she left this morning, I was having the most delicious dream. All of my friends were with me— Nanook, Bones, Luc-Marcus, and Clea. We were holed up in an igloo faaarrrr away from chaperone and terrier intervention. Being only half-Husky, it was a little cold for Clea. So, obviously, she was wearing a sweater. Playing, telling jokes, laughing, it was an epic party! There was a knock at the door, "Special Delivery from Il Laboratio for one—"

"Nikita. Wake up, wake up! Come and play with us!"

Not appreciating the interruption— Not recognizing the voice, I peeked through squinted eyes to see who was there. Two Weimaraners were running around our living room.

Impossible. Maybe, I was still dreaming.

"I see you checking us out, sweetie. I wasn't born yesterday, neither was he! We're twins you know. Now, come play a little game of tag with us!"

Who are you? How—

"I'm Lucy. He's Lucius. He doesn't talk much, which is fine by me. I prefer my men to be the strong, silent type. Wouldn't you agree?"

Nodding my head in agreement, she kept talking.

"We used to live here, so we know all the tricks and secrets. Your mistress is totally gone and the little boo boy is snoring away. You can go back to playing in your dreams or you can play with us!"

Given my options, playing with the old tenants seemed like the choice to make— And, a most excellent one at that! They had so much energy and were very good at hide-and-seek, able to appear and disappear seamlessly. I was having trouble keeping up with them. It was good to be challenged, so much better than playing with Shamus—

Shamus! You're awake!

"Nikita, who are you playing with?"

Lucy and Lucius. They used to live here. Come say hello.

"Nikita, there's no one here but us."

Right.

I looked behind me and my friends disappeared into thin air.

"Niki, should I be worried?"

No, no. It's all good. I must have been sleep-playing. You know like sleep-walking, but playing. Some medications have side effects and can make you a little wonky.

"But, you stopped taking the antibiotics two weeks ago."

Right. It must just be the residual effects. It takes time for the body to filter out toxins from your system.

"Ok, if you say so. It's actually a relief. I'm a little embarrassed to say, but I was a little jealous. I thought that you had a new imaginary friend."

Oh Shamus, all of my friends are very real indeed. And then, there's you.

"Yes? Go ahead. Use your words."

Oh, Shamus. Sometimes you are a real Dorkus Maximus.

"Huh?"

It's Latin, for—

"Oh Niki, I love it when you speak to me in a foreign language! You make everything sound so wonderfully exotic! Listen, since you're awake and feeling okay, I have a question to ask you."

No.

"Stop being silly Nikita. I haven't asked you yet."

How was it that he was always finding new ways to test my patience?

"I'm looking into doing an intensive yoga training. The Shala requests that students observe a vegetarian diet. Do you think that they'll accept a second-hand vegetarian?"

Second-hand?

"You've seen my t-shirt. I eat cows. Cows eat grass. I'm a sec—"

THWAP!

"Niki! That hurts!"

Yes, that's the intention. It hurts my head hearing you talk like that, so now we're even!

"Oh Niki. I'm so sorry. I was just trying my hand at random humor. You've been so blue lately. I miss your laughter. And, I was hoping that a little smile and serotonin release would help your headaches. Will you please forgive me?"

And then, right on schedule came the Pucker-Up Puppy Express— Ughhhhhhh.

*

Filtering into my quiet, special place was the sound of drum circle beats and feet shuffling. Never certain what they were up to, not certain if I even wanted to know, I decided to take a peek on my way to the kitchen to get a drink of water— Oh, my! This certainly falls in the realm of "curiosity-killed-the-husky!"

In our living room, a portal to a peculiar ring of visual hell had opened! *PL*-ease, do not ask me to verbally revisit the horrors of that memory! It's for public safety— There are some things that you just cannot un-see. Mistress Boum-Boum-

Boum attempting belly dancing is one. Another, is The Terrier Mimic shim-shim-shimmying along. Trust me, neither is appropriate for any audience!

"Niki, don't be so melodramatic. I was not belly dancing."

Then, what in blazes were you doing?

"Drying off!"

Apologizing to myself in advance for entering the terrier reality bubble, I nodded for him to continue.

"A little dog like me needs to shake much faster and much harder than a big dog in order to remove any excess water."

Ok, Trivia-Night Terrier. That's interesting. It might even be true, but you're dry now.

"Oh yeah. The first song she played was percussion only and super-duper fast. I was dry long before the end. But, she kept playing more and more songs! So, I just kept shimmying along working on toning my mid-section. All those gelatos are really getting to me. And, I want to look good for you!"

Turning quickly before the adoration attack, I continued into the kitchen for some water.

Not to be so easily thwarted, Train Car Terrier was only a step behind.

Looking up, I saw Lucy and Lucius at the water bowl. I stopped dead in my tracks sending Shamus barreling into me.

"Niki? What's wrong? Why'd you put on the brakes?"

Obviously, he still did not see our visitors who did indeed live here— Until, hit by a car on Lafayette AND that was three whole years ago! Nanook had filled me in on the backstory. It was neighborhood lore. One moment, the brother and sister were playing. The next, a car swerved up onto the sidewalk slamming into them both before fleeing the bloody scene. They died instantly. He said the whole neighborhood was shocked by the brutality of accident, saddened by the loss.

Lucy winked at me before they both disappeared—Ughhhh. Why was I seeing ghosts?

"Niki? Aren't you thirsty? I bet if you drank more water your headaches would go away. In fact, all of your symptoms indicate dehydration."

Is that so? And, pray-tell, when did you receive your doctorates degree or is it "still in the mail?"

"Niki, I'm just trying to be helpful. I'm worried about you."

You know what? Sometimes, I'm worried too.

Shamus's eyes bugged out of his head at my admission. On the brink of a complete breakdown, I had to intervene quickly before he detonated, verbally and mentally!

But, the worrying? That doesn't help anything. Not at all. So, pick a day.

"Huh?"

Choose a day of the week.

"Saturday."

A very good choice. Now, pick a time of the day.

"3pm"

Very wise choice, again. I was afraid you'd pick an early morning hour. Now, this is the deal.

"We're making a deal? What kind of deal? Do we shake on it or need to have it notarized?"

Shamus, please just let me finish. You and me, together, we are making a pact. Now, listen-up very closely to the terms. When you feel like things are overwhelming and you're getting super worried, I want you to place those thoughts aside in a special place. O-kay?

I waited until his lips stopped twitching and he nodded in tacit agreement.

Excellent. From now on, every Saturday, at 3pm, go to your special place and visit all the worries from your week, for only one hour.

"But, what if that isn't enough time?"

Shamus, that "worry" is now a topic for Saturday's "fret session."

"Oh. Okay. If you say so, Niki."

What you'll find, is that by the time Saturday arrives, your worries will be smaller or completely resolved. And if not, I'll be there with you.

"With your worries, too?"

Yes.

"Ok. Since you're doing it, I'll give it try. But, I don't see how this is going to work."

Shamus. Keep your heart and mind open. Make space for the metaphysical, you allow the magic to happen.

"Oh, Nikita! You have been practicing yoga! I am so proud of you! You're my idol, my shining star, my one-and-only!"

And this time, I didn't even bother to escape the inevitable puppy "love."

Puppy-love, how adorable. I came home to find Shamus and Niki snuggling up together on the couch. Of course, there were the less adorable moments, too. Like the other night, Shamus fell off the bed, landing smack on Nikita, and I thought she might kill him. But, like water on a duck's back, the anger rolled off and they'd go back to playing or "hunting" in the kitchen for mice or sharing ice cream or, like tonight, just hanging out together.

It never ceased to amaze me how much this mis-matched pair cared for each other.

*

Snowmageddon hit New York! Overnight, an early winter storm dumped 30 inches of snow. Sunday mornings were usually quiet, but from my windows the city looked like a ghost town. No souls brave enough to navigate the unplowed streets, even the brunchsters weren't venturing out.

Waking Shamus up, I took him outside and dropped him in a snowdrift to do his "morning business." The snow was so deep that only his head peaked out. His eyes affirming that he was not a fan of the current weather. He tinkled and then hopped-hopped-hopped back to door.

Back upstairs, I prepared to take Nikita out. It was sunny, but the temperatures were well below zero. She was made for this weather, her beautiful coat insulating her. On the other hand, I needed several layers and a facemask to protect against the windchill. Once I was all suited up, I called her over to put on her snow boots to protect her pads against ice and chemical salt.

I had hoped that Nanook and his father would join us, but they were sleeping in. Heading west without them, we tromped through the snow.

A few places had shoveled, but the Soho streets were still unplowed. I had never experienced New York like this, at a total standstill. With no one around, it was almost like being on a movie set. Simply magical.

Niki was having a blast tromping through the deep snow. But still, it felt like I was holding her back. Reaching an open spot near 12th Avenue, I pulled slightly on her lead and said, "mush."

Niki turned back to look at me with her head cocked.

Staring her square in the eyes, I snapped her lead hard and shouted, "Mush! Mush!"

Oh, My Goodness!

That word activated some primal instinct in Nikita. She took off plowing through the snow with a force

I'd never experienced before. Somehow, I managed to slide along, balancing on my heels until she stopped several blocks later. From that point on, I kept my mouth shut. We walked the rest of the way to the dog park.

I had never let her off-leash inside the park. Even though the fence was too high for her to jump, I didn't trust my "want to be alpha" to not assert herself. Today no one was there, but the snowdrifts made it possible for her to clear the fence.

Deciding to take the chance, I unleashed her. Today was about Nikita having fun in her element.

Her eyes popped when she saw the unattached leash in my hand.

A heartbeat later, she was making a mad dash for the fence.

Oh, Holy Buggers!

Stopping just short of her launch to freedom, she turned, winked, and then made a beeline for me. Instead of running into me, she veered to the right and did a few circles before running off again, this time "hiding" behind a large snowdrift.

My Nikita wanted play? With me? I could hardly believe it!

Slowly walking up to the drift, right before I reached it, she sprung into the air. I acted surprised. She ran a few circles around me before hiding behind another large drift. Again, and again!

Stopping for a moment to check the time, I realized that my fingers were already a little numb. Even if it warmed up from brutally cold, to frigid cold, we still had a long walk back and better get a move on. Niki ran up to me and instead of running circles, she sat down and looked at me.

Her clear blue eyes held such emotion.

In that very moment, for the very first time ever, I felt a connection between us. My heart so full of love, it could've melted all the snow in Manhattan

Oh please, let's not exaggerate. There are plenty of things that Mistress Melodramatic does that I appreciate. This particular girls' day out, running down the unplowed streets of

New York City to the dog park, just happens to be ONE of them! No reason to make such a fuss or to encourage this love fest— Exactly! We've all seen the way Mistress Smother Mother is with Shamus, coddling him all the time. And, that is certainly NOT for me!

So, Mistress Frozen Fingers, how about we go home before the arctic air turns your sensibilities into permafrost! I do believe hot milk with a drop of honey is on the menu today. And, that is very definitely for me!

*

As the snow melted, so did my hopes of staying in New York until Christmas. Mistress Francophile needed to return to Paris— Ridiculous! Why was she always so selfish? If New York City was out of the question, we could zip down to Florida and spend the holidays with family like ALL the other Americans do.

As usual, turning a deaf ear to my sound reasoning, at least this time she let me say good-bye to my friends— And, Sans-Shamus!

Out with Nanook for our last walk together before my drug-induced sleep, as we rounded the corner back home, usually the silent type, Nanook started talking.

"Yo, Niki. I got dis ideaaa."

Ok, look before you judge him, he was really good-looking and super-sweet. He just had a little Brooklynese accent from spending too many weekends in the hood.

"So baby-baby, I was tinkin' maybe you not a Siberian Husky. Ya know what I'm sayin?"

No, I actually have very little idea of what you're saying. I rarely listen to you. I like the way you walk, not the way you talk.

"Boom baby, yeah baby. You like da silent type. Dats cool. Dotally down with dat. So, back to dis ideaaaa. You sooo fine, you sooo smoooooothh. So classy, but not sassy. I dink you a *Parisian* Husky. Oh yeahhhh, dats right. Oui ouiii ouiiii!"

Once I was safely inside and away from The Yes Man, I was beginning to see the wisdom of leaving without long, drawn-out, painful goodbyes. Yes, there's something to be said for "ghosting."

"Are you seeing the twins again? I thought that you were feeling better. You know, if you're still having any sinus issues, it's best not to be on a plane. The pressure changes might cause an embolism. You could—"

Shamus. Is it Saturday? Let me answer for you. No! So, shut your front door and lock it!

"I am not worried. I am concerned."

Well, then let me assure you, that everything is fine.

"But, I know you're still having headaches and—"

AND, your gratuitous anxiety is not helping right now. So, listen up Spoon-Fed Terrier before you say another flipping word! You have no idea, absolutely zero concept of what it's like to be locked in a confined space in complete, total darkness while suffering the constant din of the engines for an entire 7-hour flight! So. do me a solid. Let me have a little peace before Mistress Pharmaceutical Enthusiast drugs me up and throws me into cargo-hold!

As he slinked away to go mope somewhere, I felt a little ashamed for being so harsh.

Truth be told? I was actually looking forward to the drugs and a decent night's sleep with the white noise drowning out the thumping in my head.

Not wanting to spend my pre-flight time A.K.A. still awake-and-aware sobriety hours feeling bad for Shamus, I

went looking for him. Not that hard to find, as expected, he was throwing a pity party for one in my donut bed upstairs.

Careful not to step on the melancholy mutt, I snuggled in with him. Not in the mood for any terrier commentary, I gave him a little warning grumble from the back of my throat.

"Oh yes, Nikita. You are perrrrrrrrrfect."

Perfect. Everything was in order and ready for us to go back to Paris. Tomorrow morning, we'd be at the St. Jean having an espresso. And, the day after that, Nikita had an appointment scheduled with the veterinarian.

Her nosebleeds had stopped, but she was still sneezing. Something wasn't right. I trusted our Parisian doctor would be more aggressive finding the root of the problem and its remedy.

Paris

As soon as I saw the domes of Sacre Coeur come into view, my heart smiled. We were back home. I could hardly wait to grab a coffee and a croissant and walk with the dogs around the neighborhood.

On our way down to the St. Jean, we were behind a father and daughter holding hands as they walked to school. She must 've been around 4 years old. It was the cutest thing watching her being pulled forward while she kept swiveling her head backwards to look at the dogs.

Tugging at her father's hand, she asked if Nikita was "un chien traineau?"

Finally compelled to see what was behind that was capturing her attention, he turned to look. Smiling, he turned back to her confirming, "Yes. In fact, they are both
sled dogs."

"Really, Papa?" This time, fully turning around trying to get a better look at Shamus.

Pausing the rush to school, her father winked at me. Then, squatting down to her level, he continued. "Yes, sweetheart. However, it takes about one hundred of the little ones to pull a single sled."

Her eyes widened as she smiled at the thought of 100 teddy bear dogs pulling her through the snow.

I burst out laughing at the image of 100 Shamuses trying to agree and be able to focus long enough coordinate anything! The dry French humor was the perfect welcome back to Paris.

*

Seeing the vet the next morning was another nice welcome back to Paris. How could one man be so good-looking, so sweet-sounding, and so freaking nice? I wondered if all the men from the Basque region were like him. If so, I'd be in serious trouble if I ever traveled there.

His brow furrowed as I recounted our experience in New York and Nikita's symptoms. Once I finished the story, he turned his attention to Nikita giving her a thorough check-up including blood and fecal testing. With the lab in office, he was able to confirm immediately that all was within the normal range.

Before he would order further tests, a course of antibiotics was the first step. Without the ability to confer with the American vet, he said they were required as due diligence.

Not happy to have to start again from scratch, I understood that he was methodically ruling out possibilities and trusted that he would pursue it until he found the cause and the cure. It was such a relief to know that she was finally in good hands.

Good hands, indeed. Finally, an appointment with a doctor who was much more perceptive of what was happening. Why she ever bothered with that other vet, I'd never know for sure— However I'd bet anything that it was a yet another manifestation of her affinity for impromptu canine torture.

While Mistress Questionable Motives was busy with the receptionist, Docteur Pays-Basque whispered that he could sense my discomfort. The antibiotics he prescribed where in fact a

little "cocktail" that included an anti-inflammatory and a painkiller— Like I said, much more perceptive even knowing NOT to alert Mistress Worry Wart to the extent of my malaise.

Taken twice-a-day with a wedge of Camembert, the pills worked their magic! No nausea, no wooziness, and thankfully, no more headaches! Happy to be back in Paris and under the care of Dr. Beaux Mains, once again life was grand with the usual exception— Exactly! S-h-a-m-u-s, Shamus!

Why, oh why, did she insist to bring this uncouth, possessive, tote-sized terrier back to Paris? Our very first week back, he threw such a conniption fit over Bones ignoring him that now ALL of my Parisian beaus disappeared! Simply ridiculous! Maybe on our next visit, the good docteur would prescribe anti-tantrum meds for the little scrapper.

Luckily, I was sans-Shamus when I discovered Pascal. The newest addition to the hunk factor in our neighborhood, he was 100lbs of pure muscle with the cleanest, shiniest, blondest coat I had ever seen— Grrrrrrrrr!

His father, a hair stylist from Milan, left him to his own devices during salon hours. Finding him glowing like the sun outside the salon door, I "accidentally" bumped into him.

Pardon me. I didn't see you there.

"No, not at all Bella. One must never apologize for such a happy accident. In fact, one might say that it was not an accident at all. But rather, divine intervention.

"You see, I happen to be in search of a special companion. Someone unique, who is beautiful in body and mind. And here you, an angelic vision, appear on my sidewalk. Coincidence? I think not. Perhaps, I may entice you to meet up later? A simple apéro. Nothing too complicated, just a casual, little get-together. A get-to-know each other. If you're inclined, I'd like to share with you my sketchbook. In fact, I'd love to sketch you, to attempt to capture your essence.

"Scusami Bella, if I am too forward. It's just, I'm compelled by your beauty, your grace. Please, per favore, si te plaît, be my inspiration, be my muse Parisienne."

Sighhhhh.

Mistaking my exhale as a Parisian snub, Pascal retreated back into the salon.

What a disappointment! All words! No tenacity, no stamina— Humph! Oh well, at least I was spared the humiliation of explaining my current situation— Exactly! Curiosity, I most certainly had. The ability to escape the confines of Mistress Ironclad Shackles, I most certainly did not.

As we walked away, I took one last look. My Italian Stallion was back in the doorway, holding his sketchbook! Catching my wistful glance, he seized the initiative to join us in Place d'Abbesses. Unfortunately, Mistress Limited-Social-Skills started to freak out a little at the unleashed company.

Ah, come on! Let me have a little fun. Let me make a new friend!

Leaning into me, Pascal whispered how he wanted to sketch me. Details more graphic than I care to share. Finished with the proposed horizontal-tango choreography, his wet tongue tickled my earlobe— Ughhhhhhhh.

Not happy with the breach of propriety from unwanted company and concerned that it might escalate, Mistress Conservative Sensibilities marched us straight back to the salon and insisted that they hold the frisky canine until we were out-of-sight.

This was one of the very, very rare moments that I was happy to have a short lead and an overprotective mistress! Of course, as always, my happiness was short-lived. This time lasting only until we returned to a homebound humming terrier.

What are you doing?

"I'm working on a serenade for you!"

Thank you, but no thank you! My head is finally feeling a little better. No need to—

"It's an original piece. The bridge is giving me so much trouble. Maybe, I should go pester her to take me out for a walk. You know, that's when I get my very best ideas. As I stretch my legs, I stretch my mind. And as soon as I pee—"

T-M-I, Shamus!

"I create more space for thought!"

Seriously?! Let me ask you something, Piddle Paws. If that's true, then how can you be certain that you're not emptying yourself of your very best thoughts?

An excellent question in theory, it became disastrous when spoken— Exactly! Literal Interpretation Puppy and refused to tinkle for an entire day! I was genuinely concerned that if he waited any longer to empty himself, his coat might turn a pungent shade of yellow or he'd permanently suffer from owl eyes!

Taking an epic 10 minutes to finally empty his bladder— The very moment that the flood of yellow stopped, the torrent of words began. My ears ringing.

"It didn't work for me, Nikita. The only thought in my mind was not to sneeze or cough. Thank goodness, she didn't try to tickle me. That would have been a total disaster and ruined the experiment! Now that my bladder's empty, my mind is full. I have all sorts of ideas. I'm just going to need a moment to prioritize them."

Take all the time you need.

"I'm ready now. Since we're already out and by the nice stationary store, we should pick up a postcard for Nanook. It'd be nice for him to know that we're thinking of him and I didn't get the chance to say goodbye. I think that he really likes me. I mean really likes me. You know, the same way he likes you!"

PL-ease, do not confuse his kindness with interest, Crossed-Wires Puppy. He might spend time in Brooklyn, he might live in the coolest place in Manhattan, he might be a part of the Hollywood crowd, but allow me to reassure you 113% that he is not poly.

"What do parrots have to do with anything? Except crackers and pirates. Ooh, I'd look so cool and super-tough with an eye patch. Maybe, we could get one on the way home? Which reminds me, I'm empty, I need to refuel. I'm super-duper hungry with all that extra space. We've already walked past the rotisserie and the Chinese traiteur. Do you think that she forgot about dinner? I'm not prepared to begin my intermittent fasting. What if I starve? Niki-Niki-Niki, this has catastrophe written all over it!"

It's not Saturday!

"But—"

But, nothing! Seriously Shamus, don't waste your time worrying. It means you suffer twice.

"But, Niki! What are we going to eat?"

Stop focusing on food or you'll end up like Gizmo

"There's nothing wrong with Gizmo."

Really? The Waddling Wonder was so miserable that she had to be exiled— And, the only place willing to grant her Boom-Boom-Boom booty asylum? Grandma C and God's Waiting Room!

"Nikita, you know very well that there's nothing wrong with Florida. Lots of people live and vacation there. And, Nana makes the very best grilled-to-a-burnt-crisp cheese sandwiches!"

That last part might be correct— However, it does mean that you will be living without me!

-silence-

Ah yes. Heaven on Earth! That simple, precious Nikita-less existence thought nugget offered me a rare, worth twice its weight in Platinum moment of silence.

-end of silence-

"You're right, Niki. I need to stay positive. Maybe, we're going to one of her friends for a little apéro!"

And just when the Straight-Jacket Terrier was in a more manageable state, she said "the" word.

"Cat! Did you hear that? Where is it-Where is it-Where is it?! I can't see it anywhere!"

There is no cat. She's messing with you, Shamus.

"No, she wouldn't do that. She knows how sensitive I am. And, this is Paris. There has to be a cat somewhere. Wait! Look! She's pointing towards it. It must be at the top of those rocks. I'm going to go investigate with or without you!"

Then, that would be without me, Spidy-Wannabe.

This certainly was not our first rodeo. Charging at the slate rock wall again-and-again, Mountaineering Mutt made it up about halfway before sliding back down— And, each and every time, filing his nails on stones the entire 4-foot descent. Predictable amusement and a clever way to ensure diva doggie's nails stayed properly trimmed— But, today was different.

In an unintentional stroke-of-genius, he charged up the incline at a wider angle. His pads found indentations just deep enough that he could propel himself forward. Adrenaline charged by success, dimple-by-dimple he made his way to the very top!

Way to go Shamus! Bra-Vo!

"Niki, the cat's gone! It totally disappeared. Not a single trace. What a tricky kitty. Did you see where it went?"

Not wanting to rain on his singularly proud moment, I sugar-coated the bitter truth.

It must've slid through the fence and scampered down towards rue Lepic. Why don't you come down and we'll check for suspicious felines on the way over to the rotisserie? The chickens should be ready by now and you deserve a celebratory dinner.

"Chicken! My second favorite! Do you know what my 1st favorite is, NIki? It's you! Hey, what's wrong with your right eye?"

Nothing.

"Then why is your windshield wiper out? Is there something in your eye? A piece of dust or hair? Were you crying? Let me get a little closer to check."

Please, absolutely no. Everything's fine.

Something's wrong. Her third eyelid visible, something must be irritating her eye. With the new course of antibiotics, there had been no more sneezing and no more nosebleeds. Even her energy level was back to normal. Maybe, it was conjunctivitis, or she really did suffer from allergies.

In any case, as soon as we got home, I called the vet and made an appointment for the next day.

Once again, her vitals and lymph glands were normal. With a large sigh, he said that he'd like to start at the very opposite end of the spectrum. An MRI would show any abnormalities and from there we would work backwards to the cause.

He made a few calls and arranged an appointment for 11am. We had just enough time to drop Shamus off and make it to the 7th arrondissement.

Arriving at the facility only a few minutes late, they immediately took Nikita into the back to prep her while I signed release papers. Understandably, she'd need to be put under anesthesia to keep her motionless for the scan.

The technician asked that I come back no later than 1:30pm. They'd do her testing immediately and would like to have her picked up before the office closed for the afternoon lunch break.

Finding a cute little bistro with an open table on the terrace, I sat down.

Sit down, Shamus. We need to have a talk.

"Huh? Sure, whatever you want, whenever you want, wherever you want. I'm all ears, all the time, all about you, my Nikita."

No. None of your sweet-talking shenanigans, my little boo. This is serious. I need you to listen closely.

"Ok-ok-ok."

Have you noticed that I still have headaches?

"Yeah, I've been— "

Please listen to me, Shamus.

"Ok-ok-ok."

Have you noticed that my nose still bleeds a little?

"Yeah. Of course, Nikita. I notice everything about you, even when you try to hide it! You're just dehydrated, perhaps a little tired, maybe still suffering from that sinus infection which was probably, definitely aggravated by the plane ride. Didn't the antibiotics help at all?"

No, Shamus. Listen to me. This is different.

"Different?"

Yes, different.

Taking a few deep breaths, I needed to clear my thoughts before I continued.

There's a tumor, a cancerous tumor growing at the base of my nose.

"Ok. So, what's the game plan? Surgery?"

No Shamus. Cutting off my nose is not a realistic option.

"Ok. So then, chemo? Radiation therapy? Will you need to stay overnight or can they treat you in out-patient?"

No. None of that. The cancer is very aggressive. It's too late for any intervention. The tumor has already grown into my skull. Its tendrils woven into my brain. It's only a matter of time before it affects my neurological impulses.

"Huh? A matter of time? And then what?!"

I leave.

"Leave?"

Yes, leave. Our Mistress and I have spoken. When it's time— not today and probably not tomorrow— But, within the next few weeks, I will tell her to take me to see the good doctor. And, I will not come back.

"Are you thinking to move to the 9th arrondissement? Live with our veterinarian? That's just crazy talk, Niki! You can't be serious."

Oh, my sweet, little Shamus. I am dying. It's as simple as—

"No. Don't say it like that. We're all dying, Nikita. She will think of something. She will find some specialist, some experimental treatment, something! The two of you have had your differences, but that's ancient, ancient history. I know that she'll think of something. Trust her."

No. It's beyond her. It's beyond me.

"What about your God-line connection?"

No, Shamus. It's beyond intervention.

"No! Nikita, you need to try something, you need to have faith, you need to believe!"

Shamus, you need to accept that one day I simply will not come home.

"No-no-no-no-no-no-no."

No, no, no. Please God, no.

That refrain repeated through my mind as I looked at the results.

Somewhere in the background, I heard the technician's explanation of the images as he choked back tears. "She's such a beautiful creature. It's an aggressive form of cancer. I'm so sorry. The tumor has already breached her skull. I'm so sorry. There's nothing to be done. No treatment, no cure. I'm so sorry. She's so beautiful. It's a matter of weeks, a month if you're lucky. I'm so sorry."

Numb. I was completely numb. Unable to move, I waited in my seat transfixed by the images of the tumor as he left to bring Nikita out from the recovery room.

The thought of losing her…

The anticipation of the heartache to come…

Completely lost, wallowing in my sorrow. On auto-pilot, I took Nikita back home on the Metro. Thankfully, the train car was empty. I could cry, letting the tears fall unseen.

From out of nowhere an old man appeared, walking towards us down the length of the car until he took the open seat to my left. I wondered where he came from and why was he sitting next to us with a hundred other seats available. He seemed normal enough, but there was something odd.

Simply dressed, his clothes were freshly pressed. He had beautifully thick, pure white hair with perfectly tousled curls. A well-trimmed beard framed his face. A soft smile crinkled his eyes. Surrounding him was the scent of freshly ground herbs and spices. The smell of him, along with his smile, put me completely at ease.

His left hand rested on top of a walking stick. A truly stunning piece made from polished, gnarled wood and topped with an elaborately-detailed golden lion's head.

Tapping his stick on the floor just close enough to get her attention, his smile beamed when she looked up. Speaking in French, he asked her age.

Not waiting for my response, his smile widened as he remarked on how delicate her ears were. Then lightly touching them, he said in a whisper, "She is the most beautiful creature, I have ever held in my eyes."

At the next stop he exited, turning to wink at Nikita before the doors closed.

For the second time in less than an hour, I sat speechless. Dumbfounded by this man's appearance, his energy, his scent. It was surreal.

Before the train pulled out of the station, he disappeared into thin air. A heartbeat later, I realized that he was an angel.

Whether it was a blessing for her or a sign for me, I don't know. However, after that moment, my perspective shifted. Instead of dwelling on the inevitable goodbye, I would enjoy the time left with this beautiful creature who had graced my life.

Getting out of the metro, we went straight home. I let the dogs have some time together while I made arrangements for the next few weeks.

That evening, the veterinarian called. The results had been messengered over to his office and he had just gotten off the phone with the lab. Other than prescribing pain relievers, there was nothing that he could do. The sadness, the defeat in his voice was gut-wrenching.

Thanking him for his call and his concern with Nikita's well-being, I hurried him off the phone hanging-up right before I broke down into uncontrollable sobs.

It was real. If we were lucky, she'd live through Christmas.

Christmas in Strasbourg?! The city that celebrates my favorite holiday with the biggest and oldest market in Europe?! Holy Moly! This promises to be the best Christmas, ever! Maybe, we'll even bump into Santa Claus!

"Niki, not to be a party pooper but I sincerely doubt that Santa will be there. He's super-duper busy this time of year. Even though he does delegate certain responsibilities like making and wrapping presents to the elves, he has to be at the North Pole to train the new reindeers. Now, if we were in Norway, we'd have a better chance of bumping into him. You do know that Norway is short for North Pole Way. Of course, how silly of me! Absolutely everyone knows that! If we come back in July or August, there's an excellent chance of bumping into him feeding the swans. After all, Strasbourg is his summer home."

Really? Tell me something Dirty-Diaper Doggie, when did you become an expert on anything?

"You know, Niki, there are different levels of expertise. Even a beginner is a master, a master of nothing."

Please stop right there! My meds just kicked in making the pressure in my head manageable. They will not accommodate your rubbish rhetoric— Sighhhhhh.

My holiday trip through the Christkindlmarkts of the Rhine river valley would be EPIC without the useless information expert in-tow. Look, I fully understand the concept of family time at the holidays and the importance of not excluding Touchy-Subject Terrier— However, he was trying too hard to avoid the elephant in the room.

But then, as mentally exhausting for me to listen to his nonsensical chatter, it was physically exhausting for her— Exactly! Mistress Self-Designated-Puppy-Trolley had to transport him absolutely everywhere! The markets were way, way too crowded for the pedal-pusher puppy— But, wait! It gets even worse— Precisely! With Stocking Stuffer Terrier wedged into her tote bag along with our purchases meant fewer presents— Ughhhh. Complete. Total. Bummer.

"Niki, that's okay. I don't need any presents! In fact, there's only one thing on my list this year! I'll give you a hint. It doesn't come from a store, it isn't handmade by elves, and it can't be wrapped."

That's 1-2-3 hints my mathematically challenged tag-a-long. How about we take a moment and I'll help you count your blessings?

"Thanks for offering your help, Niki! I am very blessed indeed. It might just be the luck of my Irish name! Anyway, one more hint: What is want is priceless!"

Everything has a price-tag my utopian terrier.

"Nopes. Because, in-fact, what I want, I already have! Time away with you!"

Time away from the routine was exactly what I needed to forget the "countdown."

Boarding a train to Strasbourg, we left Paris. But, that wasn't far enough. So, after a few days, we rented a car and crossed the border into Germany. Passing through Baden-Baden, we drove deeper into the mountains. Navigating the serpentine roads at dusk, just as we reached the summit our hotel came into view. Snowflakes floated through the sky around the chateau. A Black Forest storybook moment.

In the morning, we awoke to a winter wonderland. The blanket of fresh snow was exactly what I had hoped for to explore the hotel's extensive grounds and paths. After a quick coffee and bundling up Shamus and myself, the 3 of us set out on the trails.

As soon as she stepped on the fresh snowfall, Niki's eyes lit up and she pulled ahead. Afraid that she'd get it in her head to run as far as Switzerland, I kept hold of her leash while we hiked farther and farther into the woods. To see her happy, frolicking in the snow was priceless.

Less happy with the current weather conditions was Shamus. I knew that he was much more of a fun-in-the-sun dog, but then this trip was not for him.

A little trooper, he refused to be picked up. A little prima donna, he also refused to budge. Not wanting to tug him through the drifts, knowing he wouldn't go very far, I let him off leash. It was hilarious to watch him hopping behind us like a grumpy bunny.

By the next day, the roads were cleared and we continued through the forest. Seeing signs for the German Clock Museum, we toured their extensive cuckoo clock exhibits before heading back up to Triberg.

Known for the intricacy and workmanship of their clocks, just outside of town also happens to be the highest waterfall in the region. The force of the waters not hindered by winter's ice and snow, the cascade was impressive and definitely worth the little detour.

Continuing into town, the wide range of cuckoo clocks available was unexpectedly overwhelming. We spent the rest of afternoon going from store to store trying to choose a souvenir. A much needed diversion with Black Forest Clock Association Certified retail therapy.

Certified Cuckoo Bird is what she is!

Not able to fit inside her purse, I thankfully escaped the whole museum experience and got a little beauty rest. However, woken up from my snooze by Mistress Neophile, I should have been immediately suspicious of her actions when she offered me more medication— But, considering her age, I assumed it was a pre-senior moment where she forgot administering my morning dose.

Second flag? In the car with the two of them cuckooing the entire ride from the museum into town! The day's double-dosage was nowhere near enough to cover my throbbing headache— Especially when the 3rd flag was dropped— Exactly! You guessed it! I was their un-willing, un-interested companion., forced to go shopping in town with them!

PL-ease do not get me wrong, I do like to shop for shoes, for clothes, for accessories— And, who doesn't enjoy stepping into a biergarten with the pungent smell of hops, pretzels, and sausage! However, never, ever, ever have I wanted to, have I dreamed of, have I insinuated that a cuckoo clock is on my wish-list! I already live with TWO!

"Niki, come over here and check this out. This one has Yorkies dancing around every hour singing the 'yodeling connection!' Get it? It's the 'Rainbow Connection' Swiss-clock style! Of course, I dance and sing much better than these mechanical creations."

That is a matter of perspective.

"That's what I thought, too! But, I've spent the last 10 minutes checking it out from every single angle! They're very amateur. Anywho, the one over here has Siberian Huskies singing 'Winter Wonderland' which gave me this idea, an inspiration really. It's a little out-of-the-box."

No.

"Wait. Just hear me out. It gets better."

Doubtful.

"Close your eyes and imagine this."

Close my eyes, I did. Unfortunately, my ears picked up every single detail— My mind delivering a hauntingly frightful visual.

"A custom piece with Yorkshire Terriers and Siberians Huskies! One singing and the other yodeling, alternating between the hour and half hour, except for at 12noon and 12midnight."

Peeking one eye open, I inquired what happens at the witching hours hoping the details would be more mind-numbing than painful. Sadly, I was wrong.

"I'm so happy that you asked! That's when the grand-finale happens! A real showstopper where they all come out! Right? The entire ensemble! Everyone singing and yodeling and dancing together! I'm trying to think of what song to use. It has to highlight both of our artistic ranges and talents. Wait! That's it! A compilation! It starts with all the Siberians singing 'What a Wonderful World' and at the end of the refrain a few of the Yorkies will pop out and chime, 'With Nikita!' Once they are all on stage, the melody will transition into one chorus of 'Hallelujah!' Oh yes, that's absolutely perfect! Thanks for brainstorming with me, Nikita! You're the very, very bestest ever! I love you!"

And with that, he disappeared in search of a salesperson. So absorbed by his latest obsession, he neglected the puppy kisses.

Closing my eyes, I tried to forget the pain not certain what hurt the most— My head from the tumor? My ears from the cacophony of 100 cuckoo clocks? Or, my ego, from the bittersweet absence of Shamus-smooches? All I knew is that it sucked a little to be me right now— Sighhhhh.

*

My car snooze interrupted, as usual, by her questionable driving skills. It amazed me that Mistress Typical-American-Driver was allowed to legally operate a car in Europe!

"Niki-Niki-Niki! Look! We're here!"

Looking out the window, all I saw was just another fancy hotel.

"No, not just a hotel— A thermal spa! Badenweiler is world-renowned for its curative waters! I told you that she'd think of something! Now, let's get you a bowl of water and start your treatment. There's no time to waste. The sooner you begin, the sooner you'll be healed."

Shamus, I am not thirsty.

"It doesn't matter. Just give it a try for me."

Shamus, back off. The headaches, the eyestrain, the fatigue, it's all wearing me down and fancy water is not the solution. I don't mean to be difficult, but—

"Nikita, there's no need for you to apologize. It's of little surprise to me that you're so difficult."

Pardon you? Quickly explain yourself while you can still talk.

"Well, the French have an expression: The more beautiful a woman, the more difficult she is. Since you are by far the most beautiful creature that I've ever known, it makes perfect sense that you're the most difficult, too!"

Tears welled up in my eyes. Overwhelming, uncharacteristic emotions? Probably just a side effect of the medication, but it seemed the sweetest, most genuine thing that he'd ever said.

Blinking my tears away before he saw them, I got up and gave him a big kiss— MUAHHH!

Stunned. Completely frozen in place. Even, his loose lips were rendered immobile.

All it took to muzzle Mini-Mutt was a little peck on the cheek. How ironic.

How frightening. I woke up to find Nikita standing on the bed looking intently out into the darkness with complete focus on something. But there was nothing there... nothing that I could see.

My heart sank. The veil was beginning to lift between the worlds for my Nikita.

Throughout our road-trip, I had kept a watchful eye for signs that she might be suffering. She had slowed down a bit and was eating less, but was as stoic as ever. Never, showing any pain or any discomfort.

Originally, I had planned to travel farther south and cross the border into Switzerland. Lake Constance was a beautiful area and she'd be surprised to spend a few days in Basel with my friend. But considering what I just witnessed, I did not want to be on the road, far from Paris and our veterinarian. It was time to go home.

Slowly reaching out so as not to frighten her, she snapped out of her daze. Bringing her to me, I wrapped my arms around her, and said a little prayer that she would live until we made it back to Paris and through Christmas.

*

No matter how short or long the time spent away, there's nothing better than sleeping in your own bed that first night back. We didn't arrive in Paris until late and since the heat had been turned down while we were away, the apartment was a little chiller than usual.

Shamus had already buried himself under the covers. As I snuggled into bed, I was happy to find the little foot warmer.

Nikita was still dawdling in the kitchen. I was about to call her when I heard the chimes ringing. She'd never rung the chimes, before! Throwing the covers off, I jumped out of bed and ran into the kitchen where I found her sitting in the middle of the kitchen, waiting for me.

Asking her what was wrong, she sighed and hit the chimes once more before looking up at the chicken tender jar on the counter. The treats were her special surprise for Christmas tomorrow morning.

I glanced at the time. She was right. It was 12:01am, Christmas already.

By the time I finished laughing and reached for the container, Shamus was sitting next to her. What a couple of characters!

Walking through the neighborhood Christmas morning, it was quiet, really quiet. I hadn't been planning on returning to Paris until after the holiday and was hoping to find one boulangerie and a market or rotisserie open to grab a few things for Christmas dinner.

Stopping in the middle of the street for a moment to decide which was the best way to go, Flirt appeared from his doorway.

Since we had returned from New York, Niki's friends were noticeably absent. And, not like they went away for the holiday. They'd pop out to say hello when it was only Shamus, but they were avoiding my Nikita as if she had the plague. So, I was a little surprised to see Flirt coming over to say hello.

Looking around, I didn't see his father anywhere. Oh jeeps, Niki really didn't like him. I hope this goes— Ahhhhh. He gave her a couple of kisses and then wrapped his neck over her shoulders as if giving her a hug. How sweet.

How sad. My "friends" were hiding in the shadows. What Total Jerks! Just when you need some support—

"Joyeux Noël, ma belle."

I responded in kind, but could not hide the disappointment from my face.

"Ees dere anyting, aïe may do for you?"

I glanced over towards the sunny-day friends.

"Ah oui. Da boyz. Ma belle, da seekness, eet ees so strong da scent. Bonze, Otis... Voilà! Dey adore you, but stupid, silly boyz... juste boyz! Rememberrr, you da most belle chose! Come 'ere. Si te plaît, let mee 'old you, juste one time."

Perhaps, I had misjudged Flirt.

"See, I told you that Bones and Otis were not—"

Mr. Obvious, this is not the time! This is Christmas. You put on a happy, smiling face this very moment or so help me, I'll— ACCHHHOOOO!

"Niki! Wow! Look at that! You just sneezed the tumor straight out! This is simply amazing! I told you that those waters were special! This is a Real Christmas Miracle!"

Holy Buggers. How could I tell him that it wasn't true? That there was no miracle? The look of hope on his sweet, little face. How could I tell him? Hoping that the God-line connection was still working for me, I placed a last-minute holiday request— Please God, let me enjoy my last Christmas. Just one more day. Please.

Acting like nothing had happened, I pulled Mistress Emotional Tightrope and her terrier safety-net to the rotisserie. It was open and I needed to eat a little if I was to keep any strength. Luckily, our favorite boulangerie was on the way. Not that I was opposed to stretching my legs a little, I just wasn't certain if there was any blood splatter on my bib. After all— Holiday or no holiday, cancer or no cancer— This is Paris! Appearance is De Rigueur, tout les jours!

*

After a good meal and a little sleep, I can't say that I felt any better. My head pulsed even though she doubled my medication. I don't know which was more painful— watching both of them scramble around trying to figure out ways to make me feel better or just feeling worse with every passing moment.

Mistress Last Resort played her trump card taking me to the groomer for a shampoo, rinse, and blow-out. Sadly, that only temporarily washed away my pain. By the time we walked back home, I was feeling miserable and thoroughly exhausted.

Waking up from a little snooze, she asked me to come into the kitchen and presented my favorite comfort food— rice with an egg-over-easy.

My tummy said yes, but no.

"Come on, Niki. She made it just for you. I think that your blood sugar is a little low that's why you're so tired. Of course, a little magnesium would help with your post-holiday blues. It's a natural anti-depressant. So, how about you try some white rice!"

Nibbling on a few grains, they finally left me alone.

How was I supposed to tell them? How do you explain a pain that never goes away? How you say that it's become intolerable? That everyday tasks are exhausting? How do you say good-bye when you know that there's not going to be another hello? I just didn't— Interrupting my train of thought, My Mistress came back into the kitchen jabbering about heating up some milk.

It was time.
I gave her "the look."

She gave me "the look."

It was time. We had made an agreement.

Continuing through the motions, I heated up some milk for all three of us in the hopes that we would fall asleep and she might change her mind. But, there was little rest.

In the middle of the night, her breathing became shallow and rapid. I held her and prayed that she would live until the morning.

Seemingly oblivious to what was happening, Shamus woke up his usual, happy little self. Niki was finally asleep, so I took him out for a walk alone.

I tried to take him to the bistro for a coffee and a little talk, but he only wanted to get back to the apartment, back to her.

When we returned, she was awake and in good spirits, like yesterday was just a bad dream. But, I knew that it was never going to get any better. Not by a long shot. With the tumor growing into her brain, it would eventually affect her neurologically. A dog of her size, strength, and will could be very dangerous under those circumstances.

She had been such an unexpected blessing in my life. And, throughout her entire sickness she held her head up high with dignity and grace, never complaining until last night. The very least I could do was keep my promise to her.

Without calling in advance, we walked to the 9th arrondissement. I was afraid to call and lose my resolve. She might be ready to say goodbye, but I wasn't. Not at all.

Long before we reached the veterinarian's office, her interest in the treats in my pocket evaporated and she was completely exhausted. This was not "my Nikita."

Seeing the two of us, the receptionist ushered us into the exam room and closed the door. As we waited for him, Niki rested her head in my lap. Again, this was not "my Nikita."

When the doctor came in, Niki lifted her head happy to see him and moved to sit next to him. Her head rested on his lap. Now, that was "my Nikita."

As soon as I tried to explain why we were there, the tears flowed faster than the words. Reaching for my hand, he just said, "Breathe, it'll be okay."

The receptionist tentatively knocked. A scheduled appointment had arrived. He apologized and excused himself.

Here I was the imposition and he was apologizing. Such compassion. I started to cry all over again. By the time he returned to the exam room, I had gone through an entire box of tissues, but was no longer sobbing.

He explained "the process," slowly stroking Nikita's back the entire time.

Asking if I was ready, I could only nod my head.

He dimmed the lights and began to administer the drugs. After the second "cocktail," he placed a stethoscope to her chest.

In a hushed voice, I heard the words, "Au paradis."

I wasn't sure if the whispers were to himself, to Nikita's soul, or to the heavens.

With a deep sigh, he looked at me and said, "She is gone."

Slowly, he backed out of the room, leaving me in peace to sob over Nikita's lifeless body.

A few months had passed since that last time I held Nikita in my arms. Driving back to The Farm where it had all began, I now found myself embracing her ashes.

The house was an empty shell. No one lived there anymore. The once well-manicured landscaping, now forgotten, was overgrown creating the illusion of enchanted gardens from another place, another time.

As I walked across the backyard, I could see Niki running and playing, hear the soft tread of her footsteps, feel the rush of wind as she tore past hell-bent on her way to something.

Wrapping my arm tighter around the canister, slowly I turned the lid.

From my heart came a silent prayer and a final goodbye. Ohh, I loved her so very, very much.

Turning the container upside down, her ashes found their freedom. The wind now carrying Nikita to all the places she loved to roam and explore.

*

The first few days, Shamus had not minded Niki's disappearance. They had been separated before. However, when he saw me packing up her things, that changed.

He refused to come anywhere near me in the apartment. From his perch, ironically enough on my campaign chair, he watched my every movement. When I took him outside, he was just as difficult not wanting to leave sight of the building.

After a week of fighting with him to take a walk and having him stare at me with hateful eyes, I made arrangements for us to leave Paris. Perhaps, a trip would be good for both us. A change of scenery and time with family might be just the thing to shift perspective.

Flying first to Florida to visit my mom and Gizmo, after a couple of weeks we hit the road traveling north visiting friends and family along the way. By the time we arrived in New York, Shamus was back to his usual quirky self, attacking skateboards, looking for cats, eating ice cream, and even enjoying playtime at the dog park with Nanook.

So, when I returned to the New York apartment after releasing Nikita's ashes, I was surprised that my little boo was not there to greet me. Usually, I'd find him sleeping at the door.

I called and called, but he still didn't come. His collar and leash were at the front door which meant he had to be somewhere in the apartment. I began my search, calling his name as I made the rounds.

"Shamus!" Not in the kitchen.

"Shamooo!" Not in front of the TV.

"Shmooo-Boo!" Not by the fireplace.

Finally, in the upstairs bedroom, I saw his furry little body in Nikita's old bed. His face buried in a memory.

My heart sank.

When I went over and touched his back, he lifted his head. A tuft of Nikita's fur was glued to his nose. His face was all crunched up, his eyes squinting as if holding back tears. I could hold mine no longer. Curling up with him in her bed, we cried together.

She was never going to come home.

Epilogue

I found myself back in Paris. Ohhhh, so much had changed since I lived there with my gruesome twosome… Not only the city, but me too.

Shamus had eventually forgiven me for Nikita's "disappearance." By the time we settled in Florida, he had found his own way… made a few friends, loved bike rides from his basket, hanging out at yoga studios, and running along the beach. Just shy of his 18th birthday, a few strokes rendered him completely muddled, unaware of his surroundings and bodily functions. Once again, the difficult choice was made. His ashes now joined Nikita's at The Farm.

As I watched a young couple walk by on their daily errands with their "mis-matched" dogs, my eyes welled-up a bit. The tears hidden by my sunglasses. Some things never change. I had loved Nikita and

Shamus so very much and still missed them every single day. They'd brought so much light and laughter into my life.

My Parisian melancholy was disturbed by texts blowing up my phone. Obviously, someone was excited about something.

Looking down at the screen. I was surprised to see my nephew's name pop up. Not that often does a 25-year-old young man has time to text his auntie.

The text read, "Meet Luna!"

Thinking that he had a new girlfriend, I opened the message to see a photo of a puppy winking at me. Quickly, I scrolled down reading the full message.

My nephew had found and adopted a Siberian Husky. Her mask a little darker made her eyes a little bluer, but there was no mistaking that wink. Nikita had found a way back to her "little master."

"There's more…" Came the next text.

"Yes, please! More! Send more photos!"

"Not just photos! News too!"

"Yes, yes, yes!"

"My new housemate comes with a dog."

The next photo? Luna and Peque chilling in the kitchen. Luna looking annoyed at the camera; Peque focused on Luna. Peque was the housemate's Yorkshire Terrier.

Shamus had found his Nikita.

The End.

Made in the USA
Middletown, DE
06 January 2023